PRAISE FOR T. K. LUKAS'S *ORPHAN MOON*

"Highly recommended! An exciting, breathless read with well-developed characters and a plot that keeps you guessing."
—Elizabeth

"Excellent read! The story grabs you from the very beginning and keeps you wanting more!"
— Aubrey

"You should read this book. It is a great story of overcoming hardship with a love story threaded throughout lots of adventure."
— Ron

"Gritty, raw American history…I felt like I was there. LOVE that in a good novel."
— Gary

"Loved this book! Gripping story grabs you from the very start. T. K. Lukas does an amazing job of creating characters. You love them or hate them but you feel like you know them all."
— Sherry

"Highly recommended.The author makes the characters come alive with exquisite details and dialog…I feel like I know them. I can't wait for the next book in the series!"
— Beth

"T. K. Lukas's writing reflects the kind of maturity that will shine more and more with each passing novel. Kudos to her!"
— Grammar Dowager

ORPHAN MOON

By

T. K. Lukas

Book One of the Orphan Moon Trilogy

Chevalier Publishing

ISBN-10: 0-9962356-1-2
ISBN-13: 978-0-9962356-1-7

Chevalier Publishing

Note:
This book is a work of fiction. Names, characters, places, and incidents either are the product of the author's imagination or are used fictitiously, and any resemblance to actual persons, living or dead, business establishments, events, or locales is entirely coincidental.

Dedication

For Baron, my husband, my friend, my lover, my real-life hero…

Your unwavering support and encouragement—your unshakable, never-ending belief in me—is the source of my strength, my joy, and my smile.

I'm grateful for your love.

CHAPTER ONE

SEPTEMBER 27, 1860

High upon the Brazos River ridge, bare-chested warriors on war-painted horses gathered with lances, bows and arrows, and tomahawks in hand. The fire-holder, the elder and revered medicine man, sat astride his decorated pinto in the middle of the assembly, his mount indifferent to the flaming torches his rider gripped in each hand. Other horses stomped up puffs of fine caliche dust that glittered in the moonlight. One hundred or more in strength, they waited in patient surveillance of the quiet farmhouse below, while those in the farmhouse watched them.

The moon cast shadows where there should have been none, as if the sun instead had reached full bloom. A lone white stallion stood on the highest point of the ridge, silhouetted against the silvery backdrop, its rider sitting tall. He held his hand high above his head, as if connecting to some lunar spirit. His arm dropped, the signal was given. The rocky ridge came alive with horses pouring over the edge, sliding and tumbling down the steep slope, racing across the valley. With terrifying war cries filling the air, gyrating circles of mounted warriors constricted in an ever-tightening noose around the ranch.

Brilliant arcs of light erupted in the night sky like blazing traces of shooting stars falling from the heavens. Barleigh Flanders stood transfixed in the barricaded window of her bedroom, peering through the gun port as arrows streaming fire rained down all around. Dread rooted her feet to the floor.

1

Henry's hands shook his daughter's shoulders. "Run to the goat shed, Barleigh. Get in the cellar. Take Birdie and the baby and Aunt Winnie. Now! Uncle Jack and I'll give cover till we can make a run for it."

"No, Papa. I'm staying with you." Barleigh picked up the shotgun, thrust it through the port.

"Don't argue, girl. No time to waste. Keep hold of your gun —take it with you."

Winnie ran out of Birdie's room carrying the baby. Born two days earlier on the first night of the full moon, Barleigh's half-sister wailed with hunger. "Birdie's too weak to run *or* walk. Having this child took all of her strength."

Henry shouted instructions as he shoved them out the back door. "I'll carry Birdie down in a minute. Don't open the hatch unless you know it's me. Hurry now—run."

They ran, Winnie clutching Birdie's and Henry's baby, Barleigh the shotgun. Noble the hound bounded alongside, his black hair bristling in alarm. From the back of the house, past the horse corral, then to the goat shed, they raced the roiling cloud of dust churning in from the ridge. Barleigh threw open the secret hatch in the floor, and after Winnie and the dog made their way down the angled earthen steps, she slipped into the cool darkness below. Henry had dug the cellar and crafted a secret door for it as their hiding place to seek shelter from dangerous weather or even more dangerous men.

"Hurry. Close the hatch," Winnie whispered. She bent forward, shielding the baby's tiny body with her broad, sturdy back as hooves pounded the ground all around, dirt sifting down onto their heads.

"But Papa's coming with Birdie." Barleigh peeked out the hatch, straining to see. A cavalcade of horses passed in front of the open door of the goat shed. All she saw were fast hooves and painted legs, but that was enough. She knew what was above. She secured the latch.

In the safety of the cellar, they clung to each other, the baby nestled between them. The huge black dog sat on his haunches, watching the hatch with a keen alertness, a low rumble steady in his throat. Bloodcurdling cries lingered on the wind; thundering hoof beats echoed; gunfire exploded, diminished, faded away, and the sharp smell of things burning found its way underground.

"Shh, shh. . . ." Winnie cradled the hungry, crying baby against her ample bosom, placing a finger in her mouth to hush it. "Be quiet, Noble," she commanded the curious dog that howled in unison.

"The nanny goat is just outside the shed door in the pen," Barleigh said. "I can make a run for it. Grab the goat and duck back inside. This baby needs milk. Birdie may not—"

"No. It's too dangerous for you to go outside. I'll let the baby suck some peach nectar off my finger. Can you find a jar of peaches in the dark?"

The baby's hunger was greater than the nectar. Her wailing intensified into piercing, balled-fisted spasms. Winnie tied a rag around Noble's muzzle to keep him from joining in again.

"We need that goat." Barleigh crept up the steps and cracked open the hatch, her determined blue eyes peering outside. Dreadful noise reverberated in the distance, but overhead quiet filled the darkness. She crawled outside, found the milking stool, and wedged it in place to keep the hatch propped open.

"Stay in the cellar on the steps with the gun pointed out the hatch," Barleigh said to Winnie. "Don't be afraid to shoot if something needs shooting. If I don't come back in two minutes, push the milking stool away and bolt the hatch."

The words echoed in Barleigh's mind. *Don't be afraid to shoot if something needs shooting.* Those were the words of her father, Henry's parting phrase when leaving Barleigh at the ranch alone, and the words he'd said when he'd handed her the new shotgun three months earlier on her nineteenth birthday.

"I'm not afraid to shoot, but I don't like this plan. I should be the one going for the goat. You should be in here with your baby sister." Winnie brushed a dirty-blonde curl off her worried forehead, the wide streaks of pre-mature gray matching the color of her equally worried eyes.

"You're the midwife. You know babies. I know animals. I can catch a goat."

"All right." Winnie sighed the deep sigh of one giving in. She placed the baby in a basket of rags and grabbed the shotgun. "I'm ready."

Clinging to the darkness, pressing her back against the wall, her thin frame almost as thin as her shadow, she inched toward the door that led outside to the attached pen. The nanny goat should be just inside the gate next to the feed trough, she thought.

Barleigh rushed to the gate, searching. *Where is she?* She listened for a moment, making out the sound of faint bleating. Thick, choking smoke hung in the air. She coughed, covered her mouth and nose with her hand, trying not to make a sound. Ignoring the shouted songs of triumphant celebration in the distance, the eerie orange glow, the flickering light from fire burning all around, she opened the gate, groping, and made a blind grab. Her hand settled on the goat's bell collar. The happy tinkling sound it made rang loud. Barleigh grabbed the brass clanger, snatching it in her clutched fist to quiet the convicting noise.

Running back inside the shed with the goat in her arms, she heard a noise coming from behind. She turned to see the silhouette of a warrior framed in the doorway, a dark figure braced against the backdrop of flames and smoke.

Winnie screamed.

Barleigh dropped to the ground, clutching the goat to her chest. A shotgun blast split the air. She looked up to see the Indian, tomahawk raised, flying backward, with blood spurting from a hole in his chest. He fell to the floor, dead.

Handing the goat off to Winnie, Barleigh rolled his body up against the wall and then covered him with empty feed bags. She scattered loose hay over the tomahawk and the wide pool of blood, fearful of the evidence and the story that the scene would reveal to another passing by.

*****

They milked the goat, taking turns letting the baby suck the sticky sweetness off their fingers. Satisfied, she slept. Taking a risk, Barleigh lit the oil lamp, dialed the wick down to the lowest height before it extinguished itself, the flicker of light allowing a quick reminder of their surroundings before she snuffed the flame.

Birdie's preserved fruits and vegetables lined the shelves. Barleigh's preserved thoughts and dreams lined her journals, which she kept stacked below the shelves. She counted eight bound books, one each year beginning when she had turned twelve. The cellar was her writing place. Her dreaming place. Her hiding place.

Noble sat like a sentinel guarding the hatch while the little goat paced. "I'm sorry, Nanny Goat, but if Noble wears a muzzle, so must you." The goat's confused bleating had grown louder, her frantic striding more vigorous. "Sorry."

Barleigh and Winnie ate the jar of peaches. Like the nervous goat, they paced. Winnie used a bucket of old wash water to relieve herself. It seemed as if the night might never end, but eventually it stretched into the quiet stillness of morning.

"I can't stand this any longer," Barleigh said, the silence of the previous few hours becoming too heavy. "I need to know what's out there. If Papa and Uncle Jack were able, they would've come for us by now."

Winnie nodded agreement. "Yes. Jack—" She let the sentence trail away.

They ascended the steps, cracked open the hatch. In contrast to the violent chaos that was the night, dappled sunlight bathed the earth, songbirds sang to one another, and the peaceful world seemed normal. Barleigh's eyes adjusted to the morning's light. She looked around . . . and realized her world would never be normal again.

Smoke curled from the ashy heap where once stood the horse barn. The corral's charcoaled planks sparked in the breeze. What little that remained of the house stood under the protective arms of a singed cottonwood tree. Green pears gathered the previous day from the orchard sat piled in baskets, the shiny red pushcart sitting next to what used to be the kitchen porch. There in its place was now a gaping black hole opening into the gutted, smoldering house.

"Oh, dear God," Winnie cried out, laying the baby in the pushcart next to the pears. She ran to Jack. His body lay sprawled and motionless on the ground. A dozen arrows sprouted from his chest, with a lance securing him from ever moving from that position again. From the waist down, he was stripped of clothes, his most private parts sliced off. Winnie reached to close his eyes, his gruesome death stare frightening to look at, but it was impossible—his eyelids were cut away, too. Stubby, bloody palms were all that remained of his hands, with all of his fingers and thumbs chopped off. And, from ear to ear, his scalp was sawed from his head.

The sight caused Barleigh's stomach to lurch. She spun away, fisted her hands, and pushed them hard against her eyes. The sound of Winnie's soft voice drew her back around.

Winnie was on her knees, kneeling next to her husband's body. "There, there, there." She soothed him, kissed him, and caressed his bloody face. Speaking tender words to him, she eased his trousers up, belting them with gentle hands.

They removed the arrows from his body but could not pull the lance from his chest, so deeply was the spear impaled into the ground. Together, leaning with all their weight on it, breaking it off, they managed to lift his body off the jagged shaft embedded in the rocky soil. The lance caught a piece of Jack's shirt, tearing it, keeping hold of it, and Barleigh started to pull the fragment of his shirt free.

"No!" said Winnie, sharply, emphatically, her eyes glazed and staring at the flapping fabric. "Leave it. Let it be a banner. This marks the place where a good man died."

*****

They gathered as much of Birdie's and Henry's remains as they could. Their charred bodies were found together in the bed where Birdie had given birth just days before. It appeared as if Henry was bent over her, his body covering, protecting, shielding hers. A Comanche's piercing lance affixed them to one another for eternity.

With their ashy remains folded together in a blanket, Winnie and Barleigh carried them to the goat shed where they had pulled Jack's body. The dead Indian was dragged out of the shed and left for the scavenging vultures already hovering over the pierced and impaled cattle carcasses dotting the pastures. They piled straw on top of their dead, snaking a trail outside. Then, splashing kerosene all around, they tossed lit matches onto the soaked straw, watching as fire raced into the shed. The loud crackle-pop of the funeral pyre drowned out their sobs.

Wind gusted, stoking the flames into a frenzy. Flakes of ash drifted down, the cremated ashes of their beloved. Barleigh turned into the breeze, tears streaking the grime on her face, the wet, ashy mixture seeping into her pores, melting into her skin. She imagined a part of Papa and Birdie forever becoming a part of her, going with her always.

Some ashes flitted and twirled high in the air, blown into the late September sky by the fire's hot breath. "You're free to fly away now, Birdie," she said as the ashes swirled above the treetops. "You and Papa are now free to be together."

*****

"Is there anything to save from the house?" asked Winnie. She picked up the black and red woven Navaho blanket Papa had kept on the front porch chair, shaking ashes from it, sniffing it, pounding it hard against the railing before folding it over her arm.

What could be salvaged? Memories? "There's not much left." Barleigh walked out to the front porch, clutching two tintype photographs.

"I remember seeing your papa with this blanket around his shoulders the night Birdie gave birth, him pacing out here on the porch. The moon spotlighted him like an actor on a stage performing for cactus and cattle." Winnie's dark eyes appeared hollow and sunken, pulled inward from the terror. Her gaze drifted, unblinking, to the Brazos River ridge.

Barleigh followed her stare. It was more than cactus and cattle watching, they both knew. They'd overheard Henry and Jack speak of the growing number of warriors on the ridge each night. Henry had spotted the first hint of a raiding party on Wednesday, the beginning of the time of the Comanche moon, the night Henry and Birdie's baby chose to enter the world.

"I found these," Barleigh said, showing Winnie the tintypes. "Birdie looks almost white in this one, don't you think?"

Winnie nodded, taking the photograph from Barleigh's

7

hands. "She was beautiful. It's no wonder your papa fell in love with her, despite the circumstances. I know you loved her, too."

"Yes. I loved her. She was like a mother to me."

Looking at Birdie's photograph, her silky black curls to her waist, her fine features, her almond eyes, was like looking at the negative image of herself. Barleigh had learned at a young age, though, not to ask foolish questions as to why a half-Negro, half-French Cajun slave of her grandfather and she, whose blood was Irish and French, shared a likeness.

The few salvaged items—two tintypes, Henry's black church hat, Birdie's Bible, and the Navajo blanket—were placed into the pushcart along with the pears. A small load. Barleigh marveled at how little she now possessed. She thought about things taken for granted yesterday. The day before the attack. The day before her world turned dark. The day before her heart was inflicted with a wound so severe she expected it would never heal.

The canopied road that led east to Winnie's house was a narrow, rolling, and dusty lane. It was a two-hour ride on horseback, an hour in an emergency. Barleigh had whittled it down to less than that the day she'd galloped for help when Winnie's midwifery skills had been needed. They walked in silence.

From behind, a noise startled them from their private thoughts. Jumping like frightened rabbits into the woods, pulling the cart, the dog, and the goat in with them, they hid behind a thicket of cedar. Shaking. Waiting. Peering through branches. Each holding her breath.

It was Barleigh's horse, Deal, with his unmistakable whinny. His was not a high-pitched whinny but a deep, throaty rumble—a rat-a-tat grunting more like the sound of a person clearing their throat. Lame, limping badly, his left foreleg bore a zigzagged gash that tore deep into the muscle. Most of the hair on his right hip was burned away, leaving angry black blisters on his skin. But he was alive.

"I can poultice those wounds," said Winnie. "The injuries are severe. They'll take a long time to heal. The scars will be ugly, but they're not fatal wounds." She gave Barleigh's hands a gentle squeeze.

8

Dark, cloudy thoughts gathered in Barleigh's mind. Was Winnie trying to convey that the same was true for her? That her heart's wounds would heal but would leave ugly scars? She doubted that any heart could survive what hers had suffered, fearing instead that her heart would turn to vapor.

*****

Everyone from Palo Pinto to Fort Worth called Winifred and Jack Justin "Aunt Winnie" and "Uncle Jack." Barleigh pretended she was her real life aunt. Sometimes, she pretended Winnie was more. Sometimes, Barleigh called her "Momma" when she knew Winnie wouldn't hear, just to see how the words felt falling from her mouth.

She never knew her real mother, and each birthday Barleigh celebrated was a guilty reminder of the loss. But she had Birdie. Though she was *like* a mother, it was forbidden that Barleigh consider her *as* a mother, or even as *family.* A *simile* was all Grandfather allowed. However, Henry changed all that after Grandfather died.

"I've made you breakfast." Winnie put the coffee kettle on the stove, then sat down.

Barleigh stared at the food on the table, her stomach unsettled. "I'm not hungry. But . . . thank you."

"At least drink some milk." Winnie got up and poured a glass without waiting for Barleigh to answer. "You need to put something in there besides coffee."

"The horses that weren't burned alive in the barn they stole, except for Deal, who they left for dead. But, why did they have to kill the cattle?" She pushed the heels of her palms against her eyes, trying to rub away the horrific memory.

The barn had been full of mares with foals. Barren mares, stallions, and geldings had been separated and turned out to pastures and paddocks. All in the barn died. A few fleeing horses had been killed in the melee. Hundreds of cattle carcasses were left scattered across the pastures, arrows embedded in their silvery gray hides, their brown-eyed vacant stares going on forever.

"They can gallop away with horses. Cows are too difficult to control. They turn into a dangerous stampede. They may keep

9

one or two for food. But what they can't take, they kill or burn. Or both." Winnie stared into her coffee, slipping away to her silent place.

A silent place—Barleigh longed for one. Day or night her mind screamed over the horror—waking, sleeping. She'd open her eyes and see it all again. She'd close her eyes, and the images would remain. If it would've made the terrible visions stop, the memories fade, she'd have clawed out her eyes and fed them to the dogs.

Barleigh wandered upstairs to her room, leaving Winnie to her thoughts. Wrapping the Navajo blanket around her shoulders, she sat in the rocking chair next to the window, the photographs of her papa and Birdie displayed on the sill. Outside in the paddock, she watched her horse as he limped feebly toward the water trough, stopping short, the pain from his wounds too much for his effort. The sight was her undoing. It shattered her, broke her apart, and she buried her face in the blanket and wept.

*****

Winnie had taken to wringing her hands when she talked. "It's been two weeks since I sent word to my sons' regiment commander. Surely he'll approve their leave. Jackson and Jonah will bear the news on strong shoulders. I fear it'll be hardest on little Jeddy."

"While you're inquiring at the militia headquarters," said Barleigh, watching as Winnie fretted with her hands, "I want to pay a visit to Mr. Goldthwaite at the bank."

"Yes. I understand. That's another reason to leave your baby sister here. We have too much to do in Fort Worth."

"But I'm worried—"

"Esperanza is capable. She helped raise my three boys. Now don't go looking at me like I'm suggesting you leave her for a year. It'll be one day. She's better off here with Esperanza."

"I'm all she has in this world. What if something happens?"

"There's no need to worry. She'll be fine," said Winnie, winding and unwinding her hands.

"It's no good luck, a baby going this long with no name," Esperanza said. "To no call her by her own name can no be good."

She bent and lifted the baby from the cradle.

Barleigh looked at Winnie, panicked. She had dreaded the thought of her having been born under a Comanche moon, had feared what bad omen that may have foretold. What kind of misfortune had she added by not naming her? "Have I brought her bad luck?"

"No," said Winnie emphatically. "But she does need a name, no matter the reason. What have you considered?"

"I haven't considered anything. You're a mother. You're good at these kind of things."

"I named three boys. She's your sister. You should have the honor."

Barleigh tried out a few combinations in her head as she watched Esperanza tease a smile from the baby's mouth with a warm bottle. She wanted something that would remind her of Birdie and of her Papa.

"Starling, for Birdie, and Henrietta, for Papa. What do you think?"

"Starling Henrietta Flanders. That's perfect." Winnie took the baby from Esperanza. "Starling, you now have a beautiful name."

*****

When they arrived in Fort Worth, the town was an axis of excitement, folks joined in animated conversations about the upcoming presidential election three weeks and one day away. Barleigh once entertained opinions about such matters as politics. They'd seemed important when her papa had engaged her in spirited debates. She'd have argued that the Republican Abraham Lincoln would make the best leader, even though many in Texas favored the Northern Democrat, Stephen A. Douglas. However, her focus on this day was what she had to do to rebuild her ranch.

Barleigh hurried toward the bank, a hand keeping her hat from blowing away while the gusty wind fluttered her skirts. She reached down to straighten them, and as she did, she noticed a piece of paper being carried aloft on the breeze. It settled at her feet as the wind blew itself out. She saw that it was an advertisement. Picking up the paper, she read:

WANTED. Young, skinny, wiry fellows. Not over eighteen. Must be expert riders. Willing to risk death daily. Orphans preferred. Wages $25 Per Week.

Apply: Pony Express Stables, Saint Joseph, Missouri

It's too bad I'm not a fellow, she thought, folding the paper and tucking it into her pocket as she stepped through the bank's heavy, barred doors.

Mr. Goldthwaite was cordial, escorting her into his office, offering sincere condolences on the death of her father and of Jack Justin. He never mentioned Birdie. Then, he propositioned her.

"Your father," he explained, tobacco juice staining the corners of his mouth, "was no businessman. He was a breeder of fine equines, a knowledgeable cattleman, but he lacked business acumen. Myself? I'm an astute businessman, quite clever with stretching the dollar." He winked.

She remembered from what seemed a lifetime ago, although it had been only five years past, her initial encounter with this man the first night they'd made it to Fort Worth. She, her papa, grandfather, and Birdie had left the Gulf Coast behind, had spent three long weeks in a covered wagon before reaching the Fort, and she recalled his inclination for expressing significant meaning through the dramatic blinking of one eye. She still found the peculiar habit annoying.

"I came to you for advice, Mr. Goldthwaite," she said, her hands folded in her lap. "My plan is to rebuild the ranch." She envisioned a small barn to start, then a serviceable house, adding a few breeding animals as she could.

"My dear girl," he said. "When I heard about your tragedy from Captain Goodnight, I straightaway inspected your father's account and I went over his legal papers. Via his will, you've inherited outright all of your father's estate. That means all of the debts as well as all of the assets."

"I don't believe my father had any debts. His custom was to

pay cash for everything."

"He owned the ranch outright, free and clear. However, he let accrue the taxes on the property. Last year it was to offset the purchase of breeding heifers. This year it was to offset the purchase of those fancy thoroughbreds your late grandfather was so fond of and your father, er, late father, liked to use for brood mares."

A weedy panic began to take root. "Can't you use the money that's in the account to pay the taxes? Get them caught up until I can find a way to earn some money?" *Let the taxes accrue? Why would Papa do that?*

"I have an idea on how we can take care of the taxes." Mr. Goldthwaite, in his wrinkled gray suit with silver watch fob dangling too low from his vest pocket, waddled from his desk and stood behind her chair. His stumpy, liver-spotted hands massaged her shoulders in a fashion too familiar for casual acquaintances.

"I'm a lonely man. I miss having a wife, God rest her soul. I miss the pleasures that a wife affords a man." He massaged harder, his fingers working forward and downward from her shoulders, brushing over her chest.

A red-hot blush blossomed on her face. "Mr. Goldthwaite! Please stop what—"

"If you'd consent to my proposal of marriage," he said, plunging ahead, "well then, I'm sure I could persuade the board of trustees to grant you an extension on the taxes, in light of your recent tragedy."

Her body shuddered with the absurdity. "Marriage? As in, me marry you?"

"Of course once married, I'd transfer your land to my name in order that you'd not have to worry about the taxes in the future. As your husband, I'd take care of all that business nonsense for you. I'd give you a handsome allowance, of course, to buy yourself pretty little things."

She unfolded her hands from her lap, clutching the arms of the chair in a white-knuckle grip. "Mr. Goldthwaite, your offer is generous, but, I prefer to take care of matters my own way. Now, please remove your hands from my shoulders."

"Miss Flanders, take some time to think about my offer. You're still grieving. Give serious consideration to the options and the consequences."

"Consequences?"

"Particularly to the consequences." He leaned in, whispering his sour breath in her ear. "Take until the beginning of the year when taxes are due. January may come around and cause you to see things in a different light. By the way, your father's account has a little over two hundred and fifty-seven dollars left in it. Taxes past and present amount to four hundred and six dollars, give or take."

Barleigh's heart felt as if it might pound from her chest. Her throat constricted and burned as she swallowed, trying hard to push down the rising swell of panic. "I pledge all the money in my father's, I mean, in my account, toward taxes owed. I'll have the rest to you by the end of January."

"Miss Flanders, you do realize that this bank can foreclose on your property for delinquent taxes and sell the land to satisfy the debt? Consequences." He kneaded her shoulders harder.

"Mr. Goldthwaite, you do realize that you can die a miserable death and rot in hell?"

She shoved away from the chair, sending him tottering and stumbling backward, and then marched out of his office. Between his embarrassing actions and her own surprising words, a prickly heat blushed her cheeks. With as much dignity as she could muster, she left the bank, head high, and elbowed her way down the crowded sidewalk, somehow managing to reach the alley before losing the contents of her stomach.

Reaching into her pocket for a handkerchief, her hand instead came out with the advertisement she'd found earlier. With the paper unfolded, she read the words again, the writing seeming to jump of the page. She was young, skinny, and wiry. Only slightly over eighteen. An expert rider since a child. Willing to risk death? For such generous wages? Yes. She qualified as an orphan, in the technical sense that both parents were now dead. There was only one conspicuous concern. She was not a fellow.

Refolding the paper and tucking it into her pocket, she set

off to find Winnie.

Deep within, where pretense and truth come together in a battle of wits, she knew this waybill was meant to find her. The gods who govern the winds deposited this paper at her feet. Or, angels scooted it toward her via a gentle current from their fluttering wings. Perhaps some invisible force in the universe slowed the earth's orbit long enough for *this* to catch up to her. Any theory, plausible or not, fit, because she knew this was her answer. This was her hope. She knew, without a doubt, this was her destiny.

*****

Clutching the paper tightly in her hands, Barleigh reviewed her thoughts, getting her ideas in order. The kettle of coffee she'd made earlier as she waited for Winnie to come down for breakfast was half gone, as were her chewed-off fingernails.

Winnie yawned as she shuffled into the sun-filled kitchen. "Good morning. You're up early."

"I haven't slept."

"Are you hungry? I can fix pancakes."

She shook her head as she held out the paper, releasing the breath she'd been holding. "I want to show you what I found yesterday, or what found me. This is how I'm going to save my land."

On their return from Fort Worth the day before, Barleigh had disclosed to Winnie what she'd learned from Mr. Goldthwaite about her financial situation, the taxes due, and her father's apparent mishandling of his money. She'd purposely omitted the things that induced her to blush.

Winnie took the paper, studied it, and then handed it back. "It says they're looking for young skinny wiry fellows. *Fel-lows*," she said, elongating each syllable as she puttered around the kitchen, Starling sound asleep in her crib by the window. "You, Barleigh, while young, skinny, and wiry, could never pass as a *fellow*. It's a crazy idea. Put it out of your head. We'll think of something else. I'll sell another cow."

"You've only four cows left and still have dairy customers to think of."

"With all the men and boys leaving to join the army, my dairy business has all but dried up. For crying out loud, we'll come up with something more logical than you passing yourself off as a *fellow*."

"Logic be damned!" Barleigh threw a hand over her mouth. "I'm sorry, Aunt Winnie. I didn't mean to curse at you." She ran over and wrapped her arms around Winnie. "We'd need to sell a whole herd of cows to come up with enough money. This is all there is."

"I wish I had a herd left to sell. I'd give them all to you."

Barleigh held the advertisement up, reading again the words that were written for her. "It's destiny, this paper finding me."

Winnie pointed to the sleeping baby. "Your destiny's curled up in that crib. It's folly to think that that advertisement is your destiny. Folly. Pure and simple."

*****

Later that evening as the dark house grew quiet, Barleigh lay in bed in the disconcerting arms of another sleepless night. Tossing and turning, a gauzy vision crept in. Stealthy, it settled against her like a secret friend. Wrapped around her. Took shape. Formed. Warmed her. Urged her. Inspired her. She understood what she must do.

She slid out of bed and tiptoed downstairs to where Winnie kept her midwifery kit. Taking the scissors in one hand, holding her hair out straight with the other, she cut. Chopped. Whacked. Made another cut. The growing pile of chestnut curls on the floor looked like a small sleeping animal.

Rummaging through a chifforobe, she found some clothes that must have belonged to Jeddy, Winnie's youngest son, close enough to her size. She pulled them on. She smudged the lower half of her face with coal—just a little—the shadow hinting at the beginnings of a boy's first beard. With a bit of ingenuity and effort, she'd transformed from Barleigh Flanders, nineteen-year-old landowner and debtor of taxes, into Bar Flanders, not-over-eighteen-year-old orphan boy, soon to be Pony Express rider, and willing risker of death.

She put on her papa's black church hat, and it fell over her eyes. Stuffing the inside brim with rolled-up paper kept it in place. The mirror on the chifforobe reflected her passing image as she strolled by, stealing glances. With each pass, she tried to blend her new reflection with her mind's image of how her papa walked.

As soon as the smell of coffee wafted up to her room, she ambled down the stairs, thumbs hooked through belt loops, eyes half concealed with low-pulled hat. She sneaked around the kitchen with the caution of an imposter, trying to stitch her shadow to her new boy-self.

Winnie forked bacon and eggs onto a plate, her back turned as Barleigh stood behind her. Clearing her throat, and with her deepest, most masculine voice she could summon, she said, "I'll take my coffee black, thank you."

"My God," Winnie gasped as she spun around, a hand clasped over her heart. "For a second I thought it was one of my boys."

"But you knew it was me." She plopped down onto a chair. Heaving a frustrated sigh, she tossed her papa's hat onto the table. "I stayed up all night practicing my voice and my persona. I have to become a boy."

"And I stayed up all night last night too, worrying that you'd be doing exactly that." Winnie sighed. "What you're proposing to do is irrational. It's going to be near impossible rolling a rock up a mountain so steep."

"Near impossible. *Not* impossible." She ran her fingers through her chopped-off hair, the shortness of it making her blue eyes appear larger in her face. "Please, Aunt Winnie? Help me with this?"

Winnie twisted and rubbed her hands together, her shoulders lifting and falling with each deep sigh. "It's rash and foolish and I'll no doubt live to regret this." She sighed again. "The first thing we have to do is fix that hair of yours. Bring me my scissors, child."

Barleigh threw her arms around Winnie's waist. "Thank you. I'd live to regret it if I didn't try."

Winnie set to work giving Barleigh's hair a proper boy's

17

cut as she had done for her sons and her husband. "There. Much better. Now. The tone of your voice wasn't bad, but I knew it was you by the way you stood. If you're going to be a boy, you have to stand with your legs more apart, less fussy, not so, um, not with your knees pressed close, like you're hiding an important secret between them." Winnie let out a hearty laugh.

Barleigh started laughing, too, and the laughter carried them away for a moment. Drying her eyes, she said, "That felt good. Laughing. It's something I used to take for granted but now add to my list of things for which I'm grateful."

Winnie dried her eyes on the corner of her apron. "Laughing and crying both are good for the soul."

Barleigh thought about that for a moment, thinking she'd rather laugh. "What else do I need to fix?"

"Well, the way you're sitting, all upright with your pelvis tilted forward, back arched. Boys don't sit like that. Sit back on your pockets, pelvis rolled back and rounded, like you're cradling a rare treasure in your lap of which you are most proud, but pretend casual indifference."

They both busted out laughing. Snorting through noses, tears streaming from eyes, laughing.

"And how's my walk?" Barleigh demonstrated as she moved from the table to the coffee kettle.

"Too girly. Turn your sashay into a saunter. Slow down your steps. Yes, there, like that. And every now and then, scratch your privates and make a readjustment. Act as unintentional about it as if you're blowing your nose."

Barleigh feigned shock.

Winnie looked at her, eyes wide. "What?" she asked. "A husband, three boys, a nephew, and a slew of ranch hands, and I can tell you, that's what they all do." She proceeded to demonstrate, exaggerating every nuance, the sauntering, the scratching, the readjusting.

Barleigh doubled over again in laughter that took her breath away. Regaining her composure, she grew serious. "If I leave tomorrow morning, ride to Little Rock, catch the stage to Saint Joe, I can be there by the end of the month. But, I'll need to borrow a horse."

Winnie's brow wrinkled in concern and she chewed her bottom lip. "Are you *sure* this is what you want to do? One hundred percent sure?"

"This is what I *must* do."

"I wish there was a way to talk you out of this, but I know there's not. I'll take good care of that baby sister of yours, and your horse. You don't worry about that, Barleigh."

"It's Bar. From this moment forward, I'm Bar Flanders."

*****

Journal Entry—Tuesday, October 15, 1860

> *Tomorrow morning, I set off on my journey to Little Rock, then on to Saint Joseph, Missouri. I have this new journal, (a gift from Aunt Winnie), three sharpened pencils, a Colt revolver with plenty of ammunition, and a good and steady horse, even though he's a slow, milk wagon horse. But, he is accustomed to working all day. I'm counting on Deal being well mended by the time I come home in January to make my tax payment to the bank. Then, Deal and I will return to Saint Joe, continue to ride for the Express, then when summer comes, ride home with lots of money in my pocket to begin the process of building a home to raise my baby sister.*

> *This is my plan.*

> *Destiny dropped the Pony Express way-bill at my feet. What I do with it is beyond destiny—the next part is up to me. I'll hold fast to my dream of saving my land and rebuilding the ranch, not through an act of folly, but through hard work and determination. I'll ride fast and hard to reach my destiny's reward.*

> *But for now, sleep is calling. What lies beyond destiny is a blink and a nod away.*

T. K. Lukas
Yours ever faithfully,
Bar Flanders

CHAPTER TWO

SEPTEMBER 26, 1860

Like a giant he moved across the land, each long stride claiming ownership of the ground beneath his boots. According to the yardstick that measures a man in feet and inches, he stood six and two, but according to the benchmark that measures a man against his peers, Hughes Lévesque stood alone.

The evening's shadows and the cooling night air made turning back toward San Antonio an easy decision. He had departed the river town earlier that day, midmorning, half sober, and fully committed to his mission of picking up a federal prisoner in Fort Worth to escort him into the waiting arms of justice in Austin, Texas.

Hughes, lean and taut with muscles firm from use, slung his saddle over his shoulder and started walking. He figured he would make it back to San Antonio by sun-up. He hadn't gone very far before the old gelding up and died on him. It would've been thoughtful of him to have picked a better time than in the middle of a full gallop, Hughes thought, rubbing his sore backside. He walked with a slight limp from receiving the full impact of his landing on the hardscrabble ground.

Clouds flitted across the silvery sliver of a moon, blotting out the meager offering of light. The trail was dim and wildly inhabited by coyotes and other nocturnal creatures that prowled in the shadows. He knew he was not alone. He was being followed.

Hughes shortened his stride and emptied his mind of

distractions. He slowed his breathing, filling his lungs with the pungent warmth of the night, taking notice of the new smell that hung heavy in the thick, humid air. He detected the smell of a group of horses flanking his right—more than one mare was in heat. The riders wore buckskin leggings, just like Okwara used to. Hughes couldn't mistake the odor of horse sweat on oiled deerskin leather.

Okwara, the skills you taught me still come in handy, old friend.

His eyes darted left and right in a visual sweep of things that moved in the shadows. Lying to the side of the trail, a branch broken off of a mesquite tree emerged in his peripheral vision. A fresh break. He scooped it up without changing his stride, snapping off a long green thorn from the branch to pick at the dirt embedded under his fingernails.

The call of an Eastern Screech Owl caused him to shake his head—it should have been the sound of a Great Horned Owl in these parts. A coyote yipped. Another yipped its response. Hughes considered throwing his own "yip" to the wind to see what might happen. He tossed the mesquite thorn aside.

Taking stock of his weapons, he felt the heft of the Winchester repeating rifle hanging from his shoulder. Designed by longtime family friend Benjamin Henry, it was one of the first models produced. Hughes's father had it engraved with the family crest and a miniature scene of their sugarcane plantation as a special gift for his eighteenth birthday. The engraving was a nice touch, but it was etched with guilt. His father would have tried anything to keep Hughes marching in his footsteps.

Concealed under his vest, the carved antler hilt of his large hunting knife pressed against his lower back. His favorite knife, the much smaller Rezin Bowie, was strapped to his leg inside his right boot. It pinched and chaffed when he walked, but knowing it was there comforted Hughes like a double shot of whiskey. Usually in the saddle and not walking like some farmer, he could ignore the momentary distress.

Both of the .44-caliber black powder revolving pistols holstered at each hip held full rounds, as did his .36-caliber Navy

Colt, which he kept tucked inside his vest in a pocket hidden in the lining. The secret pocket was made of red velvet, crafted and sewn in by his favorite whore, Lydia, whom he thought of each time he pulled on his vest and tucked in his pistol.

Hughes dropped to the ground on all fours just as he heard the unmistakable sound of a rope hissing and slicing through the air. He dodged the first lasso, but the second, third, and fourth found their target. Yanked to the ground, he kicked like a wildcat, but his arms were bound tight to his sides. He scrambled to his feet but was snatched back down to the ground, again and again.

"A man is no match for four ropes, Texas Ranger." Except for the words "Texas Ranger," which were pronounced with perfect English and polished with a soft drawl, the rest was the guttural language of the Comanche.

"I count three ropes on me," said Hughes, speaking fluent Comanche in return. "The first was thrown too high and too quick. I could give you girls some lessons on lassoing. Next time, you'd need one good rope to take down your man instead of three or four."

A dark figure sitting on a white horse rode into view, coming within a breath of where Hughes lay on the ground. The horse almost stepped on him. Hughes didn't flinch.

The bare-chested rider wore beaded, fringed buckskin leggings. Black and red paint evenly divided his face left from right through the midline of his strong, straight nose. His horse bore red and yellow handprints on each hip, the mane and tail adorned with eagle feathers to match those woven in the rider's long black hair.

"Get up, Texas Ranger."

Hughes scrambled to his feet, the tight ropes biting into his arms. He looked around, tried to assess how many figures on horseback he could see. Four throwing ropes at him, and the one on the white horse in front made five. No telling how many others were hiding in the shadows.

The mounted Indians on the other end of the ropes that bound his arms stepped their horses closer, giving some slack to the bindings.

"I thought we had you, Texas Ranger, back when your horse grew tired of carrying you and decided to die instead. But you are quick like a cat and smart like a fox. You hid yourself away until the moon smiled. Then you came out of your hiding place to travel in the dark, like a wolf."

"Maybe I am a wolf," said Hughes. "A wolf in a man's body."

The Indian dismounted in one fluid movement, sweeping his right leg forward and over the horse's neck, dropping to the ground. Walking up, he pulled the badge from Hughes's vest, tossing it to the man behind him who let out a high-pitched laugh as he fastened it to the rawhide catch-rope around his horse's neck. "Are you the Texas Ranger they call Hughes Lévesque?" he asked, now speaking fluent English.

"At your service." Hughes gave a slight nod.

Studying him for a moment, the Indian walked around him, taking his time, running a finger down the rifle that hung useless and bound to Hughes's side. Coming back in front of Hughes, he stood toe to toe, both men equal in height. He took a hard hold of Hughes's chin, turning his face left and right, looking deep into his eyes as if divining a secret. "Yes. I've heard stories about you. We call you *Asgaya gago agatiha gudodi waya agatoli*. Man Who Sees With Wolf Eyes."

"You should call me *Waya Agatoli*, for short. Be easier to remember."

Hughes had heard the stories, too. His light, amber-colored eyes sparked many discussions, giving way to his Lahcotah/Siouan nickname. Who started it or how it began, he didn't know, but a man who saw with wolf eyes would be respected and revered, if not feared, in most tribes.

"Do you know who I am?" asked the handsome Comanche, whose Parisian nose and gray eyes hinted at his white mother's heritage. He thumped his bare chest with his hands flat, opening his palms outward, showing he held no weapon.

"I've heard about you, too," said Hughes, looking him in the eye. "I believe you are the infamous *Isa-tai*, also known as Coyote Vagina."

High-pitched laughter rippled through the mounted warriors, who quickly fell silent except for one. The squat, pudgy Indian hooted, cackled, and pointed. His uncontrolled amusement caused him to list sideways in a precarious slant that threatened to tumble him from his horse.

In a flash, the Indian standing in front of Hughes spun around on his heels, drew a knife from his waistband, and then hurled the gleaming blade at the laughing warrior. His life ended, his laughter silenced, in that one fluid move.

The barrel-chested Indian turned back to look at Hughes with eyes that showed no emotion. Gesturing over his shoulder with his chin, he said with casual indifference, "*He* was Coyote Vagina. Now he's No More."

"Much to No More's misfortune." Hughes looked over at the dead Indian lying on the ground whose blood had begun to pool dark and wet beneath him. "I had you mixed up. You must be Quanah, Chief of the Noconis."

"At your service." Quanah gave a slight nod.

"It must get tiresome, a great Indian chief like you, fighting unworthy opponents like that dead man there."

"That was no fight. I just killed him. I was tired of the way he laughed. I was tired of him stealing my breathing air, which is a gift to me from the Spirit of the Trees."

Think fast, Hughes, or you're a dead man. "Well, it's the Spirit of the Stars that's offering you a gift tonight." Hughes, his voice calm and steady, kept his wolf eyes focused on Quanah.

"What does a white man know about the Spirit of the Stars?"

"The star is a symbol I wear as my badge. But you took my star away. Now, I'm like the man in the moon. And like the stars that outnumber the moon up in the heavens, I'm also outnumbered down here on the ground."

"And that is my gift?" Quanah snorted. "We are the many stars outnumbering your moon?"

"Look up at the moon, Chief. See how the one moon still outshines the many stars? Your gift tonight is the chance, the rare chance, to outshine the moon."

"You speak like a crazy man. How does a star outshine the moon?"

"By overpowering it. The star needs a worthy opponent for its true glory to shine. I'm that worthy opponent. Loosen these ropes, then you and I go hand-to-hand, *mano-a-mano*. If I win, I walk away free. If you win, your star will shine bright and you can do whatever you want to with me. But you won't have to rack your brain deciding which of your favorite torture tricks to play on me. This fight I'll win."

"You speak the bold talk of a man who is used to winning. But my ropes beat you. I could cut your heart out now and be done with it," Quanah said. "Feed it to you before the blood stops pumping."

"Where's the sport in that?" Hughes challenged. "A man doesn't come along very often who's worthy of you. Show your warriors what a heroic leader they have, one who's not afraid to defy the moon for its luster."

"I have nothing more to prove to my men," said Quanah, walking past Hughes to converse with his three mounted warriors, stepping around the dead man on the ground. They conversed in their native tongue, several times looking over and laughing at Hughes.

Hughes listened intently, picking up a few words that he could make out—*waya agatoli, hanhepi wi, unze*. Sees with wolf eyes, something about either the moon or his anus. Whatever they were discussing, he just wanted his ass out of this mess and to not lose his scalp in the process.

Quanah returned to where Hughes stood tied. "I will take you up on your challenge because I am bored. Yours is an interesting proposition, one I've never encountered." He gestured to the Indians behind him to loosen the lassoes from around Hughes. "No guns. One hand weapon. If you win and take my life, my men will spare yours and let you walk free. If I win, I will add your scalp to the ones hanging from my lance."

Hughes shook the ropes off his arms and tossed his guns aside. "Your warriors will consider it bad *pejuta* for their leader to be outmaneuvered and die in front of their eyes. Seeing *bad medicine*, they'll high-tail it out of here to the Llano Estacado, where they left their fat kids and ugly squaws."

Like an animal circling his prey, Quanah began to pace, tossing his tomahawk back and forth from hand to hand. "You won't have to figure anything after you're dead. I'll let my warriors take your body back to their fat kids and ugly squaws for them to eat. They'll use your intestines to lace their moccasins."

With his hunting knife gripped in his right hand, Hughes faced the chief of the Comanche, pacing, circling, crouching low. Hughes's knife was long enough to be drawn as a sword, heavy enough to be used as a club, and sharp enough to penetrate bone.

The gray-eyed Indian chief and the amber-eyed white man circled each other, each staring down his opponent, waiting for the other to make a move, make a mistake, blink. An owl hooted in the distance. A horse whinnied. A wolf howled. Quanah's warriors began a low hum, then a soft chant, rising in volume until all the forest was alive with a vibrating song of death.

Focus—think like Okwara. Hughes slashed out with his knife. Quanah jumped sideways, then lunged forward, bringing his tomahawk down, landing a misplaced blow to Hughes's left shoulder. Hughes felt the sting of the glancing blow hitting an old wound, felt the warmth of blood on his arm. Nothing serious.

Chanting voices of the warriors hiding in the shadows blended with the songs of warblers and screech owls, the cooling night air filling with an eerie choir. On their knees, they pounded the ground with rocks, stones, a tree limb, their bare hands, anything, creating a rhythmic beat, strong, repetitive, and loud.

Blood and sweat ran down Hughes's forehead, stinging his eyes, a deep gash above his left brow full of grit and dirt. He lunged at Quanah, knocking him off his feet. Then flinging himself on the Indian, he pinned him to the ground.

In the dirt they rolled, locked in a death duel, panting, grunting, each man fighting for his life, Hughes on top one minute, Quanah the next. Then, on their feet, throwing punches, landing blows, an elbow to the side, a fist to the chin. Pulling, kicking, clawing, they fought like animals.

Quanah brought a knee up, swift and hard, to Hughes's

groin. Hughes stumbled sideways, trying to stay on his feet, to keep breathing through the gut-wrenching pain. Doubled over at the waist, he saw the Indian diving toward him, tomahawk raised.

Hughes swang upward with his knife, butt end of the handle first. It struck against Quanah's temple, knocking the man to his knees. With a quickness, Hughes struck again, this time to the other side of the head. Quanah fell sideways, unconscious, his tomahawk slipping from his fingers and dropping to the rocky ground.

Removing his belt, Hughes cinched Quanah's wrists, binding his hands tight behind his back. He then rolled Quanah over, face up. "Quanah Parker, chief of the Noconis. You don't look like much more than a napping baby. Except for the blood covering your face. And the war paint. "

Hughes walked over to where his saddle lay next to his guns and removed his canteen, taking long gulps of water, still panting, trying to catch his breath. He went back to Quanah and straddled him, knelt down with knees either side of his waist, and poured water onto the Indian's face. He tossed the canteen aside and waited. "I'll be the first thing you see when you come to."

Coughing, sputtering, Quanah opened his eyes, seeing Hughes on his knees straddling him, arms upraised, both fists gripping the knife, ready to land the final blow. "*Waya Agatoli,*" he said, his voice choked and harsh. "Wolf Eyes. You fight like a warrior."

"I *am* a warrior. You fought an honorable fight, Chief. But you lost."

"Yes. I lost. You can now release my spirit to the moon, who still smiles on you." Quanah called out to his warrior who held his horse. "Honor my words. Send Wolf Eyes to ride away into the land of no harm. My horse now belongs to him." He looked at Hughes and said, "Our spirits will fight again in the secret world of the dead. I will not let you win the next fight." He smiled. "Go ahead now. I am ready."

Hughes lifted his arms higher, tightening his grip on the knife. With a force that took all of his breath, he plunged the knife down as hard as he could into the ground, inches from Quanah's left ear.

Unflinching, unblinking, unsmiling, Quanah's eyes remained focused on the stars.

"Maybe I'd rather fight you again in this world of the living, on a day when I'm in the mood to throw a few punches. An honorable opponent is hard to come by these days." Hughes removed his knife that was hilt-deep in the stony ground. "Thanks for the use of your horse. You can come steal him back next time you're in San Antone."

"If I had won, I would not have let you live. Man Who Sees With Wolf Eyes must be a little *loco*."

"There're worse things in life than being a little *loco*, like being a lot dead." Hughes strapped on his guns, threw his saddle onto the back of Quanah's horse, and before mounting said, "I think I'll keep this as a souvenir of our fight." He picked up Quanah's tomahawk, lashing it to his saddle. "You can keep my belt that's around your wrists as yours."

Warm night air rushed against his face as Hughes galloped the white stallion south. The crescent moon slipped through the silky sky high overhead on its westward journey, ignoring the thin clouds that strayed across its path.

*****

The streets of San Antonio were dark and deserted when Hughes rode into town, few lamps burning in any buildings except for the saloon where the windows never went dark. The piano plinked out a tune. Painted women laughed in bawdy peels of delight, cards slapped the tabletops face up, face down, and sweet tobacco smoke hung thick in the air as serious men puffed fat cigars and tried to out-bluff one another.

Tying the horse's reins around the hitching post in between two large slack-jawed, droopy eared, half asleep nags, Hughes dismounted, muscles aching from his earlier fall and fight. Exhausted, he strode into the saloon, his spurs clinking on the plank floor pockmarked from years of rowel-inflicted wounds.

He elbowed his way through the lively crowd, back to the bar that had been carved out of a single slab of live oak wood. The barkeeper maintained the shellacked surface to a high polished gloss, as shiny and reflective as the mirror that hung on the wall behind it.

"Double whiskey, on the double, *por favor*." Hughes kept a close watch on the mirror, making sure no one sneaked up on him from behind. He picked up a burnt matchstick someone had tossed aside and began scraping at the dirt and blood under his nails.

"By the looks of you, a double won't scratch the surface. I thought you were headed to Fort Worth to pick up a prisoner," said Tandy McMurrough, setting a shot glass and the rest of the bottle in front of Hughes with one hand, the other hand buffing out a thin smudge on the bar.

"Was. I hope he likes his accommodations in Fort Worth. He'll have to stay put another week or two."

Tandy slowed his polishing hand and eyed Hughes with curiosity. "Week or two? I thought he was wanted in Austin."

"First, I want to pay a visit home to New Orleans and get one of Mother's fine thoroughbreds. I miss riding a good horse. A good, fast horse. It's been way too long since I've visited home, and way too long since I've had a good, fast horse."

"You seem edgy," said Tandy, leaning across the bar to fill the shot glass.

"It's been an edgy kind of night," said Hughes, slinging back the whiskey.

"What happened to that brown horse I saw you ride out on this morning?"

"He was neither good nor fast. He was just a horse who decided at the wrong time to die."

"That was inconvenient of him," said Tandy, shaking his head.

"Have you ever ridden a *really* good horse, Tandy?" Hughes sipped his whiskey, his eyes lingering on the mirror.

The bartender pondered this, pushed his glasses up off his bulbous nose with one hand, rubbed the rag around on the spotless bar with the other. "Well, let me think about that. I recall one time —"

"If you have to think about it, then the answer is no, Tandy. You have never ridden a *really* good horse. A man who has ever ridden a *really* good horse never forgets *that* horse, *that* experience. Compares all other horses to *that one*. It's like making love to a beautiful woman, or sipping a fine, expensive wine. The cheap ones never live up to the best of your memories."

"Or fantasies," said Tandy. "You have memories. Men like me have fantasies."

"Well, here's to memorable fantasies," Hughes said, lifting his shot glass in a toast.

"I'll drink to that," agreed Tandy, pouring himself a whiskey. "Your face and clothes are a bloody mess. What happened?"

"I'll spare you the boring details, but I had a run-in with an Indian chief. Quanah Parker himself. I got away with my life and his horse. He looks very inconspicuous out there tied amongst the other rangy mounts."

Tandy stopped wiping, his rag motionless. He looked at Hughes with eyes wide, mouth agape. "You stole Quanah's horse?" he asked, his voice loud above the noise of the crowd.

The piano went silent.

A hush fell over the saloon. Everyone turned curious eyes on Hughes, wanting to hear the story. Several men eased themselves nearer, a few women in fancy dresses with feathers in their hair leaned in, and Tandy absentmindedly began pushing his rag in circles over the spotless bar.

"I didn't steal Quanah's horse. You could say I took him up on his generous offer," said Hughes, pouring himself and Tandy another whiskey.

"Quanah Parker is a murderer. He tortures and scalps and burns and steals. You want us to believe he benevolently handed his horse over to you out of the goodness of his heart?" asked Jerry Allsup, the obese blackjack dealer, still shuffling cards midair from one pudgy hand to the other, stumpy cigar clenched between yellow teeth.

Hughes sipped his whiskey, glancing at the mirror, checking his back. "Well, Mr. Allsup, Quanah may be all those things you say he is, but he's still a man who honors his word, not unlike some white men I know. And he didn't hand his horse over.

It was a verbal offer. My belt . . ." Hughes pointed to the empty loops encircling his waistband. ". . . had his hands secured behind his back. I took him up on his offer after my horse died. Sure as hell beats walking back to San Antonio in the dark."

Jerry Allsup pressed in closer, his sour tobacco breath hot in Hughes's face. In a loud, smoker's rasp, he said, "Looks like he almost had the best of you. Mark my words, but you'll regret not killing that son of a bitch while you had the chance."

Hughes rubbed his throbbing left shoulder, his shirt torn and stiff with dried blood. "I'd be a dead man, minus my scalp, if I'd killed Quanah. His warriors would've seen to that." As far as regretting not killing the chief, Hughes considered regrets something old men sitting on porches in rocking chairs had time to fret over. Right now, it was time to pay Tandy for his fine whiskey and make his way to the Menger Hotel. A hot bath and his bed was waiting.

"I can help you with that nasty gash on your head," whispered a sweet voice. A small, soft hand stroked the side of his face and brushed the dark hair back away from his eyes and off his forehead. The wound over his left brow was caked with dirt and dried blood.

"Lydia, my lovely," said Hughes, taking her hand, kissing it. "What a nice surprise. I was thinking about you when I was checking my pistol before I got sidetracked by an Indian chief."

"I often find myself thinking about you and your pistol," teased Lydia, her large brown eyes sparkling. She wore her thick, blond curls piled high on her head, pinned in place with a gold and diamond barrette in the shape of a star, a gift from Hughes.

"Is that a fact?" He smiled, dimples framing his sensuous mouth.

"A fact," she said, batting her lashes in a coy, shy fashion before spouting rigid instructions. "Tandy, Mr. Lévesque's drinks are on the house tonight. Send next door for Oma Klein to come over and run a hot Epsom salts bath and bring some bandaging materials. Have Little Billy unsaddle that horse out there and take him down to the livery yard. I don't want that painted Indian pony standing in front of my saloon scaring away business. Bring

Hughes's saddle in and leave it behind the bar for safekeeping."

"Yes ma'am, Miss Lydia. Anything else?" asked Tandy as he sent Billy out to take care of the horse.

"Yes. Send up a bottle of champagne. Two glasses." Lydia took Hughes by the elbow, leading him from the bar. "I have some doctoring to do."

Hughes smiled, allowing Lydia to pull him away. "I love an in-charge woman, especially one who owns a saloon and can nurse a man's wounds."

Little Billy, the twelve-year-old orphan whom Lydia had discovered the previous winter shivering under the back porch of the saloon, flea-covered and stinky as an abandoned pup, burst through the swinging doors, carrying Hughes's saddle. "Mr. L-L-Lévesque! That horse a-a-a-ain't out th-th-there," he stuttered in a loud, excited gush of words. "Ain't no Indian's h-h-horse out there. J-J-Just your saddle lying on the gr-ground."

Hughes ran out of the saloon doors, followed by Lydia, Tandy, and the others who crowded around the hitching post, staring at the vacated spot where Hughes had tied the white stallion. The tomahawk he had kept as a souvenir from his fight with Quanah was now embedded in the wooden rail, his belt swinging from the weapon's handle as if it had just been tossed there moments ago.

The empty street held no sign of the white stallion, or of the chief, or of the other warriors who rode with him. Not even a speck of dust hung in the quiet, still air. The crowd pressed together, looking left and right, searching for a clue. There was none.

"It appears that our visitors didn't care to stick around, but I'm happy he returned this." Hughes threaded his belt through the loops, tightening the buckle that bore his family's crest. The heirloom symbol was a small gold *fleur de lis* centered in front of a larger silver Maltese cross embedded on a background of black onyx, its border a thin line of crushed red rubies. "I'm fond of this particular buckle."

"How rude of our visitors not to stay. Oh. . . . You had another today," said Lydia, feigning revelation. "She's staying at the Brazos Guest House. Oma Klein told me that she put her into the master suite next to the rose garden. Oma never lets just anyone stay in the master suite. Your visitor must be important."

Hughes looked perplexed. "She? My visitor? Did *she* leave a name?"

Lydia teased out the narrative. "She indicated that she was an old friend of yours. I told her you left for Fort Worth and I didn't know how long you'd be gone. She was very pretty, but thin and frail. She looked ill."

Hughes raised his brows in curiosity. "An old friend of mine? Here? In San Antonio?"

"Yes," said Lydia, peering up at Hughes who towered a foot above her head. "A somewhat older lady, yet lovely nonetheless. She said her name was Leighselle Beauclaire."

Hughes stopped. "Leighselle? Here in San Antonio? My God if that doesn't take me back. I haven't seen her in, hell, almost eight years."

"Are you happy that she's here?" Lydia pouted, her voice thin with jealousy.

"Happy—yes. And curious. She was like a big sister to me. She saved my life many years ago when I left New Orleans."

"Saved your life? That frail thing? How?"

"By telling a crafty lie." Hughes took Lydia by the elbow and escorted her inside, a sliver of a smile twitching the corners of his mouth.

CHAPTER THREE

SEPTEMBER 27, 1860

Leighselle sat straight-backed, high-chinned, and perched on the edge of her chair, a queen presiding over her court. She reigned at the head of an empty table that took up most of the space in the sunny breakfast room at the Brazos Guest House. Her black woolen shawl was pulled tight around her thin shoulders despite the warm breeze that fluttered the gingham curtains. The windows were thrown wide to the garden to invite in the scent of musk rose perfuming the morning air.

Sipping from her teacup with her left hand, pinky finger extended, her right hand lay tucked in her lap. In it she clutched a black silk and lace handkerchief embroidered with her initials in bold red script. The long skirt of her black receiving dress puddled at her dainty feet, which were buttoned up in fashionable leather boots. She wore dark mourning colors, though not to show a lady in bereavement. She preferred yellow, but yellow was the color of her youth. Dark fabrics served a practical matter. It was easier hiding the speckles of blood that often accompanied her cough these days.

"Miss Beauclaire, your guest stands at the door." Oma Klein stepped into the entryway of the breakfast room, her curly white hair springing from her head like tightly wound spools of wire, her soft hazel eyes sparkling with curiosity as she regarded her lodger. "Ja, he looks much better than when he rode in last night. Hard to tell it was Mr. Lévesque underneath that blood and dirt."

A cough tickled Leighselle's throat. She fought to repress it, dreading the quaking spasms that had grown more troubling. "Blood and dirt? My heavens. Please, show him in. And bring some more tea if it's not too much trouble."

"Ja, no problem." Oma Klein retreated into the kitchen, returning holding a tray heaping with an assortment of pastries and strudels, a clean-scrubbed, fresh-shaven Hughes Lévesque on her heels.

Hughes looked at Leighselle and smiled, his amused eyes crinkling at the corners. He took both of her gloved hands in his and kissed each one. "You're as lovely as the last time I saw you, Leighselle. When I left New Orleans for good, you made sure I landed on my feet instead of landing myself in jail, or worse."

"No one ever leaves New Orleans for good. You'll be drawn back someday. It's been too long, Hughes. You look well. Handsome. You're not the scrappy youth I remember."

"A lot changes in eight years." He pulled up a chair and set next to his dear old friend, a look of worry and curiosity on his face.

And some things never change, thought Leighselle, some things like the heartache of a lifetime of shameful secrets. A cough bubbled up but she held it back with her handkerchief, allowing just a small sound to escape this time.

Leighselle smiled. "You've filled out and hardened around the edges, but it suits you."

"Besides tutoring me in German, Oma feeds me wonderful pastries. She wants to fatten me," Hughes laughed. "I tutor her in English. The Germans insist on pronouncing every letter, so, her even getting my name right was a challenge. I had to spell it for her as 'Hu Le Vek' before she understood the pronunciation."

"You've always excelled in unique linguistics. It was bird calls and wild animal sounds when you were a boy, and of course, French. Then Creole and Navajo dialects, from what I remember. Any other languages since coming to Texas?"

"Spanish. Comanche. A few other tribal vernaculars. It comes in handy on the job."

With a look of pride, Hughes tapped the five-point star pinned to his vest lapel. It was forged, like all Rangers' badges, from a silver Mexican peso. As essential as a knife or a gun, a Texas Ranger's badge opened doors quicker than a polite knock or a forceful kick.

As Hughes spoke, Leighselle studied his face. She considered his square jaw, the fine angular slant to his nose, and his intense, wide-set eyes. Sunlight streaming in the window reflected off the honey gold strands highlighting his dark brown hair.

His countenance reminded her of a lion, powerful and majestic, although in Hughes's case, almost too handsome to be dangerous. But she knew better. She knew the truth behind the manicured nails, the scholar's vocabulary, and the well-placed manners. He was a gentleman, yes, but dangerous and capable of audacious deeds.

"It's difficult for me to reconcile the precocious young boy from New Orleans with this rough-and-tumble lawman sitting before me." Leighselle laughed at the memory. "Not one to be told 'no,' you kept showing up at my saloon until one day we tired of chasing you away. Oh, how my girls doted on you."

"I'm not always rough-and-tumble, wearing this badge." He leaned in close. "I'll tell you a little secret. Sometimes, when not Rangering, I'm employed by our federal government. I take care of business that others don't want to."

"Ever the chevalier," she whispered. There was no point in asking or in saying any more. She assumed he'd shared with her as much as he was able to divulge.

A violent cough erupted with a sudden force that wracked her body, bending her forward, shaking her shoulders. Her entire body heaved as she fought to catch her breath. Leighselle covered her mouth with her handkerchief, wiping at speckles of blood she feared marred her face.

"My dear, are you all right?" Hughes was at her side, patting her back. He took the handkerchief from her and dabbed at the blood that stained the corners of her mouth. "Here, sip some tea. Can I get you something else?"

"No. No, I'm fine. Thank you." Her shoulders rose and fell in slow motion as she took deep breaths, trying to refill her lungs.

"Ladies who are fine do not cough blood. There's a doctor in residence at the Menger Hotel where I keep a room. I'll send for him." Worry was etched in deep lines on his forehead.

"No, please don't trouble yourself. More tea would be lovely." The smile she gave was weak and unconvincing.

"You should let me send for the doctor, Leighselle. That cough concerns me."

"It's too late for a doctor, Hughes." She cupped a hand over his, her pleading eyes telling him to let go of the idea. "My doctor advised that there is nothing more to do short of easing my pain."

Hughes swallowed, and then took her hands in his. "Is that why you're here, Leighselle? Did you come to see me one last time? I should have come back—"

"I came to San Antonio to ask a favor of an old friend. Your brother told me where to find you. I didn't want to write. I wanted to see you, to ask you face to face. I need your help, Hughes, in tracking—" Another cough even worse than the first rattled Leighselle's emaciated body, her tiny frame seeming as if it might break in two. "Please excuse my coughing. Today is the worst so far."

"Would sitting outside in the fresh air help?" Hughes offered her a glass of water.

Sipping it, she nodded. "It would. Let's take a short stroll."

Hughes took Leighselle by the arm and steered her outside where the warmth of the late September morning's sunshine hinted at an afternoon suitable for siestas. An umbrella stand that Oma kept on the front porch held a lady's parasol. Hughes opened it, carrying it over Leighselle's head, shielding her from the rays of the Texas sun. They walked, unhurried, arm-in-arm, passing by the Spanish Mission where the Battle of the Alamo had occurred.

As they strolled the esplanade that hugged the San Antonio River, Hughes pointed out the Menger Hotel. Amid Spanish Colonial architecture, it was a conspicuous European-looking building, thanks to a German immigrant who built the hotel next to his beer brewery.

"What a grand building. I would very much like to tour it later," Leighselle said, accepting the chair that Hughes pulled out for her.

Adjacent to the hotel, a cluster of tables sat under the sweeping arms of cypress trees lining the river's banks. Hughes sat across from Leighselle, studying her drawn face. "As you wish."

A man dressed in a gray morning coat with a gleaming white towel draped over one arm approached. Hughes greeted him with a smile. "Hello, Jameson. This is a dear friend of mine from New Orleans, Miss Leighselle Beauclaire. She was more like a big sister, really."

"Pleased to make your acquaintance, Mademoiselle Beauclaire." Jameson bent at the waist.

"Enchantée." Leighselle smiled and nodded, impressed with Jameson's manners and French pronunciation of her name.

"Bring us two lemonades, if you will, Jameson. A small shot of whiskey on the side for me," Hughes requested.

Leighselle held up two fingers.

"Make that two shots of whiskey, Jameson, and also send word to Doctor Schmidt that I'd like a moment with him, at his convenience." Hughes winked at Leighselle.

"Of course, Mr. Lévesque, right away, sir." Jameson bent, whispering something to Hughes, while at the same time tucking a note into Hughes's vest pocket. Then, turning on his heels, he marched away with purposeful strides.

Hughes said, "Please, indulge me."

"There is nothing a doctor can—"

"Please? Indulge me. Let Doctor Schmidt have a look at you. What've you to lose?"

"Time. A commodity of which I have precious little. But, I'll agree to see your doctor just so *you* will feel better."

"Thank you," he nodded. "You'll like Doc Schmidt. He's well respected. And, he's an avid though rather inept poker player. If nothing else, you might persuade the good doctor to cut the cards with you. Who knows, you may walk away with a little spending money. Maybe go buy yourself a new petticoat, parasol, or pistol."

"I have plenty of undergarments and umbrellas, but a new little pocket Derringer might be fun." Leighselle's laugh melted into a blood-red cough, her thin shoulders lifting with the weight of each spasm.

Jameson returned with a tray of refreshments and a new folded note for Hughes. After pouring the lemonade into tall tumblers with sugared rims and serving the Old Crow in short whiskey glasses, he stepped back and clasped his hands in front of him, waiting for further instructions.

"Excuse me, Leighselle. This needs my attention. I'll be just a moment," said Hughes as he put the second note into his vest pocket.

"Of course." She poured the whiskey into her glass of lemonade. "I have a suspicion that this will treat a cough better than tea with lemon and honey."

"Fix mine up like that, too, if you will. I'll be right back." Hughes stepped away from the table, Jameson following.

Leighselle watched as they stepped into the shade of the walled patio at the side of the hotel, Jameson speaking, Hughes listening. Nodding his head, Hughes took the notes from his vest and studied each one before handing them back to Jameson who then marched away, disappearing from view into the dark doors of the hotel.

Hughes returned to the table, apologizing. "I hope you'll forgive the interruption." He sat and leaned back in his chair, taking a sip of the potent lemonade concoction. "Mmm. Refreshing. Intoxicating. This may become my new favorite beverage."

"It's mine, without a doubt." She waited for a moment, wondering whether or not Hughes would volunteer anything about the secretive notes, but decided that he would not. Men like Hughes kept secrets. Women like her understood.

"All right, my dear, you have my undivided attention." He leaned forward, elbows on knees, fingers tented, eyes alert and on hers. "Tell me what favor you came all this way to ask of me."

Leighselle brought her handkerchief up to her mouth anticipating a cough that never materialized. "Must be the new medicine," she said, sipping her drink. "I came here to ask you to help me find my daughter."

"Your daughter?" Hughes leaned back in his chair, shaking his head. "I didn't know you had a daughter. And she's lost?"

"Only a few people knew I had a child. Most of them, if not all of them, are dead now. And she's not lost. She was taken from me when she was an infant just days old. I was drugged and blackmailed into giving her up. It's such a long, complicated story, I . . . I don't know where to start."

"At the beginning. Start there." Hughes leaned forward. He took her gloved hand in his, giving it a gentle squeeze.

"The beginning. I was fifteen. My father sold cattle to a Texas rancher. He wasn't a Texan. He was an Irish immigrant who settled in Texas. He would come to our ranch in Vermillion Parish to purchase our pure-bred Brahman cattle and have them shipped to his ranch in Corpus Christi on the Texas Gulf Coast."

Hughes listened, watching Leighselle's confident posture weakening as she spoke, her hands twisting and untwisting the lace handkerchief in her lap.

"He visited several times a year, and every time I would catch him staring at me. Long stares, not casual glances, but vulgar stares so intense that I felt his eyes left a stain on my skin."

"Your father and mother—did they notice his unusual attention to you?"

"Yes. Mother couldn't stand to be in his presence. She would make sure I was kept busy upstairs with my tutor or someplace out of sight. Father tolerated him because he was a rich cattleman who was good for business. Father talked about buying more land, about importing more bulls. He couldn't afford to turn away a wealthy client."

"Did he hurt you, or try to hurt you?" Hughes's voice lowered and darkened.

Leighselle's eyes brimmed with tears. "It's been so long since I've spoken of what happened at Vermillion Bay."

*****

August, 1836

Rusty red soil clung to the slippery banks of the Vermillion River, which flowed into the tepid coastal waters of Vermillion Bay, the river snaking its way south before spilling its murky iron ore into the Gulf of Mexico. The rich dirt oozed a blackish, brick-red slime. Seasonal tidal waters pushed inland and crept upstream through the marshlands, at times causing the river to appear to run backward heading north toward its source, as if the river were swallowing itself in one thirsty gulp.

Everything in the small Louisiana parish—the river, the bayou, the bay, even the parish itself—claimed the name "Vermillion," while the vermillion iron ore claimed the air, the water, the land, the animals, anything else that stood still too long, tinting all within its reach in varying shades of red.

Armand and Jeanine Beauclaire's only child was never still long enough for the color red to claim her. Leighselle La Verne Beauclaire was an active girl, and the minutes spent sitting still were minutes wasted. She hated sitting still; stillness was not something for which she had any patience, and she hated the color red.

"I prefer yellow, Mama, like the sunflowers."

"Then you shall always wear yellow," her doting mother would proclaim.

Leighselle was aware of how the sun's yellow rays could distract her from the ugliness of Vermillion Parish, where everything was a dusty, rusty red. As she grew, Leighselle also gained a keen awareness of how it felt to distract a man from his business, though not through affectation. At the juncture when a young girl crosses over to womanhood, she was a natural beauty. Chestnut hair fell in silky waves past the small fullness of her hips. Flawless porcelain skin provided a palette on which to showcase pink lips too sensuous for a young girl's face. A straight, narrow nose turned up a fraction of a degree at the tip and seemed to point upward to her most dramatic feature: gold-flecked emerald green eyes that edged on the side of being too large for her face. Fringed in thick ebony lashes that grew thicker and longer at the outer corners, the effect was feline.

Seamus Flanders, an Irish immigrant who settled in Texas

and conducted business in Vermillion Parish, was not immune to her charms, despite the twenty years that separated them. His business dealings with Leighselle's father could have been accomplished in a single yearly visit, but he came to Vermillion Parish more often, looking for any excuse, purchasing more cattle than he needed, because it meant another chance to eye the object of his desire.

On the occasions he insinuated himself to be a guest for a meal, he would study Leighselle as if she were an objet d'art meant to be inspected and admired. His intense stares and undue attention made her uncomfortable. She couldn't help but notice that during those times, he often kept his hat strategically placed across his lap.

*****

Leighselle and her little dog, a small white terrier with brown ears and a brown spot at the root of its tail, skipped down toward the river bridge. Her mother had promised she could have a swim and a picnic if she were a good girl and completed her lessons for the day.

The woods thickened. It became dark and cool despite the heat from the near-noon-day sun. Leighselle stopped at the rock where the others had taken off their dresses and took hers off, too. Splashing into the water, her white skin was almost translucent compared to the nut-brown skin of the two slave girls who splashed and played alongside her.

"We supposed to be dyeing them linens, Miss Leighselle. If Massah Beauclaire catches us a swimming and not a working, he sure enough going to be mad." Esther dove into the water. Addy-Frank followed, matching the younger girls' playful exuberance with her own.

"I can handle Father. I'll tell him I was drowning and you both jumped in to save me. He'll award both of you a work pass for snatching his daughter from the jaws of death."

"He ain't going to believe a word a that." Addy-Frank and Esther splashed Leighselle while Jacques raced along the shoreline, barking.

The expensive ivory linens imported from Paris floated in

tubs of ocher water made deep mustard yellow by an abundance of iron oxide in the soil, the mineral-rich dirt a treasure hidden in secret pockets along the riverbank.

Where everything else in Vermillion Parish was red from the prevalent hematite, the soil in the inlet where the girls bathed and washed clothes was infused with the yellows, oranges, and browns of ocher. Using the mineral as pigment, colorants were made to dye the linens and other fabrics of the Beauclaire household in beautiful shades of yellow.

"Come on. We best be getting back with them linens. You mama tell us to have them pinned to the line 'fore noon so the sun can bake that color right in," said Addy-Frank.

"Go on back without me. I'm staying a little longer." Leighselle, chest deep in the slow-moving waters of the Vermillion, flung her head backward and forward, streaming a spray of water from her long hair onto the bank where Jacques jumped and barked, trying to catch the water droplets in his mouth. Leighselle and the girls laughed at the little dog in his tireless efforts, jumping many times his height into the air.

"I reckon that be OK, Miss Leighselle, but don't you be too long," said Addy-Frank. "Your mama get worried if you ain't home 'fore lunch."

"I brought a picnic lunch. Mother's not expecting me back until later." Leighselle splashed the girls as they scampered out of the river. Jacques twisted and twirled in the air and scraped at the water droplets as they sank into the sand. With furious energy, the tenacious pup rooted and scratched where the droplet disappeared from view, his paws and nose turning a bright ocher yellow.

After the girls hurried away with one of the tubs of linens, Leighselle sat on the bank of the river, rubbing the warm ocher sand onto her legs and arms. "Jacques, look. I'm not white anymore. I'm yellow, like your nose. I think I'll stay yellow the rest of my life—it's such a fine color. Much better than red. When I'm old, I shall ask to be buried in a yellow dress."

Pulling on her lace underslip, she reached into the small tote, bringing out a sandwich. She halved it, giving the generous portion to Jacques. It disappeared in an instant. "We must work on your manners, *petit chien*. Maybe teach you to say *please* and *thank you*."

"If I say *please*, will you let me kiss you? Or, will I have to take what I want?" Seamus was on her in an instant, grabbing her from behind, clapping a hand over her mouth before her scream was out. He pushed her onto the wet sand, pinning her to the ground with his weight.

Leighselle struggled but was powerless against the brute force of a man intent on taking what he wanted.

His hot breath panted against the back of her neck, his words—grunts—groans loud in her ear. She wrenched one of her arms free from under her, clawed backward at his face, his hands, but he pinned her arm again. Ripping at her underslip, his rough hands scratched and bruised her pale flesh.

Jacques raced in circles, barking, lunging, biting at his bootleg, grabbing the fabric in his teeth, pulling backward. Seamus shook the little dog off, then kicked hard, booting him a solid blow to the side. Jacques landed in the sand, quiet, unmoving.

Leighselle screamed. His hand over her mouth muffled her cries. The more she struggled, the rougher he got. "I see the way you look at me, teasing me, begging me for this. It's in your eyes that you want me to fuck you. Say it. Say you want me to fuck you."

Leighselle shook her head, frantic, tried to say no, tried to scream, but his hand clamped down on her mouth again. Sand clogged her nostrils, grated her eyes.

"You're mine, Leighselle. After today, no one else will want you. You'll belong to me." Seamus took her in the roughest way he could. "Do you understand? Mine."

Pain ripped through her body. With each push and shove, Leighselle felt as if she might slip into unconsciousness—she prayed that she would. A silent cry formed in her throat and stayed there, even though her mouth, wide open in horror and fear, allowed for its release.

A noise coming from the trail leading down to the river drew Seamus's attention. He pressed his hand hard against Leighselle's mouth, and it covered her nose. She struggled to breathe.

"We forgot one basket of your mama's linens," said Addy-Frank as she stepped from the dense overgrowth of the trail onto the sun-drenched bank. "The big ol' heavy one. Massah Beauclaire say he going to send Ole Isaiah down with the wagon to lift it 'cause it be— Oh!" She stopped mid-stride, frozen, her eyes taking in the graphic scene.

Seamus shoved away from Leighselle, fastening his belt and slipping like a shadow into the darkness of the thicket. Moments later, the clattering of hooves echoed down into the ravine as he galloped across the wooden span. The commotion flushed a murder of nesting crows into the sky.

Addy-Frank splashed across the river, grabbing Leighselle, pulling her up off the sand. "What he done to you? He hurt you?"

Leighselle opened her mouth but no words formed. No one could ever know about this. No one. She pulled away from Addy-Frank's grasp and tugged at the torn slip that was ripped down the front, trying to cover herself.

"Who done this? You know him?" Addy-Frank grabbed Leighselle's shoulders. "Who?"

"He comes from Texas to buy cattle." Leighselle began to shake, a sound like that of an injured dove rising softly from within. "I couldn't stop him. I tried to stop it, but I couldn't."

"Your daddy's shotgun sure stop him. I go get Massah."

"No! You never saw anything. Father—his business. We can't speak of this to anyone. It'll shame him. He—"

"Miss Leighselle, you need to tell your—"

"Tell no one. Go back to the house like you never left."

Addy-Frank opened her mouth to speak, hesitated, and then walked back up the trail toward the house, leaving the river behind.

Leighselle knelt by Jacques, who was whimpering, his paws twitching. She stroked the dog's side, feeling for broken ribs. "You'll be all right. Lay still, little dog, and catch your breath."

Stepping into the warm current, she located the large flat-topped boulder that sat partially submerged under the water's surface, the rock she played on and dove from—the rock that snapping turtles sunned themselves on and where frogs would sit and catch dragonflies.

She lay on the rock, letting the warm, slow-flowing waters of the Vermillion wash the ocher sand from her slip, her hair, her skin. She imagined the water washing away the nightmare, purging it from her body and flowing it out to sea.

Leighselle closed her eyes against the glaring sun, against the indigo sky, against the red river, against the ocher sand and sunflowers bending over the banks, and against all that was fine and vibrant. Nothing would ever be fine or vibrant again. Something died. It was the death of yellow.

*****

"My God, Leighselle. I want to kill him." Hughes pushed back from the table, knocking his chair over as he moved to her side, crouching down next to her. "Tell me where this monster is. I'll put a bullet into his black heart. That son of a bitch is a dead man."

Leighselle coughed into her handkerchief, patted each corner of her mouth clean, and then took a sip of lemonade. "If I recall, defending a woman who had been brutalized by a man was what led you to flee New Orleans in the first place."

"That wasn't a man who brutalized Monique. That was an animal. So was the creature who attacked you." Hughes dropped his fist hard down on the table, sending the silverware clattering. "Nothing tightens my jaw faster than seeing a man hurt a woman. I had a gut full of that as a kid, seeing my mother cower from her own husband."

"What happened to me seems a lifetime ago. I do have an idea where Seamus Flanders lives, if indeed he's still living, but it's not him I want you to find. It's my daughter."

"Your daughter would be close to my age, then, or a few years older," Hughes said.

"Oh, no. That grievous incident didn't result in a pregnancy. Seamus is not the child's father. He's the child's grandfather. I fell in love with Seamus's son, Henry, but I wasn't aware of the connection. Henry had just arrived in America at the Port of Orleans from Ireland. I told you it was complicated."

"That's putting it mildly." Hughes righted his toppled chair, taking a seat close to Leighselle.

"Indeed. And, all that I just told you is the easy part of the story."

"The easy part? Good God." Hughes shook his head and gave Leighselle a long, hard look, his eyes moving slowly over her thin face.

Her emerald green eyes were jaundiced, sunken, and accentuated by dark circles underneath. The angular sharpness of her cheekbones protruded from parchment paper skin. Lips, once supple and pink, were drawn into a thin, pained slit in an attempt of barring coughs from escaping.

"Did you ever marry or have a family of your own?" she asked, uncomfortable with how he studied her with such intense concern. She knew she was dying—she had hoped it wasn't that obvious.

"In my line of work, it's better not to." Hughes waved at Jameson, indicating more lemonade. "Having a wife would leave her vulnerable. If someone, an enemy, wanted to get to me, all they'd have to do would be to threaten the woman I loved."

"Do you have many enemies?" she asked, her eyebrows raised in surprise.

"A hired gun always has enemies. It's my aim to never leave one standing."

Leighselle shuddered, pulling her shawl tighter. "Concentrating on a job would be near impossible, I would guess, if you had someone at home to worry about."

"I don't have a permanent home, anyway. Another reason to stay single." He gave a casual shrug of his shoulders.

"There are many reasons men choose to remain single. Yours sounds like one of the better ones." A small cough tickled the back of her throat, lingering, never erupting into a full spasm. She waited, expecting it to explode, but the moment passed, leaving only the metallic aftertaste of blood.

CHAPTER FOUR

Journal Entry of Bar Flanders:

"A boy straddles a saddle differently than a girl" *were the parting words Aunt Winnie called to my back when I rode out of Hog Mountain this morning. She's right.*

In my mind's eye, I see my papa sitting tall in his saddle, reins in his left hand held loose between his fingers, a lariat gripped in his right, his preferred hand for shooting, too. He sat a saddle with the confident, casual attitude given to men born to ride. Given to girls born to ride, too.

I must remember to ride, sit, dress, eat, laugh, spit, talk, walk, and think like a boy—all while acting naturally. However, through trial and error, I have determined it is impossible to stand and pee like a boy.

Today's travels brought me a few miles east of Fort Worth. Not a bad start at all for a wagon horse. We put a respectable dent in the three hundred and fifty miles left to go. If we average fifty miles a day, then we can make Little Rock, Arkansas by this time next week. From there to Saint Joseph, Missouri is another four hundred seventy-five miles. However, the Overland Stage can cover one hundred miles or more in twenty-four hours since it makes quick stops to change drivers and horses and to allow passengers comfort breaks.

By my calculations, I'll be applying at the Central Overland California and Pikes Peak Express Company by the end of October. As Aunt Winnie cautioned, I'll refrain from referring to it as the COC & PP Express Company. Pronouncing the name as the cock and pee-pee express company would send Aunt Winnie into another fit of laughter.

If I pocket twenty-five dollars a week all of November, December, and January, I'll have at least three hundred dollars to finish paying the taxes due on the ranch, plus some. Won't ol' Mr. Goldthwaite swallow his teeth when he sees that?

We (King and I) made camp just at sunset. Bone-deep weariness saps my appetite. My desire for food hides itself behind my ribcage. Papa used to say that. "What's wrong girl? Your hunger hiding behind your ribs?" I'd laugh, he'd laugh, I'd feign starvation. His eyes would twinkle—his grin would spread across his face. Papa's smile, his ear connecting smile. . . .

I look west and my thoughts tangle. I wonder what's wrong with me—wrong with my heart. Did I leave it in Palo Pinto? I wasn't sad this morning leaving Starling. I should have been, but I wasn't. All I could think about was getting on that horse and riding. Not riding away from her, but riding toward this opportunity.

The township of Dallas is tomorrow's target, so I should close my journal and sleep. I wonder if I'll have that dream again, that recurring dream I've had these past few nights. A

*wolf, silent and powerful, watches over me and
I'm not afraid. He keeps the nightmares at bay.*

*Tomorrow, I'll forgive myself for not
feeling sad about leaving my baby sister. I'll put
emotions aside. I'll concentrate on one thing:
being Bar Flanders.*

*****

October 17, 1860

The township of Dallas was abuzz with activity as Barleigh rode
through the middle of the square. Everyone was pitching in to
rebuild the business district, which had been torched the previous
July. Only a few buildings were completely functional. Others
were half-gutted shells, although still operational. Most, however,
were nothing but charred heaps of blackened rubbish.

Seeing the destruction, smelling the scorched remains of
wood and plaster, caused her blood to cool. The memory of *that
night* came rushing back with the sooty breeze that swept through
the burned-out streets.

Barleigh rode King past the blackened buildings, looking
for the livery stables. A helpful stranger pointed her down Main
Street, indicating the building adjacent to Bennett's Mercantile.
Barleigh tipped her hat, said "Much obliged," and kept riding.

A pinch-faced elderly woman, along with her homely
daughter who was approaching old maid status, was at the stables
waiting for the stagecoach. "My widowed sister lives here, but
we're going back home to Austin," the mother informed Barleigh.
Her busy hands fussed at the closures on her dress, with her
daughter's dress, and with the ribbons that held her hat to her head.
"You know who did that, don't you?"

"Ma'am?" Barleigh peered from under the brim of her hat,
following the woman's pointed finger toward the rebuilding
project. "Uh, no, ma'am, I don't."

"Wasn't lightning did that," she said, flipping the handle of
her carpet bag back and forth. "Nope. Local slaves rebelled and set
fire to those buildings. Abolitionists were run out of town, three
Negroes hanged, and a judge ordered all the rest of the slaves in

51

the township whipped for good measure. No telling who really done it. But they all got whipped." She tugged at the fingers of her gloves, then settled her brown, pin eyes on Barleigh. "You aren't an Abolitionist, are you?"

"I, uh, I just stopped here for water and to check my horse's shoes, ma'am." A cold sweat broke out on her brow. Her hands shook as she fumbled with untying the leather straps that attached the canteens to the saddle.

The mother continued her nosy inquiry, asking where Barleigh came from, where she was going, and might the mother and her daughter be fortunate enough that her destination might also be Austin. "A male escort would be most welcome, given the unrestful atmosphere. Two helpless women traveling alone. . . ." She fretted again with the ribbons on her hat, the frayed ends betraying an old habit.

"I'm Bar Flanders, ma'am. Headed to Saint Joseph, Missouri, to hire on with the Pony Express." She kept her words and eye contact to a minimum, though the mother tried hard to engage her in a staring contest. The daughter, however, never raised her eyes off the ground or her voice above a whisper.

"Mirabella, wouldn't he make a fine young suitor for you?" The mother elbowed her daughter, eyes wide, and her gloved hands fluttered in the air like two seizured birds. "I think he should come to Austin instead. He can work on the ranch, if he wants to ride horses for a living."

Barleigh tipped her hat, politely declined, made her excuse to be on her way, tipped her hat again, and aw-shucked her way out of there.

While she spurred King away at a fast trot, her mind played with the notion of who she'd have become, if she'd grown up with a fussy mother like that. Would she be an old maid, quiet, shy, and afraid of her own shadow like Mirabella? Maybe fate had it right that she should have grown up without a mother, with Papa raising her as he did, in a saddle, on a horse, under the wide-open sky, just as at ease with a pistol as she was with a pencil.

With the first close encounter a success, she was nearer to becoming Bar Flanders, perfecting her persona, growing ever more natural with her boy-self as each hour passed. Sinking into this new somebody she was becoming, she found the clouded image easier to hide behind.

A small stand of towering cottonwoods lined the banks of a creek where she made camp for the night, their leaves pale yellow with the approaching autumn chill. The place reminded her of where her horse, Willow, was stolen by an Indian boy on the wagon trail north when they had left the Gulf Coast behind. Making a small fire, she sipped coffee from a tin cup, remembering.

It had been along the Brazos River between Waco and Fort Worth when she had broken her papa's number one rule of the wagon trail, to always stay together. She'd ridden off alone like a hotheaded fool.

*****

"What am I hearing coming from inside that wagon?" Seamus Flanders, Barleigh's grandfather, shouted as he brought up the team of horses to be harnessed for the day's drive. "Barleigh, what are you doing in the wagon? Birdie is supposed to be repacking breakfast supplies."

"She's through with packing. I'm reading to her. And, I'm teaching her to read, too, just like Papa taught me." Barleigh poked her head through the flap in the canvas that covered the wagon and smiled at her grandfather.

"Slaves can't read. They don't know how. Come out of there at once, Barleigh." His face reddened with anger.

"Birdie can read. I taught her. Go on, Birdie, show Grandfather how well you pronounce the words." Barleigh crawled out of the wagon and perched on the seat, motioning for Birdie to follow. She held the book out for Birdie to take, but Birdie refused.

"That not be a good idea," said Birdie, a slight catch in her voice. "Your grandfather a busy man this morning, getting the horses and wagon ready and all."

"See," Seamus said with a smirk. "Even Birdie knows it's a farce. She's memorizing what you've read to her. She's not reading. Slaves are incapable. Their brains don't function the way ours do."

"Birdie can," Barleigh insisted. "Here, read this next paragraph that I haven't read to you. Show Grandfather you're not memorizing. Go on." She handed the book to Birdie, pointing out the next paragraph.

Birdie shook her head 'no,' clamping her hands behind her back, refusing to take the book.

Seamus laughed, his words caustic. "See. I told you. Darkies are ignorant. You can show them a task, but you can't teach them complicated skills."

Barleigh pressed the issue, insisting that Birdie demonstrate her command of reading, proud of how she'd taught her. "Birdie, show him he's wrong. Go on, now."

Birdie hesitated, and then took the book in her hands. She read, her voice slow and steady, enunciating each word:

"This is God's curse on slavery! A bitter, bitter, most accursed thing! A curse to the master and a curse to the slave! I was a fool to think I could make anything good out of such a deadly evil."

Seamus spun on his heels, pulling Birdie from the wagon, slapping her hard across her face with the back of his hand, knocking her onto the ground. She landed in a heap at his feet. The book slipped from her hands and lay open in the dirt, its pages flapping like a tiny flock of white birds trying to take flight.

He kicked the book into the dying embers of the campfire. "You are never to pick up another book again. Do you understand me?" he shouted, pointing his finger at Birdie who lay on the ground, an angry welt beginning to swell across her cheek.

Birdie held a fist to her bleeding lip, tears welling in her eyes. "Yes'suh. I won't never."

"Grandfather, don't!" Barleigh shrieked. "Stop!" She leapt from the wagon and attached herself to her grandfather's arm as he lifted Birdie off the ground with one hand, his other slapping her across the mouth.

"What the hell?" Henry came at a run to see his father with one hand a twisted fist gripping the front of Birdie's dress, the other upraised, ready to inflict another blow to her already swollen face. Barleigh clung to his upraised arm, swinging like a monkey from a branch.

Henry's voice growled low with a trembling fury not to be ignored. He spoke each word as a single imperative. "Let her go, Father. Never again lift a hand to her. If I ever see you or hear of you striking this woman, it'll be me you face."

"Know your place, boy. Birdie is my slave. It's my prerogative to punish her as I see fit. Any slave caught reading deserves punishment."

"That's a damn coward's way, a man striking a woman. If you wish to hit someone, hit me, *Father*." Henry spoke the word '*father*' without a trace of respect. He balled his fists, ready to receive or to land a blow.

"Birdie is not a woman, she's a slave. And she's my slave, lest you forget." Seamus spat out the words as if they tasted bitter in his mouth.

"She's a human being." The veins that formed a V on Henry's forehead and that crept their way to the surface when he showed anger pulsed hot and red. "Let the punishment fit the crime. If her crime is reading," he enunciated each word with crisp indignation, "then take away the book."

"I took that away, too. She is never to read again. Never. Do you all three hear my voice and understand my words? I demand you respect my rules," shouted Seamus. "My slave. My rules."

"You're ashamed that Birdie can read—something you never learned. You pretend, all right, with your library full of precious books." Henry's hands fisted and unfisted at his sides.

"I've never been ashamed of anything." Seamus turned and stomped back to the wagon to finish hitching the team.

"I have," Henry shouted at his father's back. He took a rag, wet it with water from his canteen, and began washing the blood from Birdie's face.

"I'm sorry, Henry. I didn't know what the next line be. I just be reading for him like he say to. I'm sorry." Birdie whimpered, wincing as Henry dabbed at the blood oozing from her swollen lip.

"It's not your fault, Birdie. I should have put a stop to Barleigh teaching you. I was afraid something like this would happen if my father found out."

"No," Barleigh said, stomping her foot. "You should not have put an end to the reading lessons. You should've put an end to Birdie being Grandfather's slave. Don't you understand, Papa?" She ran to the campfire and tried to pluck the burning book out of the coals.

Henry grabbed his daughter by the shoulders and spun her around. "You read and get ideas about things you don't understand. What were you thinking, reading *Uncle Tom's Cabin* to Birdie? Letting her read it aloud? You should have known better." He kicked at the remaining pages that smoldered and glowed red around the edges.

"You bought me the book, Papa, so I'd have something new to read on our journey. Now you say I shouldn't be reading it. I don't understand . . . ." Barleigh tried to pull away.

"Look at me, daughter. I do understand your desire for the world to be fair. But darling, you're only fourteen and too young to understand the world. This is a complicated issue that has no easy solution."

"The solution is easy, Papa. You and Grandfather are making it hard."

Barleigh didn't want to listen to him. She just wanted to ride, to ride away from him and her grandfather and the things she didn't understand. Untying Willow from the wagon, she swung into the saddle.

"I can find my way to Fort Worth. I don't want to ride along with you. I hate that Grandfather won't let Birdie be free, Papa, and I hate you for not insisting on it."

As soon as the words left her mouth, they hung like black darts in the air—sharp and hurtful. She wanted them back.

"Barleigh," Henry shouted. "Don't even think about riding off from here by yourself. It's too dangerous to ride alone. Barleigh, do you hear me?" He kicked the ground hard, twice, sending a spray of rocks flying. "Damn it, girl. Why are you such a hothead?" He stood, fists on hips, glaring at his daughter.

"It's not just slaves, Henry, who should not be taught to read," Seamus shouted over his shoulder, the horses now hitched, the wagon ready. "Impudent, young teenage girls should learn sewing and cooking and leave education to men like us who know what to do with it. It was a foolish thing for you to teach that girl to read. You should've known better."

"There're lots of things I should've known better. I don't count this as one of them." Henry spoke to his father, but his eyes were on his daughter. His blue eyes were not shining and lively, but hurt and dark.

Barleigh turned away, reining her mare around, spurring much harder than what was needed to escape from the pain in her father's eyes, from Birdie's bruised and swollen face, from the madness of her grandfather's wrath. She wished she hadn't spurred Willow so hard, wished she hadn't thrown those hateful words at her papa. She could do nothing now but ride for Fort Worth.

Spurring the horse into a fast gallop, Barleigh smacked the latigo against the mare's hip over and over when she didn't have to. Willow dug down, running faster, trying her damnedest to comply with what was being asked of her. The little mare ran near to exhaustion, trying to please her rider. The harder the horse tried, the more Barleigh sobbed.

How could her grandfather be so brutal toward Birdie? Barleigh wondered if she was like him? Did she have it in her, too, whipping and spurring her poor horse as she did? Could that evil streak run through her own blood and harden her bones? The thought terrified her.

"Easy, there, easy now." She stroked Willow's neck and slowed her to a walk, bending forward, burying her face in the horse's mane. "I'm sorry, girl, I shouldn't have made you run so hard." Leaning sideways in the saddle, she ran her hands down the horse's sides, checking for blood. She heaved a sigh of relief at the sight of her unstained hands.

A gathering of trees a half mile or so off the trail indicated water. Cottonwood trees edged the banks and offered their long branches to shade the ground. She reined Willow to a stop, unsaddled her, but left the bridle on keeping the reins tied around her neck to make it easy to catch her.

"I'm sorry, Willow, please forgive me. I'll never do that again. I promise." She breathed deeply the smell of the horse's sweaty neck and stroked the star that swirled at the tip of her blaze. Willow nickered, then dropped her head to the ground and began to graze on the sweet spring grass growing at the edge of the wide creek, its water cool, clear, and inviting.

After filling the canteen, Barleigh poured water on her head, splashing her face, washing off the dusty streaks from her tears. She laid down on the saddle blanket and watched as the horse nipped the green grass clean at the root while ignoring the cattails and bitter weed sprouting along the water's edge.

Stretching out in the warm sunshine, Barleigh shut her eyes, her mind unsettled. The breeze whispered as it rustled through the cottonwood leaves. She mused: does the tree own the dirt around its roots, taking from it what it wants, or does the dirt own the tree, holding it against its will?

Her eyelids grew heavy and she drifted off to sleep, pondering a world out of balance—a world she didn't understand.

The snap of a twig awoke Barleigh from her nap. She rolled over onto her side, propping her head in her palm, yawning. "Willow, we better get you saddled and ourselves back on the trail before . . ." Her breath caught in a startled gasp.

At the water's edge, a young Indian boy crouched on all fours, drinking straight out of the pond like a thirsty horse, or a coyote. His dark skin glistened in the sun, while his brown eyes, darting between Barleigh and Willow, looked wild. He was a predator sizing up his prey. He sprang to his feet with liquid grace and ran toward the horse. Grabbing a handful of the mare's mane, he leapt onto her back in a singular bound, digging his bare heals into her sides, and was gone.

"Willow!" Barleigh screamed, running after the pair, feet tangling, falling, hands out, catching, cactus quills sticking. But it was no use. A trail of sepia-colored dust rose above the trail quite a distance away as the Indian boy galloped the stolen horse from view.

ORPHAN MOON

Henry and the wagon caught up with Barleigh as she walked, carrying her saddle. His fear of what could have happened to his daughter turned his initial relief that she was all right into blistering anger. Barleigh had broken her father's number one rule and had ridden off alone. She knew that she deserved his rage, and more. She had let her horse be stolen.

The remainder of the journey to Fort Worth, she rode in the back of the wagon, curled up with her head resting in Birdie's lap. She lost herself to the rhythmical sound of Peaty and Boss's large hooves striking the ground at a fast trot. In a soft, hushed voice, Birdie crooned lullabies just as she had when Barleigh was a small child, while the swaying wagon rocked and soothed her. The canvas cover, pulled open and tied to the sides, showcased the milk cow following behind, trying her best to keep up. The bell Barleigh had tied around the cow's neck clanged with each desperate stride.

The infinite horizon shimmered as it stretched in an unbroken line. Barleigh kept her eyes alert to any sign of something breaking that line—a lone rider on a stolen horse; a group of riders looking for trouble—but all she saw was dust and dirt and sky.

A searing wind twirled around the wagon, dust swirling, twisting upward. "Wind hot as the devil's breath be a bad omen," Birdie said half to herself. Barleigh's spine tingled with a creeping chill. A single white cloud as billowy and fluffy as cotton passed overhead, erasing the wagon's shadow.

*****

They arrived in Fort Worth as the long-reaching orange and pink fingers of the setting sun stretched out to greet them, the sky an inky blue-black to the east. It was June 25, 1855. The journey had taken three weeks and three days.

If fort is a shortened version of the word fortress, Barleigh thought they must be in terrible trouble. Little remained of anything recognizable as fortress-like. High up on a north-facing bluff overlooking the Clear Fork of the Trinity River remained a portion of a wall bearing gun turrets, the heavy wooden shutters thrown open as a bold invitation to the night sky. If stars were the enemies, a clean and clear shot would be certain.

Mr. Simon Goldthwaite, the attorney and banker who had corresponded with Henry regarding the property in Palo Pinto, greeted them upon their arrival. He was quick to say that Fort Worth had been disbanded and evacuated over a year prior when the Army had ceased its operation as a fortified military outpost. Remaining settlers took over the fort, setting up shops and businesses, using the timber from the fortress walls to build homes, a schoolhouse, and additional buildings for commerce. One unique business, something he called Leonard's Department store, deserved special mention.

"Imagine a large store with an entire department of boots and shoes, another section full of hardware, and another of women's finery," he said with a theatrical wink and a nod. "Over here you have a department for men, over there, a department for children. Everything you need and don't yet know you need, all under one roof!" He winked again, slow and deliberate.

"All of the Hostiles have been pushed back farther west," he explained as reason for the fort's dismantling. "The Army, with wisdom and forethought, relocated all garrisons to points deeper into Indian Territory."

"Not all Indians," Barleigh informed him, "have vacated the area." In a gush of words, she spouted, "One is at this very moment well mounted on a fancy little palomino mare named Willow. She stands fourteen and a half hands, has a star and a narrow blaze, four white socks, flaxen mane and tale, with a coat that is a deep autumn leaf gold, just in case you find her."

Henry told Mr. Goldthwaite about the morning's encounter a few miles north of where the Brazos River flowed through the town of Waco. Mr. Goldthwaite said he would inform the Texas Rangers of the incident, but he assured Henry that folks in Fort Worth were safe.

Mr. Goldthwaite had planned for the next day a trip to Palo Pinto, a small community half a day's ride west, to show Henry the new ranch, causing Henry to smile for the first time since having left Corpus Christi.

Barleigh hoped Palo Pinto smelled like it sounded—like a horse. Like a sweaty horse. That wonderful, woodsy, smoky smell reminded her of campfires on cold mornings.

"The land, eight hundred acres and more to be had if you desire," said Mr. Goldthwaite, "lies between a fork of the Brazos River and the Coffee Creek, the creek getting its name because it turns dark reddish brown when a storm churns and muddies the water. It foams on top because of the loose silt from the caliche beds, like someone added a helping of cream. I don't know about you," he winked again, "but I sure do like cream with my coffee."

Barleigh asked if she could name their new home "The Coffee Creek Ranch." Henry, turning aside of Goldthwaite, gave a comical wink and a dramatic nod, sending Barleigh into a fit of laughter.

*****

Riding through the township of Dallas, Barleigh had spied a palomino horse tied at a hitching post, and she thought of Willow. Yellow horses and pale yellow cottonwoods putting on their fall colors were nostalgic symbols that triggered melancholy memories.

She poured water on the campfire and covered it with a scoop of dirt. Huddled deep in her bedroll, she wrapped the black and red Navajo blanket around her shoulders, wondering what the next day's ride might bring.

CHAPTER FIVE

SEPTEMBER 27, 1860

Jameson appeared with a tray of beverages and an assortment of ripe fruit. After tidying the table and laying out clean, pressed linen napkins, he asked in a clipped British accent, "Will there be anything else, sir?" The fullness of his dark mustache covered his mouth and hung well below his square jawline, his furry caterpillar eyebrows arching upward to accentuate his inquiry.

"Thank you, Jameson, that'll be all for now," said Hughes, centering the tray on the table.

Leighselle watched as Jameson retreated into the shadows of the hotel, his uniform impeccable. The old cloud of doubt and guilt crept into her mind, and she wondered again what it might be like to own a reputable establishment like a hotel, instead of the rowdy saloon, La Verne's Tavern, that bore her middle name.

She folded and refolded the crisp white napkin, moved the glass of lemonade an inch this way, two inches that way, and picked at the ripe, red strawberry on her plate. "So," she sighed deeply, eliciting a rattling cough that shook the table, "the rest of my story won't tell itself, will it?"

"No." Hughes shook his head. He waited, giving her time to collect her thoughts.

Leighselle's gaze drifted across the scenic landscape, settling on a point somewhere along a bend in the river. "After the attack, I wanted to die. I felt horrible guilt that somehow I *had* brought it on. But it wasn't me who died. Typhoid fever was taking its toll in the poorer quarters, and it spread throughout the parish, soon claiming my mother, father, and most of our servants."

"Good God, Leighselle. I had no idea. How did you survive, after what you'd been through?"

"I had no choice. The next morning, after a night of wishing *I* were dead, I awoke to find the household quiet, mother and father in bed, and *they* were deathly sick. I somehow pulled myself together and found the wherewithal to ride into Vermillion Parish to fetch Doctor Bronstein. He came right away, and for three days we did all we could for my parents. Then I got sick with the typhoid, too." The memory of typhoid's deadly fever caused a visible shudder, and Leighselle dotted her forehead with her handkerchief.

Hughes moved his plate aside and poured two cups of coffee, passing one to Leighselle. "What year was this? You were —?"

"Fifteen, almost sixteen. It was September of 1836. Doctor Bronstein called it 'the month of death.' I remember waking up, looking out the window, with the sensation of being in a very bad dream."

*****

The sky is on fire and the sun has gone black. Lying back on the pillow, Leighselle drifted in and out of dreams. Fiery dreams. Dreams of panic, terror, and pain. Running. Falling. Drowning. A hand over her mouth. Suffocating. Screaming. Fading to nothing. Nothing.

Big Betty walked into the room and sat a tea tray at the foot of Leighselle's bed. "Wake up now, Miss Leighselle. Time for afternoon tea. I brung you cinnamon scones. You gonna like them scones, um-hm. I done buttered them for you."

Leighselle sat up. "Where am I?"

"You's at Doctor Bronstein's house. I done told you the same thing every time you ask, but that's fine. You been sick a good while. You bound to forget what you done ask." Big Betty fisted her hands on her ample hips. "But today I see the ol' Leighselle shining through them eyes. Thank you, Lawd."

"I thought I heard Jacques whimpering. Is he sick, too?" A

wave of panic washed over Leighselle as she looked around for her dog.

"He fine. He right here on the floor licking up crumbs." Betty lifted the little dog onto the bed and he burrowed under the blanket. "What spread round here ain't affecting the animals. Only the peoples." Big Betty opened the window on the opposite side of the room. "But only some peoples. Addy-Frank and her child, Birdie, they all right, but Addy-Frank's twin babies, they too weak and young to fight something like this. Doctor Bronstein be all right too, 'cause he say God protect him so he can treat those that be sick."

"Mother and Father? Where are they? Are they at home? Are they all right now? I remember they were sick. I helped take care of them. I remember . . ."

Doctor Bronstein rapped on the bedroom door. "I see you are awake, Miss Leighselle. May I enter?"

"Yes, please come in," she said, setting the empty teacup aside.

Big Betty poured another cup. "Drink more, baby, if you can. You need strength. Doctor, you want I should wait outside?"

"No. No, Big Betty. I think you should stay."

"Yes'suh."

"Leighselle," he said, pulling a chair up to the bed, "we must have a serious discussion about your circumstance. Let me listen to your lungs first."

After a brief exam, Doctor Bronstein patted her on the back and said, "Well, child, you are on the road to recovery. No fever. Eyes and throat clear. A slight rattle in your lungs but much improved even over yesterday. You'll be fit to travel within the month if you continue improving."

"Fit to travel? Where am I going? Where are my parents?" She sat up straighter. The serious tone of the doctor's voice caused an inner alarm to begin chiming.

Big Betty sat on the bed and took Leighselle's hand in hers, Doctor Bronstein taking the other. With his free hand, he pushed his glasses back up on his nose, then changed his mind and took them off, tucking them into his coat pocket. Beads of sweat glistened on his bald head, which he blotted with his shirtsleeve.

"This is unpleasant, my child, but there is one way to deal with tragedy, and that is straight on. The fact is that your parents did not recover from their illness. I'm very sorry. We did all we could, but it was not to be for them to get well."

A sob tried to form in the back of Leighselle's throat. A tear brimmed but then settled back into place, as if the effort was too taxing for her exhausted body that had spent the last month hovering close to death. "When?" she asked, her voice a whisper.

"A month ago, just before I brought you here to my house. You were gravely ill, too. I wasn't sure my medicine would pull you through."

"I see. And the slaves?"

"All gone, except for Addy-Frank and her eldest child Birdie. I'm afraid that they are all you have left." The doctor patted his forehead again, blotting the perspiration.

"All I have left? What do you mean? I have the animals—the house—the property." That's not logical, Leighselle thought. The doctor was making no sense to her.

Doctor Bronstein looked hard into her eyes. "Let me be quick with this. It's best to be quick. On his deathbed, I promised your father I would look out for you. He sent for his attorney to witness me becoming your guardian. Do you understand?"

Leighselle nodded her understanding.

"Both your father and your mother loved you very much. It was their final wish that you should not have to worry about the future, if you survived. They asked that I sell the ranch and put the funds in a trust for you. Do you recall your neighbor to the north, the man whose plantation borders your property?"

"Yes, I know him. My father called Monsieur Baptiste a braggart and a crook and a cruel excuse for a man. Father said he once beat a horse half to death for sucking in air and refusing to be saddled."

"Yes. He has a reputation for being rough. But he offered a fair price for your property, including the cattle and horses." Then, looking at Big Betty, he said, "Please bring me a glass of water, Betty."

"Yes'suh."

Doctor Bronstein tapped his pocket as if remembering where he put his glasses, and then slid them back onto his face, nudging them into place. "Monsieur Baptiste's one stipulation was that the buildings be set afire. I could not convince him that the air in your home was not tainted, that this disease did not come from bad air. But, he insisted."

Leighselle looked out the window. "The sky was on fire this morning. I saw it from my window. I thought I was dreaming. That was my—"

"Yes, that was your house. The carriage house and the slave's quarters, too. He sent his men over. I had no choice. Besides the money from the land, you've retained ownership of Addy-Frank and Birdie."

"Ownership? I don't know the first thing about taking care of slaves. I'll set them free. I recall Father tell Mother that others are doing so." Hearing clearly her father's voice in her head speaking to her mother seemed surreal. *They're gone now. I'm all alone.*

"In some northern states, yes. But it's against the law in Louisiana to emancipate a slave. You could go to jail right along with the slave you were trying to free." He reached for the glass of water. "Thank you, Betty."

"Yes'suh," nodded Big Betty as she moved to the side table and began her preparation of medicinal tea.

"Besides," the doctor continued, "you'll need Addy-Frank as your handmaid to help you with personal, day-to-day requirements. I've enrolled you in school up in Shreveport."

Leighselle's stomach lurched. "What kind of school? I've never been to *school*. Mother hired tutors." A cold sweat began to form on her brow. She reached for the cup of tea Big Betty offered, her hands unsteady and weak.

"I understand this is a shock, so much information to take in at once. But this is best. You'll not be tied to a place of bad memories. The ranch would be impossible for you to undertake on your own. You'll be going to school at the Medical Hospital in Shreveport. That's where I studied to become a doctor. It's one of the finest facilities to learn medicine outside of Virginia Military Institute, which doesn't allow females. Shreveport will allow female students in their nursing program." The doctor emptied the glass of water, refilling it.

"But I don't like to be around sickness," Leighselle protested, trying to keep her voice even despite the adrenaline pushing it higher. "The smell of vomit gags me. The sight of blood makes me swoon. The sound of pained wailing terrifies me. I—I cannot."

"Don't be afraid, child. You'll be fine. It's all settled. I've paid your tuition with the proceeds from the sale of your property, and you have a tidy sum remaining in a trust fund that I've set up for you at the National Bank in New Orleans. Once you are out of school, you can open a clinic of your own. Of course, you'll have to hire a doctor to run the clinic. But, technically, he would work for you. Now, is that not a fine idea?"

Leighselle lay back on her pillow, staring at the ceiling. "Mother and Father dead. The ranch sold. Mammy Hannah, Johnny Boy, Esther, all the others gone, too. Me in nursing school with Addy-Frank and Birdie? I need time to think this all through."

"Of course, my dear. When you awake tomorrow morning, I trust you'll see I have done my best for you. You'll have an education. Money in the bank. You can leave this sorrowful place and put your sadness behind you." Doctor Bronstein stood up, steadying himself against the doorframe.

"My sadness will come with me. It's stitched to me like my own skin."

"In time, that sadness will diminish. Your heart will find ways to refill itself with other joys. Rest, drink the medicine Betty prepared, and continue getting stronger."

"Yes, Doctor. Thank you."

Leighselle rolled over, scooping Jacques up from where he'd burrowed under the covers, placing him on the pillow next to her. Looking out the window, she tried to envision this red land without her parents, without the slaves who had always been a part of her life, without her home, her horses, where nothing remained but red death.

She felt vacant, hollow, as untethered as a free-floating balloon. There was nothing left for her in Vermillion Parish. She must find her own way.

A plan began to piece itself together in Leighselle's mind. She knew she was not suitable for nursing—she didn't have what it must take to be a good nurse. There stood a high probability that she might harm her patients, if for no other reason than for desertion. Surely there were laws against that.

Jacques scooched closer and whimpered, then poked his nose into the palm of Leighselle's hand, his signal for more attention. As she stroked his silky, triangle ear, she considered her future. With a quiet reckoning, it came into soft focus, like fog gradually lifting over the Vermillion River, transforming the red dirt banks and bends and ocher shoals into something definable.

"I'll be damned, Jacques, if we're going to Shreveport. My money is in a bank in New Orleans. By God then, that's where we shall go."

*****

Hughes studied the frail woman sitting across from him. "I'm trying to imagine you as a frightened yet determined teenage girl embarking on such a journey. It would take gumption for an adult to undertake what you were considering. You were just a child."

Opening her parasol, she rose to her feet. "I was a girl with gumption. I just didn't fully realize it yet. I'm getting a bit stiff, sitting. Let's take a walk, shall we?"

"Of course. And so you set off for New Orleans." As they stepped away from the table, Hughes waved at Jameson, indicating they'd be back soon.

It wasn't pleasant, the leaving, Leighselle recalled. There had been other deaths to contend with first. "By the time I was well enough to leave Vermillion Bay, both Doctor Bronstein and Big Betty had succumbed to the typhoid, too."

So much death in such a short period of time had left only a few remaining souls who were able to help bury the dead. "Addie-Frank sent for help from the neighboring plantation, but the only help available was a skinny, eight-year-old boy. The graves dug for the doctor and Big Betty were shallow and inadequate, but it was the best we could do."

As they rounded the hotel, Hughes opened the gate to the patio, ushering Leighselle inside. "I can imagine how terrified you must have been."

"Terrified, yes, but the strange part," she recalled, a smile warming her face with the memory, "was that I began to feel stronger and more self-assured than I had ever felt before."

"We're molded by our adversities." Hughes motioned for Jameson and requested coffee service, noticing that he'd appeared at the patio. "Was that a long enough walk?"

"Yes, perfect." She took the seat Hughes pulled out for her. "And if you allow, adversity will mold you into a better, more enlightened version of yourself." She sipped the cup of black coffee Jameson had poured from the sterling silver service.

"When I left Vermillion Parish behind, all I had were the two letters of introduction from Doctor Bronstein, one for the school in Shreveport, which I had no intention of using, and the other for the banker who held my trust in New Orleans, which I had every intention of using."

"How did you get to Orleans?" asked Hughes, his curiosity bending him forward.

"I helped myself to the doctor's buggy and cart horse. First, I went through his desk and bureau. I was penniless until I could get my hands on my trust. I knew the good doctor wouldn't mind me taking whatever I could find. There was no one left alive for him to give it to. He had almost eight hundred dollars hidden in the back of his shaving toilet."

"You were a very brave girl," said Hughes with admiration. "You grew up in a hurry."

"Yes. In the blink of an eye, I went from being the very spoiled only child who never wanted for anything to having two people and two animals who depended on me. I didn't have time to be a puddly, teary mess. I had to get us to New Orleans, despite the fact that I had at best only a vague idea of where New Orleans was."

*****

Early November 1836

70

Addy-Frank's thin, gray shawl hung limp around her bony shoulders; her dark brown eyes, sunken and vacant, stared off into the distance. "Just keep on a heading this buggy south, Miss Leighselle. I know I heard folks say N'Awleans be south."

Five-year-old Birdie lay curled in her mother's lap like a sleeping kitten, while her mother stroked the child's soft, light brown cheek with her finger. Addy-Frank had wept for an hour when they left Vermillion Bay. She'd cried until her body was limp and empty of tears from having to leave her twin babies behind in the red dirt grave that held the other Beauclaire slaves.

"Thank you, Addy-Frank, but we can't go any more south than we've already gone or we'll end up in the Gulf and needing a boat instead of a buggy." Leighselle drew the reins up short, slowing the horse. "We need to make our way east. We should head east. I'm certain. Or, maybe we should go north first a little way to find a stage road or railroad we can follow, one that goes east. What do you think?"

Leighselle had tried to adopt an air of confidence—she wanted to feel certain about where she was going, but the only thing she felt assured about was leaving Vermillion Parish. The place smelled of death.

"What I think? I think you the white girl and I the black girl and you need to start acting like it and quit asking me what I think. I don't want to think. All I want to do is go back to the time before that ol' typhoid took my babies away." Addy-Frank drew her shawl around her shoulders and turned her chin the other direction.

"Oh," Leighselle said, stunned. She pulled hard on the driving lines and reined the cart horse to the left, heading east.

*****

January 1, 1840 – Four Years Later

Leighselle called to Addy-Frank, "We have two more. Please attend to their wounds and see to it they have a hot meal and a bath. These girls look worse off than the first three." Leighselle's pulse throbbed in her temples—her head ached as anger percolated just below the surface. "It's worse every year, these girls coming in

71

here abused and beat up, then dumped on my doorstep. New Year's Eve should be outlawed."

"Yes 'sum, Miss Leighselle, but ain't much left to feed them poor girls. We's about outa food in the pantry," said Addy-Frank. She headed to the back of the Sew Beauclaire Shoppe, where girls in need hid out until wounds mended or memories faded. She muttered to herself, "Lost girls showing up with a sob story or a split lip, them working girls from the tavern, ain't no wonder we ain't got much left."

"Miss Leighselle," said Birdie, "they a gentleman knocking at the front door. He wearing a torn topcoat. Spec he needs it mended." Birdie, small for her age, had silky black curls that hung in long, thick spirals down her back. Her fine exotic features were pulled into a serious frown. "Why someone wants to do business on a holiday? Miss Leighselle? Want me to show him in?"

"No, Birdie, my hands are full this morning. Tell him we're closed in observance of the New Year," said Leighselle from the kitchen as she sorted and washed apples.

"Closed?" shouted Addy-Frank from down the hallway. "Miss Leighselle, we ain't never closed. We need the money. You say the rent be due soon and—"

"Calm yourself, Addy-Frank, it's all right." Leighselle sighed with frustration. "You're correct. We need the money. Show him into the parlor, Birdie."

The customer stepped into the front room, removing his topcoat and hat, handing the garment to Birdie. "Top three buttons are missing and lapel is torn." He turned, a sardonic smile spreading across his face, and stared at Leighselle, who stood in the kitchen doorway.

Leighselle drew in a quick breath of surprise. "You. What are you doing here? You must leave at once. Take your coat and leave."

"I saw the sign above your door, 'Sew Beauclaire.' I couldn't help but notice the name. Your business, I assume?" Seamus Flanders strolled into the kitchen, his hard blue eyes scanning the room.

Leighselle backed away, a cold fear washing over her. "I

said to leave."

"I went back to Vermillion Bay. Everything was gone, even your house. The entire parish, vaporized." Seamus folded his hands across his chest, staring at her. "I had gone back for you, to take you to Texas, to make you my wife. My ranch settled, a home built for us, money in the bank. Everything was ready."

Leighselle continued backing away, feeling the color draining from her face, the heat from her body.

"I was told everyone died except for a few slaves. I guess I was told wrong." His smile was cold.

"Yes. Now all that's left are unwelcome memories and ghosts." She leaned further away as Seamus inched closer, a wave of panic shooting through her. "You must leave or I'll scream."

"Scream? Then what? Frighten the pretty little child that answered the door? Summon to your aid your darkie and drunken whores? I'll be happy to put them all in their place."

Seamus reached for Leighselle's hand but she swatted it away. She groped behind her back, trying to feel for the paring knife she had left lying on the counter beside the bowl of apples.

"I dreamed of this—of you being alive, of me finding you. I saw the graves of your mother and father, but not one with your name on it. I knew in my heart you weren't dead."

"You don't have a heart," she spat out the words, her fear congealing and hardening into righteous anger.

"I told you on that day, Leighselle, that you belonged to me, that you'd always be mine." With rough hands he seized both of her wrists and pulled her toward him. "Remember that day? I think about it all the time."

"I'm not yours. You—you took something that didn't belong to you. You're an evil person who attacked an innocent child." The horrible memory sickened her.

"Thank God I came to 'Orleans for the New Year. Thank God I tore my coat. Thank God someone pointed me in the direction of a good seamstress shop." He gripped her wrists tighter. "Thank God I found you and you're still alive. Maybe now I've got enough reasons to start believing in God."

Leighselle struggled against him, trying to free her wrists

from his grip. Turning her head left and right, she fought to resist his sloppy kisses. Whiskey and cheap cigars flavored his breath. His clothes looked and smelled as if he had slept in them.

She managed to pull one hand free and reached behind for the knife. The heavy bowl of apples tipped off onto the floor and clanged like a bell as it hit, the red fruit rolling out like shiny children's marbles across the black and white checkered tile floor. The loud noise caught Seamus off guard long enough for Leighselle to slip out of his grasp and run past him.

"You all right, Miss Leighselle? I heard a noise." Addy-Frank walked into the kitchen and saw the bowl of apples strewn across the floor. "What happened here?" She looked from Seamus to Leighselle.

Birdie walked into the kitchen behind her mother and began picking up the spilled fruit. "I wash them off, Miss Leighselle. It's all right."

"I was clumsy and knocked them to the floor, Addy-Frank." She kept her voice calm. No need to alarm anyone. "Do you have our customer's mending finished?"

"Almost. Just need to put a few more stitches in. Be just a minute." The small man with copper hair and russet freckles seemed unimposing until she looked into his eyes; then she shivered. She gave him a hard stare before walking back to her sewing room.

Seamus raised his eyebrows, his silvery blue eyes darkening. He nodded toward Birdie. "You sure are a pretty little girl. What's your name?"

"Birdie," she said, fidgeting on her feet, the apples now back in the bowl.

"My, if you don't favor Miss Beauclaire. You both look enough alike to be sisters." Seamus studied the child a moment longer. "How old are you?"

"She's not my sister, she's Addy-Frank's daughter, and she's none of your business," said Leighselle, stepping between him and Birdie. "Now take your coat and leave."

Addy-Frank walked in with Seamus's coat and handed it to him. "You all fixed up now. That be five cents, please."

Seamus ignored her. "Don't you agree there's a strong family resemblance to the Beauclaires?" He turned to Addy-Frank. "You belonged to Leighselle's father. I remember you as one of their house slaves."

"Enough with the questions," Leighselle said. "Leave now. Never set foot on my threshold again or you'll be sorry."

"Save your threats. But understand this. I'll be back." Seamus grabbed his coat as he marched toward the door. Before leaving, he tossed a twenty-dollar gold piece onto the counter. "Keep the change."

He disappeared into the loud, boisterous crowd that clogged the street in front of Leighselle's shop. Some revelers were singing, some laughing, and some looking for a place to duck out of the heavy rain that had begun to fall.

"Take your damn money with you!" Leighselle screamed, scooping the coin up and throwing it against the slamming door.

"Don't be a fool, Miss Leighselle," said Addy-Frank. "Be a long time before we earn this amount, just mending folks' clothes. We need medicine an such. Our food is mostly crumbs an scraps. Rent be due. This money take care all that."

Leighselle glared at her. "You have no idea what you are saying. That money is evil. It's bad money. It—" Leighselle's voice was high and shrill, the dark memory sinking her, sending her to the floor on her knees. "I don't want his money."

"I spec that you paid a horrible price for this gold coin," said Addy-Frank, dropping to the floor, taking Leighselle in her arms. "There, now. You go ahead an cry. Get it all out, but get it over with," she said, rocking Leighselle in her arms, "cause we have more important things to do than think about that foul man who walks in the devil's shadow."

Leighselle ran a hand across her face, wiping at the tears. "He's not finished. He'll be back, now that he knows I'm still alive —that I'm here."

"I smelled his wickedness when Birdie brung me his coat to sew. I knew he be bad news even 'fore I remembered his face. But he won't be back here bothering you. I took care a that." She continued to rock Leighselle in her arms.

"You took care of what, Addy-Frank? What do you mean?"

"I mean I took care a that evil man. I sewed a curse into his pocket. Sewed it tight. First five stitches take away his health, happiness, love, money, an family. Six be the number of Evil. Sixth black stitch make it final. Satan his self gonna steal his breath an escort him to hell."

Leighselle paled. A chill shivered her spine and cold beads of sweat dotted her brow. "Addy-Frank, what have you done? A man with those curses is a man with nothing to live for—with nothing to lose."

Pulling away from Addy-Frank, Leighselle moved to the window and stood with her forehead pressed against the cool glass panes. She stared at the widening puddles on the ground, watching big drops of rain plop, sending echoing ripples across the surface. Rain poured from the darkening sky, making the first day of January a lucky day. Rain on the first day meant showers of blessings all month long, but she feared a storm was upon her. She drew the velvet curtains closed against the dreary scene.

*****

Six Months Later – July 4, 1840 – Port of Orleans

The port city sweltered in high noon's heat and humidity, the stagnant salty air hospitable to mosquitoes and malaria. Cargo ships that weren't moored to a dock clogged the Bay of Orleans, waiting their turn, riding the easy swells that lifted, rocked, and splashed the vessels' eager sailors.

Creole and Negro dockworkers bent shoulder to sweaty shoulder unloading imported goods while others toiled at loading the cargo meant for export. All along the bay, there was a revolving *pas de deux* of crates of tropical fruit and coffee coming in, and cattle and cotton going out.

The rowdy, fetid piers and sidewalks around the docks were jammed with restaurant chefs, hotel cooks, and haggling house slaves hoping to snatch a bargain on a broken crate of spoiled fruit or spilled coffee, while hawkers barked their daily offerings of fresh Gulf Coast red snapper and bay lobsters. Small, round birds on quick feet dodged cats, broomsticks, and boots as they snapped up scraps of fish scales and breadcrumbs.

"Miss Leighselle," said Addy-Frank, fingering the coins in her pocket. "I done bought all the coffee we can stand for a month. At a good price, too."

"Look, Addy-Frank. Brahman cattle are at the livestock dock. Those are the cattle that my father raised." She paused at the memory, a faint smile crossing her face. "Father loved their beautiful gray coats, and I remember the little calves' sweet faces, their large eyes, with their long, floppy ears. Oh no, look out!"

A silvery-hided bull had busted through the warped planks of the holding pen and was barreling down the narrow passage between seller's booths congested with shoppers and hawkers. The two thousand-pound beast with his cone-shaped horns split the crowd in two, left and right. Frightened people stomped, pushed, shoved, and shouted in their attempt to save themselves from the rampaging animal.

As she screamed out a warning to Addy-Frank, the bull struck Leighselle a glancing blow, sending her sailing through the air. Landing in a heap, Leighselle lay unconscious, head bloodied, unmoving.

In an instant she was scooped up in the sturdy arms of a tall man whose face seemed to reflect the sun. He yelled at the crowd to watch out, that the animal was coming back. The bull was causing all sorts of destruction, tossing people, tables, and chairs into the air, trampling booths, knocking down tents.

"He's turning and coming back! Stand aside," the man shouted in an accent heavy with Irish brogue. Laying Leighselle down on top of a vendor's table, he turned, pulling his revolver as the horde of people scattered in mass panic. Taking careful aim, he fired once, dropping the raging bull moments before it came within goring distance of where the red-headed stranger stood his ground.

Turning back to the unconscious figure lying on the table, he took her again in his arms and began walking toward the town square. "Where might I find a doctor for this woman?" he called out to no one in particular.

"The doctor be this way," said Addy-Frank. "I'm with her. Her name Leighselle Beauclaire. Whoever own that bull you just shot an killed be mighty angry with you, no matter the destruction he be causing." Addy-Frank walked at a fast clip, talking and motioning as she moved through the calming crowd.

"I own him. I'm not pleased that I had to kill the poor animal, but allowing him to trample and gore a crowd of shoppers didn't seem like the neighborly thing to do."

Leighselle stirred, eyes fluttering, moaning. "What happened? What are you doing? Who are you?"

"You ask a lot of questions for an injured woman," said Henry Flanders, his bright blue eyes flashing a mixture of amusement and concern. "You near came to be trampled by a bull. I'm carrying you to a doctor to see about your injuries. My name's Henry and today's my first day in America. So far, I'd say it's been an exciting one. There you have it, and there it is."

*****

Leighselle coughed into her handkerchief. "That was the moment I fell in love with Henry Flanders." She would always love him— would take that love to her grave.

Hughes poured coffee, sipping his steaming and black. "I don't mean to sound obtuse, but how in the hell did you fall in love with the son of a monster?"

"I didn't know Henry was Seamus's son." If she had learned the truth, would it have made a difference? She'd asked herself that question many times. "I didn't learn Seamus's name until later, so I didn't connect the two of them."

"I see. Why was Henry in New Orleans?"

"Henry decided to immigrate here, too, to follow his father who'd come to Texas many years earlier. His father had him go to England first to select a bull to bring with him, since his original source, my father, had been long out of business."

"After the incident on the wharf," asked Hughes, refilling his cup, "what happened?"

"For three months, we were together while Henry arranged the shipping and receiving of a replacement bull. We were never apart a single moment. I became pregnant, and we married right away."

Hughes leaned forward and poured Leighselle another cup

of coffee. "And this is the daughter that you want me to find?"

"Yes." Leighselle nodded.

"What happened to Henry?"

"There was a delay in the receiving of the replacement bull, a problem with the paperwork. Henry received a telegraph from his father stating that Henry was to travel to England and get the problem straightened out. I begged him not to go, or to take me with him. Henry was certain that everything would be fine, that he would return before our child was born." Leighselle shook her head at the memory, a cough rattling her frail body.

"But?" Hughes asked, gesturing with his palms face up.

"But things weren't fine." Leighselle looked across the table at her dear friend and wondered why she'd never spoken of her past with Hughes—he was so easy to talk to— and the more she talked about it, the less it seemed so horrible. So staining. "Things weren't fine at all. Seamus made good on his threat. He came back—just like he said he would."

*****

Early afternoon was siesta time in San Antonio, and Leighselle was exhausted. Hughes escorted her to his room where she settled in for an afternoon nap. Then, he hurried downstairs to meet with Doctor Schmidt in the Colonial Room, making arrangements for her care.

He would have just enough time before meeting with Jameson to make it to the telegraph office. There, he would send word to his federal contacts in Washington that they could expect him in Saint Joseph, Missouri, by the end of October.

Saint Joseph, the first home station of the Pony Express, was rife with suspicious activity. Important people in Washington were unhappy that their letters urging the thirty-first state to remain loyal to the Union were not being delivered to their equally important recipients in California—recipients whose deep pockets were lined with shiny gold nuggets.

CHAPTER SIX

OCTOBER 20, 1860

Thursday passed without Barleigh crossing paths with another soul. On Friday, she met three going in the opposite direction. Three young men heading to Dallas to join the Texas Militia. They reminded her of Aunt Winnie's sons, all eager to go to war. "It's coming," they shouted, pumping their fists in the air with excitement. "War is on the horizon. Turn around and join us."

They spoke of "war" as if it were a destination, a happy ending to a pleasant journey. Their exuberance to kill or to be killed revealed the sweet naiveté of one who has never been exposed to the reality of death, especially to the kind of gruesome death that war would reveal to their innocent eyes.

Time does not heal. The clock can never be dialed back. Permanent scars will remain, Barleigh wanted to tell them. Instead, she tipped her hat and kept riding.

After a monotonous morning, the day was changed by a pleasant happenstance when her path crossed that of another lone rider, a gray-haired, gray-bearded gentleman on an elderly horse just as gray as its rider. They made quite the striking pair.

He introduced himself as Mr. Templeton and said that he was headed south for the winter. Like a Canadian goose, he wasn't stopping till he came to a large, warm body of water, specifically the Gulf of Mexico. When Barleigh mentioned that she used to live in Corpus Christi right on the Gulf coast, he offered to share his lunch if she'd share her stories of Corpus.

She tried to edit her thoughts to alter her stories, making them suit that of a boy's history. A few times she slipped up. Mr. Templeton was sharp. She could see the suspicion growing in his eyes—and in his expression, the confusion of following such a tale as she was weaving.

"I understand needing to be believed that you're a boy, what with traveling alone," he said, "but your secret is safe with me. I sense there's more to your story. You can tell me, if you wish, why the disguise."

So, she did. She poured out everything. They talked for hours. It was a needed break from the hard riding, the hiding, and the pretending. She was prepared to make up the time somewhere down the road.

Before they parted, he offered this advice. "From now on, don't offer folks a glimpse into your past, even if asked, though I'm honored you told me. But for others, tell them you don't have a past. That way, you won't run the risk of revealing yourself. Keep the truth hidden in a shroud of sadness. Most folks don't want to rub up against sadness for fear it's contagious."

He's right, she thought, as she guided King onto the trail. It's difficult to speak of the past without getting emotional. Better to keep all of that buried. Sharing stories with Mr. Templeton, the hurt had become real and raw again. She would become the sad, mysterious Bar Flanders whose unspeakable past caused too much pain to share with others.

And wasn't that really the truth?

Mr. Templeton had given her a parting gift of a bag of roasted coffee. She decided to make a toast to him each morning and to think of him and to remember his kindness. She felt certain that Mr. Templeton was more how grandfathers were supposed to be than the one she had known.

The Texas-Arkansas border was where Barleigh pitched camp for the night. Despite feeling more tired than she'd ever been, her spirits were high. In this border town called Texarkana, she learned of a well-traveled cattle route that headed due north into Fort Smith, Arkansas, where she could pick up the stagecoach into Saint Joseph, Missouri. By not having to travel to Little Rock, she could save two days or better of riding.

Looking forward to a good night's rest and to roasted coffee in the morning, Barleigh jotted a few notes in her journal. Perhaps her dream wolf would appear in her sleep tonight, she wrote, sketching the four-legged creature in the margins of her book. His watchful company would not be unwelcome.

*****

She wanted a bath. Oral hygiene was easily adapted to life on the trail, but she wondered how much longer she could go with simple, discrete sponge baths of certain body parts. At least it wasn't her time of the month, she thought. That issue would take some clever planning after taking on life as a Pony Express rider.

Oh, the things I didn't consider. . . .

One-third of the way to Fort Smith, she found herself behind a herd of Mexican cattle headed to market in Kansas. She followed along for a while before the dust and the flies became a nuisance. Pulling off the trail, she took an afternoon nap, something of a guilty pleasure, but an hour's rest gave her and her horse an extra boost of energy, so they traveled well into the night.

Judging from the moon's heavenly path, she knew it was far past midnight. She made camp, feeling lonely. Homesick. Thinking of Aunt Winnie and Uncle Jack and their three boys. Missing Starling. Papa and Birdie. A long, monotonous day in the saddle left her mind numb with too much time to dwell on those she loved and those she longed for.

Removing her bedroll from the saddle, she was reminded of Papa's friend, Charlie Goodnight, who had visited the summer before Starling was born. He'd presented her papa the Navaho blanket as a gift. There had been many Indian uprisings that year, brutal attacks on settlers, even more brutal retaliations at the hands of white men. White outlaws were performing all kinds of unspeakable atrocities against white settlers and blaming them on the Indians. It had been a bloody summer.

*****

"These lawless acts of white men preying on settlers are being blamed on Indians. The white desperadoes responsible are making sure folks see it that way. We must keep a watchful eye on any suspicious character, be he red or white." Captain Goodnight was thoughtful when he spoke, choosing his words carefully. He surely would have chosen more censored words had he known Barleigh hid behind the door, listening.

"While most reservation Indians are agreeable to learning how to farm the land which the Government has set aside for them, there are those that refuse to relocate to reservations. Tonkawa Indians, they'd rather kill and eat a farmer than to become one, while the Cherokee and Comanche would be happy murdering, mutilating, and scalping the farmer, along with the farmer's wife, and worse."

"Indians are different here than the friendly local Indians we encountered on the Gulf," Henry said to Charlie. "The Atakapa and the Karankawa ate turtles, ducks, geese, and deer. It seems your plains tribes have different appetites."

"Not all of them, Henry. But some do. Just remember to keep a watchful eye. The kidnappings, murdering, the cattle rustling, the horse thieving are increasing. The mutilations are becoming more gruesome. Everyone must stay vigilant. Anyway, Henry, I didn't stop by here just to scare you. I wanted to bring Barleigh this Navajo blanket from the trading post. She mentioned to me the last time she saw mine how pretty she found it. They do weave a nice pattern."

Captain Goodnight left Barleigh with a beautiful black and red woven blanket along with a mind seared hot with images too troubling to sleep that night.

*****

After a restless night of fitful dreams, she spent another lonely day on the trail without an encounter of the human kind, though she saw plenty of rabbits, squirrels, opossum, and deer. The piney woods of east Texas and western Arkansas abounded with wildlife. The antlers on some of the white-tail stags would have set her papa's trigger finger to twitching. She could picture him grinning from ear to ear.

Her mind wandered, although she remained vigilant of her surroundings. But the trail was easy to follow, with King staying on task. One more day's ride would place her within sight of Fort

Smith, Arkansas. Though she'd miss King and would hate leaving him at the livery stables, she was eager to board the stagecoach that would take her on the next leg of her journey to Saint Joseph, and to her destiny.

Making excellent time, she figured they were averaging better than fifty miles a day, despite a few afternoon naps and one very long lunch along the way. It was interesting that most people she encountered, Mr. Templeton being the exception, readily accepted her as a boy riding alone, no questions asked. Had she taken this journey alone as a girl, she wouldn't have made it past Fort Worth without someone stopping or accosting her.

Storm clouds rolled in, the smell of rain thickening the air. In the distance, lightning streaked across the evening sky. Thunder rumbled. She'd never before slept outside during a storm and was thankful for the small tent that Aunt Winnie insisted she bring along. This was the first indication of bad weather since leaving Hog Mountain and the first time she'd felt the need to pitch a tent. Making camp in a dense pine thicket just off the trail, she hoped that the trees' thick umbrella would offer more protection against the storm.

Writing in her journal next to the campfire while eating a dinner of beans and cornbread (with a little rabbit cooked over the fire this evening) had become the one thing she looked forward to at the end of the day's ride. She wrote quickly, finishing her thoughts before the thunderstorm snuffed out the light.

*****

Lightning crackled, the sky bursting with bruised shades of green and purple. Deafening reverberations crashed and echoed throughout the thick piney woods, as if every demon that stalked the heavens shouted curses in unison, and through their fists shook thunder from the sky.

King whinnied in a shrill, high-pitched alarm, stomping and rearing. Barleigh raced to untie him from the line picket, afraid that lightning would strike the trees and him, too. Then, she made a mad dash back inside the tent. It proved to be a useless shelter against the mighty gale, for the powerful winds snatched up the tent and hurled it away. All she could do was huddle under the saddle blanket until the squall passed.

The night woods were too dark for her to see farther than the hand in front of her face. She sat until morning, dozing a little, wet, shivering, and waiting for the sun to come up. The fear that she wouldn't find her horse caused a gloom to darken her spirit, a gloom as gray and damp as the sky.

Walking in circles for hours, calling King's name, whistling, looking everywhere for him, proved fruitless—he was gone. Barleigh told herself that the storm no doubt frightened him so badly that he ran all the way to Hog Mountain and back to Aunt Winnie. She liked to think that's what he did.

She couldn't leave the saddle behind. It had belonged to Uncle Jack. So, off she went, saddle over shoulder, bedroll and blanket attached, and she footed it into Fort Smith, stumbling into town as the sun was setting over the wide Arkansas River, its slow current murmuring soothing, welcoming sounds.

A boardinghouse with a room for the night and a hot bath were the two things she wanted most in life. She found them, the room costing two dollars, the bath ten cents. It was a boomtown and prices were high. She'd have paid twice that not to have to sleep in the woods again. Thoughts of Indians hiding in the shadows kept her unsettled and restless. Rare were the nights when her dreams were free of fearful images of painted faces, painted war horses, flaming arrows, burning buildings, and worse.

Though physically exhausted, she imagined that writing about her fears and placing them in her journal would fix them to pages so they couldn't trouble her sleep. She began to write.

*****

Journal Entry – It's hard to believe it was a month ago, the night of the Comanche Moon, the night so bright, so full of promise and life and death.
Even as midnight approached, the sky was so bright that the stars refused to shine, their incandescent light no match for the huge, silvery orb. High overhead, the moon cast shadows where there should have been none, miniature shadows as if from the noon day sun.

I took Papa another cup of coffee and my Navajo blanket to warm him against the cooling night air. Papa wrapped it around both of us, and we sat shoulder to shoulder, waiting for the tiny cry, the signal that Aunt Winnie had successfully delivered Birdie's baby. We looked out over the pasture dotted with grazing Brahman cattle, their fair hides shimmering in the vivid lunar light.

"Do you know the Indian name for what we call the harvest moon?" asked Papa.

I shook my head no.

"Wasuton wi," he said. "They call it 'the moon when calves grow hair.'"

Our calves and foals had indeed begun putting on early, thick winter coats. Nature was preparing them for a harsh winter.

The lusty sound of a baby's cry pierced the night, startling Papa and me with its sudden intensity. We bolted for the door, running into the bedroom to see Aunt Winnie wrapping a blanket around a squirming, crying bundle. The figure in the bed lay motionless, the sheets soaked with blood.

"Take the baby and go on out. I need to attend Birdie. She's lost a lot of blood. Your baby girl's fine and healthy. Go." Winnie bent to her work and Papa and I went back out to the porch, Papa cradling his new baby daughter in his arms.

I pulled back the blanket to see my new little half-sister, wondering if she'd favor me, or Papa, or Birdie. "Look at all her thick, dark hair," I mused.

Papa laughed. "It's the moon when babies grow hair, too. She's beautiful, just like her big sister. Here, you take her. I'm going to see about Birdie, even if Winnie tries to run me out."

I rocked the baby, letting her nuzzle against

my neck. Papa's words gave me a chill. Was this baby, like the calves and the foals, in for a harsh winter? How could this happen to her, too, I wondered? Would she be cursed like me, with a lifetime of guilt that her birth caused her mother's death? Please, I prayed to anyone up there listening, to anyone behind the moon when calves grow hair, please don't let this baby grow up not knowing her mother.

*****

Wednesday, October 24, 1860

From the second she awoke, Barleigh had coached herself for this moment. With confidence, thinking and speaking like a man, she asked the clerk behind the counter of the Fort Smith Mercantile and General Store for what she wanted. "One ticket on the next stage to Saint Joseph, Missouri, please."

The clerk, whose girth equaled his height, studied Barleigh from down his bent, warted nose for a long moment before answering. "Well, son, this is your lucky day. Just so happen to have one seat left."

"Good. Thank you, sir." She breathed a quiet sigh of relief.

"You'll be the ninth and final passenger. One piece of luggage is allowed, but you got to hold it on your lap. Underfoot will be the mailbags. You carrying anything other than that saddle?"

"No, sir. It's all I got." She looked him in the eye, man to man, unashamed of her meager net worth. The saddle had belonged to Jack Justin, but Aunt Winnie had insisted she take it. Its value was far beyond the leather, wood, metal, and stitching that went into its construction.

"That's a fine saddle, but it's still considered a piece of luggage. On your lap it goes, or it don't go." He shoved his finger into the air to accentuate his point.

"Yes, sir, I understand," Barleigh said, jutting her chin in what she hoped was a show of masculine determination.

"Fine. List of rules is posted over yonder on the wall. Read and commit them to memory. There'll be stops four times a day and twice at night to change out the mule teams and to allow comfort breaks for the passengers. Food at these comfort stops is extra. Expect at least four days to make the destination. That'll be forty dollars for a through ticket. Yes, or no?"

"A through ticket?" Barleigh swallowed hard, shifting her weight from foot to foot.

"Yes, a through ticket. Besides the comfort stops, the stage stops along the way to pick up mail in Rogers, Bentonville, Bella Vista, Neosho, Joplin, Carthage, Kansas City, and Liberty. To go all the way *through* to Saint Joe is a *through* ticket. Forty dollars, yes or no?"

She handed over the money with a slight hesitation. Fifty dollars was the sum total in her pocket, a gift Aunt Winnie insisted on and that Barleigh insisted would be paid back once her taxes were settled with the bank.

The steely-eyed clerk handed Barleigh the ticket along with a piece of advice. "For some of your journey you'll be traveling through Indian Country. The safety of your person cannot be vouchsafed by anyone but God. Iffin' it were me, I'd make sure my guns were loaded and in good working order. Read those rules now, boy. You got just ten minutes before the stage pulls out."

"Yes, sir." She tipped her hat and turned to the wall, where the rules for proper stagecoach etiquette were posted.

1. Abstinence from liquor is requested, but if you must drink, share the bottle. To do otherwise makes you appear selfish and unneighborly.
2. If ladies are present, gentlemen are urged to forego smoking cigars and pipes as the odor of same is repugnant to the Gentle Sex. Chewing tobacco is permitted but spit WITH the wind, not against it.
3. Gentlemen must refrain from the use of rough language in the presence of ladies and children.
4. Buffalo robes are provided for your comfort during cold weather. Hogging robes will not be

tolerated and the offender will be made to ride with the driver.

5. Don't snore loudly while sleeping or use your fellow passenger's shoulder for a pillow; he or she may not understand and friction may result.

6. Firearms may be kept on your person for use in emergencies. Do not fire them for pleasure or shoot at wild animals as the sound riles the horses.

7. In the event of runaway horses, remain calm. Leaping from the coach in panic will leave you injured, at the mercy of the elements, hostile Indians and hungry coyotes.

8. Forbidden topics of discussion are stagecoach robberies and Indian uprisings.

9. Gents guilty of unchivalrous behavior toward lady passengers will be put off the stage. It's a long walk back. A word to the wise is sufficient.

Around the back of the general store was the livery and blacksmith shop, where six replacement mules were brought up two by two. They were hitched in pairs to the celerity wagon, the type that was lighter and faster and thus more uncomfortable than the storied Concords, whose reputation was that of a cradle on wheels.

The large, rawboned mules matched in size and color, all of them black, and they shuffled into their places in the hitching line. This coach didn't look like a cradle on wheels, Barleigh thought, but looked instead more like a contraption suitable for rattling teeth and jarring bones.

Inside the stagecoach, three rows of passenger seats accommodated three passengers each. On the back and middle row, passengers faced forward, but the front row faced rearward. Thus, these passengers faced the folks seated on the middle row. With not much room between rows, the knees of passengers in the front and middle rows interlocked. The narrowness of the stage caused the passengers sitting on the outside of the rows to want to dangle their outside leg out the door to gain legroom, putting their feet precariously close to the wagon's wheels.

A family of six sat stuffed on the front and middle rows: a taciturn preacher dressed in black, his somber gray bride, and their four dour, supplicating children. They were relocating to Joplin to build a church of a denomination Barleigh wasn't familiar with, the father himself having a difficult time clarifying for the rest of the passengers this new church's doctrine.

On the back row, Barleigh sat wedged between two passengers. To her right, a long-legged beanpole of an Army captain whose uniform smelled like cooked cabbage bragged that he had "been directed by President Buchanan himself to travel to Kansas City on official government business." To her left, a slight-built, blond-headed young man beamed with pride. He claimed he was "going to Saint Joe to show them other Pony Express riders what riding's all about."

Barleigh's heart sank to her stomach. This couldn't be good, she thought. She looked down at the saddle in her lap, fiddling with the latigo straps tied around the bedroll, pretending not to hear the question the captain was asking, trying to gain a few minutes to compose a response.

"Cat got your tongue?" The captain nudged her with his sharp, bony elbow. "We all said our 'howdys.' Now it's your turn."

"Howdy." *Breathe. Relax. Don't seem nervous.*

"That sounds mighty unfriendly, don't you think?" the captain asked, his words sliding into a slur. "We shared our names and our stories of why we're on this little journey. The rules of polite society say that one must reciprocate. Do I need to teach you a lesson on the rules of polite society, boy?" The captain studied Barleigh with hard, bloodshot eyes.

"Reciprocating wasn't on the list of rules," said the other Pony Express rider, leaning across Barleigh to address the captain directly.

"Who are you?" asked the captain in a haughty voice.

"I already introduced myself. I guess you forgot. I'm Stoney Wooten, from Frog Level, Arkansas. I recall the rules mentioning not spitting into the wind, and not cursing or snoring or hogging the buffalo robes. Don't recall nothing about having to share names and stories—just sharing your liquor if you brought any. I see that you brought some but you ain't sharing. You done already broke a rule yourself, as far as I can tell." Stoney eased back into his seat, giving Barleigh a friendly nudge of his elbow.

"Are you his protector and appointed spokesperson?" the dark-haired, mustached captain asked in an agitated voice. He took a sip from his whiskey flask, making a big show of re-pocketing it.

"Name's Bar Flanders. I'm a Pony Express rider, too. Or soon will be." She reminded herself to not act intimidated or afraid. Be direct.

"Well, ain't that something?" Stoney put out his hand. "Maybe after we get hired on, we'll be on the same relay. Wouldn't that be something?"

Barleigh shook his hand. *Full, firm grip. One pump.* "Pleased to meet you, Stoney. Yep, that'd be something." She shifted her body position a degree to put the captain more at her back as best she could, given the tight quarters.

The captain retreated into his flask until he coaxed the last drop of alcohol from the container. Soon, a rattling snore filled the air, reverberating inside the small, closed coach. The family of six withdrew into their prayers and their Bibles, a humming drone of devotions blending with the whiskeyed wheezing coming from the captain.

"I'm from down a ways in Frog Level. Lived in Arkansas all my life. My pa's sending me off to get a paying job so he won't have to. He says I should help with feeding the other eight young-uns at home. Where you from?"

Stoney's friendly blue eyes and ready grin reminded Barleigh of her papa's. She fought down a wave of longing that caused her eyes to burn. "I'm from Texas. Don't have any family."

"Hell, I got enough to go around. I'll share."

"I may take you up on that." Barleigh attempted a lighthearted smile, but it was thin.

The four days it took to get to Saint Joseph were long, dusty, and monotonous, the nights cold, cramped, and uncomfortable. Trying to sleep while sitting upright and holding your baggage in your lap induced little rest, yet provoked lots of stress. Friendly chitter-chatter dwindled to near silence.

No Indians, though. Thankfully, no Indians.

Even so, Barleigh kept her revolver in a firm grip, her hand hidden under the McClellan saddle at all times. The saddle straddled her lap the entire journey. This must be how a horse feels, she mused.

After the praying family disembarked in Joplin and the Army captain stumbled off in Kansas City, Stoney and Barleigh stretched out. As she relaxed for the last day's ride into Saint Joe, her thighs felt light without the stress of a saddle pressing on her lap.

Stoney pulled back the canvas flap covering the window opening of the wagon; it had remained lowered most of the four days to keep the fine caliche dust out of the coach. A bandana over mouth and nose was still required, as the mules kicked up clouds of dust on their gallop into Saint Joseph.

"Well, ain't that something," said Stoney as he poked his head out the window.

When he retreated back into the coach and removed the red bandana covering his mouth and nose, the lower half of his face was clean. The upper half of his face was sifted in a soft, white, chalk-like powder that made his eyelashes and eyebrows look like they belonged to a dusty ghost.

"Look at all them people. I ain't never seen so many people all at once, just ambling around in no apparent hurry." Stoney shook the dust from his bandana and then washed his face with water from his canteen.

Saint Joseph, on the fringe of settlement, was the farthest outpost for travel and commerce. There the railroad ended its journey toward western expansion. A hub of activity, trade, and exchange, it was raucous with cowboys bringing in massive herds of cattle to market. It was where settlement bloated outward from the city center, and where the Oregon Trail picked up just over the banks of the Missouri River that wound its way across horizontal plains, over ragged mountains and through verdant valleys before reaching California and the Pacific Northwest.

And it was here Barleigh Flanders had a rendezvous with

destiny.

CHAPTER SEVEN

SEPTEMBER 27, 1860

The wait staff at the Menger Hotel set a decadent evening buffet of smoked hens and wild game, savory cheeses, ripe fruit, yeast rolls and whole-grain breads, chocolate pastries, and a variety of imported wines and sparkling French champagnes. The lavish spread invited gluttony. Hughes and Leighselle sat on the shaded patio, sipping chilled Veuve Clicquot.

"How was your siesta?" Hughes asked, setting the champagne bottle into an ice bucket, the ice also a luxury import.

"Refreshing," Leighselle said, noticing that she hadn't coughed in quite some time. She attributed it to the siesta. Then again, the champagne might have played a roll, she thought, taking another sip.

"Do you feel like picking up the story where you left off?" Hughes asked. "Or would you rather just enjoy the evening?"

"I feel like it, yes, though this may be the most difficult part to tell." Leighselle looked at Hughes, wondering if he would rather just enjoy the evening instead of listening. "Are you sure you want to hear my tale of woe?"

Squeezing her hand, Hughes raised his glass. "That's what friends are for."

Leighselle raised her glass, clinking it against his. "Thank God for dear old friends."

*****

Leighselle clutched tightly to Henry's arm. She leaned into his side as they walked to the pier, a dark sense of foreboding dimming her mood. "Why do you have to go to England, Henry? I don't want you to go."

"I don't want to go either, Leighselle, but I have no choice. My father wants a Brahman bull to replace the one I shot. He wants it from the same breeder, so back across the pond I go." Henry wrapped his arm tighter around his wife.

"Why can't he go?" Leighselle pouted.

"He claims poor health. Besides, I'm the one who shot and killed the animal in the first place, with good reason of course. It's my duty to see to its replacement. Father said shooting the bull was an act of folly. I need to save face and make it right."

"An act of folly? Nonsense. It was an act of bravery." She cast a sidelong glance at her husband, remembering the day she fell in love with him, and her heart filled with pride as it always did when she recalled that day. "You saved more people from getting hurt." Leighselle closed her eyes and fought off another wave of nausea.

"Morning sickness again, darling?" Henry asked as they reached the end of the crowded pier. He pulled Leighselle close to him as they stepped away from the sidewalk, letting others pass.

"Yes, but I'm fine. I'm just afraid you won't come back, or something bad will happen. I'm worried that—"

"Don't worry, my love. I'll be back before the baby arrives. I need to impress my father and show him I can accomplish this task. If I work hard and prove myself worthy, I'll be handsomely rewarded."

"He's a father you haven't seen in over fifteen years because he walked out on you and your mother. All you have are his telegraphs and bank drafts from Texas. How can you know that he's reliable or trustworthy?" The more Leighselle thought about it, the more anxious she became. "Why hasn't he come to New Orleans to meet you and discuss these business dealings face to face?"

"His bad health keeps him from traveling. Leighselle, we have to take this on good faith. He's followed through on everything so far."

"I could go to England with you. We could live there. Not come back." She fisted his coat lapels in her hands and placed her head against his chest.

"I have nothing in England to offer a wife. There's nothing in Ireland to go back to since Ma died. My future is here. It's in Texas. At least working for my father I have an opportunity to own a part of something, to support a wife. And a baby." Henry touched Leighselle's stomach, which hinted at an almost imperceptible bump.

"Near three months," whispered Leighselle, her eyes brimming with tears. "Do you wish for a girl or a boy?"

"Oh, God, please, a daughter who's as beautiful as her mother. She should have your green eyes and auburn hair, your fair skin. I won't stand a chance. You'll both have me wrapped tight around your dainty little fingers."

"I wouldn't mind a son with your cinnamon hair and freckles, and your silver-blue eyes. If he has your dimples and ready smile, he'll have me wrapped around his tiny little finger."

The horn on the ship gave three long blasts, the smoke stack belching gray steam into the ashen sky that was almost the same hue. The smoke blended into the sinking clouds as a light drizzle began to mist the air.

Leighselle clung to Henry's coat, the brimming tears now spilling down her cheeks. "I love you. I don't want to be without you."

Henry's smile stretched across his face. "You won't be. You're keeping a part of me with you."

Henry encircled Leighselle in his arms and kissed her with a lingering kiss full of promises. A couple strolling head to head and arm in arm passed; they cleared their throats and raised their brows but kept walking. Sailors on the ship whistled. Leighselle didn't care. She pressed into Henry, inviting the kiss to go on forever.

"I hate to, my darling girl, but I must go." Henry gave her one last kiss, then pulled away and sprinted toward the ship.

Standing at the salty, wet railing that separated the pier from the dock, she watched Henry tread up the swinging rope-and-plank bridge that connected the walkway to the ship. She saw him on the top deck, hat in hand, waving at her. She saw the ship being tugged out to sea and felt as if her heart were being pulled along with it. The steamer cut a slow turn away from the dock, then made its way to the outer harbor. The rippling wake trailed behind, connecting Leighselle to Henry in a widening *V*, until a tugboat crossed the wake's path, severing the tie.

Leighselle wept. She stood transfixed with her eyes on the horizon. Her hands gripped the rail that kept her from toppling into the dark and murky water, and she watched until his ship was a small dot disappearing into the gray, choppy sea.

"Almost three months along?" asked a familiar voice from behind her shoulder. "I guess I should congratulate my daughter-in-law."

Leighselle drew in a sharp breath and spun around, fear filling her heart. "You. What? What do you mean, congratulate your daughter-in-law?" All the heat, all the blood, all the air in her body drained in a sudden rush to her feet, leaving her lightheaded and swooning. A reckoning washed over her—a dawning of something dreadful—something her subconscious had suspected, yet pretended was nothing.

*****

San Antonio, Texas, September 27, 1860

Hughes shook his head in disbelief. "So Seamus sent Henry out of the country on a mission to purchase a bull. To what end, though?"

"If Seamus couldn't have me, then no one else could, either." The horror of those days never lessened. The memory, the pain, the terror was vivid and raw each new day. "And he would take away any chance of me ever being happy or having a part of Henry with me."

"How did he do it?" Hughes asked, his eyes drawing narrow slits.

"He drugged me with laudanum. But his evil didn't stop with Henry and me. He loaded me along with Addy-Frank and Birdie into a wagon, and before leaving New Orleans, he made a few stops first. I learned these terrible details later from Addy-

98

Frank."

*****

Seamus guided the wagon to the corner of St. Louis and Chartres Streets and reined the team of horses to a stop next to one of the many slave pens that lined the busy lane. Inside the squalid pen, which normally held up to one hundred slaves, a dozen Negros remained. The group consisted of adult men of varying ages, all wearing new but cheap suits. The two women wore calico frocks with matching scarves tied about their heads, while a young boy of twelve or thirteen wore new shoes too big to stay on his feet. They all pressed against the far side of the pen trying to claim the meager shade offered by the side of the hotel's walls.

"If she stirs or starts to wake up," he instructed, "give her a sip of tea from this canteen. Don't let me catch you drinking from it. Do you understand me, girl?"

Birdie nodded her head. "Yes'suh."

"Get your good-byes over with here, but do it quietly. I don't want prospective buyers put off by a bunch of wailing and carrying on."

"Please, Massah Flanders, please let me go with my Birdie. She all I have. My other two babies I done buried. I can help take care of Miss Leighselle. I been doing it ever since the day she was born. Birdie too young to help much with a baby. She ain't but ten herself." Addy-Frank's eyes were red and bloodshot from crying, her shoulders sinking under the heavy weight of what might become of her.

"She's old enough to learn. Remember, no agitating prospective buyers." Seamus turned and strolled inside the opulent building. He soon returned, a small man in a white suit in tow.

"I have one to be sold," said Seamus to the auctioneer's assistant. "She's chained to the back of my wagon. I don't have time to wait until she sells. I'm on my way out of town. Can you handle this and deposit the proceeds into my bank account?"

"Indeed, sir. That's how most prefer to handle it. Just sign this document detailing name, age, and abilities of your property, then your bank and the name on the account." The man gave a cheerful smile, offering Seamus the document to sign.

"Hell, I don't know her age or abilities. I'd prefer if I just sign the document and you fill in the blanks however you wish. My name's Seamus Henry Flanders. First Federal of New Orleans is my bank in town."

"Yes, Mr. Flanders. Sign here." The assistant pointed to the signature line. "She'll fetch a better price if she's clean and wearing a fresh dress. It doesn't have to be expensive. The men need to be shaved of facial hair, and the women's hair must be covered with a scarf. If you want to get the best price, you need to demonstrate—"

"Just get what you can." Seamus signed the document and took his receipt.

He released the bindings and led Addy-Frank into the holding pen. Just before the door closed, she bolted, running to the wagon, clutching Birdie in a tight embrace. "Be good. Watch out for Miss Leighselle. Don't give Mistah Flanders reason to be angry with you. You understand, child? That's the most important thing of all." Her tears fell on Birdie's face.

"I understand, Mama. But I want to come with you," sobbed Birdie. "Why can't I come with you?"

"Here's a secret to take with you, Birdie." Addy-Frank hugged her daughter one last time, whispering in her ear. ". . . and never forget that, baby. Always remember that."

"I won't forget, Mama," Birdie said, dodging Seamus's slaps.

Grabbing Addy-Frank by the arm, Seamus tried to drag her back to the pen but first had to pry Birdie's hands free. "Be quiet, girl, I said no commotion." He pulled them apart, forcing Addy-Frank back to the holding pen, shoving her inside.

"Best to remove the child from the mother's sight so the woman can calm down before going up on the auction block. A hysterical mother never brings much money. Is there anything else I can assist you with, Mr. Flanders?" asked the assistant auctioneer as he finished bolting the lock on the pen.

Without answering, with no backward glance, Seamus climbed up onto the driver's seat, took the reins in hand, and snapped them against the horses' backs. "Move it on out," he commanded as he headed the wagon up Royal Street, then north toward Alexandria.

As Seamus's wagon disappeared from sight, a shiny black buggy passed by the slave holding pen, stopping just beyond the hotel. Doctor Flemings emerged, medical bag in hand. With quick strides, he made his way to the entrance of the rotunda. As he passed the holding pen, he paused, recognizing the frightened woman on her knees, wailing, her hands folded in prayer.

"Addy-Frank? What are you doing at the slave auction? Where's Miss Leighselle?" He sat his bag on the sidewalk and stepped next to the fence, lacing his fingers through the wire enclosure. "Come here. Tell me what's happened."

She rushed to the fence, grasping the doctor's coat sleeve. In a gush of words and tears, she explained the nightmare of the past twenty-four hours. "Please, suh, I beg you. Please buy me. I can work for you, be your nurse an seamstress. Please, suh." Her thin face was haunted, her eyes pleading.

The doctor looked stricken. "I'm not a slave owner. I didn't come here for the purpose of buying slaves. I came to treat a sick guest at the hotel. Are you sure that Leighselle has been taken away by her father-in-law?"

"Yes'suh. An he took Birdie, too. He stop at Judge's house afore bringing me here. I heard him say Judge made it legal for him to do what he do, for him to sign for Leighselle."

"That doesn't make sense. Leighselle doesn't need a guardian or an executor."

"Leighselle ain't herself. She acting like she out of her mind, or something. I be worried sick 'bout her."

The auctioneer's assistant, with sharpened cane in hand, strode out to the pen. "All right, you there, come along. Look lively and smart." He pointed the stick at Addy-Frank. "Dry your face. No crying on the auction block."

"Please, Doctor. Please take me with you," she implored.

"I'm sorry, Addy-Frank. I'm not in a position to buy a slave. I'm a poor country doctor. I don't know how I'd manage."

Addy-Frank backed away from the fence, her expression fervent. "Please, I beg you, suh. Please." Her words trailed off as the assistant prodded her with his stick toward the rotunda.

"Once you are up for sale, tell the buyers what all you know how to do. Sound smart, look sharp. You'll go to a better owner the more you can demonstrate all the ways in which you can perform," instructed the assistant.

The bright room smelled of cigars puffed on by well-dressed men who paced the room, assessing the goods to be sold. A faint smell of bacon lingered on the air, the grease used as a body gloss. A fine sheen on black skin was preferred; grayish, dull skin meant tuberculosis, which could kill a sale. The auctioneer's assistant applied a variety of tricks to get the bids climbing until he heard, "Sold!"

The crowd was lively, the buyers anxious to snag a bargain at the end of the selling day. Addy-Frank walked to the block, head high, her face glistening with tears.

"She may look frightened, but there's wisdom in those eyes, I can see that right off," claimed the auctioneer. "Tell these buyers what kind of work you'll do for your new master. Speak up."

"I a nurse, an a nanny, an a seamstress. I can cook some, too. But mostly household duties." She thought, chiding herself, she could also sew curses into a man's pocket, but not tight enough to keep it from coming back and landing on her own head. She ran her hands into the pockets of her thin dress, feeling for the threads of a curse someone might have secretly sewn.

"Let's start the bidding off at one thousand dollars. A nurse, nanny, seamstress, and cook, all rolled into one. Do I hear a thousand? One thousand dollars. All right, how about seven hundred. Seven hundred dollars for a lifetime of wisdom."

"The price for a skinny bag of bones should start at two hundred," said a whiny female voice in the crowd. "She looks frail enough to blow away, and then what? Lose your investment, that's what."

"I'll give two hundred," shouted Doctor Flemings, his hands in a white-knuckle grip on his medical bag. He swallowed hard, clearing his throat. He kept his eyes on the auctioneer and away from looking at Addy-Frank.

"I have two hundred here with the good doctor. Two twenty-five anyone? Two hundred twenty-five?"

Someone across the room raised the bid.

"Two hundred fifty is now to you, Doctor. Yes? No? Will you go?"

Doctor Flemings nodded.

Back and forth the bidding went, climbing in increments of twenty-five dollars. Bidders dropped off until two remained. The echo of the gavel banging hard on the hickory dais concluded the sale.

"Sold, to Doctor Flemings, for three hundred and seventy-five dollars. Congratulations, Doc, you now own a fine piece of property there."

Doctor Flemings assisted Addy-Frank into the front seat of his buggy, his voice a thin attempt at cheerfulness. "We have patients coming into the clinic all afternoon. I used to tell Miss Leighselle that I could use a good nurse. I expect she would be pleased to know that you'll be working with me."

"Yes'suh. Thank you, suh." Addie-Frank looked straight ahead, pressing the back of her fist against her mouth, holding in the scream that begged to be released.

"And if you don't like nursing, I can put you to work sewing gowns and blankets for the Women and Children's Hospital. How would you like that?" The doctor took up the driving lines, turning the cart horse away from the slave pens.

"I like that fine, suh," she said, tears streaming down her face. The back of her fist pressed harder against her mouth, the silent scream shattering her heart.

*****

Birdie shook Leighselle by her shoulders. "Wake up, Miss Leighselle. That man be here again."

She referred to Seamus Flanders as "that man," and every Tuesday he paid a visit to the nunnery in Alexandria where he had Leighselle ensconced for the purported reason that he needed a private place to allow his daughter-in-law, who suffered from severe psychosis, to have her baby in safety and seclusion. Seamus made a generous donation to their orphanage, ensuring their cooperation.

Leighselle, sitting in her rocking chair, blinked open her eyes. "I'm awake." Indeed, she was wide awake. Clear-headed. No longer in a drug-induced fog, thanks to Birdie.

When they had arrived at the nunnery, Birdie was allowed to sleep on a floor rug at the foot of Leighselle's bed. Every morning and evening, Sister Francis would knock on the door. Birdie, answering the knock, would receive a tea tray, the instructions never changing.

"Put the sugar cube in the tea cup before you pour the tea. Make sure Madame drinks it all before you bring the tray down to the kitchen."

But on Tuesday mornings, there were two sugar cubes. And, on Tuesday mornings, Birdie would notice Miss Leighselle behaving strangely. She would stumble her steps, mumble her words. She would fall asleep while she was eating, while she was bathing, even while she was on the chamber pot. She'd say things and use words Birdie didn't understand. She'd stare out the window, crying, clawing at her skin.

Other sisters prayed over her, invocations lasting all day long. The scene frightened Birdie, the strange litanies that combined oils and incense and chanted readings. Their raised voices calling on God's healing power, calling on God to enter the body to guard the soul of the unborn child, propelled her to a terrified silence.

One day when Birdie was scrubbing the pantry, she overheard Sister Francis speaking to Massah Seamus about something called laudanum treatments for Miss Leighselle. The conversation she heard between the two—how the drug affected Leighselle, how to wean a baby from the drug's addiction—frightened her more than the sisters' chanted prayers to an all-powerful God who could cast people into burning pits of fire.

Birdie began crumbling the sugar cubes into the chamber pot to empty with the waste. As Leighselle started showing signs of clarity, Birdie confided in her, telling her what she had seen and heard and how she had been taking care of Miss Leighselle by not putting the strange, brown sugar cubes in her tea anymore.

"Ain't nobody's baby need to be born addicted to God and laudanum," Birdie had said, after Leighselle had explained to her what the word *addicted* meant.

They made a plan. So as not to draw suspicion, Leighselle would behave as if she were still under the influence of the drug until she felt recovered enough that the two could escape. They hid clothes and food. When the moment was right, they would sneak away. Weak, her legs unsteady, Leighselle figured it would take a month before they could put her plan into action.

Sitting in her rocking chair, she looked at Birdie, her eyes clear and bright. "After the usual meeting with Seamus, when you remove the coffee service and take it to the pantry, leave the pantry unlocked." Leighselle spoke with clarity, her voice strong. "The small valise you packed is still there, right?"

"Yes, Miss Leighselle, behind the flour sacks. I'll check again when I go down to empty your chamber pot, but there's nothing to empty. Wasn't nothing in there to hide the sugar cubes. You sure you don't need to go?" Birdie asked, her voice anxious.

"I'm sure. Just pour some water in there and cover it with paper. It'll be all right. Wait. Shhhh. . . ." Leighselle pressed her finger across her lips.

A knock. Sister Francis opened the door. "I'm ready to escort you to your meeting. You look well this morning." She smiled.

*****

"Thank you, sister," said Seamus, looking up when he heard them enter the receiving room.

Leighselle shuffled into the room, her billowy, flowing gown a discrete cover-up for her eight-and-a-half-month pregnancy. As was the custom, she took the chair opposite Seamus, and as always she stared at him with hollow, sad eyes and a vacant expression.

He sat in a chair by the window overlooking a pond with a fountain, its spray fanning out high into the air. Swans and ducks floated in languid circles under its misty umbrella.
He looked on as some of the orphans skimmed the moss and trimmed the cattails growing at the edge of the pond.

"Hard work builds character. Better they learn it young," he said.

"Yes, sir." Sister Francis gave a generous smile of agreement. "May I have a word with you out in the hall, Mister Flanders?" She motioned for him to join her, and Seamus followed.

Leighselle stared at the chair vacated by Seamus and waited, anxiety churning her stomach. Did Sister Francis overhear her conversation with Birdie? She glanced out the window at the swans, wishing for wings that she might fly away.

After what seemed an eternity, they reentered the room, Seamus taking his seat, Sister Francis serving their coffee and sandwiches. All seemed normal. Their smiles were pleasant, their voices cheery, their conversation about his donation to the orphanage the apparent reason for their tête-à-tête.

Leighselle breathed a sigh of relief, secretly pocketing two sandwiches as Sister Francis excused herself from the room, allowing her and Seamus their privacy.

"Week after week, Leighselle, and we go through this silent face-off all over again." Seamus drummed his fingers on the wooden armrest.

Sipping her coffee, Leighselle ate the sandwich on her plate, saving the cookie for Birdie, following the same routine as every Tuesday. With half-closed eyes, she let her head sway, portraying the actions of one under the influence of laudanum. She knew the behavior well.

Seamus glowered at her. "Sign these papers and I'll have Henry on the next ship to America, where he can raise his child in luxury and comfort. His heart will be broken that his wife died in childbirth, but he'll get over it. Don't sign, and Henry will never see me or this child again. I'll send him a letter that you're a whore unfit to be the mother of my grandchild and that I'm raising it myself."

Leighselle darted her eyes between the pen and the document. Her fingers began to itch. Her scalp tingled, as if a thousand needles pricked the surface—not enough to draw blood, just enough to irritate. A metallic taste lingered in her mouth, an all too familiar sensation that she remembered from before. In a sudden reckoning, she dropped her coffee cup and it clattered to the floor.

"I'm not a whore." Leighselle's eyes wanted to close, but she forced them to remain open, to focus. *The coffee…*

"I can describe your body intimately for Henry, the triangular scar on your backside low enough for me to smell your womanhood, the large mole on your right breast just above your nipple. It was common knowledge that you let whores sleep in your sewing shop. It wouldn't be hard to prove you an unfit mother."

"You know my body because you forced yourself on me." Leighselle's head throbbed, her pulse speeding the blood too quickly through her veins.

"You asked for it, Leighselle. You seduced me. You seduced my son. I'm sure there have been many other men." He sat back and crossed his legs, his voice conversational. "My good friend, Judge Reeder in New Orleans, would swear to anything I asked. He owes me many favors."

"Henry would never believe that about me," she said, her shoulders drooping a fraction, her posture curving inward.

"It would be better to be thought dead than thought a whore. Sign this document giving me custody of the child." He held out the paper and pen. "You'll have a nice, tidy sum to get on with your life. I'll get on with mine and put you behind me forever."

"If I don't sign, you take my child. If I do sign, you take my child and let Henry raise it. Either way, I lose—you win." She pressed her hands against her ears, trying to quiet the ringing. "If I sign, it appears I've signed away my child for money, like some common whore."

Seamus leaned forward, his eyes a hard, blue slit. "You were mine, Leighselle. You were always mine. I told you I was coming back for you. But finding you with my son—knowing you *gave* to Henry what belonged to *me*—now the grandchild."

"I didn't know Henry was your son. I—I never belonged to you." The room was stifling. Prickly heat inflamed her skin, perspiration beaded her brow—the room began to close in.

Seamus stood, looking down on her. "I can allow Henry and this grandchild in my life. I *will not* allow you ruining my life. Removing you . . . is the only alternative. It's the cost of making you pay for what you've done." Then, he turned and strode to the door, opening it. "Bring her in."

Sister Francis stepped into the room, Birdie in tow—her eyes streaming tears, her bare legs covered in the stripe marks of a whip.

Seamus strode back to where Leighselle sat, clutching the arms of the chair, steadying herself. Leaning close to her ear, his voice harsh, he pointed to the door. "Take a look at your darkie. We both know the truth. She's what happened when your father fucked Addie-Frank. Sign the papers, Leighselle. It'll make life easier on your little half-sister, Birdie."

Leighselle, gulping quick breaths, her head floating light, took the pen in hand. She touched the sharp gold tip to the paper. The cloven, diamond-shaped end left an ink mark that spread out like a bleeding wound. She studied the blot blossoming on the line that waited for her signature. Whore, the stain seemed to say—a stained woman. Next to the ink's blemish, she signed Leighselle La Verne Beauclaire Flanders. She opened her fingers, allowing the pen to roll out of her hand and fall to the floor.

Seamus picked up the papers and turned to Sister Francis. "She's near enough term. Isn't there some concoction you can give her to hurry this situation along?"

"I don't think that will be necessary," said Sister Francis, rushing to Leighselle's side.

Pushing herself out of the chair, Leighselle stood, clutching her swollen belly. A pool of amniotic water puddled on the floor at her feet.

*****

September 27, 1860

A rattling cough erupted from deep within Leighselle's core, a cough full of death. The sun, no longer warm, had turned tepid, the sky a dull, chalky white with a hint of pale pink to the west.

"And that, my dear old friend, is my story." Leighselle stood and stretched, fisting her hands against her lower back.

Hughes stood and put his hands on Leighselle's shoulders. "You've been living a nightmare that's lasted a lifetime. I wish I'd known. I'd have been a better friend. God knows you needed one."

"I had Addy-Frank. We had each other. When I returned to New Orleans, Doc Flemings released her and she came to live with me again."

"Let's take a walk." Hughes crooked his arm through Leighselle's and guided her into the lobby of the hotel. "What happened after that?"

"After that?" Leighselle said. "As soon as the baby was born, he left with my child and Birdie. He gave the sisters instructions to keep me sedated until he returned for me, telling them he feared the travel so soon would not be good for me. He never returned, of course."

"Leighselle. There are no words—" Hughes swallowed, forcing back emotion. "Sorry." He cleared his throat. "So. What did you do next?"

"What I've always done. I picked myself up, dusted myself off, and woke up the next day. And then the next. And then the next after that. My heart was broken. I'd lost both Henry and Barleigh. What kept me sane was knowing my daughter would be raised by Henry, and Birdie would be there to help." She held up one hand to indicate she needed a moment to compose herself.

Hughes nodded, walking in silence, holding onto her arm.

"I knew where the nuns kept the laudanum. There were times I considered ending my life—my baby's life—before it entered the world. I prayed to God He would end it. But, I didn't—I couldn't."

"Jesus, Leighselle." Hughes drew a deep breath and looked up at the ceiling, blinking, swallowing. "I hope this son-of-a-bitch is still alive so I can have the pleasure of making his acquaintance."

They walked in silence, making their way around the well-appointed lobby to the pride of the hotel, its grand piano. As they stopped to admire the piano and listen to the musician's masterful rendition of a popular waltz, a crowd had gathered. Leighselle motioned to Hughes that she was ready to go.

"Sorry to interrupt, sir," said Jameson, meeting the pair as they made their way back to the patio. Leaning close to Hughes's ear, he said in a quiet voice, "Your package has arrived. I placed it in your room, sir."

"Thank you, Jameson. I'll look it over later."

"Yes, sir." He turned but stopped short. "Should I arrange for a carriage for your guest?"

"No. If I can talk Miss Beauclaire into it, she'll take my room. I'll feel much better with her staying here so that Doc Schmidt is immediately available if she needs him, and you can assist her as well. Leighselle? Is that all right with you?"

"I can't put you out of your own room, Hughes."

"You already have, my dear. You're sending me on a mission—an adventure, really."

Jameson cleared his throat and tapped his vest pocket.

"I haven't forgotten, Jameson. I'll take care of that business before I leave."

"Fine, sir. I'll send for Miss Beauclaire's things from the guest house and have them brought up to your room." And then he was gone.

Hughes turned to Leighselle, concern wrinkling his brow. "Are you all right? Surely, this has been difficult talking about."

"It was more difficult *not* talking about it. I'm praying now that you can find her. The last I heard was Seamus Flanders sold his Corpus Christi ranch to a Captain King. They may have settled in the area of Fort Worth."

"Well, my dear, that's what I'm good at, finding people. You'll have your daughter back in no time, I promise."

"Oh! No, no, no." Leighselle held up both hands, pushing the thought away. "I don't want you to bring her to me. I just want you to find her. I don't wish to disrupt and complicate her life. I just need to know that she's alive and well. And happy. She doesn't need to know anything about me or my life—my past."

"What—I don't understand."

"Please promise me, Hughes, that you'll keep my secret.

Please."

"Don't you think your daughter would love to know that her mother is alive and and is searching her?" Hughes looked confused.

"After all these years?" She shook her head. "No. If she's happy in her life, I want her to stay that way. Knowing I'm alive would surely hurt and confuse her. There're things about me she might find offensive, or not understand. No, it's best this way."

Leighselle hoped it was best. She accepted Hughes's promise to keep her secret, ignoring the fact that he insisted he would try to change her mind. Her mind was set. Some events lost to the past should stay buried. Though try as she might *not* to dwell on it, she often dreamed of seeing her daughter, of touching her, one more time.

"After the baby was born, what did you do?" Hughes reseated them at their table, where Jameson had left a bottle of brandy waiting for them.

"As soon as I recovered, I simply told them I was leaving. I wanted to go back to New Orleans, where I might feel close to memories of Henry. My parting gift from Seamus had been left in the priest's care. A suitcase full of hush money. Five thousand dollars to keep me quiet and out of my daughter's life."

Hughes sucked in a breath. "Five thousand. Seamus was evil but he wasn't stupid. He made sure you wouldn't cause trouble."

"What trouble would I have caused to jeopardize my daughter or Birdie?" Leighselle's voice was sharp. She found the thought profoundly ridiculous. Seamus *was* stupid. He could have paid her a penny and she would have walked away if it meant ensuring no harm would come to either Barleigh or Birdie.

"None, of course," said Hughes. "Though in Seamus's mind, you would have caused plenty."

"No . . . I busied myself. I opened La Verne's Tavern. No more Sew Beauclaire and working for pennies. And, I bought back Addy-Frank. Doc gave her to me, really. He wouldn't touch the money, so I made a hefty donation to his hospital."

"Addy-Frank, Birdie's mother." Hughes flicked a speck of

dirt from under his thumbnail, drummed his fingers on the table, and shook his head. "How in the *hell* did the both of you cope, having lost your daughters to the same man?"

"We clung to one another, supported one another, cried on the other's shoulder when the grief would overcome. I miss her." She sipped her brandy, both hands cupping the snifter.

"How long ago did she pass?"

"Last year. She encouraged this little endeavor of mine. I promised her I'd try. . . ." Leighselle pressed a napkin to her eyes, blotting the tears.

Hughes looked up at the darkening sky. "My dear, it's getting late and I'm feeling anxious to get on with this new mission. We should get you inside, too, before the evening chill sets in."

"Evening chill? Here in San Antonio? It still feels like a hundred degrees to me."

Hughes laughed. "You're right. Well, we should get you in before the ghosts start making their rounds. I told you the Menger Hotel is haunted, didn't I?"

"Haunted? Ghosts?"

"Yes, ghosts, and lots of them from what I understand, though I've never had the pleasure of an encounter."

"Who and how many?" asked Leighselle, a chill running up her spine. A smile tickled the corners of her mouth. "I've always wanted to meet a ghost."

"Soldier ghosts, many of them, most likely from the Battle of the Alamo that was fought here. The Spanish fort was originally called Mission San Antonio de Valero, and this hotel sits on what is considered sacred ground. If you're lucky, you'll hear the muffled boot stomping of spirit soldiers as they march around during the dark of night—still on guard duty."

"I welcome the sound of a man moving about my room in the dark of the night," said Leighselle with a wink. "It's been too long."

The evening's stars reflected like a thousand sparkling fireflies in the San Antonio River. Ancient cypress trees lined the banks, knobs from their roots peeping up out of the ground like snooping gnomes. A lone weeping willow stood sentry next to the Alamo's west wall, sweeping the ground with its long, thin arms. The air was rich, pungent, and thick with the spicy smells of south Texas. Crickets and cicadas sang their praises to the night.

Hughes escorted Leighselle up to his second story room overlooking the Alamo Plaza. "If you need anything, Jameson is in the room just below mine. The signal is to stomp on the floor by the window three times. He'll hear you. He's a very light sleeper, one eye and one ear always open."

"Hughes, I can't begin to thank you. I know you'll find her. I just hope it's in time."

"Yes, me too. I'll keep you posted on my progress. The telegraph office will deliver messages to you here at the hotel, a courtesy to Menger guests."

As they strolled through the arched double doors, past a polished wood and brass entryway, and into the marble-tiled reception area, they chatted like amiable old friends who might be discussing the beautiful artwork on the walls or the fine European furnishings of the Menger. With its fifty guest rooms filled to capacity, there were plenty of visitors discussing these trivial topics and other matters less important than stolen children, hush money, clandestine missions, and death.

"I have Barleigh taken care of, financially speaking," said Leighselle, holding onto Hughes's arm. "I've given that topic a lot of attention throughout the years. Besides the majority of the money from Seamus, of which I spent very little, my business is quite profitable. Too, there was the refund from the nursing school in Shreveport which I never attended. That was an expensive school!"

"Ah, the Shreveport School of Medicine, I forgot about that," said Hughes, giving her arm a squeeze. "I'm glad you chose New Orleans instead."

"If something happens to me . . ." Leighselle's voice turned serious. ". . . Barleigh will inherit a respectable amount of real estate and liquid assets. My will is on file with my attorney, a Mr. Bertram La Mont in New Orleans. A copy is with me in my valise."

T. K. Lukas

"If something happens to you? What I expect will happen is that you'll rest, recover your full health, and enjoy a passel of grandkids one day, each one having inherited your beautiful green cat eyes."

Clutching his lapels in her weak grasp, she said, "Be careful, Hughes. I wish I could tell you that this is without risk, but I cannot. If Seamus Flanders is still alive, there will be danger."

"I don't shy from danger," Hughes said, a sharp edge to his words. "I hunt down outlaws for a living and bring them to justice. I think I can handle Seamus Flanders if we cross paths, and I hope to God we do. But I know my mission. I've given you my word that your secret is safe with me."

"Thank you, Hughes." Leighselle blinked away tears.

"I'll respect your wish for privacy until I hear otherwise from you. Remember, stomp the floor three times by the window if you need Jameson. I'm off. I don't want to miss the midnight train." He kissed Leighselle on each cheek and embraced her before turning and disappearing down the stairs.

"Your package," called Leighselle after him. She ran out into the hallway with a large, thick envelope in hand.

Hughes looked up from the lower landing. "Drop it."

She did and he caught the package with one hand, saluted her with the other and blew her a kiss.

She saluted, sending an air kiss back, her gesture awkward and clumsy, which made her laugh. The laugh dissolved into a racking cough, the blood bright red and metallic in her mouth. She stumbled to her room, closed the door, and leaned her back up against it, waiting for the dizziness to pass, waiting for coolness. Her vision became fuzzy, the room's furnishings out of focus. She leaned forward, moving her hands through the air for a place to lie down, like a blind person groping for something familiar.

Slow feet shuffled and scraped their way across the wooden floor to the canopied bed. She eased herself onto the downy duvet cover, her breathing shallow and fast. "Please find her. Find my Barleigh," whispered Leighselle as darkness closed in. "But please keep your word. . . ."

Boots on the ground—stomp, stomp, stomp—ghost

114

soldiers on patrol. She heard the echo of their heavy footfalls, the noise muffled in her ears like a throbbing pulse. Stomp. Stomp. Stomp. A faint smile eased across her mouth moments before she fell unconscious, a trickle of blood staining the white pillow.

A Comanche moon lit up the Menger Hotel and bathed it with a brilliant radiance. Guests lingered on the patio, enjoying the dazzling splendor of the remarkable lunar display. Privileged companions danced in the moonlight and toasted its magical spell, while the moon gilded the hour and all below with its otherworldly light.

CHAPTER EIGHT

SEPTEMBER 27, 1860

Hughes gave the coded knock: two fast, three slow, two fast. When Jameson answered the door, Hughes stepped into the room, giving him a list of instructions regarding Leighselle's care, a note for the doctor, and a telegram for Jameson to send to New Orleans ahead of his arrival.

"Yes, sir. Anything else?" asked Jameson.

"I've looked over the package. I'll study it further on the train," said Hughes. "I'll be in Saint Joseph by the end of next month, but I've encountered a minor delay." He *hoped* it would be minor, anyway. He considered himself among the best when it came to tracking wild animals. How difficult could it be finding a nineteen-year-old girl?

Hughes gave Jameson a brief description of his impending search mission once his visit to Louisiana was complete. He expected it would take a few days to find the girl. Then, he would send Jameson a telegraph once he'd accomplished Leighselle's mission and he was on his way to Missouri.

"Very well, sir," said Jameson, taking notes. "One other question. Should Miss Beauclaire's condition become dire, what should I do beyond sending for the doctor?"

"She's already beyond dire. I'm sure the doctor will do his best to make her comfortable." What else was there to do, thought Hughes, besides hope like hell she had the strength to hang on until he found her daughter?

The San Antonio to New Orleans train chugged east, yet Hughes's thoughts drifted west. With few passengers aboard the midnight freight run, the car was quiet except for the clanking of wheels on metal and the occasional whistling of the horn. He closed his eyes and lost himself in the rhythmic cadence of the rails.

His plan was clear. He would depart Louisiana late the next day riding a fine horse, head back to Texas, be in Corpus by week's end, head north to Fort Worth if required, and then before you know it, have word to Leighselle that he'd located Barleigh. How difficult could it be?

He made a pillow of his topcoat, stuffing it between his shoulder and the window. Resting his head against the cool glass, he tried clearing his mind of his troubled thoughts of Leighselle. It was easy to picture his dear friend as she was when he left New Orleans those many years ago—stunning, vibrant, sassy, funny, intelligent. And clever. That woman was clever. He drifted off to sleep, his memories melting into vivid dreams.

*****

February 24, 1852

Winter Carnival season was in full swing, La Verne's Tavern a hotbed of activity. It was Fat Tuesday, and all around the French Quarter, parades clogged the streets, passing in front of the tavern, bringing in customers, revelers, and troublemakers alike. The final masquerade ball celebrated Mardi Gras and the end of frivolity before Ash Wednesday ushered in Lent and the Holy Holidays— and along with it, the expectation for decorum. But for one last night, unbridled pleasures for all the senses abounded. Exuberant revelers didn't have to look far to find them.

Leighselle was draping the final strand of an English ivy and eucalyptus garland around the life-sized oil painting of a charcoal-gray and silver Brahmin bull. It took up most of the wall above the mahogany bar. She had commissioned the painting when she'd purchased the business, adding a brass nameplate on the bottom of the frame. The plate was etched with the words *Henry's Folly*.

"You need a hand with that?" asked Hughes as he strolled through the swinging doors of the saloon.

"You're early. Did your father shut down Lévesque Sugarcane and Shipping in honor of our Mardi Gras masquerade?"

"He'd drop dead before that would happen. Hop down off that ladder and let me help you. You're making me nervous way up there."

Leighselle climbed down, handing the garland to Hughes. "Drape this over the top of the painting, please."

"Henry's Folly. I've always wondered if there was a story behind the name." Hughes climbed the ladder, finishing the decorations.

"Yes, a long story." Leighselle's bright green eyes darkened, her smile faded.

"I'm sorry. Did I say something wrong?" Hughes climbed down and then folded the ladder, stowing it behind the bar.

"It's all right. I get asked that question often. I should be used to it by now." She smiled, but the smile sat flat, not reaching her eyes.

Hughes studied her face and her petite, graceful form. The way she looked, the way she moved, reminded him of a cat, but a sad cat on the verge of tears. "All finished," he said as he put away the ladder. "Anything else you need done while I'm here?"

"Just a few more decorations." Leighselle placed candles on each table. "Thank you for helping. I'm glad you managed to sneak away from work. Your father's grooming you to take over the business is taking you away from being my handyman and security guard. I'm sure I'll be in need of your services tonight. The crowds the last few evenings have grown more boisterous."

"It'd be wiser if Father groomed John-Pierre to take over. Even Mother sees that he's better suited to running the business," said Hughes, handing candles to Leighselle for placement.

"Won't your father consider what your mother thinks about the situation?"

Hughes snorted. "Listening to a woman's point of view, even if that woman is his wife, ranks just below his shutting down business for a holiday."

"You're twins. Why can't he groom John-Pierre for the business?"

"That would go against tradition, God forbid. I'm the elder by a whopping two minutes." Hughes adopted a comical, mocking tone, causing Leighselle to laugh.

John-Pierre *was* more suited. He didn't act like an 'irresponsible eighteen-year-old always looking for trouble,' to quote Father. He acted more like a 'responsible young man on the cusp of adulthood.' But, Father would try anything, including guilt and bribery, to get his way—to try to force his eldest son into fitting into the mold that shaped all the men of the Lévesque Sugarcane and Shipping dynasty.

"What I want is to know if you brought your mask for the ball tonight?" asked Leighselle, putting the finishing touches on the bar's centerpiece. "I want you to mingle. I don't want you standing out as the hired gun. That would put a damper on the festive mood."

Hughes shook his head. "I respectfully disagree. I think having visible security would help keep things from getting out of control, like it did last year."

"You worry too much," chided Leighselle. "Dress up, wear a mask, mingle, have fun, but be on your guard for anything that needs tamped down."

"Yes, ma'am." Hughes helped finish decorating the tavern with crepe paper and colorful streamers before going out to watch the parade.

A comical troupe of men and boys, women and girls, on foot, on horseback, or riding in wagons, carts, or buggies, paraded past La Verne's. Grotesque, horrible, diabolical masks seemed to be the theme. Some costumes were human bodies with heads of beasts, fowl, or fish. Others were animal bodies with distorted human heads made of papier–mâché painted wild, graphic colors. All sorts of garish beasts wound their way up and down the street in rich confusion and with much foolish laughter and singing.

Some revelers wore disguises of mermaids or monks, some were beggars or robbers, while a few opted for body paint that left many guessing if they were clothed underneath. The carnival spirit had erupted over the French Quarter, spewing decadence and debauchery all around.

Later that evening at the tavern as the masked party crowd swelled to capacity, Hughes moved through the room, elbowing his way around the bar. Jostling and pushing his way across the dance floor, he made his way toward Monique. Peacock feathers masked half her face, with the other half covered in blue and gold glitter paint.

"Having a good time, Monique?"

"I'm in disguise. You're not supposed to recognize me."

"I'd recognize your fiery red hair anywhere. You should have worn a powdered wig, like that one over there."

He pointed to a tall, beautiful woman in a gold brocade gown cut low in the back, showcasing her exquisite form. Her mask was black feathers that formed a beak-like point over her nose, giving her a dramatic avian appearance. Her costume kept one guessing if she were a well-dressed raven or King Louis XV's mistress with a feather affliction on her face.

Monique laughed. "It's Madam Pompadour all right, but the king will be shocked when she disrobes. *She* is a *he*."

"A *he*? Are you sure? But, her back is so feminine. A he?" Hughes cocked his head for a look from a different angle.

"Positive. That's Liberty's cousin Boyd Guzzleman, in from Mobile."

"Well, I'll be damned. He's prettier than Liberty, but don't tell her I said that."

"I won't, although she says as much herself. I'll catch up with you later." She glanced over at the bar and saw Leighselle pointing a man her way.

"Be careful tonight. There are people in town we don't know." Hughes studied the man walking toward Monique.

"Yes, big brother, I know the rules." Monique gave him a peck on the cheek and slipped away. Dressed as a cowboy, a red bandana pulled up over the lower half of his face and wearing six-shooters at his hip, the man took Monique by the arm and led her upstairs.

Hughes had never been with her. Monique and Leighselle

were like sisters, Leighselle the older, wiser sister and Monique the younger, naïve one who caused him to feel protective. He had been with a few of the other whores who worked at La Verne's, had lost his virginity one enjoyable, drunken night to Liberty, cousin of Boyd the cross-dresser, but Leighselle and Monique were off-limits. They were family.

After midnight when the masks came off and the crowd thinned, Hughes made his way to the bar for a whiskey, the one drink he allowed himself when on duty. He was all coffeed up, jittery, and in need of a calming spirit. The small splash of water swirled in a sensual fusion with the dark amber liquor. He sipped, sighed, enjoying the warming sensation that melted away the tension as he swallowed that first taste.

Spying Leighselle presiding over a game of poker, he strolled over, his soft black leather mask tucked into the breast pocket of his wine-colored vest. His white tuxedo shirt was rolled at the sleeves, exposing masculine wrists, his evening coat long ago discarded. He was handsome and comfortable in his casual elegance and despite his youth, turned the heads of women and men alike.

Leighselle looked up and smiled. "Like I told you, nothing to worry about tonight. Thankfully, no repeat of last year's Brawl at the Ball."

He watched as Leighselle dealt the cards with deft, quick movements, placing one face down, one face up, then waiting for hit-mes or stays or folds from the men around her table. Dealer's face card was the queen of diamonds. Half the players folded; the other half wished they had when Leighselle flipped over the ace of spades.

"Let's take a break, gentlemen. I'll be back in half an hour. Spend your money at the bar or on the dance floor with your favorite girl, but save a little for me and the queen of diamonds." Standing, she hooked her arm through Hughes's. "Fresh air would be nice. How about a walk outside?"

Hughes finished his whiskey. As he set the glass on the table, his amber eyes swept across the room one last time before escorting Leighselle out onto the sidewalk. Despite the late hour, it was crowded with costumed people in high carnival spirits.

"It's been a great night for La Verne's Tavern," Leighselle said with a smile. "The bar's been doing a brisk business as usual, the card tables are lively, and the girls have a steady stream of escorts twirling them around the floor and up the stairs. Have you had any problems?"

"Everything seems peaceable enough. I've tried keeping track of the girls and their escorts. I haven't seen Monique since early evening, though. Have you?"

"I think the last time I saw her was when she accompanied her first client, the man disguised as a gunslinger."

A sinking feeling came over Hughes, a sense of dread chilling him from the inside out. He recalled the man's red bandana mask and how the man walked with the six-shooter at his hip like a gunslinger—it was not a costume. *Fuck.* He spun around, racing back into the tavern and up the stairs, taking them two at a time.

Monique's door was locked. Hughes could hear muffled voices inside the room. A faint whimper, a sharp word—a slap— stifled moaning. Pounding the door with his fist, he demanded, "Open up. Security."

"Go away, I'm busy," said a male voice, mumbled and slurred with alcohol.

"Monique? Are you all right? It's Hughes. Open the door." He pounded again with his fists, rattling the knob. "Goddamnit, I said open the door!" he shouted.

A hush fell over the crowd downstairs. They collectively looked up, straining to see what was happening in the room at the head of the stairs. The tavern grew quiet except for the player piano, which continued to plink out "Molly Will You Be My Bride," the thin notes seeming to levitate and ride on the heavy cigar smoke choking the tavern's space.

Stepping back, Hughes raised his leg and kicked his booted foot against the door, splintering the frame into pieces. What he saw revolted him—enraged him—the grotesque scene hitting him like a sickening gut punch that displaces oxygen, leaving one gulping for air.

"Move away from her," he said through gritted teeth,

easing his gun out of its holster.

Monique was tied to the bed, a rag stuffed in her mouth. Her breasts had been slashed, clumps of her hair chopped off, the red curls strewn in shiny tufts on the floor. Round, angry cigarette burns dotted the length of both arms, but it was her face he couldn't bear to look at. Blood smeared the blue and gold glitter paint on half her face; the other unpainted half where the feathered mask had been removed was now covered in dark purple bruises. Both eyes were blackened and swollen shut, while her nose streamed blood. Her bottom lip, ripped half off, exposed several missing teeth.

"I wouldn't draw on me if I were you," the man said with a drunken slur, his body wobbling with the effort of standing. "You ain't got no idea who you're dealing with, do you?"

Hughes eased into the room, finger steady on the trigger. His eyes darted around, making a quick assessment of the situation. On the nightstand by the bed stood a near-empty bottle of whiskey. A revolver lay next to it. Another pistol was positioned on the bed between Monique's legs, employed, he was sure, in all kinds of horrors. The man he held steady in his sight was dirty and small, his mean eyes bloodshot and watery, his hands twitchy and empty and hovering.

"I don't give a damn what your name is," said Hughes in a dead-calm voice, not wanting to alarm the half-conscious Monique, who moaned quietly in between gasping for breath on the blood-soaked bed. "Raise your hands, slow and easy. Walk toward me."

"My names Whitt. Dalton Whitt. Me and my brothers Monroe, Raymond, and Arthur make up the Whitt Gang. I'm sure you've heard about us. My brothers'll come looking for me if I don't make it back to camp."

"I said get your hands in the air, you son of a bitch." Hughes stepped farther into the room, blood pounding in his head like a drum. "Walk nice and easy toward me. Now."

Dalton Whitt raised his hands, his body swaying with the exertion. He cast a glance at the table and his gun, then back at Hughes. "I believe this'll be your last day to live without worry or regret. Go ahead, take me in, but my brothers are even more unpleasant than I am." He laughed and wiped spittle and Monique's blood from the corners of his mouth, his shirt sleeve already a dark rusty brown.

Looking back at Monique, he gestured over his shoulder, "She had it coming. The bitch laughed when I dropped my pants. Laughed at me! Can you fucking believe it?" He lunged toward the table, hands outstretched, grabbing for his gun.

Using the calloused heel of his left hand, Hughes pounded the Colt .45's hammer in rapid-fire succession He emptied his six-shooter into the man, the first bullet taking care of the job, the other rounds spent for good measure. He pulled Dalton Whitt by his shirt collar and dragged him out into the hall, away from the bed and Monique. Then, with the butt-end of his gun, he pummeled the face and head of the lifeless Whitt.

"Stop, Hughes," Leighselle said as she ran up the stairs. She grabbed his arm, pulling back on it with all her weight. "He's dead. You can stop."

"He's not dead enough." He hit the man one last time across the face, crunching teeth and bones. With one final kick to Whitt's side, Hughes fell back against the wall. He took deep gulps of breath, blinked hard against the white-hot rage melting his vision, trying to focus on Leighselle's face, not on the bloody mess lying unmoving at his feet.

I killed a man. He turned aside, hands on his knees, and vomited.

Leighselle rubbed his back until the heaving stopped. "I should have come up with you but Smitty said to let you handle it. What happened?"

"He went for his gun. I shot him. I . . . I killed him."

"You did what you had to. A man defending himself is not a killer. Do you hear me? This does not make you like him."

"When I saw what he did to Monique, I knew I was going to kill him." Hughes stared at Leighselle, his words hanging in the air between them. "I'm glad he went for his gun, the stupid, drunken fool. Monique's bad off. He tried to kill her, too."

"Tried? You send for the sheriff and the doctor—I'll do

what I can here." She turned to enter the room but Hughes stretched his arm across the doorway to block her.

"It's bad. Don't go in there—don't look. Just send for the doctor." He tried to pull the door closed behind him but it bounced against the splintered frame.

Leighselle gasped. "Oh! I did. I saw." She turned quickly, pressing her face into Hughes's vest.

Hughes took her in his arms, a hand cupping the back of her head, and he held her against his chest while Leighselle wept.

*****

After the sheriff and undertaker left with Dalton's body, most of the revelers departed, too, in search of a livelier party to end the evening. Hughes felt edgy and alert. He wanted the night to be over. The three other Whitt brothers, no doubt, would come looking for him. Fine. He would wait for them.

He allowed himself one more whiskey. Then, to Leighselle, "Close down business for the night. Take Addy-Frank and go upstairs to your rooms and lock your doors."

Leighselle nodded. "The doctor and Addy-Frank are up with Monique. That's where I'm headed now."

"I'll come check on you in a bit, but don't open the door unless you know it's me. You're armed?"

"Always." She ran her hands down the outside of her ball gown, feeling her garters. She kept single-shot pistols, one each side, just above each knee.

A shadow moving caught Hughes's eye, but before he could react, a knife sliced the air between where he and Leighselle stood, missing his face by inches. Hughes pushed her to the floor, pulling a table in front of them for cover.

"We got word that someone here killed our brother Dalton," shouted a voice outside the swinging doors. "We're not here for nobody 'cept who done it. You step forward, and we'll leave everyone else alone. You don't step forward, and we burn this place to hell."

"Don't do it, Hughes. I'm sure the sheriff's moments away."

"He's probably tied up or dead if these three got past him.

Stay down behind this table. Don't make a sound."

Leighselle nodded.

Hughes rose from behind the overturned table. His hunting knife, with its gleaming blade and carved antler handle, pressed against his lower back. He knew within a fraction of an inch where his hand would settle on the heavy weapon. He knew how fast he could get to it, how fast he could zip it through the air to meet its target. Perfecting the move was something he'd practiced since he was a small boy learning to hunt wild boars with Okwara, the half-Negro, half-Navaho plantation slave who'd taught Hughes how to slice the air clean through.

"I'd rather you take me prisoner than see this fine establishment go up in flames." Hughes stood with his arms hanging casually at his sides, hands relaxed, fingers open and ready. "Well, here I am, girls. Come on in and take me."

Without a word, the Whitts eased into the room, the three standing shoulder to shoulder, barring the door. Boots shuffled and spurs clinked on the wooden floor strewn with streamers and glitter. Dust motes floated in the air, illuminated in the golden glow of the gas lights. The only sound was heavy, measured breathing.

Hughes waited. The reward goes to the patient hunter. *Yes, Okwara, I remember.*

Then, with an almost imperceptible gesture, a slight dip of the head from the brother in the middle, nodding to the one on his right, the largest of the three brothers made a quick move for his gun.

Hughes was quicker, drawing the knife from the back of his waistband, flinging it at his barrel-chested target, hitting the man square in the heart. The big man sank to his knees and fell sideways, dead before he could close his surprised eyes.

The two remaining Whitt brothers went for their guns. Hughes filled his hands with his Navy Colts, firing both pistols simultaneously, each one aimed at its own target. He hit one brother in the gut, but his other shot missed its mark.

Hughes continued firing, moving away from the table where Leighselle crouched in hiding, drawing the gunfire away from her. He tried to make his way to the safety of the heavy mahogany bar. Firing his last shot, he leapt on top of the serving counter, scattering glasses and bottles, taking a shot to his side as he went over.

"I been hit," said Monroe Whitt as he dropped to the floor, "get me outta here." He clutched his belly, his hands turning dark with blood.

"What about Arthur?" Raymond pointed to the man with Hughes's knife buried hilt deep in his chest. "We can't leave him."

"He's dead. Leave him. Get me out of here." Monroe tried to stand but sank back to the floor, blood pooling around his feet.

With one pistol reloaded, Hughes rose up from the shadows, clutching his right side with his left hand, and fired. He hit Monroe again, a direct shot to the thigh. Hughes collapsed onto the slick, cool surface, semi-aware of hearing another shot, knowing more than feeling his body flinch.

"Goddamnit, Raymond, I said get me outta here." Monroe was losing copious amounts of blood from both wounds. "My leg . . ."

The shot that struck Hughes was from Raymond's gun, aimed and fired in a quick panic just before he grabbed Monroe by the collar, dragging him out of the tavern and down the stairs. Throwing his brother onto the saddle, Raymond heaved himself up behind him, the horse crow-hopping in protest at the weight of both men. Raymond dug in his spurs. The horse galloped off, with a spray of blood misting the midnight air.

"Oh dear God, Hughes!" Leighselle rushed to him, wiping the blood from his face. "Please, someone, help me!"

"I'll run upstairs and get Doc," said Smitty, the beefy-armed blacksmith who'd taken refuge behind the bar.

"No need to come up," said Doctor Flemings as he peeked out the door. He made his way down the stairs. "I'm sorry, Leighselle, but Monique . . . she lost too much blood. Her injuries were too severe. I'm sorry."

"Hughes has been shot. Please hurry." Leighselle's eyes filled with tears. "Oh, my dear Monique." She shook her head; words stung her throat.

Doctor Flemings and Smitty stretched Hughes out on the

bar. "Head wound appears to be superficial. The one to his side is another story. He won't make it if I don't get in there and stop the bleeding. Smitty, can you help load him into my wagon?"

Hughes moaned, his eyes opening and closing, his breath shallow, his skin cooling and becoming pale as the men carried him out. Blood left a sticky red trail on the plank floor strewn with discarded masks, feathers, and bright streamers in every color of the rainbow.

*****

Leighselle placed the tray of fresh compresses and strips of gauze on the bedside table. "Stand still. Let me finish redressing these bandages. I wish you wouldn't go. You're not ready, not strong enough."

"Three weeks is enough time for healing. I can't let their trail go cold." Hughes gritted his teeth, pain shooting through his side. He thought for a moment that she might be right. . . . Then he shook his head against the notion. No. He had to go.

"Go back home to Lévesque Plantation, hide out there for a while till all this blows over." She wiped her forehead with the back of her hand, shoving a stray curl back into place.

"Hide out?" Hughes snorted. "You saw what that bastard did to Monique. He and the other one may be dead, but there's two more who tried to kill me for the effort."

He was prepared to chase those sons of bitches to Hell if he had to. They'd be back gunning for him—of that he was certain. What kind of man would he be if he ran and hid—was afraid to face the fight? He'd be the kind of man he wouldn't want to know.

"Ouch." He winced as Leighselle tightened the bandage.

"You're barely on your feet. You think you're ready to chase after two outlaws? You don't have the strength."

"I'll find the strength."

Hughes strapped on his guns and reached for his hat, pausing while Leighselle finished buttoning his shirt, a fresh bandage covering the wound on his side and secured around his waist. He shoved his shirttail into his waistband and then put both hands on her shoulders.

"I'll be fine. Besides, you know I'm not welcome at home

anymore. Father's decree." He took a deep breath and let out what sounded like a growl. "I need to finish packing a few things, then I'm off."

"I can't persuade you otherwise?"

"No." Hughes opened his saddlebags, taking stock of what to pack.

"I'll see you downstairs, then. You'll need a bottle of whiskey—for medicinal purposes." Leighselle stepped out the door, shutting it behind her, her taffeta skirt swishing around her ankles.

Turning, she saw someone approaching. "May I help you?" she asked in a loud voice.

"I'm looking for someone. A man named Hughes Lévesque. Heard he might be here." He eyed the trash can Leighselle was holding, looking closer at the bloody bandages. "He's wounded. Those his bandages? Is he in that room you just came from?"

Leighselle tightened her grip on the trash can. "That's my room and this," she said, holding the can out for inspection, "this is —uh—it's my time of the month, is all. See?"

Raymond Whitt lurched backward, turning his head away. "Is there a man here named Hughes Lévesque that you're hiding?"

"I'm not hiding anyone. You're welcome to look around. I heard Lévesque left for Tennessee, though, about a week ago. You might catch up with him, if you hurry." Leighselle took a step closer, batting her eyelashes.

"Tennessee?" He took a step backward.

"Um-hm. Might you be interested in a little play time? Discounted, today, of course." She patted the trash can and offered a coy smile.

"Hell no, woman. I'm interested in finding Lévesque." Whitt took a few steps backward, eyeing the door behind Leighselle.

Leighselle pursued. Then, feigning surprise, dropped the trash can. It landed on Whitt's feet, the soiled bandages spilling on his boots and splaying across the hallway. The mess created a bloody barrier that might as well have been a brick wall between

Whitt and the door Hughes stood behind.

"Goddamnit, woman." He danced backward, shaking his feet free of the bloody bandages. "What in Christ's name are you trying to do?"

"My goodness. I'm a bit clumsy sometimes." She dropped to her knees, bending forward, allowing Whitt a generous peek at her cleavage. Picking up the bloody strips of gauze, she asked, "Can you give me a hand here, please?"

Raymond Whitt backed away and made quick progress retreating down the stairs, his spurs tangling together. "Tennessee?"

"Yes. Chattanooga."

*****

Hughes was standing behind the door, listening, when Leighselle returned to the room. "You clever, clever girl," he said, shaking his head in astonishment. "That's what I call an out-foxing maneuver."

"I was afraid you'd come out, guns a-blazing."

"Boy, did I want to," Hughes said, twirling the loaded chamber of his Colt. "Biding my time is best. I plan on catching them off guard when they're not on the hunt. But you—you deserve an honor—what a brilliant performance."

"I think on my feet. Coming up with a spontaneous plan when there's trouble brewing can mean the difference between life and death."

"I'll remember that." Hughes moved to the side of the window, the chiffon curtain lifted a fraction. "The other brother's out there—guessing the one I gut-shot. He's not sitting too tall in the saddle."

He watched the man as he exited the saloon and mount his horse. Then, the two Whitt brothers aimed their horses north out of the French Quarter, the horses' galloping hooves splashing through the rain puddles that rutted the muddy lane.

"March is still cold at night. Take warm clothes. Did you pack a blanket?"

Hughes smiled at her. "Yes, mother."

Leighselle winced. "I'm not your mother," she said, piercing him with a sharp look.

"I'm sorry. What did I say?" Hughes looked stricken.

"Nothing. Never mind. I'm concerned about you."

"I appreciate your concern. I grew up roughing it when Okwara would let me tag along on hog hunts. I think I can handle Texas in the spring. Come here." He wrapped his arms around Leighselle, then kissed the top of her head. "I owe you my life. If you ever need anything, I'm forever in your debt."

"Will you be coming back?"

"I don't know. Father made it clear after what he called my 'latest shenanigans,' that I'm not welcome at home. He stuffed my pockets full of money and then showed me the door. Thank God my brother brought me here." He shrugged his shoulders, his eyes clouded with pain.

"You're always welcome at my door. Come, I'll walk you downstairs. You'll need that bottle of whiskey when it comes time to changing those bandages."

Hughes sprinted the four blocks to the livery stable to fetch his horse, not wanting to put too much time between himself and the Whitts. Holding his side, feeling lightheaded, he fought off waves of mind-splitting pain and gut-emptying nausea.

*****

Smitty rubbed his dirty hands down his apron as the fire box behind the anvil glowed bright orange. He picked up a red-hot horseshoe with heavy wrought-iron tongs and laid it on the anvil. After giving it a few whacks with a flat-headed hammer, he immersed it in a bucket of water. A gray circle of steam rose, eclipsing his round, bald head.

"They were here," said Smitty. "Asked if I knew you— asked how long since you left for Tennessee. I said, 'Tennessee? Hell, he didn't go to Tennessee. That boy went to Texas.' I think that confused 'em a bit."

Hughes led his mare out of the stall and threw his saddle across her back, wincing as he did so, tying the blanket and rain slicker behind the cantle. "I wonder which way they went."

"Oh, they argued. Almost came to blows. One said Tennessee, but they sure as hell didn't leave here headed east. The other'n, the one with the gut shot and leg wound, said Texas.

Guess he's the boss. They rode west."

*****

Their trail proved too easy to follow. Hughes reined his horse back a few times to avoid riding up on the reckless pair who left careless clues. Crickets, owls, and coyotes filled the frosty night with their songs as stars filled the expansive darkness from corner to corner with their sparkling light. Spring was still a few weeks away. The nighttime cooling of the earth at night left a heavy dew on the ground, creating a wet snaking track where the horses passed.

Hughes yawned and stretched, ignoring the pain pulsing hot on his side. He thought of changing the bandages as he touched his wound and felt a wet stickiness through his shirt. He would have changed it if the Whitts ever stopped to rest, but it appeared as if they planned on riding all night. The other wound from the superficial grazing of the bullet just above his right ear left a faint scar, his hair already growing over it.

Dawn washed the eastern horizon in shades of night-dissolving pink, the forest sounds hushing as the sun rose into a silent sky. The Whitts pulled off the trail and led their horses into a thicket of old-growth pine so dense the sun's rays strained to reach the ground. There they made camp.

Hughes rode his mare in the opposite direction a safe distance away, putting her on a picket line to graze. Then, wrapping himself in a blanket, he lay down next to where his horse was tied. He fell into a light, feverish sleep.

The screeching of a hawk high overhead awoke him, the sun halfway through its arc across the sky. Hughes sat up, listening to the piney woods, orienting himself. The pain in his side radiated out in fiery hot fingers that tugged on every nerve. A gulp of whiskey from the bottle in his saddlebag numbed the pain and cleared his head just enough.

He'd change the bandages later. It was time to see what was happening at the Whitt camp. Guns in hand, he sneaked through the woods, careful not to make a sound.

Hughes smiled and thanked the stars above for making this so easy. Raymond and Monroe Whitt lay on the far side of their fire next to a rocky outcropping, an empty bottle of whiskey between them. The injured man moaned in his blanket, which was bloody and wet with a darkening brown stain. The small campfire offered up a thin string of pale gray smoke.

"I'm cold, Raymond. Get up and stir that fire back to life." Monroe's voice sounded raspy and weak. "And I'm thirsty. Gimme a sip of whiskey."

Raymond Whitt rolled over, the blanket that was covering him falling away. He sat up, cursing. "Well, shit. Can't a man even get some sleep?" He hobbled over to the fire and began to poke it with a stick. "Ain't no more whiskey."

"I'm thirsty, brother. I'm hurting. Just put a bullet in me and get it over with," Monroe begged.

"Hold your horses. I'm stirring the fire."

Hughes crept in further, ducking behind the trunk of an enormous pin oak tree. Assessing the situation, forming a plan, he picked at the dirt under his nails, scraping them clean with a twig. Go on, Raymond, he thought, give your brother some water. Step on over there, nice and close.

"I'm thirsty. . . " Monroe's voice faded away to a whimper.

"Well, I'm cold. I want coffee." Raymond busied himself with the task at hand, stirring the ashes, the fire crackling to life once again.

"Water. Now."

"Damn it, Monroe, we should a headed to Tennessee." Raymond spun around, stir stick in hand, thrusting it in the air for emphasis. "That bitch at the tavern said that's where Lévesque went. But no. You took the blacksmith's word. We've been in goddamned Texas a day and a half now and ain't seen a single sign. Not a one. Now you're dying, and it'll be on me alone to find Lévesque and kill him, wherever the hell he is. We should a gone to Tennessee."

"I'm the one with the gut wound and you're the one bellyaching—"

"Tennessee," insisted Raymond. "Tennessee."

"Put a bullet in me and get it over with," he pleaded again. "At least I won't have to listen to you harp on about Tennessee." Monroe, feverish and moaning, rolled back and forth in his blanket, clutching his distended belly that oozed blood. "Water. I'm thirsty . . ."

"You got a gun. Do it yourself," said Raymond over his shoulder.

"Goddamn you," moaned Monroe. "Suicide's a sure ticket to hell."

"I think murdering your brother'll get you there, too."

Hughes watched as Raymond picked up a canteen and rose to his feet, shuffling to where Monroe lay shivering on the ground. He opened the canteen and lifted his brother's head with one hand, pouring a trickle of water into his mouth.

Now. Go.

Hughes rushed from behind the oak tree, a pistol in each hand. He covered the distance to the Whitts in long, ground-clearing strides. "Get your hands in the air, both of you," he shouted, "or I'll shoot. I've had enough of all your fucking arguing."

Raymond dropped both the canteen and Monroe's head, then stood up, hands in the air. "Don't shoot, mister."

"You on the ground, ease your hands out of that blanket. Let me see them. Nice and slow."

A noise coming from behind, twigs snapping, a horse nickering, caused Hughes to divert his eyes to the side a fraction of a second. In that moment, Raymond drew his gun, fumbling, pulling the trigger too soon. The bullet struck the ground at Hughes's feet, spraying dirt into the air. Hughes fired back. The bullet ripped a hole through Raymond's heart, sending him sprawling backward, spread-eagled to the ground.

A white-hot, searing pain tore through Hughes's left shoulder—the flashing of a gun—the loud pop echoing in his ear. The force from the blast spun him around, knocking him off his feet.

On the ground, Monroe crawled out from the blanket, gun in hand. He stood but sank down to his knees, struggling to hold the weight of the weapon. He brought the pistol up, gripping it in both hands slippery with blood. Unsteady, shaking, he blinked his eyes in rapid succession in an apparent effort to keep his target in focus.

Rolling over on his belly, ignoring the pain underneath the bloody bandage on his side, Hughes took quick aim. He fired, sending Monroe Whitt to join his brothers in hell.

The whoosh-click of a shotgun being readied just behind his head caused him to freeze—and then to comply with the "get up on your feet and put your hands in the air" command. The voice was patient and pleasant, gentle yet assertive, the kind of voice that could talk a kid into giving up a piece of candy or convince a hornet into not stinging.

"Toss your guns over here, then hands in the air," said the pleasant voice.

Hughes stood and did as he was told. Two men he could see, one with the shotgun, another behind in the trees. He tossed his guns on the ground, shoved his hands in the air.

"What's your name, mister?" The tall, thin man stood under a large brown hat that hid his eyes and the top half of his face, while his thick, black mustache covered his mouth and the bottom half. His slow, easy words dripped like thick, rich molasses.

"Hughes Lévesque."

"Where're you from, and why are you here?" he asked with a nice tone to his voice.

"New Orleans. Tracking these outlaws."

"You're as sparse with your words as you are your bullets."

"I'm efficient."

"Looks like you tracked them all right—tracked them to the gates of hell."

"They tried to kill me first. I shot in defense. My plan was to take them back to New Orleans where their brothers Dalton and Arthur paid the same price for trying to kill me. These two are Raymond and Monroe Whitt."

"We know who they are, son, and saw what happened," said a gravelly voiced man stepping out from the trees. "We've come from Orleans. Heard what happened there. We suspected it might be you who was following these two."

"We've been after the Whitts for some time," said the pleasant, hatted man holding the shotgun. "Looks like you made tidy work of them in short order."

"Hell, I didn't know who they were until two or three weeks ago. I had no quarrel with them, until what happened to Monique. Then I had a quarrel." Hands still in the air, Hughes's shoulder throbbed. He ignored it.

"Well, son, you did us a favor," said the man with the gravelly voice. "Seems you have a knack for tracking and killing. You ought to think about joining up with us."

"I'm not some common brigand looking to join up with an outlaw gang," said Hughes, the wound to his shoulder dripping with blood.

"We're not outlaws, son. We're Texas Rangers."

*****

September 28, 1860

The train pulled into New Orleans Station, its shrill whistle drawing Hughes out of a deep sleep. He pressed his forearm against the foggy window, swiping a clear circle, allowing a watery, distorted view of the platform. John-Pierre stood shivering, hands in pockets, hat pulled down, coat collar turned up against the autumn chill. He never did take to the outdoors. It wasn't even that cold outside.

Hughes stepped onto the platform and the brothers shook hands, then embraced in a quick hug. Exchanging pleasantries, they made their way to the station's café where they spent an hour drinking coffee, telling stories, and reminiscing.

Before long, John-Pierre pulled his watch from his pocket, apologizing for having to leave so soon. Business demanded it. The two brothers embraced again—longer, tighter—before John-Pierre departed, disappearing through the crowd of uniformed soldiers milling about the train station.

Hughes sat a while longer and sipped another coffee. Everywhere he looked, he saw soldiers. Young, fresh-faced boys pumping fists in the air, eager for excitement, eager for adventure, eager for the chance to prove their manhood. *Eager to die.*

They spoke about going to war, their voices filled with the enthusiasm and energy of youth, as if "War" were a welcoming place to put your bags down and stay a while. Some would stay—for eternity. But maybe there wouldn't be a war. Maybe this next presidential election would steer the country away from that. These boys should stay boys a little longer.

Hughes saw lovers kissing lingering good-byes, mothers and fathers embracing sons eager to pull away and board the trains, and teary-eyed wives and children waving as soldier-fathers disappeared into thick crowds. A feeling he was missing out, that he was not reaching for something that he should take a tighter hold of, washed over him as he thought about his brother.

But he couldn't have that. He couldn't have what John-Pierre had—a wife and a child, with another on the way. A family. People who needed and depended on him. His brother had the luxury of worrying about the safety of his wife and child. Hughes would never know that luxury. Worrying about someone who needed him would alter the way he thought—the way he reacted—with dangerous consequences. He knew the luxury of unencumbered work, and the excitement of a new mission.

He drummed his fingers on the table, a familiar restlessness rising up from within. His mother had sent a message of her love without an invitation for him to come home for a visit. Father was at home, ill and resting, his brother had said. All these years later and he was still not welcome there. He understood. And really, he didn't miss it, that place he used to call "home."

Hughes slugged down the rest of his coffee and then strolled out of the station café over to the mare who stood tied. She was saddled in expensive hand-tooled tack with roses, oak leaves, and acorns carved into the dark, oiled leather. The polished brass fittings gleamed, the stitching straight and perfect. Matching saddlebags hung on both sides, and a bedroll and slicker were affixed to the cantle. She was shod and ready to go, just as he'd requested.

Hughes opened one of the saddlebags to store his small valise inside. There was barely enough room. The saddlebags were stuffed full of his mother's usual gifts she mailed to his hotel: linens, money, gold coins, pewter plates, things every Ranger might need on the trail.

Shoving his left boot into the stirrup, he swung over and settled down into the saddle. *Now this—this feels like home.* He smiled. Turning away from New Orleans Station, Hughes relaxed into an easy trot, the fine morning mist burning away as the early autumn sun warmed his back, following him west.

CHAPTER NINE

OCTOBER 26, 1860

The robust stage driver pulled the frothy mules to a stop and climbed down from his perch. He swung the coach door open, grabbing the closest bag of mail in his gloved hands. "Well, boys, this is the end of the line. Welcome to Saint Joseph."

"Can you tell us where we can find the Pony Express stables?" Barleigh lowered herself from the dusty cab of the wagon, hefting the saddle onto her shoulder. A mixture of anxiety and excitement bubbled within, and she took a deep breath, hoping to keep those feelings subdued.

Stoney followed close behind with his dirty bedroll. Two thick straps of greasy brown leather held his belongings together, keeping the contents inside from spilling out—a tin cup, a fork, a threadbare, button-less coat.

Without slowing his rhythm, the driver tossed mailbags into the waiting arms of a lanky kid wearing a postal clerk's uniform. He grunted a few words as he thumbed over his shoulder, indicating the large cedar and brick structure behind him.

"Much obliged, sir, and thank you for the ride," said Stoney, tipping his hat as the two strode over to the stables.

The building's arched entryway was wide enough to accommodate a wagon or a team of horses being moved about. An overhead sign read "Pike's Peak Stables." Inside the cavernous barn, the smell of sweaty horses, manure, sweet oats, oiled leather, and alfalfa hay mingled together to create a heady aroma. The aroma induced both melancholy and feelings of comfort at the same time. Barleigh felt right at home.

"Excuse me, sir," Barleigh said, greeting a sprite, balding man using a quick pitchfork to fill hay troughs. "We're looking for the Pony Express Stables. This sign here says Pike's Peak—"

"You're in the right place. The Central Overland California and Pike's Peak Express Company, also known as the Pony Express. Name's August Olsen. What can I do you for?" He kept forking hay into the feed troughs, yet his welcoming smile and friendly style invited conversation.

"Well, sir, Mr. Olsen, sir, I'm Stoney Wooten. This here's Bar Flanders. We came to hire on as Pony Express riders." Stoney held out the waybill advertising the job, the same type of paper that had blown down the street in Fort Worth and landed at Barleigh's feet.

"You can call me 'August.' I'm the station manager," he said with a slight Swedish accent. "You need to see Mr. Waddell about applying for a job. He's the owner. One of 'em, anyway. There's three of 'em."

"Where can we find Mr. Waddell?" Barleigh asked, keeping her voice measured.

"Over yonder at the Patee House. The big four-story hotel two blocks east 'o here on the corner of Twelfth and Penn Streets. You can find the Pony Express office there. Tell Mr. Waddell I sent you."

"Thank you, sir," they both said, turning to leave before Olsen's words drew them back around.

"Dangerous job, you know. What makes you boys so eager to be Express riders? Risking death daily? Orphans preferred? Those aren't just words on paper." August Olsen leaned on his pitchfork, his clear gray eyes not blinking.

Barleigh shuffled her feet, kicking at a clod of dirt on the ground, waiting for Stoney to answer. Letting Stoney act as the spokesperson was going to be the best strategy in keeping her identity hidden, she'd decided, and Stoney never seemed shy about speaking up.

"It's mighty good wages for sitting on a horse," Stoney

said. "Hell, I done that for free all my life. Now someone's willing to pay me to race a pony back n' forth? That's a risk I won't mind taking, considering the high wages offered."

"Know what you're getting into, boys. This ain't a frolicking pony ride in the park," said August, raking a dirty sleeve across his bald head. "There's many risks to consider. The harsh weather—your bones freezing in the winter—the sun baking you alive in the summer. Monotony. Boredom. Riding fourteen hours— hunger. Long stretches of teeth-itching thirst. Thunderstorms. Blizzards. Midnight, galloping full out over hazardous terrain where you can't see shit. High noon, the glare of the sun burning your eyeballs that are already scratched to hell from dust and sand. And, if that's not enough risky excitement for you—you'll be ducking from angry Indians and dodging gun-slinging outlaws."

"I've faced bigger risks dodging my pa's drunken fists," Stoney said as he turned on his heel and hurried out of the barn.

"Much obliged, sir." Barleigh rushed after Stoney and they headed east toward the Patee House Hotel.

The red-brick, four-story building, with white wooden arches and ornate carved window moldings, was a short two and a half blocks from the stables. On its wide, columned front porch, ladies under parasols sipped afternoon tea; they were seated at dainty tables to the left and to the right of the center steps leading to the double arched entryway doors. A hectic network of hatted, suited men scuttled about as if on critical business, moving up and down the stairs as they entered and exited the hotel.

Upon entering the hotel, Barleigh glanced around and spotted a door at the end of the main hallway. The etched glass on the upper half of the door showed a mounted rider bent low over the neck of his pony running at full gallop.

"That looks promising," Stoney said, pointing down the hall. "Let's try that office." The boy from Frog Level, Arkansas, dirt and dust marring his face and clothes, marched with his shoulders back, head high down the fancy corridor among the well-suited businessmen. He walked with the posture of one moving among his peers.

The brass nameplate on the door read "Russell, Majors, and

Waddell – COC & PPEC." A shadow moving against the etched glass—a muffled voice stammering on the other side of the door—paused when Barleigh knocked.

"Come in," boomed a voice from inside.

Taking a deep breath, Barleigh filled her lungs, letting the air seep out slowly. Her hand on the doorknob, she breathed in again, held it a moment, then, turning the knob, strode with purpose into the light-filled room, light that seemed to shimmer in the late afternoon sun.

"May I help you?" The nameplate on the desk belonged to Mr. William Bradford Waddell. The stocky man sat in an ox-blood leather upholstered chair with brass nail-head trim. He had a pleasant face despite the corners of his eyes and his mouth being slanted downward in a perpetual pout.

"Yes, sir. We're here to apply for the job." Stoney held out the waybill advertisement. "We're your new Pony Express riders. Sir."

Mr. Waddell leaned back in his chair, chewing his unlighted cigar between clenched teeth. "You with the saddle, what's your name and age?"

"Bar Flanders, sir. Eighteen."

"And you?"

"I'm Stoney Wooten, sir. I'm also eighteen."

"What's your story, young Mr. Flanders? Orphan? Runaway? Experienced at riding and shooting?"

"Orphan. Expert rider, accurate shot." A blush began to blossom and she fought hard to force it down. Bragging on herself was awkward, but the truth was the truth.

"You're small for eighteen. I took you for fourteen, maybe fifteen. But the smaller the better for faster riding. Less weight for the horse to haul around. And you, Mr. Wooten. What's your story?"

"I ain't no orphan, just not welcome at home no more. I growed up on the back of a horse and ain't never fallen off. Mounted, at full gallop, I can shoot a rabbit and only waste one bullet. That's if I don't have a rock and a slingshot to use first—which I prefer. I'm pretty handy with hurling stones. That's how I got my name, Stoney. I don't remember my given name. It wasn't used much. I think it was Walter. Or maybe I just hoped it was that and not Owen. Owen's my pa's name."

"One of you is mighty sparse with your words, the other quite generous," said Waddell. "Well, tell you what. We're holding tryouts a week from tomorrow morning at eight o'clock. Be at the Express stables on time, if you're interested in applying for the job."

"Yes, sir. What's the tryout?" Barleigh asked.

"We hold tryout races every other Saturday of the month. It's become quite the spectator event—a popular opportunity for friendly wagering among the locals. So far, there'll be five riders competing, including you two. You'll mount your horse, ride to the Ellwood ferry, and take it across the river—race to the Troy relay station, dismount, shoot at two marked targets, remount a fresh horse, and then race back here. If it's a tie for first place, which hasn't happened yet, the winner will be the rider who returns with his horse in the best condition as determined by August Olsen, our station manager. Any questions?"

"How many riders out of the five get hired on?" Stoney asked.

"Two. One other we might use as a stock handler. Anything else?"

"How far is Troy Station?" Barleigh asked, shifting the saddle from one hand to the other.

"Fifteen miles from Ellwood Ferry. Fifteen miles back. My curiosity's gotten the best of me. Why are you carrying that saddle?" Waddell asked, using his unlit cigar as a pointer.

"A midnight storm spooked away my horse. This belonged to Uncle Jack. He's dead now." Hearing herself speak those words aloud gave Barleigh a peculiar sensation, and she lowered her eyes.

"I see. Well, if you need a place to sleep, tell August I said to give you an empty stall in the barn. The hay's soft and the company's better than what you might find at the local tavern. I'll see you both there a week from tomorrow morning. Good luck in the race. And, try to stay out of trouble for a week. That's the hardest part for young riders."

"Thank you, sir," they said in unison.

After leaving the office of the COC & PPEC, Barleigh decided a bath after four days of dusty traveling in an enclosed coach would be the perfect end to the day. She dropped her saddle off at the stables and was directed by Mr. Olsen where to get a bath.

"I can't afford a bath," said Stoney, jingling the coins in his pocket. "I'll just head down to the river and wash up there. Save your money and come with me. River water's free."

"Thanks just the same. A long, hot soak in a bathtub is five cents well spent." She'd have paid twice that.

*****

Most businesses in town were decorated in red, white, and blue bunting in anticipation of the presidential election a few days away. Doors and windows were draped, posts were wrapped, ribbons hung from awnings, and contentious arguments filled the air.

"Let's go to the saloon," said Stoney. "We've been here all week eating nothing but beans and cornbread. I need something more substantial before the tryouts tomorrow morning. I think I can afford a slice of baloney if they slice it thin."

Walking to the saloon from the stables, they passed several different groups of men standing around on sidewalks or gathered around porches, all involved in heated debates about the election. Barleigh kept her ears open and her mouth closed, though she was tempted to throw her opinion into the argument. She felt in her heart that Abraham Lincoln would be the best leader for the country. If she were a man, that's who'd get her vote.

"Take your pick of tables, friends. The place is pretty quiet tonight. So far." The bartender continued to wash glasses as he spoke, looking up once when he first heard the doors swing open and shut. "What can I get you?"

They sat at one of the two tables by the front window to watch the people walking by. In town a week and both Stoney and Barleigh still marveled at the mass of people moving about. The one other person in the bar was sitting at the other window table, apparently also enjoying the view.

"Bring us two steak plates and two beers, please." Barleigh wondered what beer tasted like. "And two coffees." A manly meal.

"Steak? We're not Pony Express riders yet," Stoney said, laughing out loud. "Make mine a plate of fried taters and a thin slice of baloney if you have it, and a glass of water." He jingled the change in his pocket. "Baloney budget, not steak budget."

"I'll buy. You can reciprocate after we get hired on tomorrow. We'll be numbers one and two coming back. I know it." There was no doubt in her mind that she and Stoney would win the race.

"I'll let you be number one, then, since you're buying the steak," Stoney said with a grin. "Thanks, Bar. Been a long time since I've tasted steak."

The gentleman at the adjoining table to Barleigh's back leaned in close. "Excuse me for intruding into your conversation. Did I hear you say you were Pony Express riders?"

Stoney chimed in. "Not yet. We try out in the morning. But by noon tomorrow, we will be, you can bank on it." He leaned on the back two legs of his chair, grinning.

Barleigh remained quiet, hoping the man would turn back around to his table.

"Ain't that right, Bar? We'll be the best two riders that company's seen. We'll show them others a thing or two 'bout racing ponies." Stoney brought his chair back down on all fours, still grinning from ear to ear.

"That's right, Stoney," Barleigh said, fidgeting in her chair.

"May I introduce myself?" the gentleman asked. "I'm writing a letter to a friend of mine back home about the Pony Express. I'd love to be able to say I've met a couple of the riders, especially if they're going to be the best in Pony Express history." He scooted his chair away from the table.

Barleigh sensed him standing behind her. Anxiety knotted her stomach. She didn't welcome this stranger's intrusion. But she told herself to relax; everyone's accepted her as a boy—no need to worry. She half stood, half turned around, half looked up, gave half a nod, and stuck out her hand.

"Bar Flanders. Pleased to meet you." *One pump, firm*

manly handshake, sit back down, eyes on the table, let Stoney do the talking.

"Hughes Lévesque. Pleased to meet you, too. I'd be honored to buy your dinner for a chance to interview two actual riders and get some firsthand facts for my letter." He smiled and looked at Stoney.

"Ain't riders just yet." Stoney stood, offered his hand, and introduced himself. "But given your generous offer, you're welcome to sit at our table. I'll talk as long as you want to listen. I'll tell you all about our interview last week with Mr. Waddell and about the tryouts tomorrow."

Hughes, taking the window seat, said, "It's my pleasure, Stoney."

"I think I could get used to this, getting paid to talk, then getting paid to ride a fast horse—two things I'm naturally good at." For a poor country bumpkin, Stoney had the true polish of a politician. He told a story that lasted far longer than the actual interview.

Though Stoney was the one talking, every time Barleigh chanced a peek, she caught the gentleman looking at her. Not staring, just a few easy glances. Something about his eyes, something in the way he wasn't shy about looking at her, wasn't quick to move his eyes away, gave her the feeling that this could be trouble.

*****

Stoney and Barleigh woke before dawn and shared a small breakfast of hard biscuits and the last of what remained of the French roasted coffee beans. Lingering a moment, enjoying the final aroma and taste, Barleigh toasted to Mr. Templeton with the last sip from her tin cup, remembering his kindness and hoping he found warm waters.

"I slept like a stinking dead man. Belly full of steak and beer is how a man should go to sleep every night. Even better, if in a woman's arms, to boot." Stoney rolled up his bedroll and shook the hay from his clothes.

"Yep." Barleigh put her cup away.

"Course, spending four nights and five days sitting in a

goddamned stagecoach, and then a week sleeping in a feed trough with horses nipping at your hair, will do that to a man, too. You sleep all right?"

"Yep," she said, pulling on her coat.

"You don't waste too much energy on words, I've noticed."

"Don't need to with you around." Barleigh smiled and clapped Stoney on the back.

"You two ready to join the others?" asked August Olsen, leading a yellow dun mustang mare and a dark seal brown gelding out of their stalls. "The other two riders already picked out their mounts. Which of you wants Big Brownie?"

Stoney and Barleigh looked at each other and shrugged.

"I'll take Brownie. Reminds me of my old horse back home," said Stoney, taking the lead rope from August. With gentle yet assertive hands, he checked the gelding's legs and feet, looking for heat or tenderness. "Big boned—I like that in a horse."

Barleigh took the dun mare and ran a hand down her front cannon bone, over the fetlock, and tried to pick up her hoof. The mare, with ears flattened, swung her head around, nipping Barleigh's shoulder hard enough to draw blood.

"Ah, a little feisty, eh?" Barleigh said, wincing, rubbing her shoulder.

August laughed. "Don't turn your back on her, but once you're in the saddle, you're safe enough. She's fast—hang on tight. Big Brownie's fast, too, though he don't look like much."

"I thought there were five of us trying out," said Stoney as they led their horses out into the morning's soft gray light.

"One's already dropped out. Said his ma and pa didn't want him gone. So, just the four of you left. Tie your ponies over yonder next to them others, then all you boys come on over here." August waved the other two over.

"Our odds just got better. We only got to beat two now," whispered Stoney with a big grin on his face. "We can box them in. You and me'll stay out front. Work as a team. Keep them two in our dust."

"It'd be unwise to underestimate you country boys from Frog Level," said Barleigh, and she meant it.

"Here's how this works," said August. "When I say 'Go,' you run to where the saddles and bridles are set out over yonder lined up next to that water trough. Pick out your gear and get your pony tacked up. Get your ass in the saddle, then hightail it down Francis Street to the Ellwood Ferry, where it's waiting for you. Take it across the river and then hightail it to Troy Station. It's a fifteen-mile straight shot off the ferry down the California Road. Once there, get off your horse. There'll be someone there to hand it to who'll have another horse similar in color to the one you rode in on. That's how you'll know who to ride to. They'll point you to your target. Shoot your target—not someone else's. They'll give you a score on a piece of paper. Bring it back or it's counted a zero. Hightail it back here. First one back wins. Take care that you don't run your horse into the ground. A dead horse always makes it back last. Any questions?"

"Yes, sir." Barleigh stepped forward. "Will the ferry be waiting on us when we get back to return us to this side of the river? And what's the allotted time?"

"The ferry will have made its round-robin before you get back from Troy Station. It will be waiting. It should take you a minimum of three hours round-trip if you use a combination of walk, trot, and gallop. Remember, don't run your pony to death. If two of ya get back at the same time, the rider on the best conditioned horse wins. If it's still a tie as judged by me, then your target score comes into count. By the way," said August with a wide, toothy grin, "besides getting hired on as a Pony Express rider, the winner gets a bonus of this five-dollar gold piece, an incentive from Russell, Majors and Waddell."

There were "whoops" and shouts of boastful challenge among the four riders as they lined up and waited to hear August shout the command "go."

"Look," Stoney pointed. "That saddle on the end's like the one you drug up here with you from Texas. You want that one?"

"Yep."

"I'll block and take the one next to it."

Barleigh saw the others eyeing it, too. Lightweight and more maneuverable than the other heavier saddles, it could mean the difference between winning and losing when pounds counted. She wanted that saddle.

The word "go" rang out. Stoney blocked the other two, allowing Barleigh to run to the McClellan that lay on the ground at the far end next to the trough. The saddle looked identical to the one that had belonged to Uncle Jack. Barleigh thought it must be a sign of good luck, or fortune smiling down on her. It calmed her, despite the swarm of activity buzzing all around.

With quick hands, she tacked up the mare without getting bitten again, hopped into the saddle, spun her around, and raced down toward the ferry in less than two minutes.

Stoney followed right behind, trailed by a long, lean, freckle-faced kid named Ford Dewar who rode a flea-bitten gray mare that whinnied and pranced, head high. The fourth chap struggled to get a saddle on his horse without much cooperation from the recalcitrant gelding.

They pulled the horses up and trotted side-by-side, the three making it to the ferry simultaneously, leaving the fourth rider behind.

"Well, ain't that something," said Stoney. "Look at all them folks lined up at the ferry. Looks like they're watching us."

The throng of onlookers yelled and waved, shouting out encouragement. Some called out the horses by name or by color. "I'll take Dunny!" "My money's on Flea!" "Don't let me down, Big Brownie!" They knew the horses. It seemed this had become a regular entertainment event.

"Apparently a friendly little wager's going on as to who gets back first," said Barleigh.

"Best bets on me and Flea," Ford shouted to the onlookers. He stood up in his stirrups, pumping his fist and waving his hat in the air. His antics spooked his horse, causing it to crow-hop sideways, further entertaining the crowd.

A gentleman in a tailored black riding outfit with a red brocade vest sat astride a fancy bay roan mare that pawed at the ground with impatience. They stood next to where the three riders lined up to board the ferry. His hand-tooled riding saddle and matching bridle with ornate brass fittings, custom revolver and holster, and knee-high black leather boots all gleamed.

Barleigh gave a slight nod in polite acknowledgement. "Morning, Mr. Lévesque."

"Morning, Bar," he said, touching the brim of his hat with a hand gloved in black leather. "I'm putting twenty-five dollars on you and the dun mare. I'll earn back double my wager if you win."

"I'll win," she said with a matter-of-fact air. "I'll be on a different horse, coming back. One similar, though, in color."

"I was told what to watch for when I placed my wager. I understand it'll be another yellow dun or a buckskin, a similar horse so folks here can cheer their bets as they race back home."

He smiled and wished her luck as Barleigh urged her horse onto the ferry. Their eyes met for a brief moment, and in that moment, something caused her breath to catch. Her heartbeat felt erratic and out of sync.

Looking away and straight ahead, she tried to concentrate on the task at hand. Had she remembered to lower her voice and speak like a man? Why had he raised his hand to his hat as a man does when greeting a lady? Did he, or didn't he? Had she failed at her disguise before even given a chance at success?

Concentrate, Barleigh—I mean Bar.

The ferry pulled to the dock at the opposite shore on the Kansas side of the river. Stoney and Ford rode ahead as the rope lowered, allowing the riders to disembark. Barleigh hesitated and looked back over her shoulder. The man on the bay roan horse sat straight and tall in the saddle, looking directly at Barleigh.

The sound of hooves pounding the ground jolted her back to reality. She spurred her horse and slapped the latigo hard against the mare's rear. The horse let out a squeal, then leapt off the ferry, landing like a jackrabbit on hind legs, her front legs pawing the air. The mare's explosive propulsion off the ferry almost unseated Barleigh, but she grabbed a handful of mane, pulling herself upright, and they galloped off into the settling dust of Big Brownie and Flea. Within a short time, they closed the gap. The race stayed neck-and-neck most of the way to Troy Station.

Taking the lead by a length as Troy Station came into view, Barleigh galloped into the paddock area and reined to a halt. She dropped to the ground before the mare slid to a complete stop. "Where's my target?" she yelled to the attendant who grabbed the reins of the sweaty, panting horse, her pistol already clearing leather.

"Bull's-eye metal square nailed to the first white post." He pointed at the target ten paces to the north.

She dropped to one knee, aimed the revolver, took a deep breath, blew it out halfway, held it, and squeezed the trigger twice in rapid succession. The distinctive pinging of metal on metal filled the air as the bullets made contact.

"Dead center, both," yelled the spotter as he ran to the target. "Perfect twenty-five point shots!" The boy holding the reins of the fresh horse handed Barleigh a square of paper marked with the number "50" scratched in pencil with a hurried hand.

She pocketed the paper and turned without waiting to hear Stoney's and Ford's scores. Taking the reins of her fresh mount, a light-boned buckskin gelding, she jumped back in the saddle, galloping away as the attendant shouted, "His name's Buckeye. Careful, he kicks."

Great. First a biter, now a kicker.

As with the race to Troy Station, the race back to Elwood Ferry was a constant shifting, maneuvering, and retaking of the lead spot. Walking a little, trotting a lot, and galloping full out where the terrain allowed was the strategy all three adopted.

Trotting up to the Elwood Ferry platform, Barleigh saw a red flag with a galloping horse and rider emblem being hoisted on the Missouri side of the river, a sign alerting the townsfolk that the riders were approaching. Soon, she was joined by Ford riding a feisty white mare, and Stoney, whose small black mare seemed unfazed by the race. What the riders didn't see was the ferry.

"What's happening? Why's the ferry not here?" Barleigh asked the dockhand as she searched up and down the length of the river, a sense of worry creeping in.

"Something's wrong with her paddle wheel. They're sending down a raft to fetch you back," said the worker. "Look up yonder. Here it comes."

She looked and was dismayed. It would take too long for

that slow, flat-bottomed raft to get down river. She looked again at the distance up the river, calculated the distance across the river, and made a hasty decision.

"Come on, Buckeye, let's go." She spurred the little gelding forward. He pawed at the water a few times and snorted at the spray, then plunged right in.

"What are you doing, Bar?" shouted Stoney. "The river's too wide here. It's too dangerous."

"I'm not waiting," she yelled over her shoulder. "We can do this, Buckeye. Easy now."

She took a fistful of the horse's mane with one hand, held tight to the saddle horn with the other, and let the horse lurch and paddle his way into the deep, cold water. The horse struggled against the swiftness of the current, and Barleigh feared that the pair might be swept too far downstream.

"Well hell fire, don't leave me behind." Stoney on his little black mare took the plunge too.

"I can't swim, for crying out loud." Ford pulled hard on his reins, trying to restrain the white mare desperate to join the herd of two swimming away from her. "Whoa, for shit's sake. Whoa now."

Halfway across the river, Stoney and his mare were closing the gap. "Come on, Blackie, swim faster, girl."

The raft on the opposite shore was pulling away from the pier, one angry, pawing, rearing white horse with its red-faced rider aboard. The flat-bottomed vessel flirted dangerously close to capsizing with the horse's overwrought behavior.

"Come on, Buckeye. You can do this," Barleigh urged. She held on for dear life, the gelding lurching forward, his feet thrashing like wild pistons in the water. Pulling her feet free from the stirrups, drawing her knees up, she tried to keep her legs away from the danger of being pummeled by the horse's sharp hooves.

Near the bank, the gentleman on the bay roan mare watched, cheering them on. The entire shoreline filled with people shouting, waving, clapping, yelling out encouragement. The boisterous crowd had shifted downstream to where Buckeye and Blackie came out of the water to raucous applause and shouts of "run, pony, run!" Neck and neck, they shot off in a flash toward the

Pony Express stables, dripping wet and shivering.

The station manager and the COC & PPEC owner were waiting at the stables as the two galloped to a stop. Stoney and Blackie, a neck in the lead, were the first, with Barleigh and Buckeye a close second. The sound of fast hooves striking the ground told that Ford was moments behind.

A large crowd gathered around, pushing in to see the triumphant return of the three riders. Men on horseback, ladies carrying parasols, children running circles around each other, dogs nipping and barking—all made for a festive atmosphere.

"What in Pete's name happened to you two?" asked August Olsen. "You're all wet."

"The ferry wasn't there," Barleigh said through chattering teeth.

"I sent a raft for you. What in the hell happened? Did it turn over?" He looked at Ford. "You're dry." August scratched his bald head, his face scrunched in a confused expression.

"Didn't care to wait for the boat. We swam." Her body trembled hard with a deepening chill.

"Well, why in tarnation did you do that?" The rotund William Waddell, with his mouth in a perpetual frown, waited for an answer.

"The sign on your office wall, sir, the Pony Express motto. 'The mail MUST go through.' I thought of what I'd do if I were carrying the mail and the ferry . . . was out." She tried to control her chattering teeth and shivering body. "I'd make sure, come hell or high water, that the mail would get through."

"Is that right, son? Why, that impresses me immeasurably," said William Waddell, eyes beaming. "And you, Mr. Wooten? Is that what you were thinking when you swam the river?"

"Partly, sir," replied Stoney, teeth chattering. "That five-dollar gold piece may have been on my mind, too."

The crowd roared with laughter and wild applause.

"That impresses me even more—an honest answer." Waddell's laugh was hearty and loud. "August, who do you pronounce the winner of our little race?"

"Well, sir, it looks like the horses are no worse for the wear for taking a cold swim. Hell, it seems like they enjoyed the plunge. Stoney Wooten wins fair and square."

August handed the gold coin to Stoney, then pointed at Barleigh. "Now you two get inside to my office. Best you strip off those wet clothes before you both catch pneumonia. I'll bring you some horse blankets until we can find something dry to wear."

"Uh, sir, but I, uh . . . ," Barleigh stammered.

"I just doubled my money betting on these two lads," said the man on the bay roan mare, easing his horse through the crowd. "The least I can do is pay for each of them a hot bath over at Miss Sallie's Boarding House," Mr. Lévesque said.

"That's mighty generous, sir," said August. "I'm sure they'd appreciate that."

"That was one hell of an exciting finish. Lunch is on me for all the riders over at the tavern, after you've dried off, of course. I'll go set it up with Miss Sallie." He turned and rode away before anyone could protest.

"Before you take off, we have an item of business to attend to." Mr. Waddell handed each rider his own personal Bible. "This Bible is the courtesy of Mr. Alexander Majors, one of the other owners of the company. Being a temperate and religious man, he requires the same of his employees and that each of you shall swear an oath of your allegiance. You all three stand together here and raise your right hand. When I've read the oath, state your name and give your verbal agreement."

The three stood shoulder to shoulder, Barleigh and Stoney shaking in wet boots, Bible in left hands, right hands raised, and solemnly took the oath of the Pony Express.

"While I am in the employment of Mr. A. Majors and Company, I agree not to use profane language, that I will drink no intoxicating liquors, I agree not to gamble, not to treat animals cruelly, and not to do anything else that is incompatible with the conduct of a gentleman. I will neither quarrel nor fight with other employees. I will be faithful and honest in my duties and will direct all

my acts to win the confidence of my employers. If I violate any of the above conditions, I agree to accept my discharge without any pay for my services. So help me God."

In good faith, her heart honest and without malice, Barleigh took the oath that said she would conduct herself *as* a gentleman. She didn't swear that she *was* a gentleman. The other parts of the oath gave her no pause: no drinking, gambling, cursing, or fighting; be faithful and honest in her duties; be kind to the animals. Easy.

"You are now all three officially Pony Express riders. Ford, you as an alternate and stock tender. See me back in my office after lunch." Mr. Waddell shook each rider's hand. "Congratulations."

"Just curious. What ever happened to the fourth chap from this morning?" Ford asked.

"After ten minutes and finally managing to get his pony saddled, that ol' horse went to bucking and put on quite a show of it," August laughed, slapping his knee. "That boy hit the dirt so hard it rattled his teeth. Said then that he'd had enough of it and was going back to his plow."

*****

A hot bath and dry clothes put Barleigh in a fine mood. The lunch, courtesy of Mr. Lévesque, was delicious and more food than she'd seen since leaving Texas. Hungry, she ate like a starving man.

Mr. Lévesque kept his attention on Stoney and Ford, his queries directed for the most part toward them. He seldom spoke to Barleigh or looked her way except for an odd question here or there. So many nosy questions. Fine. Her appetite had returned, and all she wanted was to eat.

After lunch, the short walk over to Patee House to meet with Mr. Waddell took more time than it should have. Everyone who recognized the three riders wanted to shake their hands and offer congratulatory praise, a slap on the back, or a word of advice. Old women kissed their cheeks and said quick prayers for their safety. Blushing young girls offered shy smiles and batted eyelashes, and smudged-faced little boys stepped in the shadows of their boot steps.

They'd gained notoriety for doing something they all loved to do. It came as naturally to each of them as breathing. Riding horses. Riding fast.

"I was watching from my window," said Mr. Waddell, ushering them into his office. "You're now celebrated young riders of the Pony Express whom everyone wants to touch, hoping that maybe just a little of your derring-do will rub off on them. Have a seat. Let me tell you about our mail service and what you'll be doing to help ensure its success."

Taking seats on the ox-blood leather sofa across from Mr. Waddell's desk, the three sat and listened with rapt attention as he explained what they should expect.

"At any given time along the route, I've approximately eighty riders. Additionally, there are more than four hundred other employees, from station keepers to stock tenders to route managers. You'll be assigned two home stations. Home stations are about seventy-five to a hundred miles apart. In between home stations are swing stations which are about ten to fifteen miles apart. How it works is that you'll start at your first home station, race to the first swing station where a fresh mount will await, saddled and ready to go. Switch to your fresh mount and race to the next swing station, and so on and so on, until you get to your other home station. There, you'll rest for eight hours or longer, depending on where the return mail is, and then relay the mail back to your initial home station. Questions?"

Ford spoke up. "How will the swing station know I'm coming and to have a fresh horse ready?"

"You'll be issued a bugle. When you're nearing the station, blow your horn to announce your arrival."

"How will we carry the mail?" Barleigh asked, excitement growing at the realization that she'd done it—she was a Pony Express rider.

"We had a specially designed leather sling made for this endeavor. It's called a 'mochila.' It goes over the saddle. It has a hole in the front for the saddle horn, and a slit in the back for the cantle to fit through. It can easily and quickly be removed from one saddle, then thrown over the next in a split second. The weight of the rider keeps it in place. Which brings me to my next point, Bar."

"Yes, sir?"

"That saddle you tote around needs to be stored someplace. You won't be using your own saddle. It'd take too much time to resaddle horses at each swing station. The horses will be there, saddled, ready to run. Only the mochila goes with you from swing station to swing station. You swing the mochila off your saddle, swing it on to the fresh saddle, then away you go to the next swing station. Got it?"

"Yes, sir." She nodded her understanding.

"Where's the mail go?" asked Stoney.

"At the corners of the mochila are four locked leather boxes called 'cantinas.' That's where the mail goes. Each home station manager has a key to add to or remove mail as necessary. Letters are wrapped in oiled silk to prevent water damage."

"So we ride from home base to home base about a hundred miles or so before changing riders? Day or night?" asked Ford.

"Day or night, whether raining, snowing, or in the high heat of the day, the mail must go through." Waddell pointed his unlit cigar to the wooden plaque engraved with the company's motto.

Coming around to sit on the edge of his desk, Waddell took on a serious tone as he spoke. "One thousand nine hundred sixty-six miles separate Saint Joe, Missouri, from Sacramento, California. We've proven it can be done in ten days or less. There'll be tough challenges along the way. Rough terrain. Inclement weather. You'll get hungry. You'll get thirsty. You'll face boredom. You might face a bandit or two. We've had incidents with hostile Indians."

Waddell paused and looked each one in the eye. "The job is tough, but you have to be tougher. There's no shame in bowing out now if you don't think you're up to the task. We have tryouts every other week. Someone else will gladly take your saddle if you don't want to sit in it."

"When do we start?" they all seemed to ask at once.

"First thing tomorrow. Ford, you'll be staying here to help

August Olsen with stock tending, moving horses back and forth along the line, breaking new horses, and filling in as an alternate rider when we need you. It pays less since the danger's less—fifteen dollars a week plus room and board. That sit right with you?"

"That sits right with me, sir, if I can have a shot at being a full-time mail rider when a slot opens up." Ford said.

Mr. Waddell nodded. "You'll be first in line."

Then, "Bar and Stoney, we need riders in the Utah Territory, Carson City Station. I figure if you swim horses across the Missouri without hesitation, you won't mind riding the most dangerous leg of the relay. Concerning wages, the average rider's pay is twenty-five dollars a week plus room and board. But you're not the average rider, are you, Bar? You're not like the others."

"Ex—excuse me, sir?" She looked up, eyes wide.

"What I mean is, riders who take on bigger risks, for instance, or who ride longer than their normal shift, or who carry special mail might get paid more—more than the average. I think you might be one of those kind of riders."

"Yes, sir." She let out the breath she'd been holding.

Mr. Waddell handed the riders a map of the trail. "Like I said, we need riders for the relay segment in Utah Territory. It's Indian Territory. We have a hard time keeping riders and horses out there."

"I'll ride the whole damned, I mean dang, route if you want me to, sir," said Stoney.

Waddell laughed. "Now that's the spirit. You'll become so familiar with your own part of the route that you'll know every rock, cactus, and creek along the way. Both you and your pony will be able to ride it with your eyes closed, though I wouldn't recommend it. You'll depart tomorrow morning to head for your new home stations. Good luck, and Godspeed."

Utah Territory. Indian Territory. There were a lot of miles and mountains to cross before getting to Carson City. Barleigh's hands trembled as she studied the map of the trail.

CHAPTER TEN

NOVEMBER 3, 1860

Journal Entry: Saturday night. The sun will rise at my back tomorrow as I head west into that gaping frontier that waits beyond the outer fringe of civilization. From studying the map Mr. Waddell gave us, we'll follow the Oregon Trail most of the way until it leaves us in the vicinity of the Great Salt Lake where The Trail then climbs to its Pacific north-western destination. Stoney and I will press westward.

Mr. Waddell says the Oregon Trail is well established by fur trappers, traders, and emigrants who've gone before in their oxcarts and wide-wheel wagons. Our swing stations and home stations are marked along the trail, so they'll be easy to identify.

Tonight, my restless thoughts feel as loosely bound as our fractious country. While the North and the South appear near to tearing apart, the Pony Express chomps at the bit, eager to stitch together the east to the west. Perhaps this swift mail delivery will hold open the lines of communication between America's opposite shores and will serve as the instrument that holds our tenuous Union together.

This night may be my last opportunity for some time to write in my journal, as I don't know what to expect from here forward when each day is done. My journal is the one place where Barleigh can exist. Maybe it would be best if I put away my pencils, stowed my journal, and kept Barleigh safely out of sight.

But I can't not have a journal with me. I feel itchy even at the thought. I'll take one plus a pencil or two, wrapped together, and will carry them tucked inside my shirt.

Tomorrow begins our long trek to Carson City. I'm excited, nervous, and anxious—but at the same time, blank and empty. Even laughter and polite conversation have posed a challenge. I feel like a forgery. A phony. And for good reason. I'm pretending to be a boy. Am I also pretending to be human? At present, I am a hollow shell awaiting to be refilled with feelings and emotions.

Longing is the singular sentiment that keeps me faintly tied to myself with a thin thread. I remember nights at Coffee Creek Ranch, Papa and Birdie sitting in front of the fire, me on the floor, Papa reading to us from the newspaper. Oh, Papa ...

Embers of longing, however faint they glow, are best kept buried. Feelings such as those have the potential to become disastrous distractions. I cannot afford distractions.

I must think things through. Look beyond the immediate. Keep the goal in sight. Stay focused on the Pony Express and being Bar Flanders.

Yet tonight my mind wanders ...

Hughes Lévesque is a handsome man, but there is something about him that seems intense— unreal—as if he doesn't share the same flesh and blood as other men. He is set apart. He's above it and he knows it, though his unflinching confidence doesn't give way to haughty arrogance.

It's in his eyes. They know the world's secrets yet reveal nothing of their own.

It's good that tomorrow I'll put him behind me. He'll go on about his life, and I mine. I'll not live in danger of his eyes uncovering my secrets.

I am, after all, a boy.

I'm Bar Flanders, a young, skinny, wiry fellow not over eighteen, an expert rider willing to risk death daily.

An orphan. Nothing more.

******

Early before dawn, Stoney and Barleigh filled their bellies at Miss Sallie's fancy dining table at her insistence. At her insistence, too, they filled their saddlebags with plenty of biscuits, smoked ham, venison jerky, and dried apples for their journey.

"Did you feed those boys well?" Mr. Lévesque walked into the kitchen as they finished their breakfast in the other room.

"Fed 'em well, I did," Miss Sallie said with a hearty laugh. "That blond-headed Stoney, I don't recollect ever seeing someone so skinny eat so much. And, I'm sending them off with plenty to take with them, too. Stoney and the other little 'un, Bar, who looks too young to shave, are headed to Utah Territory to Carson City."

Mr. Lévesque sounded surprised. "Carson City? I assumed they'd be assigned this station."

Miss Sallie continued. "Ford, the freckle-faced tall one, is staying here. He took off just a minute ago for the stables. I told him to come back anytime for a visit and a hot meal."

"That's kind of you, Miss Sallie. Well, I stopped by to pay these boys' tab. How much do I owe you?"

"Three dollars and seventy-five cents, for all three."

"There you are. Please keep the change. Now, I need to post a letter in the mail. If you'll excuse me, I'll be on my way."

"If you're going," Miss Sallie said to the sound of shuffling papers, "you can be a dear and save me the trip. Bar left this letter for me to mail along with mine. I was going to go later on, but . . ."

"I'd be delighted to." Hughes took Barleigh's letter. "Thank you again, Miss Sallie."

From the other room, Barleigh overheard the conversation. She wished Miss Sallie hadn't done that. Should there be cause to worry? No. Surely Mr. Lévesque would take the letter she wrote to Aunt Winnie and mail it, right and proper, just like Miss Sallie would have done. No cause to worry. Time to go. Time to head to the stables. Time to get on with being Bar Flanders. No time to think about the nosy, frustrating Mr. Hughes Lévesque another second.

*****

Standing in the shade of a large oak tree behind the post office, Hughes took his Rezin Bowie knife from inside his right bootleg and slid the gleaming tip of the blade under the seal, careful to open the envelope without tearing the paper. It was addressed to Mrs. Winifred Justin, Hog Mountain Ranch, Palo Pinto, Texas. He removed the thin sheet of paper and held it between thumb and finger, brought it to his nose, detected a faint trace of maple syrup, noticed a sweet, slanted, feminine penmanship, and smiled.

> *My Dear Aunt Winnie,*
>
> *Mission accomplished. I'm a Pony Express rider. I've been assigned a relay route in the Utah Territory. I'm traveling with another rider, Stoney Wooten from Arkansas, a fine fellow and companion who takes me at my word. It disturbs me, having to deceive such a nice and trusting person. But I have no choice. Please kiss Starling and give Deal an extra-large bunch of carrots for me. I hope you are well. I miss you and think of you every day. You may write me in care of the Pony Express, Carson City Station, Utah Territory. Please do, and tell me how you are, how your sons are, how the ranch and the cows are. There is one thing I must tell you that I am very sorry about. King ran off, frightened by a bad thunder and lightning storm. It was our last night camped on*

the trail. Things were going so well until that night. I pray you'll walk out onto your porch one fine morning, coffee cup in hand, and King will be there standing at your fence gate waiting to be let in, having found his way home.

Maybe one morning, you'll find that I've done the same.

Love and laughter,
Bar (leigh)

He replaced the letter into the envelope, then took a pencil and paper from his saddlebag and added his own note:

Dearest Mrs. Justin,

This is Hughes Lévesque writing. I've (obviously) located Barleigh. She doesn't know that I've added this letter for the reasons I shared with you the day I met you. Thank you again for trusting me, and for telling me of Barleigh's plans. I find her to be a remarkable and brave young lady, along with being a very fast rider—she stayed at least a day's ride or more ahead of me until Fort Smith, Arkansas. If there had been another seat available on the stage, I'd have taken it, but I was able to make it to Saint Joseph in good time.

I telegraphed her mother that I've found her daughter and what she is now undertaking with the Pony Express. Leighselle's immediate reply was to ask that I keep an eye on Barleigh and to keep her safe, if that's possible. As I feel I was making a promise to a friend who is on her death bed, it's the least that I can do. Although, knowing how dangerous this endeavor of hers is, I am of the opinion I should inform Barleigh of her mother's predicament and bring Barleigh back to San Antonio.

My business in St. Joseph has flexibility, so

now I'm off to Utah Territory and will do my very best to make sure Bar (leigh) Flanders stays safe while I remain in the shadows. I will write again and update you once I get to Carson City.

Respectfully – Hughes Lévesque

*****

Journal Entry: Tuesday, November 6, 1860.

While the rest of America voted on our next President, Stoney and I dashed our ponies across the plains, never once discussing it. It flat never crossed my mind, until now. Fort Kearney in Nebraska Territory is as far as we progressed today—we could muster only so much energy. One hundred miles horseback over rough terrain and at fast speeds wears on you after ten hours, which is how long it took from Saint Joseph to here. We changed to fresh mounts at Troy, Log Chain, Seneca-Smith, Marysville, Cottonwood Station, Rock Creek Station, Thirty-Two Mile Site, and then rode into Fort Kearney tired, hungry, and far too excited for our sore muscles to register a complaint.

We are Pony Express riders, the first leg of a very long ride now behind us.

We took turns bugling our arrival as we approached each swing station, and sure enough, fresh horses awaited us saddled and ready to go. The previous day's mail runner alerted the station managers there would be two riders next coming through. We would hop to the ground off our sweaty, panting horses, pull off the mochila, swing it onto the saddle of the new mount, climb back aboard, then away we would race at a gallop, taking advantage of the fresh horses' enthusiasm.

I anticipated privacy issues regarding bathroom breaks, but today, I managed to put off

166

taking care of personal business to when changing horses at the swing station during our ten minute lunch stop where an outhouse was available.

Stoney was afflicted with an upset stomach much of the day after drinking bad water at Fremont Springs station, and four times had to stop and drop his trousers right on the trail, the diarrhea hitting with embarrassing quickness. His stomach lurched and churned; however, he managed to do his throwing up from the saddle, even while at a full gallop. It troubled me that I might be likewise afflicted and I'd have to drop my trousers. My mind worried over this for a while, but my stomach didn't betray me.

Off to sleep. We ride far and hard tomorrow.

*****

Journal Entry: Fort Laramie was our intended goal today, but Chimney Rock station was as far as we progressed before exhaustion called a halt to today's ride. Rough and undulating terrain made walking and trotting the practical pace for much of the distance. Water was plentiful and prairie grass abundant, so the horses didn't suffer doing without, and we kept our canteens full.

Swing stations are stocked with grain for the horses, which gives them more energy than horses on a simple grass-only diet. If we encounter danger on the trail such as Hostile Indians, our instructions are to not fight them but to outrun them. Our grain-fed ponies are quite capable of that.

The mail must go through, and the mail cannot go through if the Express riders are busy engaging Indians in a shoot-out.

Let the pony do its job. Let the pony RUN. I'm quite content to put space between the Hostiles and me.

*****

Journal Entry: Last night my journal remained unwritten in, fastened underneath my shirt next to my skin. Sleep was the one thing my body could manage, and it managed that fully clothed and flat-out on a pile of hay out in the stables. I was too exhausted to drag myself from barn to bunkhouse, and was satisfied to sleep with the horses.

After a tedious day's ride that ended with a long descent down a steep hill, we rode into Devil's Backbone at near midnight. The jagged and broken ridge of the giant sandstone boulders, silhouetted against the moon's glowing sky, looked much like a malevolent serpent.

We slept for four hours, rose before the rooster crowed, and after a quick cup of thick black coffee and a hard biscuit, were back in our saddles. Pushing nearer to the Great Basin, we rode farther away from the valley where the Sweetwater River joins the North Platte.

The mail went on without us as it must, the relay rider assigned to this leg of the route racing off with the mochila and into the darkness of the night as we slept. Our duty carrying the letters is done thus far until we get to our permanent relay home station. Our duty now is getting there safely and with the same urgency as if we still rode astride the mochila.

We've passed hundreds of emigrants along the Oregon Trail. Many were camped at the Sweetwater River Valley where they made their final ford across before beginning their trek toward the Pacific northwest.

Stoney and I kept our ponies' noses pointed west. At day's end, we found that we'd completed an astounding one hundred twenty miles, ending up in Millersville Swales, one of the home stations along the route. The supper offered was delicious, the bed warm, and the stabling accommodations more than adequate.

We are at a convergence where the Great Plains meets the Great Basin as we prepare to leave Kansas Territory behind and enter into Utah Territory. I've enjoyed seeing herds of buffalo here and there along the trail, but didn't spy any today.

Yesterday, in the area of the North Platt River in the Sweetwater River Valley, an enormous herd of buffalo grazed on the western side of the Platt. From my advantage of witnessing the scene from a distance, it first appeared that the yellow prairie grass was dotted with shadows of clouds drifting across the plains. With a suddenness that surprised me, the clouds transformed in an instant into giant hairy beasts stampeding across the earth. The concussions from their flying hooves shook the ground beneath my horse.

I wondered what spooked the grazing animals into a frenzied stampede, wondered if it might have been Indians on the hunt. I stayed jumpy, anxious for the rest of the day, with a heightened awareness to potential dangers.

While water and grass have been abundant on the plains, the danger in the Great Basin is its dryness. The swing stations have water brought in on ox carts, but between stations, there may be long stretches where creeks, streams, and gulleys run dry.

Throughout the Great Basin, there are more rumors of water than actual water, so if you find yourself on the fortunate side of a rumor, the lesson is to drink up and fill up canteens. The next rumor of water may be false.

T. K. Lukas

*The plains Indians we've encountered
along the way have been friendly, curious, and
non-threatening, though we're always at the ready
to spur our ponies away from potential trouble.*

*The massacre on May 7th at Williams
Station in Nevada, where four station agents were
murdered, followed by the May 12th Paiute Indian
uprising at Pyramid Lake, where seventy-six local
volunteers lost their lives trying to quell the
violence, serves as a reminder to never let down
our guard. We've been reminded of these incidents
by every manager or attendant at every station
we've ridden through.*

*After the Paiute Indian War, mail service
was suspended temporarily; however, by early this
past June, reports of hostilities dropped off as
military patrols increased, allowing the Pony
Express to ride again.*

*Temperatures are dropping. Winter's frost
now covers the ground each morning, and the
mountains are capped in white. Having only seen
mountains in paintings and in books, I understand
why they inspire artists and poets. Majestic and
formidable, yet we must get to the other side.*

*****

*Journal entry: Leaving Millersville Swales this
morning left me a touch melancholy. It felt like a
home should, warm and inviting, despite the fact
that it's also a stage stop and a Pony Express home
station. The proprietor, Mr. Holmes, read aloud
from the Book of Mormon, a religion with which
I'm not familiar, and his comely English wife
played the fiddle after she served our breakfast of
boiled potatoes, sliced onions, and scones with
jam. Missus Holmes' direct personality reminded
me of Aunt Winnie, and I felt a pang of
homesickness. I thought of Starling the majority of*

the day.

At first, Stoney tried to engage me in conversations. He has since given in to my silences. "I understand it ain't your way to talk a lot," he had said. "I don't mind doing the talking. Just nod a time or two, if you will, to show you're still alive." I nodded, and he laughed.

If ever passing this way again, I must remember Cache Cave, a dark, deep tunnel in the rock just beyond the watershed of Bear River. It's a fine place to shelter away from the path of wild weather, dangerous animals, or hostile Indians.

For at least twenty miles we rode hugging the base of a tall red cliff, the area known as Echo Canyon. The road was smooth, hard packed, and descended at a graceful slope, which allowed for intervals of full-out gallops interspersed with long trots and steady walks. We covered that ground fast.

We arrived at the summit of Big Mountain early afternoon with another fifteen miles yet to go to Salt Lake City. The spectacular view played upon my senses, the dramatic colors of mountain, forest, and valley painted vibrant against the azure sky. The piney smell of clean, pure air deep in my lungs, the soft tickle of cool wind on my skin, the echo of water rushing and spilling in its fall down the mountain filled me with joy. I found myself without a need for words—there were none adequate in my vocabulary to describe the beauty before my eyes. I dismounted, stood next to my horse, and for a few silent moments, gazed upon the scene.

An Overland Stage was at that moment preparing for the seemingly impracticable descent down the perilous slope. The passengers, five of them, were made to walk. It would have been too dangerous to ride inside the sliding, bouncing coach which might at any given moment turn into a run-away. Also, lightening the load for the poor mule team, which must control the Stage's descent, was the proper thing to do.

The driver rough-locked the wheels by shoving a long wooden plank between left and right rear wheels and left and right front wheels, then roping the planks together and tying both pieces off at the tongue, keeping the wheels from turning. The mules hunkered down and tucked their tails to the ground, thus keeping the coach from hurtling down the mountain. Born to the task, the six big-boned beasts executed the maneuver without a protesting grunt.

Stoney had nodded toward the travelers, his eyes bright. "This moment calls for a wild spectacle of bravery. Let's give these fine folks something to write home about." Then, he pulled upward on his reins, causing his horse to rear up like a trick pony.

I found his exuberance contagious. We waved our hats in the air and whooped like wild banshees as we rode our horses over the pass and straight down the mountain. The passengers of the Overland Stage whooped, too, shouting out words of appreciation to the Pony Express riders' show of bravado.

I enjoyed our performance, the rush down the mountain filling me with a surge of vitality. I felt—alive.

After descending Little Mountain, steeper than Big Mountain though not as high, we changed horses at Emigration Station, and then rode straight into The Great Salt Lake City as the sun was preparing its graceful descent down the other side of the earth.

ORPHAN MOON

The Salt Lake House is a home station for the Pony Express. It's also a wonderfully appointed hotel that sits right across the street from the post office. There's a large corral out back with a long row of stables, and next door is the City Bath House and Bakery.

We checked in with the station manager, Mario Russo, a dark skinned, dark eyed, miniature Italian sporting a thick tuft of salt-and-pepper hair circling the back of his head from ear to ear. He was relieved to see us, he said, with a sincere, toothy white smile. Word from the west coast warned of an early winter storm moving in from the Sierra Nevadas. In preparation, he had sent two of his experienced riders on west ahead of us to take the vacant positions at Carson City to which Stoney and I had been appointed.

"This be as far as you go," he said with a thick accent, an excited waving of his arms punctuating his words. "Next door you get you a bath, you get you some bread if you're hungry, you don't pay for it, they charge it to our account, you then come back here. I'll show you where you bunk over at the Hotel."

I don't know if I'm relieved that Salt Lake House will be my home station or disappointed that I'll not see and experience more of the trail. Compared to some of the stations we've encountered, some no more than a dug-out or a roofless shed, I'll be living in the lap of luxury, so I should be thankful.

I'll be the rider who carries the mail west, riding roughly one hundred miles where I'll wait at Fish Springs to bring the east bound mail back to Salt Lake House. Here I'll transfer the eastbound mail to Stoney who'll ride east back to Millersville Swales where he'll hand it off to the next eastbound rider, and then Stoney returns the westbound mail to me at Salt Lake where off I go west again to Fish Springs. And so on ...

Stoney and I each have our own small beds since we're The Riders. Two upper and lower bunks are shared in the same room with two horse breakers and two barn assistants whose names I've not yet learned. This arrangement might prove tricky, but I'm learning the fine art of subterfuge.

This is "home" for now.
Goodnight.

CHAPTER ELEVEN

NOVEMBER 13, 1860

The Great Salt Lake stretched across the cold, semi-arid desert to the north and west of the city, while the rugged Wasatch Mountains lined the horizon to the east, creating a pastoral valley ripe for growing crops and crosses. Simple wooden symbols marked the graves of those who didn't survive the winter, or the desert, or the Indians, or the birthing, or the influenza. Crosses sprang from a gunslinger's bullet or a kick from an untamed mustang—from the dark, cold, silent loneliness—from the myriad ways death crept in and took what it wanted.

But crosses did not adorn The Temple.

"Those damned Mormons pulled the cross off the Baptist church again last night," said Mario Russo as he led a dark bay mare out to be saddled. "Just because they don't decorate their buildings and books with the symbol of the cross don't mean others can't."

"No, sir." Barleigh ran a hand down the mare's leg, concerned about a small cut on the cannon bone, but pleased that she detected no heat or swelling. "You sure it was them?"

"Who else would it be?" Mario worked with quick, skilled hands, completing the task of saddling and bridling the mare in less than a minute. "Latest I heard too was that they're trying to shut down all the non-Mormon owned businesses. You tell me, but that's not right."

"No, sir." She leaned her back against the horse, tucking

her thumbs in her pockets. "I remember once, back in Texas, white settlements were attacked, people murdered, homes burned, livestock stolen. Folks blamed Indians, because Indians were known to do that kind of thing. But that one time, it wasn't Indians. It was white outlaws using Indians as scapegoats. Lots of innocent people died, whites and Indians alike, because of those false accusations."

"You're saying it might be Indians? Not the Mormons?" Mario scratched his head, a look of confusion clouding his dark brown eyes.

"No, Mario. I'm just saying not to jump to. . . . Never mind. I'll get this mare some water."

Barleigh returned to the stall with a bucket of water and an apple for the horse and found Mario perched on the stall's half-wall partition, a concerned look on his face. She fed the apple to the horse, the mare chomping the sweet treat in one bite.

"Sir?" she asked, worried. "You all right?"

"You sure you're ready for your first midnight run, boy? Got the rhythm of the trail down pat? Know all your markers?" asked Mario.

"Yes sir. I know the trail," she said with confidence.

"It's different at night. The shadows, the sounds, the smells change. You swear you're coming up to a right bend in the road when a left bend will sneak up all of a sudden and throw you smack into a creek. The night, she can play games with you."

"Yes, sir." Barleigh listened, attentive.

"Bad weather's moving in, too. You'll see snow before sun-up."

"I'm ready for it," she said, wrapping her thick, woolen scarf double around her neck, tucking the ends into her waterproof, oiled canvass slicker that hung to her spurs.

"This might not be the regular run o' the mill correspondence you'll be carrying tonight. This just might be the run everyone's waiting on, the one with the big news."

"I hope so," she said. She was as anxious to hear the news as everyone else.

At that moment, the sound of pounding hooves tearing up

the ground caught their attention. Looking east, they glimpsed a horse and rider approaching at full gallop. Dust hung in the air behind the fast pair like sepia-colored ribbons, sparkling in the golden glow of gas lights that softened the frosty night.

A yellow bandana tied around the rider's neck billowed straight out behind like a banner. His buckskin shirt and coat were covered in dust. Canvas trousers, along with the leather tapaderas that attached to the stirrups and protected the rider's feet, were splattered with mud. Beaded fringe edged the outer seam of his gauntlet-style Cavalry gloves and stuck out like colorful spikes. A wide-brimmed, Mexican-style hat was pulled down tight on his head, cinched snug under his chin with a big silver dollar bolo.

"It's Lincoln," he shouted as he reined his sweaty horse to a stop, vaulting to the ground before the horse's feet quit moving. "Lincoln's our new president. Ain't that something?"

"That's sure something." She grinned and slapped Stoney on the back. "So is your fancy get-up."

"The riders back east wear this."

"They do? Along with the sombrero?"

"No. This is my special touch. I can fix you up, if you want."

"I'll save my money, thanks."

Mario already had the mochila pulled from Stoney's horse and swung in place across the bay mare's saddle as Barleigh stepped her left boot into the stirrup and mounted, ready to ride off into the night with the important news for which the West Coast hungered.

"Don't forget, this mare, she is hot. She'll buck-trot till she's good and warmed up," Mario advised. "Give her more slack than you would to most hotheads. She'll come unglued if you go to yanking on her mouth. But be ready when you feel her relax. That's how she tricks you just before she explodes. You best to be hanging on or she'll leave you embarrassed and sitting in the dirt."

Mario understood a horse's personality and work ethic after spending a few minutes in the saddle with one. He would give a rundown of each horse's peculiarities before each ride. The information was invaluable to the riders whose life depended on their horses.

Mario double-checked the figures as he marked the time of arrival on the mochila's log. "Stoney, if these figures are accurate, and Bar and every other rider on down the line makes his runs just as tight, do you know what this means?" He bobbed up and down like a piston, tapping his pencil against the ledger in an excited staccato rhythm before replacing the time log into one of the four cantinas on the mochila and locking it.

"All I know, sir, is that I think these ponies know something special's happening tonight. It's like they all sprouted a pair of wings. Every time I think one of 'em don't have nothing left, I just ask for a little bit more, just a little, and they give more than I ask for. I reckon it means California's gonna get this news pretty darn quick."

"Pretty darn quick? As quick as stink in a shitstorm. News of this election could make it to California in record time."

"We're setting a record. Well, ain't that something?" Stoney punched his fist against Barleigh's thigh, his eyes as wide as silver dollars. "That's some crazy fast riding."

"Fast, yes," said Mario. "And you could've done your run a little faster if you hadn't had all that wind-drag from that goddamned hat. Where'd you get that thing, off a dead Mexican?"

"I paid good money for this hat. It cost me two dollars, including the silver concho." Stoney loosened the bolo and lifted the large, yellow sombrero from his head, swatting the dust from his prize. Sweat and grime had plastered his thin, blond hair to his scalp.

"Well, that was four quarters too much. You should have saved them for a bath."

"A bath's a nickel," said Stoney, sounding defensive.

"Yep, and at one bath a Saturday, I wouldn't have to smell your stinking ass for a good goddamned forty weeks, longer than that hat's going to last. Now get some rest. You ride again tomorrow."

"It's a fine hat. I like my hat."

"Get some rest."

"Yes, sir."

"And you, Bar, you get out of here."

"Yes, sir."

"Abraham Lincoln!" Barleigh shouted with excitement, the thrill of the election news sending a current through her body. She reined her mare around, galloping down the dusty road toward Mill Creek Crossing, the first of ten swing stations. Throughout the night, changing to fresh horses at each station, she ended her relay 115 miles west and ten hours later at Fish Springs Site. She had pushed herself and all eleven horses to the limit.

As Salt Lake City grew smaller behind her, lights began to glow in windows. People gathered on porches and out in the streets as news of the election was shouted from neighbor to neighbor. Many stayed up all night in celebration, yet there were plenty others who snuffed out their gas lamps, closing their doors to the news.

*****

A fresh horse stood saddled, bridled, and ready to receive the mochila as Barleigh galloped into each swing station. Rare was the mount she considered gentle and well-broke. Most were wooly charges fresh off the range, some having been handled just enough to make them curious, others just enough to make them cantankerous.

The horses back east along the Saint Joe line tended toward the Kentucky Thoroughbred and Morgan types, finer and purer in their pedigrees. Farther west, the horses on the Express string were rangier, more the California mustang type, hardier, smaller, and meaner.

Once beyond Salt Lake City, she spurred hard for Mill Creek Crossing, the first of the swing stations. She lay low on the bay mare's neck and let her have her head, staying out of her mouth as Mario instructed.

The night was as black as tar pitch except when lightning punctured the darkness with its sharp flashes. The moon and the stars hid themselves behind thick storm clouds, and the smell of cold rain hung heavy in the dusty night air.

Barleigh used flashes of lightning to navigate from stone to stone, from one trail marker to the next. She knew Mill Creek wound through the flats nearby and off to her right, but she could not see the creek as the night was so dark.

As the storm front passed overhead, rolling across the valley, thunder echoed throughout the canyon while intense lightning danced off the jagged granite walls. Well after darkness had descended, temperatures plummeted and a confused concoction of rain, sleet, and snow began to pelt the earth.

Riding blind through the blackness, she found it impossible to see the trail. However, she could hear her horse's hooves striking the hard-packed wagon road. This assurance told her that all was well, allowing her the confidence to continue asking the mare to give it her all. The mare complied.

Barleigh knew that the swing station lay just beyond the plank bridge that spanned the creek, and the dull clattering of hooves on wooden planks was a relief to Barleigh's ears. She relaxed, knowing where she was, despite the blackness of the night.

Halfway over the bridge, lightning streaked across the sky, illuminating in a white-hot flash the muddy banks of the creek. The sudden brightness silhouetted two looming figures on horseback letting their horses drink water at the stream.

Indians.

She shrieked. In a panic, Barleigh yanked too hard on the reins, which caused the iron bit to dig like a sharp knife against the horse's sensitive mouth. The sudden, intense pain sent the mare into a high-headed, side-stepping prance right off the side of the bridge and into the freezing creek a few feet below.

The two Indians disappeared into the darkness.

Fear was the tight glue that kept Barleigh's seat from separating from the saddle. The mare splashed and crow-hopped out of the shallow water, Barleigh clinging tightly to the saddle horn with both hands, the reins lost and hanging uselessly at the ground. They splashed up the slippery bank and were back on the road in an instant, the mare growing more enthusiastic in her bucking the nearer they drew to Mill Creek Crossing. A lantern gave a warm, glowing welcome in the window of the stables just up the hill.

She didn't dare let go of the saddle horn to reach for the bugle. Instead, she yelled. "Franks! Help me stop this damn horse." She yelled again, louder. "Franks, grab the reins."

"What in the hell have we got here?" asked the station master as he grabbed for the bucking horse, throwing his weight against the mare's shoulder and easing her to a stop. "Why in the hell are you and your horse drenched, boy? You'll catch your death."

"Indians at the creek spooked me. I saw two, maybe more. We jumped off the bridge."

"Jumped off the bridge? Why in the hell did you go and do a thing like that?"

"I didn't mean to. It was an accident."

"Indians? Ain't been Indians this close in some time. You sure about that, Bar?"

"I saw what I saw." She removed the wet mochila from the saddle, threw it across the back of the waiting black mustang, and remounted. "Lincoln won the election."

"Don't you want some hot coffee? A quick cup to warm you?"

"No coffee. You got a dry blanket or something I can wrap up in?" Barleigh asked, a chill setting in.

"Here. Take my slicker," said Franks, removing the coat from his back. "It'll swaller you up, but that'll be all right. I'll have yours dried out when you get back."

Leaving Mill Creek, she found the territory harsh, the desert valley scattered with sagebrush, greasewood, and the bleached carcasses of oxen and cattle. Salty dust hung in the air, thirsty for the rain or snow that would wash it to earth and turn it into an oozy mud.

Throughout the stormy night, Barleigh raced from station to station, bugling her arrival, shouting the news of the election. She dismounted, mounted, and raced for the next station, taking no breaks for coffee, water, or personal comfort or hygiene. No liquid in—no liquid out. A record-breaking ride was at stake.

The Express Company had planned and built swing stations along the route where natural springs were located to provide a source of water for the stock and for the people managing the stock. In the Great Basin, good water was difficult to find, and the water at Simpson's Springs, the seventh swing station along her route, had long been used by local Indians. This was her least favorite station, the one she hurried through the fastest with the changing of the mochila.

A watery gray dawn of light and mist told that night was over. The morning was steely and damp and dull and cold, but at least it was no longer dark. The mountain peaks at her back were all but invisible in a shroud of sinking clouds as she reined to a stop at Simpson's Springs.

"Morning, Whizzer." Barleigh leapt to the ground, pulling the mochila off and flinging it across the saddle of the fresh mount that stood stomping at the hitching post. "Lincoln wins."

Remounting, she galloped off before the news settled on his ears, quick to put as much distance between herself and the Indians who, she felt certain, hid in every shadow, in every dip and hollow, behind every stone, behind every blade of grass in and around Simpson's Springs. She wanted this place behind her. Racing now for her western home station, Fish Springs Site, she faced a hard forty-two mile ride farther into Utah Territory.

"Hey! We got boiled wolf mutton and rye soup, and plenty of coffee," Whizzer called to her disappearing back. "What's the hurry? Oh. Lincoln, eh?"

From there, she changed horses at the haunted Riverbed Station. Other riders told frightening tales of this place, of how they spurred fast through the ghostly flat terrain. She'd never felt or seen one with her own eyes, but others insisted that the canyon swarmed on stormy nights with desert fairies who teased horses into spooky antics, who howled at lone riders, who snatched at their shirt collars and twisted jealous fingers in their hair.

She remounted onto fresh horses twice more, at Dugway Site and then at Black Rock Site, before at last galloping into Fish Springs Site just shy of eleven o'clock in the morning. With her first overnighter behind her, Barleigh was elated to see her western home station.

A soft snow began to fall, sifting a fine powder over the

thatched roof of the low-slung rock building, where a roaring fire blazed in the wide hearth. Gray smoke curled in a thin ribbon out of the crooked stone chimney, disappearing among the low clouds that threatened heavier snow.

Her butt cheeks were raw and felt as if they must be bleeding. Riding all night in wet clothes that freeze to your skin will do that. Craving coffee, wanting warm, dry clothes and sleep, she knew that walking was going to hurt. She braced herself for the expected pain.

"Hello, Mr. Barth. Abraham Lincoln won the election." She slid from her horse, too exhausted to help remove the mochila.

Yes. Walking. Hurts.

"Mr. Lincoln, eh? Well, don't know if I'm surprised or not. I reckon those Mormons will be glad to see the last of Buchanan, eh? All the trouble he's caused 'em?"

"I reckon. So, where's Eckels?" Her relief rider was known to be punctual, always on the spot, horse in hand, ready to take over the relay.

"Eckels ain't made it back yet. He must be caught up in the storm that's got the Sierra Nevadas all snagged up."

"What about Thomason?"

"Indians scared him off. Last week back at Black Rock Site, he was ambushed by a passel of them. They shot a bunch of arrows, even a few stray bullets at him. Thomason outran them, but it scared him bad enough not to want to come back."

Barleigh shivered. "I just passed through there. So, what do we do? We can't let the mochila stop. It has to keep moving."

"Then you have to keep on riding, boy. You're all we got right now. Can you do it?"

"Yes, sir. I can do it." She'd given her oath. The mail must go through. The thought of letting it stop on her ride was unthinkable.

"It pays more money, you riding extra," Mr. Barth said.

"That parts nice, but this is the election results. It has to keep going." Barleigh felt a sense of obligation, of duty.

"How long you already been in the saddle, son?"

"Since midnight."

"The snow will be picking up—I don't know. Don't seem safe, you not knowing this leg of the route and all." Mr. Barth shoved his gloved hands into his coat pockets, his breath hovering in a frozen cloud in front of his drawn, thin face.

"I can do it, Mr. Barth. I want to ride." She stood her ground against the station master.

"Get some coffee. Fill your canteen. There's hard biscuits on the stove to fill your pockets. Take my serape to throw over your slicker. Get some dry gloves, too, from the bunk house."

"Yes, sir. Where do I go from here?"

"Boyd's Station, due west. The road stays hard-packed if you keep close to the bluff. Don't stray far off or you'll end up in the swampy mire that's worse than quicksand. You'll bog down your horse. The only way out of that mess is a bullet."

Barleigh nodded her understanding.

"Boyd's Station is a small stone house with gun ports. They're there for a reason. If you're lucky you'll pass Eckels on the way. If not, then keep on riding west as far as you can without killing yourself or your horse. The sun will be with you unless these clouds regroup, which it looks like they're doing. You best make good use of your time, and keep an eye out for Eckels."

She didn't pass Eckels on her way to Boyd's Station. The road was flat and fast, so she tried outrunning the lowering, thickening snow clouds. Light flurries changed to fat, wet flakes, which turned to a swirling whiteout as she rode into Boyd's Station.

There she changed horses and kept on riding, the lone stock tender a skinny, apprehensive-eyed boy of twelve, pointing her to the next swing station, Willow Springs.

The boy, Ennis Julesburg, an orphan taken in by the station manager, had been frightened by the worsening blizzard. He had brought all six horses up from the corral and had led them into the boardinghouse, where they were all milling about the sparsely furnished cottage.

"They all run off once before when Injuns attacked," he explained with wide eyes as Barleigh threw the mochila over the saddle of a dappled gray mare. The horse munched sweet oats scattered on the floor in front of the hearth.

"I don't want to go out in this storm and have to chase them down," said Ennis. "What if I couldn't find them? I might get lost and might not be able to find my way back. Then I might freeze to death and no one would know where to find my dead body."

"But it stinks in here." Barleigh kicked at a pile of manure. "How can you sleep or breathe with the windows closed, the smoke from the fireplace so thick, and all this horse shit all over the floor?"

"Living with the stink is better than dying in the snow," said a very serious Ennis.

Wind blew the snow into deepening drifts, the trail becoming harder to define. Barleigh's pony leaned into the biting wind, her thick whiskers coated with icicles. Barleigh shivered under the serape—she tried to sip from the canteen, but her hands shook, splashing coffee over her chin. She pulled the scarf up and it froze to her skin.

She talked to her horse, keeping up a running dialogue to pass time as she looked for signs along the trail that might indicate she was at the very least still on the correct path. A good guess was all she could offer herself at times. Their pace slowed to a safe walk. Sometimes it slowed to a safer standstill while she reoriented herself in the blinding snow. The mid-afternoon sun was useless against the thick clouds, offering no help in finding the route.

One moment, she thought she found the road. The next, it disappeared under a foot of powder. Finding a place that was flatter and wider and then curved down into a gulley, she cautiously picked her way through the snow, following it to wherever it led.

Twice more losing the trail, she dismounted and circled back, keeping a low and close eye on the hoof prints before the fast-falling snow erased them from view. The prints led her back to what she felt sure to be the trail. Still on foot, she led the weary horse through a steep-sloping gulley where the wind had blown drifts into waist-deep heaps.

"Come on, Blaze, don't give up." Barleigh pulled on the reins and tried to coax the exhausted animal to keep moving.

The horse plodded up the steep slope, her feet falling heavy one at a time. Fatigue and brutal cold sapped her strength. Her sides heaved with each labored breath, and each one, Barleigh feared, might be the mare's last.

All of a sudden, with no warning, the gale stopped. It was as if a giant fist punched out the wind's breath. The snow, once thrashing in a horizontal blizzard, now began to float in a silent, spiraling sway. Disoriented and snow-blind, Barleigh fell headfirst over a cedar-stave hitching post all but buried in the snow.

A faint light flickered with a pale yellow glow in the window of a small stone lodge just a few yards farther to the west. The oaky smell of a wood fire scented the air. A horse nickered a greeting to Blaze—she offered a grunting nicker in return. A front door opened. Steaming black coffee in a thin tin cup appeared. Gloved hands took the reins from Barleigh's frozen fingers and led her horse away. Another's hands pressed against her shoulders and steered her into a glowing, warm, open door.

"My God, we're here, Blaze. Willow Springs. We almost rode right by it." Barleigh fought off a tear.

"Blaze was taken to the barn, if that's the horse," said Frenchie Jones, the station manager.

"Where's the mochila?" Barleigh asked through chattering teeth, her body shaking so hard that most of the coffee spilled out of the cup and onto the floor. "It's Lincoln. Lincoln won the election. I can't stop. Have to keep riding. Keep the mail going."

"It's all right, son," said Frenchie. "That was Eckels who took the mochila from you. He got here this morning but the storm kept him from going any further. He's rested up enough to take it on west for you. Your mochila's in good hands. And Louis Shoals left not ten minutes ago with the eastbound mail. You no doubt passed him."

"If I did, I didn't see him. Hell, I almost didn't see this place until the wind just . . ." She tried to snap her fingers but her frozen joints wouldn't cooperate. "The wind just stopped, just like that." After taking another sip of coffee and eating a spoonful of lamb stew, Barleigh crawled over by the fire. Curling up in a ball, she slept for twelve hours straight, her clothes thawing and drying by morning.

The sun was well established over the eastern ridge when Barleigh awoke to raw, blistered skin from riding all night and most of the day in wet, frozen pants. Chaffed skin made walking to the coffee pot a challenge, but determination and want prevailed.

"Here, son," said Frenchie, "smear this all over your legs and between your butt cheeks. It'll take a couple a weeks before you toughen up down there and get used to the constant wear and tear."

"Thanks, Frenchie," she said. "What is it?"

"Lard. And in case Cookie runs out of frying oil, just scrape it off when you're done riding and give it back to him, nice and seasoned, just the way he likes it." Frenchie walked out of the kitchen doubled over laughing, no doubt, at the look on Barleigh's face.

He was still laughing when Barleigh met up with him at the stables. She selected an easy-tempered looking gelding and saddled up, getting her mind ready for what she expected would be an arduous ride home. Feeling as greased up as a holiday duck, she rode away at an easy trot, butt out of the saddle with her weight in the stirrups, determined not to cry.

CHAPTER TWELVE

NOVEMBER 15, 1860

Journal entry: I returned to the Great Salt Lake City late in the afternoon carrying the east bound mochila I'd picked up along the way. Stoney waited at the stables, horse in hand, eager to receive the mail pouch as I bugled my way into town.

He sported a new brown hat. Cinched tight under his chin with a braided leather cord, the hat was smaller brimmed, shorter crowned, and more suited to faster riding.

Before galloping away, he informed me he still had his sombrero and asked me to keep an eye on the yellow Mexican hat. With mock horror, he said Mario threatened to throw it away first chance he found.

I promised him I would, laughing, as Stoney and Mario threw obscene gestures at one another before Stoney and his horse raced out of site.

My intention of bathing and washing the lard off my body was sincere, but once I saw my bed, my intention crumbled. I fell asleep before my head made contact with the pillow. Exhaustion must have deadened the sense of smell. I found it remarkable I slept without my own odor waking me. It's a good thing all the other riders found reasons to be away for the night.

After waking from the sleep of the innocent or of the dead, I did take a bath and noticed my skin felt soft and supple where it wasn't blistered and chapped. Lard may not be what the fancy ladies purchase for their dainty skin at Leonard's Department Store back in Fort Worth, but it worked wonders for my chaffed behind.

Weariness kept me from riding out today to the hot springs. I was afraid I'd fall asleep once there and end up drowning myself. Apparently, death's not a good excuse for not settling your tax debt with the bank.

After lunch I strolled around town and made my way to the mercantile. I thought I'd buy tobacco. I wouldn't use it, but it fit my public personality, to carry a pouch of Snuff's chewing tobacco in my pocket like a man. Honing my male persona took practice and observation every moment of every day.

At the far end of the store in front of the tobacco counter stood a man who bore a striking resemblance to Hughes Lévesque. I watched as he finalized his transaction before he turned and exited out the side door.

I saw him only for a brief moment and from a distance, but the likeness made me pause, stare, and forget my own purchase. My pocket remained tobacco-less.

I don't know why, but my heart skipped a beat. Or two. It couldn't be him. What in the world would he be doing here in Salt Lake City? I thought he said he was from Texas. San Antonio? I remember he was writing to a friend about the Pony Express, and he had many questions that he didn't mind asking.

Was his friend a lady friend? Don't be silly. What does it matter anyway?

What matters is this yawning fatigue that's washed over me, a tiredness like I've never felt before; yet, it rewards me in ways I can't describe. I've earned this exhaustion. A deep sleep will be my immediate reward tonight.

Tomorrow, I'll go to the hot springs and enjoy a warm soaking bath in the mineral spa. I'll take along some fine soaps and oils, and if only for a brief hour or two, I'll remind myself that in my previous life, I didn't smell like a filthy Billy goat. I wouldn't want my fragrance to frighten away the wolf who watches over my dreams.

Good night.

*****

"Don't soak too long in those hot springs," said Mario as he forked a thick slice of ham dripping with runny egg yolk into his mouth. "I heard those minerals will shrivel up your pecker to smaller than your little finger. Course, I've seen you in your long johns. You don't have much there anyway."

Barleigh shoved her middle finger in the air like she'd seen Stoney do, then walked out the door to the laughter of Mario and the other riders who had returned at dawn from a night of drinking and card playing. She readjusted her imaginary privates and spat on the ground.

"You bastards can go to hell." She tried not to think of what her papa would say if he heard her using such vulgar language.

"Careful you don't wake up a bear hibernating in one of them caves," shouted Big Brody, the part-time rider when he was sober enough to sit a saddle. "Or surprise a band of outlaws stowing away their loot. They hide out in them caves, too, you know."

She ignored the jokes and kept walking, giving another readjusting scratch and a sideways spit for good measure.

There were four mineral baths close to town. The nearest

and largest was patronized by tourists and high-paying guests. Not too far away were the deepest and hottest, which were favored by the locals. Emigrants and vagrants pitched their tents and camped around the farthest and most sulfuric.

The fourth, which was hidden away and known only to a few locals, was in a secret location. Down a steep path and tucked away in the belly of a cave, its entrance was camouflaged by giant boulders covering the gaping mouth. Mario shared this secret with the Pony Express riders, so they could use it on their days off.

Barleigh guided the high-stepping chestnut gelding down the snow-packed lane past the mercantile. She cast a sidelong glance in the window as she rode by, wondering if the gentleman at the tobacco counter might make another appearance. After a second glance, she chided herself for entertaining dangerous thoughts.

An easy hour's ride outside of the busy city found her at the secret cut-off for the springs. Despite the nice break in the weather, the trail was empty, with Barleigh the lone rider. Snow covered the ground, but the sun glowed in a clear blue sky, and the wind seemed content at a soft breeze.

Leaving the main trail and heading south where the three stacked stones marked the way, the secret path became narrow and steep. Barleigh dismounted, leading the horse farther down until she came to a large pine tree growing in a small, flat glade hidden behind a stand of mountain red cedars. She tied the horse and removed her saddlebag, giving the gelding a piece of peppermint and a pat on the neck.

Slipping and sliding farther down the narrow, precipitous grade, Barleigh finally came to a cluster of massive granite boulders. Long ago when the earth shook the giant rocks together, a low, tapered opening into the hidden cave was formed.

Inside, she heard the hollow echo of water dripping. She sniffed and wrinkled her nose when she detected the tinge of sulfur in the air. Through a jagged crevasse overhead, a narrow beam of sunlight filtered into the cave. The light's effect cast the semi-dark scene into an ethereal oasis of beauty: steam rising above a languid pool, and lush green ferns growing in random tufts along the slick, wet granite walls.

Throwing her saddlebag to the side, she heard it slide to a stop against the cave's wall. She felt her way with her hands and feet, moving with caution until her eyes adjusted to the near-darkness. She propped her shotgun between the bag and the wall, her pistols within easy reach of the pool's ledge.

Boots and socks were shed. She crept to the water's edge, easing her feet into the steaming pool, quick to yank them out.

"Ouch!" She listened to the echo of her voice, a surprised smile on her face.

"Ouch!" she hollered louder, laughing at the sound of her voice disappearing into the belly of the cave.

Removing her clothes, she lay them next to the pool for washing. To keep her clean clothes dry and off the damp floor, she lay them on top of her saddlebag. Then began the slow process of unbinding her breasts from the tight swaddling cloth. Aunt Winnie had given her the cloth and had shown her how to wrap herself, in order to flatten her curves.

"Ahh." Barleigh breathed in a deep, satisfying breath, rubbing herself with brisk hands to get the circulation going. "That feels good."

Filling her lungs with deep breaths again and again, she languished in the unrestrained freedom of an unbound woman. From inside the saddlebag, she removed a soft towel, lavender bath salts, lilac shampoo flakes, and oil of lilac she'd borrowed from the Bath and Bakery. She placed the jars on the towel next to the water's edge. Her picnic consisted of a small flask of watered brandy and a pouch of dried apricots and walnuts.

Holding her breath, she eased into the steaming pool, taking a seat on the sloping stone ledge a few feet below the water's surface. The steamy water didn't feel as hot the more she became accustomed to it.

After scrubbing her skin, washing and oiling her hair, then pounding and soaking the dirt out of her clothes, she sat up to her neck in the mineral pool. Sipping brandy and eating walnuts and apricots, she tried to think of what to do next besides just sit and enjoy the simple pleasure of smelling like a woman again.

As the sun changed position, light entering the cave through the crevasse glittered and sparkled off the crystal quartz in the wet granite. The cave's walls appeared to have pink, black, and white diamonds embedded in the slick surface.

Barleigh climbed out of the pool and crept to the far side, running her hand along the warm surface of the sparkling wall. The idea of exploring further into the depths of the cavern piqued her curiosity, as she wondered how far back it might go.

Uh . . . ? She drew a quick breath. *What was that?* She remained still, holding her breath, trying to discern if the noise she heard came from within the cave or from outside.

Pressing her back against the wall, she inched closer to her saddlebag and the shotgun. She moved with slow, quiet, deliberate movements, stretching her arm, reaching out her hand, extending her fingers as far as they would go. She touched warm metal, wrapped her fingers around it, but because the barrel was slick from the humidity of the cave, it slipped from her grasp, clattering to the rocky floor.

Shit!

Dropping to all fours, she crouched on the ground. Reaching for the gun and crooking it in one arm, she crawled to the water, slipping into the hot bath. Like a silent snake, she floated to the opposite side, the gun in her hands and her eyes grazing just above the water's surface. She sat perched on the submerged ledge with eyes and nose inches above the water line, the barrel of the gun resting on the edge of the pool. With her finger on the trigger, she waited, watched, listened.

How long must she stay submerged? She felt as if she were turning into a boiled prune. Maybe there was nothing—she just thought she heard something. She was being jumpy. Ten minutes must have passed. She would wait five more, then get dressed and get the hell out of the water, leave the cave, and get back to town.

Taking a deep breath, she eased out of the pool, gathering up the towel, wet clean clothes, the jars of soap and shampoo, and her pistols and shotgun. She carried her belongings to the saddlebag lying against the side wall, repacking everything for the trip back up the trail.

The swaddling cloth lying on top of the clean, dry clothes, the binding that would turn Barleigh back into the boy Bar Flanders, would go on first. She began the wrapping process, but stopped. The feeling she was missing or forgetting something vexed her.

Ah, yes.

She put down the swaddling cloth and felt her way back to the water's edge to retrieve Mario's brandy flask he'd loaned her. Barleigh had sworn an oath to guard it with her life. As she reached for the flask, the quiet darkness was pierced by the sound of a horse's whinny very close to the entrance, the noise reverberating and echoing deep into the cave.

The sudden and loud whinny startled Barleigh. She stopped her in her tracks.

"Pardon me, ma'am, but isn't it unsafe for a woman to bathe way out here, all by herself?" The man's voice was smooth and deep.

Leaping into the pool, Barleigh pressed flat against the ledge she'd had been sitting on earlier. She'd heard that voice before. It sounded like Mr. Lévesque, the nosy man from Saint Joe. Maybe it had been him purchasing tobacco in the mercantile.

"Have you drowned? Are you all right?" the deep voice asked.

"I haven't drowned," she said, the heat from the steaming pool no longer registering on her skin. She wished her guns were within reach.

"Drowning's only one concern. There're many reasons why a woman shouldn't be out here bathing alone. It's unsafe." The smooth, baritone voice moved closer into the cave.

"Perhaps it's more unsafe with you here. I felt quite safe before." Barleigh wondered how long he'd been watching. He'd clearly seen enough to call her ma'am and to know she was a woman bathing alone.

"You're safer than you were before. But, to show you that I mean no harm, I'll turn my back and guard the entrance to make sure no one is watching while you towel off and get dressed. See? I'm turning around." He turned his back to the pool.

"You're either brave, or imprudent, turning your back on an armed woman whom you've never met." In principle, true, if this was Mr. Lévesque. He'd met Bar. Not Barleigh.

"Lady, if you *are* armed, I'd like to see where you're hiding your weapon."

"Well, sir, a knife I keep strapped to my thigh at all times, just in case." She decided she should buy one of those, first chance she got.

She slipped out of the pool and tiptoed backward toward her guns, lifting the towel and rushing it over her body. Keeping one pistol in hand, she fumbled with her clothes with the other. Finding it impossible to dress quickly using only one hand, she lay the pistol down at her feet.

"My pistol *was* in my towel—now it's in my hand," she said, knowing he couldn't see in the dark and with his back turned. "My shotgun is at my side. Please keep your back turned while I finish dressing."

"Yes, ma'am."

"And could you please step to your left into that beam of light so I can see you better? No surprises. Keep your back turned."

"As you wish." He sidestepped until he was centered under the small ray of light, his hands in a casual clasp behind his back as he whistled a soft tune. "Is this where you want me?"

"Yes. That will do." She hurried with the binding, wrapping the swaddling tight around her breasts before pulling on the long johns, pants, shirt, and boots. She pondered how she was going to explain a sudden transformation from female to male. A miracle? Something in the mineral water, as Mario said, that shrivels a man's pecker?

"I'll stand here as long as you say. It's my personal philosophy never to argue with a woman who has a gun pointed at my back. Or with one who has a knife strapped to her thigh. Of course I'm just taking your word for it that you are indeed armed, as I didn't witness said weapons. By the way, I'm Hughes Lévesque, Texas Ranger. And you are?"

"Dressed. You may turn around now."

When he turned, the beam of sunlight under which he stood illuminated his face, sparkling off of the flecks of burnished gold in his eyes, and in that instant, Barleigh knew him.

My dream wolf.

She sank back into the shadows, transfixed, watching as he blinked hard against the beam of light from the sun. He tilted back his black hat and then cocked his head, listening. Scanning his eyes across the cave to the right, he settled upon the exact spot where Barleigh crouched in the shadows against the warm, wet wall.

His long buffalo coat was open, revealing polished Navy Colt revolvers at each hip. A burgundy and gold brocade vest and a crisp linen shirt looked out of place, more suitable for a dinner party in Saint Joseph than scouting out caves in Salt Lake City

"I'm standing in the light, but you're hidden in the shadows. I prefer conversations face to face." He waited for a reply. "It's all right, miss. I won't bite."

Barleigh watched and listened in silence. She remembered there had been something about his eyes that disarmed her when they'd met in Saint Joseph. That she didn't realize then those eyes belonged to the wolf from her dreams surprised her. Their intensity was unnerving.

"Would you feel better if I waited for you outside?" He began to back toward the entrance, gloved hands open, outstretched. His shiny spurs clinked against the wet stone floor.

"Yes. No. I . . . I don't know," she stammered, feeling foolish. "I'm . . . I'm mortified you saw me naked."

"The cave is dark. More dark than light. I had only the faintest idea I was seeing anything more than a shadowy, shady silhouette." He moved his hands, making an hourglass shape.

"You saw enough to know I'm a woman bathing alone," she said, embarrassment flushing her cheeks.

"It's a trick I learned from an old Indian scout. Follow the heavy scent of lilac and lavender, and there's a good chance you'll find a woman at the end of your nose." His gaze remained on where Barleigh still crouched against the wall in the shadows.

"Oh? Oh, the shampoo and soap. I, uh, I was just enjoying . . . I haven't smelled like a woman in . . ."

"Now, would you please come out of the shadows?"

"No."

"Why not?"

"Because I'm afraid."

"Afraid of what? By now you must know I mean you no harm."

"Yes, I know. It's just that, well, you see, I, uh, I've a secret. A significant secret. Once you know it, you must agree to keep it, too. Otherwise, I'll have no choice but to take your weapons, bind your hands, blindfold you, and leave you in this cave until I'm a safe distance away."

"Do you have a gun drawn on me now?" Hughes asked, a smile lifting the corners of his mouth.

"Yes. Two."

"I heard quiet shuffling and I know you just now picked your guns up off the floor. The scrape of metal against stone gave you away. And you need to see a cobbler about resoling your boots —the leather has worn somewhat thin. You tapped your toe against the wall, I'm guessing searching for your other gun. Although I can't see you, I can hear you. As both of us know, I can smell you. I can sense you. You were crouching. Now you're standing. If I had wanted to, I could have disarmed you. Or worse. But I didn't. You can trust me. You know you can." His voice remained smooth, steady, and calm.

Barleigh sighed a reluctant sigh, not convinced yet she should give in. "Swear an oath on your Texas Ranger's badge and give me your gentleman's word that my secret is safe with you."

"I'm the best keeper of secrets you'll ever need."

"Swear on it," Barleigh insisted.

"I don't know which I value more, my gentleman's word or an oath sworn on my badge, but I give you both. Whatever dark secret you reveal will go no further than the mouth of this cave." He couldn't tell her he already knew her secret. He'd given his word to Leighselle he'd follow her daughter to Utah Territory and keep an eye on her safety, while staying hushed about Leighselle's identity.

"I'm—a boy. I'm Bar Flanders. We met in Saint Joseph a

few weeks back." She walked from the shadows and over to the beam of light where Hughes stood and stuck out her hand. "It's a pleasure to see you again, Mr. Lévesque." She didn't bother lowering her voice an octave.

Hughes removed his glove and took her hand. "I'll be damned. The Pony Express rider. But you're not a boy. Just pretending to be."

"Yes. Just pretending."

Barleigh felt the weight of his intense eyes on her. She could not turn away from his gaze. In her dreams, when she was on the cloud circling around the mountain peak and spiraling back down to earth, the wolf would silently command her to look at him and not turn away. It was the same with this man.

She expected him to throw back his head and offer his howl to the moon and for the moon to accept his offering. But he wasn't a dark sable wolf, and the moon wasn't out. Barleigh wasn't hearing howling, she was hearing ringing in her ears—thin, metallic ringing—and the dark cave was spinning. She couldn't blink away the fuzziness clouding her vision. She swayed as her knees grew weak.

"Are you all right, Bar? Here, sit down." Hughes took her by both arms, steadying her.

"I'm sorry. I don't know what's wrong. I feel lightheaded and faint, all of a sudden," she said, her voice a trembling whisper.

"How long did you stay in the hot bath?" Hughes spread his thick buffalo coat on the ground and she sat down on it.

"A good while. An hour at least. And then some more when someone scared me and I had to jump back in."

"Right. Sorry about that. Have you had anything to eat? Any water to drink?"

"Some watered brandy, and some apricots and walnuts."

"Brandy and a long hot bath with not much to eat? Good God, woman, it's no wonder you're dizzy. I'll be back in a minute." And then he was gone.

Barleigh lay back and fought the urge to close her eyes and drift away to sleep. She rolled over on her side, drawing her knees up into a tight ball, pulling the arm of Hughes's coat around her shoulders. His scent was strong on his garment, smoky and woodsy, with the smell of leather, horsehide, and saddle soap mingled together with something else. She breathed in again, smelling something tempting, something spicy, like cloves, or cardamom. The shorn lamb's wool lining was soft against her face as she pressed into it and breathed, trying to identify the aroma.

Mmm. What is it?

"What is what?" Hughes walked back into the cave with a large, tooled leather duffle bag and knelt on the ground beside her. "You were asking 'What is it?' when I walked back in."

"Oh. Private thoughts." She hadn't realized she'd spoken aloud. A red-hot blush climbed up her neck and blossomed on her face. She was thankful for the darkness.

"I'm sorry. I didn't mean to intrude into your private thoughts." Hughes opened the bag and reached inside. He offered his canteen, then moistened his bandana, placing it across her brow.

"Thank you. I hope I didn't sound rude." She sipped from his canteen and took the cloth from his hand, washing her face with the cool water.

"You didn't. You sounded matter-of-fact. And private. Now, you should eat. I have in my bag some honey bread and smoked ham. More water—don't set that canteen down. Drink up."

"Do you always sound like that?" Barleigh asked, drinking more water.

"Like what?" Hughes reached into the duffle bag and took out two plates, arranging the food, napkins, and silverware as if they were dining in a fine restaurant.

"Matter-of-fact and dictatorial." She picked up the silver fork with gold filigree trim, twirling it between her fingers, then placing it on the linen napkin tucked next to the pewter plate. The center of the plate bore an engraved family crest above a coat of arms

Acquiring this type of finery wouldn't be possible based solely on a Texas Ranger's wage, she thought to herself. Was this keeper of secrets hiding a few of his own? She let that thought percolate while she watched him serve the food.

Hughes paused and looked at her, seeming to study her face in the beam of sunlight. "You've cat-like eyes, but blue. Very blue. And very feminine. No wonder you kept them cast down. It's part of your disguise, your act," he said. "It's no wonder. Your eyes might betray you."

Like Hughes's eyes might betray him—another private thought she would keep to herself.

"So you consider me dictatorial? I prefer 'commanding,' or 'take charge.'"

"I can take charge of myself." Her voice took on a defensive tone.

"I can see that. You're a brave young lady." He sat back and folded his arms around his bent knees. "May I ask you, though, why you're doing something that's impossible to sustain? This masquerade of yours is reckless, dangerous, and foolhardy."

"Reckless, dangerous, and foolhardy?" Barleigh bristled. "You wouldn't use those words to describe a man in this role. You'd call him daring, valiant, and heroic."

"But you're not a man."

"And it hasn't mattered."

"You put yourself in harm's way every time you race off with that goddamned mochila. Pardon my language. Don't you realize the risk you take? Men have died doing what you're doing." Hughes's voice deepened, his eyes darkening. "Take those words seriously."

"Mr. Lévesque, you don't know me or know anything about my life. You've no right to question me about the risks I take or what I realize or don't realize." She pushed the plate away and stood up, arms folded across her chest, pacing, irritated, and incredulous.

"What's your name?" Hughes stood up, placing a hand on her arm. He knew her name was Barleigh Alexandria Henrietta Flanders—he knew more about her than she knew herself—but he had to get her to tell him. "Stop pacing like a damned caged cat. I'm sorry—I didn't mean to rile you. What's your name?"

"Excuse me?" She stood with her arms still a barrier across her chest.

"Your name. Is Bar Flanders your real or your pretend name?"

"Barleigh. Barleigh Flanders. I shortened it to Bar."

"Miss Barleigh Flanders, you became a Pony Express rider by your daring horsemanship and bravery. I didn't mean to sound dismissive of your skills or capabilities. You've proven yourself equal to the task. But, if you were my girl, if you were my little sister, I would never allow—I would do everything in my power to dissuade you from such dangerous activities."

With hands fisted on hips, she tilted her chin to look Hughes square in the eye. "I've done my job as well as any Pony Express rider. I haven't shirked my duties once. I'm accepted. No one questions that I'm *not* a boy. I'm not a childish girl playing dress-up and make-believe for the thrill of a silly little game. I *need* this job."

A surprising urge to cry welled from within. She took shaky breaths, trying to swallow it away. All of the reasons why she was here, and all of the reasons why she shouldn't be here, conflicted, grating against her emotions.

"Hey now, come here. It's all right. I swore to you your secret is safe with me. I'm the best keeper of secrets—"

"—I'll ever need. I'm sorry, I don't know why I'm crying. I hate crying when there's no reason."

"It's not what I'd call a full-blown cry. Just one tiny little leak right here." He wiped her cheek with his thumb. "There, the leak is fixed."

"Thank you, Mr. Lévesque."

"Hughes."

"Hughes. Thank you. Please call me Barleigh, but only here, only today."

"Barleigh. I hate to be the bearer of bad news, but there is one tiny little thing that might give your secret away, that you're *not* a boy."

"What's that?" she sniffed, wiping at her eyes.

"If you ride back into town smelling like a perfumery, someone's bound to raise an eyebrow." He looked at her, one eyebrow raised in comical fashion. "Lilac and lavender are not the scents of Pony Express riders. Take your shirt off. I'll be right back."

"I beg your pardon?" She stiffened and looked at him wide-eyed.

"Just your shirt." He waved his hand around, up and down in front of her, chest level. "Leave all of your under-bindings on."

"So you didn't see anything but a shady, shadowy silhouette 'cause it's more dark than light in here." Barleigh felt the beginnings of a blush again, but began unfastening her shirt. "Where are you going?"

But he was already gone.

Hughes returned with a handful of pine cones and a few small branches, then built a fire on the floor of the cave below the crevasse. He boiled water and made a strong smelling tea with the tarry pine needles, adding thin flakes carved from the bar of oily saddle soap he'd fetched from his bag.

"Come here," he said, "and let me smell you."

Barleigh laughed out loud.

"I'm serious," he said, looking at her, waiting. "Is the smell in your hair, or on your skin, or both? Can we fix it with just a shampoo, or will you need a complete scrubbing down?"

Hesitating a moment, she walked over to the fire and stood under the beam of sunlight. "Ready for inspection, sir." She held out her arms and held her breath.

Hughes moved around and stood behind her, inches from her body. He leaned in close, grazed his nose along the curve of her neck, inhaling, and then along the other side, breathing in and out. The silky fine hairs at the base of her neck fluttered from the warm puffs of his breath against her skin.

She swayed. *Oh. My. Steady on your feet.*

With his large hands, he scrunched her hair, burying his face, breathing in. He ran his nose along the outside of each arm to the tips of her fingers, turned over the palm to trace back up the inside of her elbow, up and over each shoulder, then followed down, down along the centerline dip and curve of her back, stopping short where her unbelted trousers hung loose on her hips.

He placed his hands on Barleigh's waist, turning her around

to face him. "My dear," he said, his voice deep and husky, "the verdict is in."

"Yes?" *Breathe.*

"I detect only a faint trace of floral scent on your skin. But, your hair is something else. Your hair smells—marvelous. That problem needs fixing." He turned and walked to the pool.

"All right. What do you need me to do?" She tingled where merely his breath had brushed her skin.

"Lie down here on your back with your head over the pool, yes, like that. I'll wash your hair with this pine tea and saddle soap. It won't smell as pretty as lilac and lavender, but smelling pretty isn't what *Bar* needs."

Hughes rolled up his sleeves, kneeling beside the pool. He cupped her head in one hand while running the warm mixture through her hair with the other, massaging it into her scalp and pulling it through the short length of her hair.

That one act, holding the weight of her head in his hands and washing her hair, bonded his intent to his word and his oath. Barleigh relaxed—closed her eyes. She imagined him holding also in his hands her secrets and dreams, her thoughts and desires. His hands would not let them go but would keep them safe, protected, buoyant, free to float where destiny's winds blew them.

But, the fears. Would she ever be able to relinquish her fears to this man?

What is it about Hughes Lévesque, she wondered, that made her feel as if she'd known him all her life—and longer?

His bare arm, wet and soapy, slid against her cheek, against her forehead, and she felt a warm stirring in the pit of her stomach —and lower. Every nerve tingled, every sensation multiplied as his strong hands and long fingers scrubbed her scalp, washed her hair, effectively putting her disguise back into place.

"We can finish eating while we wait for your hair to dry." Hughes gently patted her head with the towel. "I have another canteen with some honeyed whiskey, now that you're feeling better. It'll thicken your blood for the ride back to town."

"That sounds nice," she said, taking the towel from him, rubbing her head with vigorous strokes. "I've always thought I needed thickened blood. While we're waiting, you can tell me what a Texas Ranger is doing in Salt Lake City in Utah Territory via Saint Joseph, Missouri?"

Hughes picked up a long pine needle from the floor of the cave and scraped at the dirt under his nails. "Barleigh. I'll say your name a lot, since I can *only* say it here. Barleigh, there's not much to tell."

"I don't believe that. Tell me something about yourself others don't know," she said, laying the towel aside.

"What? You shared your secret, now I share mine?" Hughes inspected his nails and flicked the pine needle away.

"Yes, something like that." She sipped the honeyed whiskey, studying his profile over the flickering fire. He looked as much like a lion as he did a wolf, she thought. "You have secrets, don't you," she said, not as a question but as a statement.

Hughes held her gaze for a long moment, the light from the fire dancing in his eyes. Barleigh wished she knew what he was thinking—what secrets he carried behind those eyes. But he turned away, keeping them to himself, apparently lost in his own private thoughts.

"All right," he said after a pause, "give me your lady's word and swear an oath on your Pony Express Bible that the dark secret I reveal to you will travel no further than the mouth of this cave."

She raised her right hand and composed a serious expression. "I swear an oath on my Pony Express Bible and give you my word to keep your secret."

Hughes took a deep, dramatic breath. "I'm deathly afraid of spiders. I hate them and their eight, horrible little legs, all creepy, crawly, and crunchy when you step on them." He shuddered.

"That's not fair." Barleigh threw her empty cup at him, tried to pull down a pout, but her mouth gave way to a grin.

"You're right, that's not fair. I should share a secret bearing equal weight to the one you've shared." His composure and his voice too on a serious quality.

"That's the honorable thing to do." She matched the seriousness of his tone.

"Yes, and I'm nothing if not honorable." He stared for a long moment at her and took several deep breaths, as if calculating the odds on a poker game. "I *am* a Texas Ranger, currently inactive. Mostly, I work for the federal government. Clandestine operations. There's a group of Southern sympathizers conspiring to censor the U.S. mail. Their special interest is the westbound mail to California. I'm working undercover to see what can be done about it."

"Is the Pony Express mail at risk of—"

"—of being diverted or tampered with? Yes. That's one of the reasons why I'm here."

"One of the reasons?" she asked, her interest piqued. "What's the other?"

"Ah, don't be greedy. One secret per customer per day, Barleigh." His voice adopted a sensual quality, soft yet masculine.

He smiled and steadied his piercing eyes on her. Barleigh was learning the futility of resisting his silent command to not look away.

She did not look away.

CHAPTER THIRTEEN

NOVEMBER 16, 1860

Journal entry: We rode back to the city together after Hughes shared the rest of his meal with me in the cave. But that's all he shared. Mr. Lévesque holds his cards close to his chest and reveals little. He told nothing else about himself except that he is indeed a Texas Ranger taking leave to work for the Government to discover who's attempting to tamper with the mail.

I have a strong intuition, however, that his mission is more involved than that of a singular assignment of discovery.

I've promised to tell no one, and I shall keep my promise as I expect him to keep his. I feel I can trust him, though I don't know why. I hardly know him. But, I have no choice other than to do so. His cover is that he is a wealthy businessman in town scouting out investment opportunities. He plays the wealthy part with comfort and ease.

Amusing, both of us incognito. He as a businessman. Me as a boy. I wonder which requires the biggest leap of the imagination.

The Salt Lake House is the only fine hotel west of the Mississippi, so Mr. Lévesque has taken a room on the second floor next door to the room kept for the Pony Express riders. This arrangement might prove useful to both of us as we discussed on our ride into town. We can keep an eye out for the other's best interest.

"Well, ain't that something," was Stoney's reply when we ran into him. He was flying down the stairs on his way out the door for his eastbound mail run, short brimmed hat in hand. Stoney reminded me again to keep an eye on his sombrero and not let Mario throw it away. I promised him I would.

Keeping my mind focused and on task will require an extra amount of vigilance. I don't know why, but thinking about Hughes sleeping in the next room from where I sleep stirs me. It's good there is a wall in between—a barrier—a physical reminder that I must keep to myself. Although, I might be tempted to press my ear to the wall to discover what sounds a man makes when he's alone .

Next weekend is the Harvest Festival, a full day Saturday of sharing food and feeding the poor. There'll be pie-eating contests, yard games for the children, a quilting exhibition, a butter churning contest, and a barn dance in the evening. The festivities end Sunday with a day of giving thanks for all our blessings and for our bounty, the 25th of November, exactly one month until Christmas.

That almost a full year has passed since Papa and Birdie's secret "ceremony of vows," then her discovery that there'd be a baby, seems impossible. But everything about last year seems impossible. I wonder if that's why I ride so fast and so hard, that maybe the faster I ride, the faster I'll put last year behind me.

I should blow out my lamp, put away my journal. I go back on duty in the morning and

back in the saddle.
The mail must go through.
*****

Barleigh left the Bath & Bakery, still damp behind the ears, washed, and wearing clean clothes. She made her way to the courthouse square, guided by the lively shouts and peals of laughter coming from the boisterous crowd in the meeting hall. Though she was tired from her earlier mail run, the festive mood lifted her spirits. Hearing people laughing, singing, and having fun put a smile on her face. It felt like a long time since she'd had a genuine reason to smile.

"There you are," she said to Stoney, tying her gelding to the hitching post. "I thought you were sick, or dead. Big Brody took the eastbound mochila from me when I rode in this afternoon. He said he took over your run."

"He didn't take over my entire run, just this one ride tonight. I had to pay him a king's ransom to get him to agree. Big Brody don't like missing out on too many pie-eating contests. You going to enter?"

"Me? No, I don't think I'd be very good at that. You?"

"Hell yes, I'm entering. The winner gets to dance with the girl who baked the pie," said Stoney, grinning from ear to ear. "Getting my hands around a girl, pulling her body close, smelling perfume on soft skin. Gets me hard just thinking about it. Maybe we should go pay a visit to the whorehouse instead."

"Maybe I'll think about the pie-eating contest after all," said Barleigh, a nervous twitch in her voice.

The pathway leading from the courthouse square to the town hall was lined with pumpkins, gourds, and square bales of hay decorated with garlands of dried flowers and leaves. The melting from the first snow of the season left muddy puddles, the chilled evening air hinting of frost as stars began to shimmer in the eastern sky.

"Seems more like winter than harvest time, don't you think?" asked Stoney, tapping a pumpkin with his boot. "Back in Frog Level, harvest is over and done with by now."

"It's over with here, too," Barleigh said. "The Harvest

209

Festival isn't welcoming it in; it's celebrating the bounty that it left behind. And, sharing it with the needy."

"We had harvest festivals, too," said Stoney as they reached the town hall doors, "but in Frog Level, we were among the needy on the receiving end." Stoney waved. "There's Hughes Lévesque by the coat table."

"Hello, gentlemen," said Hughes as he handed his coat to the girl behind the table. "I was wondering if I'd see you two here."

After depositing their hats and coats at the table, Barleigh shook his hand and said, "I'm on my two-day break, and Stoney pawned his ride off on Big Brody so he could come here tonight, eat a pie, and dance with a girl."

"I think that sounds like a fine plan." Hughes gave Barleigh a private wink. "Let's all eat a pie and dance with a girl."

"I've never been good at pie-eating contests. You two go ahead. I'll watch." The thought of dancing with a girl, and the girl thinking she was dancing with a boy, caused Barleigh to suppress a giggle.

"Oh, no you don't," said Hughes. "You're entering with us. It'll be fun. Come on. I'll even put up the quarters to buy the pies. Go on, go pick out which pie you want."

"Thank you, sir," said Stoney, hustling over to a table laden heavy with apple pies, pumpkin pies, chocolate cream pies, a variety of berry pies, and some pies undistinguishable as pies altogether.

Girls, some smiling, some shy, some confident and bold, an assortment of girls as varied as the pies they stood behind, waited to see who would buy their pie and vie for a chance to whirl them around the dance floor.

"What are you doing?" Barleigh hissed under her breath. "Don't you know what the prize is for the winner of the contest?"

"Yes, I do know, Barleigh. I'm helping you with your cover," whispered Hughes, still grinning. "These folks seeing you wolfing down a pie and dancing with a girl will be good for your image."

"Don't be crazy. And don't call me Barleigh. It's Bar. And,

I'm not dancing with a girl."

"It's harmless. I do it all the time."

"I'm sure you do."

"Let's go find our pie." Hughes strolled over to the pie table, causing a twitter among the girls. "Over here, Bar. Lots of pies to choose from." He waved with a grand gesture, drawing attention his way. Then, to the girls behind the pies, he said, "This is my friend, Bar, a Pony Express rider. Don't let his small stature fool you. Pick him out the biggest pie here."

A doe-eyed blonde behind the chocolate cream pie with thick flaky crust said, "My pie's small. Could be eaten in one or two bites, if you're hungry enough." Her eyes shuttered closed and reopened in slow motion, as if each lash weighed ten pounds. "But Dorthea over there at the end of the table, she's got the biggest pie here. Could take a man all day to get through that."

Hughes put a silver dollar in the jar and said, "We'll take three—keep the change. It's for a good cause, right?"

"Thank you, sir. It goes into the food drive fund. Now, which pies do you want?"

Stoney wasted no time in claiming the doe-eyed girl's small chocolate pie, pleasing her. She rewarded him with a beaming smile and batted lashes. Hughes scooped up the large pumpkin pie in front of Dorthea.

"Here you go," he said, handing the pie to Barleigh, avoiding her glaring eyes. "And, let's see, I'll have the nice apple pie over there."

"Not funny," she said through gritted teeth as they walked to the row of chairs lined up behind the table of eager pie eaters.

"I picked the biggest pie for you as a strategy," Hughes said under his breath. "I've thought this through. Stoney will be dancing with Little Miss Doe Eyes, not you and Dorthea. Remember, this'll be good for your *boy* image."

"My *boy* image is just fine, thank you, and this pie may, just *may*, be a fraction bigger than the others."

"Then I recommend you eat slowly."

A fast-talking man chewing a fat cigar announced one minute left for purchasing pies, but not to worry, there would be rounds two and three and perhaps four until all pies had been sold.

At the table, Stoney, Hughes, and Barleigh took their places alongside a half dozen others, hands in laps, faces hovering inches above the pies, waiting for the word "go."

"First to finish their pie wins. And, finish means the crust, too. No hands—just your gobbler. Ready . . . set . . . go!"

The crowd erupted with applause and shouts as all the competitors at the table dove face first into their pies. They shoved their heads around, grunting, slurping, and rooting through the baked goods like starving pigs.

Two faces looked up simultaneously.

"Looks like we have a tie, and in record time, too," shouted the cigar-chewing announcer. "How in the world did you boys do that so fast? And where in the world did you put it? One's no bigger than a flea, and the other could hide behind a broomstick."

Barleigh looked around, meeting Hughes's astonished eyes. "What? I'm competitive. I couldn't help it."

"And I'm motivated by something altogether different," said Stoney, walking over to the pie table to claim his dancing partner.

Hughes laughed so hard he fought for breath, holding his sides as if they might split. Wiping traces of apple pie from his face, he shouted over to the pie table, "Oh Dorthea, your dance partner awaits."

Barleigh glared at him and swiped her sleeve across her face, erasing bits of crust and pumpkin custard from her mouth as the fiddle player screeched out the first notes of a waltz. Dorthea stood at the pie table, her impatient foot tapping while she waited to be claimed for the dance. With her hands fisted on her generous hips, she cocked her head and stared at Barleigh in the manner of an enthusiastic woman not used to waiting.

Barleigh gave Dorthea a sheepish smile. Visualizing herself dancing as a man, seeing the steps in her mind—one, two, three, one two three, one two three—she told herself to simply start forward on the left foot, not backward on the right. Easy. She readied her mind for the task.

Tired of waiting, Dorthea pushed past the pie table and

strode to where Barleigh stood. Clamping a meaty fist around Barleigh's wrist, Dorthea pulled Barleigh onto the dance floor, leading and one-two-three-ing her way around the small space. Dorthea kept perfect rhythm with the frantic notes erupting from the fiddle, her eyes closed, her head and body swaying as she glided around the floor in three-quarter time.

Smiling and sweating in profuse droplets when the last note came to a halt, Dorthea gave Barleigh one final under-the-arm spin, curtseyed, and announced in a voice heard loud and clear by the appreciative crowd.

"I thank you kindly for buying my pie, but as far as dance partners go, a little romance wouldn't harm you. I might as well have been dancing with my sister." With that, Dorthea grabbed Barleigh by both cheeks and planted a wet, sloppy kiss full on her mouth.

Hughes threw back his head and let out a hearty laugh. "That was worth the dollar I paid for the pies, right there."

"I, uh, thank you, Dorthea, that was my, uh, my first pie, I mean, my first time to d-dance. . . ," Barleigh stammered in awkward embarrassment.

"Bar, you better stop while you're ahead. Explaining yourself to a woman is a losing proposition," shouted Stoney after rejoining Hughes, his comment eliciting more laughter from the crowd.

"Come on, let's adjourn this party to Whiskey Street," said Hughes, rescuing Barleigh from the dance floor and directing them toward the coat table and out the door. "If you want to dance and have some real pie, a stroll down Whiskey Street is where even the Mormons sneak off to on Saturday nights."

"Whiskey Street?" asked Stoney. "What's Whiskey Street?"

Hughes gave him an astonished look. "You've been here how long and haven't heard about Whiskey Street?"

"Apparently not long enough. Let's go," said Stoney, an eager smile on his face.

Barleigh buttoned her coat and followed them out the door, wondering what she'd gotten herself into.

*****

Main Street threaded north and south through the darkening town, and where it left the southeast corner of the Temple Square, it lead to the commerce district of the Great City, a district that buzzed with activity. The far south end of Main Street flowed from one block to the next with a lively mixture of saloons, distilleries, and tippling houses. It became familiarly known as Whiskey Street. Here, the fervor was for things other than religion.

At the corner of Main and 2nd South Street, Hughes said, "We'll turn here. The best whiskey around is a few steps away. The Baer Brothers' Distillery. They brew and barrel their own."

The saloon wasn't yet crowded. A few empty chairs sat at the bar, a billiards table stood unmanned, and a card table with vacant chairs waited to be filled. Stoney and Barleigh seated themselves at the card table, while Hughes negotiated with the bartender for three glasses and a bottle of Baer Brothers' finest.

Sitting the bottle and glasses at the table, Hughes said, "This is not a contest, Bar, so don't let your competitive side see who can finish the fastest. Fine whiskey should be enjoyed, slowly."

He grinned, handing Barleigh a cut-crystal glass of dark honey-colored liquid, then gave it a small splash of water. Doing the same for Stoney and himself, he raised a glass. "Here's to the most entertaining pie-eating contest I've personally ever witnessed."

"Here, here." Stoney lifted his glass.

A blush tried to form, and Barleigh fought hard not to let the heat rush to her face. She lifted her glass. "Here's to Hughes, a man who knows a thing or two about picking the right pie." She took a sip, waited for the burn, but was surprised by the velvety, delicious flavor of smoky caramel with a hint of orange. She sipped again.

"Smooth," said Stoney. "Not like the Valley Tan that Mario keeps at the barn. You might as well put that shit in the medicine cabinet, not the liquor cabinet."

"Ah, Valley Tan, the exclusive Mormon refresher made with imported fire and brimstone," said Hughes. "The alcohol with many uses. It was considered medicine, when it was originally distilled."

"You gents want me to send over the card dealer?" shouted the bartender. "He's stepped outside to make use of the facilities but he'll be back in a few."

"I paid Big Brody five dollars to take my run tonight. I best hang on to what I have left," said Stoney, shaking his head.

"I'm a saver, not a gambler," said Barleigh, the thought of taxes due on her land flashing through her mind. Losing a penny would be unacceptable.

"I was thinking it sounded like a splendid idea," said Hughes. "I haven't enjoyed a good game in a while. Why don't I stake you each twenty-five dollars? It'll be like me winning back my own money, no loss for me, and we all share an enjoyable evening."

"Who says you'll win?" Barleigh asked. That he'd automatically assume he'd win and she'd lose made her want to put him in his place and show him exactly how much she knew about playing cards.

"Oh? Is this another facet of your competitive nature?" Hughes leaned back in his chair and raised an eyebrow. "I detect a challenge."

"My grandfather spent a lot of time in New Orleans on the riverboats. Two things he taught me—one was how to play cards." Barleigh met the challenge in Hughes's eyes.

"What was the other?" asked Hughes, sipping his whiskey. His curious expression shifted a few degrees, darkening to a guarded alarm.

"How to wish I wasn't blood related to someone." She locked eyes with Hughes for a long moment that turned uncomfortable, and then looked away.

"I thought you was an orphan," said Stoney, swirling the whiskey in his glass.

"I wasn't always."

Hughes tapped his finger on the rim of his whiskey glass. "We'll play five-card draw. I'll stake you each twenty-five. If you win more than that, pay me back my twenty-five, then you keep the rest. If you lose, then it's my loss, too. A small risk I'm willing to take." He waved the dealer over as the man walked in through the back door.

Barleigh, feeling a little lightheaded, pushed her whiskey glass further from her reach. She imagined what her papa would think if he saw her sitting in a bar, drunk, playing poker. She might as well be chewing on a cigar, too, to complete the picture. Checking her posture, she reminded herself to sit like a man, to think like a man, to not let her guard down.

Stoney cleared his throat. "Excuse me, Bar, for interrupting your reverie. Pick up your cards. You look like you're a million miles away."

"Oh, right. Sorry." She picked up her cards, fanning them in one hand, reminding herself of the first rule of poker. Just because her hand held two jacks and three tens was no reason to reveal her luck to the rest of the table by grinning from ear to ear. She picked up her glass and raised it to her mouth to hide her smile. And then took a very small sip.

After several hands, she had doubled her money. Handing Hughes back his twenty-five, she pushed away from the table, ready to leave with Stoney who had managed to lose everything.

"I'm going back to the pie-eating contest to find my love, Elizabeth. Elizabeth Annabelle Parnell. I want to marry her." Stoney's speech was thoroughly slurred. "Elizabeth, with the beautiful, big brown eyes."

"You might have better luck wooing the heart of Miss Doe Eyed Elizabeth," teased Hughes. "The Queen of Hearts sure wasn't doing you any favors here."

"I won't need luck," said Stoney with a confident air, before hiccoughing. "I think she loves me."

"Bar, you might want to stick around." Hughes nodded toward two well-dressed gentlemen walking toward the card table. "I think the stakes are getting ready to get interesting."

"Are these seats vacant? Care if we join in your game?" The heavyset man with round spectacles and a walrus mustache grinned as he eyed the poler chips.

"I'm just leaving," said Stoney. "You coming or going, Bar?"

"I'll stay and play. If I win another twenty-five, I'll toss it over to Hughes and pay your debt."

"You're sounding pretty bold," said Hughes. "But remember, I said that if you lost your twenty-five, I considered it my loss, too. Stoney doesn't owe me."

"You two can argue," said Stoney, shaking Hughes's hand. "As for me, I'm going to find my lost love. Thank you for the poker game. It was the most fun I've ever had losing."

Another bottle of Baer Brothers was sent to the table, courtesy of the bartender. The dealer shuffled a new deck with lightning-fast fingers and declared the table now doubled, if all players agreed. All nodded their acceptance.

Under the table, Hughes bumped Barleigh's knee with his, and then whispered, "Do you want the twenty-five back you repaid me? It might come in handy with these gents. I have a feeling they're going to be loose with their bets."

"Then they'll be big losers," she said. "Thank you, but no."

Somewhere in the course of the evening, Barleigh noticed that Hughes's knee went from an accidental bump or two against her knee to his thigh resting against hers continuously. And, somewhere in the course of the evening, she went from being distracted by the touch to being even more distracted when the touch was momentarily absent.

The bespectacled walrus man lost big and lost quick after a few hands. However, his short, bald partner with the unblinking eyes held on to his money well into the night, increasing it by half before losing it all as well.

*****

"Congratulations, Barleigh. I don't know if you're good, or lucky, or both. What was your final take?" Hughes asked.

They strolled along the upper end of Whiskey Street, the plank sidewalk dark and empty except for an occasional passerby. Barleigh jiggled the gold and silver coins in her trouser pockets, feeling again the bulge of paper money wadded in the inside breast pocket of her coat.

"I quit counting at two hundred fifty or so. How can people throw money away like that? What do those people do for a living that they can lose hundreds of dollars a night and not blink an eye?" The thought of losing that much money made Barleigh nauseated.

"They're owners of silver and copper mines. A few hundred dollars is a drop in the bucket for those gentlemen. You sure took them by surprise. And me, too."

"Pardon me for asking, but did you throw a hand or two my way?" she asked, her question serious.

Hughes laughed. "I'm as competitive as you are. I don't like losing—money, or anything else. Here, walk this way." He turned left down a narrow alley that wound several yards through a courtyard before coming to a dead end behind a row of empty shops that were closed for the night.

"What are we doing here?"

"I want to talk to you in private, away from the others at the hotel. This looked like it had possibilities."

"What do you mean? Talk about what?"

"About how long you can keep this up. About how dangerous being a Pony Express rider is and how I . . ."

She placed her index finger across his lips. "Don't say any more. We've covered this topic in the cave. You don't have any right to interfere."

Hughes took hold of the finger she'd placed across his mouth, pulling it away. He ran his hand down to her wrist, his fingers easily encircling its circumference, and he kissed the underside of it. Then he pressed his mouth to her palm, lingering his lips there.

"God, I wish I had the right to interfere. Every time I watch you ride away by yourself, run after run, taking such risks, I get so —distracted. It's driving me crazy, knowing the danger you're in."

"What are you doing? What are you saying?" She pulled her hand out of his grasp. "You can't do that. I'm Bar Flanders. Pony Express Rider. A boy."

Barleigh stared at her palm where his lips had touched. She pressed her hands together, trying to rub the sensation away, the provocative sensation that left her head light, her knees unsteady.

"You're Barleigh Flanders, Pony Express rider *disguised* as a boy. But a woman who—"

"—who you shouldn't be saying these things to. Stop it. You're drunk. You're not making sense." She tried to back away, but a brick wall stopped her retreat.

"—who drives me crazy with desire. Mad with worry. I don't handle worry very well. I want to kiss you."

"That's the whiskey talking. That's nonsense, that's—"

His mouth covered hers, soft and tender at first, then more insistent, his tongue seeking hers. Entwining his arms around her waist, he pulled her close, lifting her to her toes. His hungry kisses sought nourishment from her—from her lips.

Words of caution flitted through Barleigh's mind like summer butterflies. She thought of capturing them, but let them pass unfettered. Pressing against him, enjoying the sensation, she wanted to know the taste of his mouth, the feel of his hard body, the smell of his breath. Her hands explored his neck, his back, his arms, and she pulled him closer, wanting to feel every part of him. She felt dizzy, and couldn't blame it all on the Baer Brothers' whiskey.

His hands cupped her face, tilting her head, exposing her neck. There he lingered, kissing, biting, trailing his mouth along the curve of her ear, down the side of her neck, stopping with a kiss at the base of her throat.

He groaned, pulling away. "I could go on forever kissing you. I don't want to stop, but I'd better get control of myself."

Barleigh blinked hard, trying to catch her breath, trying to find her balance against the cold brick wall she stood against. "I—that was—I don't know what to say."

"Say you'll take your poker winnings and go back to Texas. Put an end to this tomfoolery. I worry about you. I'm not good at worrying. I don't know what to do with it. It—interferes."

"Hughes," she said, releasing a deep sigh. "Thank you for worrying about me, but I can take care of myself. Besides, I'm enjoying the challenge. And, I'm good at what I do."

"Then do me a favor and consider this." He drew her near, leaning in, brushing his lips against hers. "Consider taking Stoney into your confidence. Now, don't start bristling before you hear me out."

"No. Absolutely not. Why should I even consider that?" Barleigh put both hands against his chest in protest.

"Things are heating up with this mail-tampering business and I have to leave for California first thing Monday. I'd leave feeling much better knowing Stoney was keeping an eye on you and watching to make sure you're safe."

"Keeping an eye on me? Making sure I'm safe? What?"

"The men trying to steal the mail are vigilantes who'll stop at nothing. They're Southern sympathizers who're willing to kill to keep President Lincoln's letters from reaching California. They've already killed others who've gotten in their way. The Union needs California's gold. So does the Confederacy. If we go to war, California's gold could sway the outcome."

Barleigh took a deep breath and let his words soak in. *If we go to war?* She felt a growing sense of urgency and alarm. So much was at stake getting the mail through, now so more than ever. "Tell me more."

"I've already told you too much."

"Then you're in danger, too, spying on these vigilantes."

"Yes." He placed his hands against the wall on either side of Barleigh's shoulders, forming a barrier. "That's why I'd feel much better if I knew Stoney was my backup. If things go bad while I'm not here, it'd help if he knew the truth. I know we can trust him."

"I'll consider it, though I'm not clear exactly why his knowing my secret will keep me safe. Why do I have the feeling that you're not telling me everything?" She looked up into his eyes, hoping for a satisfying answer.

"Trust me on this. Please? I have my reasons," he said, his voice deep and compelling.

"May I sleep on it?" she asked, not yet persuaded.

"Of course. We can talk about it over lunch tomorrow." He leaned in close, his hand drawing her face to his. "Don't pull back. Kiss me."

"I may have to take the eastbound run tomorrow. Eagan is training a new rider and it's Stoney's day off." She pulled further away. "But no more kisses." She knew the kissing had to stop. She couldn't risk being caught. The thought of being seen, of being found out, of losing her job, terrified her.

"All right, no more kisses," said Hughes, "after this last one."

Hughes took Barleigh in his arms and kissed her again, long and deep and slow—an illuminating kiss—making the invisible visible. Pressing her against the wall, he leaned in, moving his body against hers in a way that sent her senses tumbling, sliding, radiating. That one last kiss stole her breath and her heart.

*****

Walking toward Main Street, Barleigh and Hughes stepped from the shadows where the alley crossed through the courtyard. Near the center, three men stood together in an apparent one-sided conversation, one man speaking, the other two nodding. As Barleigh and Hughes neared, the one man who was speaking hurried away. The other two figures turned, crossed their arms, and stood in wait.

"Excuse me, gents," said Hughes as they tried to pass.

Shoulder to shoulder, they blocked the way. "You have something that belongs to my boss," the bigger one said, his voice clear and full of menace. "He wants it back. All of it."

"You must be mistaken," said Hughes. "I don't know you or your boss."

"My boss is the man you cheated at what was supposed to have been a friendly game of poker. Hand over the money." He drew his weapon, pointing it at Hughes.

Hughes raised his hands and took a slight step in front of Barleigh, who also raised her hands. Addressing the two men, he said, "Gents, that money was won, *and lost*, fair and square. No cheating occurred."

"We're not here to converse. We're here to collect. Just hand over the money and no one gets hurt. If Boss says you cheated him, you cheated him. He wants it all back." He thrust his gun forward for emphasis.

"It's not all his money," Barleigh spoke up. "I'll keep what

221

we had to begin with. You can take the rest."

"This is not a negotiation," the smaller one said, drawing and pointing his pistol, Barleigh's midsection his target. "You must be the one holding the money. Keep your hands up. Which pocket is it in?"

Hughes and Barleigh looked at each other, an understanding passing between them. They both knew where she'd put the bundle of money. It was stowed in her inside breast pocket.

The small man took a step in Barleigh's direction, pistol in one hand, the other ready to search. He fumbled in her pants pockets and frowned as he came away with a handful of coins.

"I know Boss plays with bigger stakes than this. Where's the rest?" He started to pat down Barleigh's coat.

"I have the rest," said Hughes. "It's in my inside coat pocket. There's five hundred dollars in there. You're right. Your boss lost big. But he came to the table with only three hundred. I bet if you took him back the three hundred he lost, and you two kept a hundred each for yourselves, he'd never know the difference."

The small man stopped his pat-down of Barleigh's coat, looking to the bigger man for guidance. The big man gave a nod of his head toward Hughes, and with that the search shifted.

"Unbutton your coat, then hands back in the air," the small man said to Hughes. "You," he looked at Barleigh. "You keep your hands where we can see them. I done saw that you're not armed."

Hughes did as he was told.

The man used the tip of his pistol to open Hughes coat wider. "You won't be needing this." He removed the Colt revolver hanging at Hughes's hip and placed it in his own holster. "Which side's the money?"

"Left."

He reached in and pulled out a tooled leather wallet, the initials HPL in fancy script. As he opened the wallet, his mouth moved as he counted the bills inside. With eyes bulging, he looked at Hughes.

"You lied, mister. There's not five hundred in here."

"Hey, what are you trying to pull?" the bigger of the two

asked, stepping close to look inside the wallet.

"See here? There's not five hundred," said the smaller one, holding the wallet open for the big man's inspection. "There's closer to a thousand. Looks like our lucky night. Boss gets his three, we get . . ." He used his fingers to count. "Well, we get the rest."

With their full attention drawn to the wallet and on their good fortune, they didn't notice Hughes forcing his hands down in a plummeting rush. He slammed the two men's heads together with a sickening crunch. The smaller one fell sideways, unconscious. Staggered, the bigger man tottered on his feet, eyes blinking. Delivering a swift kick, Hughes knocked the gun out of the man's hand, followed by a punch to the gut that dropped the big man to his knees, leaving him gasping for air.

"I believe this belongs to me," said Hughes, reaching for his Colt revolver in the small man's holster. As he leaned down to retrieve his gun, the big man lunged forward, knocking Hughes off balance, the gun slipping from his grasp. They struggled on the ground, trading punches, the big man groping for his own gun that Hughes had kicked from his hand.

Running to scoop up both dropped weapons, Barleigh stuffed one in her pocket, the other ready to hand off to Hughes. She was unaware that the smaller man had regained consciousness. He grabbed her ankle as she ran by, pulling Barleigh to the ground, the weapon in her hand falling from her grasp. She rolled to her back, trying to retrieve the pistol she'd stuffed into her pocket, but the man was quick to straddle her, pinning her arms to her sides with his knees. He picked up the dropped gun from the dirt, raised it butt-end first to deliver a blow to her head.

Struggling, bucking, and twisting her body, Barleigh thrashed her legs. Though he was the smaller of the two robbers, his weight was more than she could dislodge without the use of her arms.

She winced, bracing herself for the blow. Instead of feeling the gun coming down hard, she felt his entire body collapse onto hers in a dead-weight fall. Blood sprayed onto her face. Barleigh screamed. Another scream—but from where? Loud, next to her face, the pained wail had come from the man lying across her as the comprehension of what had happened shocked him out of his momentary stupor.

Hughes, having seen what was happening, had taken his Rezin Bowie from his right bootleg and zipped it through the air, aiming it at the base of the small man's skull.

"My ear," he screamed. "You sliced off my goddamned ear." Holding a hand over the right side of his head, blood poured between his fingers.

Hughes dashed over to where Barleigh lay, the small man still straddling her. He wrapped both hands around the man's arm, and in an instantaneous move, yanked him off her with such brutal force that it dislocated the man's joint. The small man dropped to the ground, holding his shoulder, writhing and crying out in pain.

Hughes scooped up his gun. Striding to where the man lay on his side, he forcefully booted the small man over onto his back. "Look at me, fucker."

"Don't kill me, mister," he pleaded, holding his shoulder, his voice ripped with pain. "Please don't kill me. I didn't mean . . ."

"I'm not here to converse. I'm here to kill." Hughes raised the gun.

"No, Hughes!" Barleigh rushed to his side. "He's not worth it. I wouldn't waste a bullet on him."

"Oh, I would. I have plenty of bullets to waste on filthy animals like him."

"I have plenty to waste on filthy animals, too," said a familiar voice coming from the far side of the courtyard. "What kind of filth are we using for target practice tonight?" Stoney, his revolver drawn, moved to Hughes's side.

"The thieving kind. The kind who do their lying boss's dirty work." Hughes lowered his gun, holstering it. He knelt and took the man's gun, then patted him down for other weapons. Finding none, he jerked the man to his feet. "Wake up your big buddy over there, then go tell your boss to stay away from games he's not good at playing."

Barleigh turned and looked at where the big man was lying,

moaning, his unsightly face swollen and bloody. He was struggling to his knees, babbling incoherent words. Hanging useless and limp, his right arm was bent at an odd angle midway between the wrist and elbow.

Stoney aimed his pistol at the small man. "You've been given your marching orders. Make haste before we change our minds and start wasting bullets."

The two bloodied men hobbled off, leaning on each other for support.

"Are you all right?" Hughes was in front of Barleigh, peering into her face. With his hand on her chin, he turned her head left and right. "You've got a cut on your forehead."

"When he tripped me, I hit my head on the ground. It's not bad. I'll be fine." She reached up to touch the cut and felt Hughes's fingers still there. "Are *you* all right? You got the worst of it."

"*They* got the worst of it."

"You almost killed them." The reality of what had happened washed over her, and she shivered.

"I aimed to kill. He got lucky. I would have finished it if he'd hurt you."

Stoney cleared his throat. "Don't mean to interrupt, but what the *hell* just happened?"

"Bar won big at poker. The loser sent those two idiots to rob us and get his money back. It didn't quite work out the way they planned."

"I'd say not. I should have stuck around. I missed all the fun." Stoney holstered his pistol.

"All the fun? Didn't it work out for you and the doe-eyed blonde?" Hughes was speaking to Stoney, but his eyes remained on Barleigh.

"No, sir, it did not. My heart's as wounded as that big man's face you pummeled." Stoney pulled a bottle of Valley Tan from his coat and threw back a slug, offering the bottle to Hughes, then to Barleigh.

"God, no. After Baer Brothers', that'd be sacrilegious. Let's walk," said Hughes, steering Barleigh and Stoney toward the Salt Lake House Hotel.

"When I found Elizabeth to ask her to marry me," continued Stoney, his breath clouded with whiskey, "she told me she's *already* married. She's wife number *seven*. Seven! All at the same goddamned time. Can you believe it? Men—Mormon men—can have all the wives they can stand. But the wives? They get just *one* husband. Now who in the *hell* came up with that shit?"

"I can bet it wasn't a woman," said Barleigh, shuddering at the thought.

As they neared the hotel, Stoney stopped walking. Hughes and Barleigh turned and waited, watching Stoney to see what he was doing. Raising a hand as if seeking permission to speak, he cleared his throat and rubbed the hand down his face, pulling on a serious expression.

"If I can see what's happening, then others can too." Stoney crossed his arms, then uncrossed them, and then shoved his hands in his pockets, clearing his throat again.

"What are you saying, Stoney?" Barleigh asked, ignoring the nagging voice in her own head that mirrored those same words of caution.

He looked from Barleigh to Hughes, then back to Barleigh, starting and restarting his words until they flowed freely. "Tonight at the pie-eating contest, then at the poker game, I saw the way Hughes looked at you. Sorry, Hughes, but I did. And the looks weren't one-sided, Bar. You tried to hide it, I could tell, but maybe 'cause I'm your friend I picked up on it quicker. And I seen the way y'all's fingers lingered on the whiskey bottle, the glass, on the cards, or the money, on anything that might lend a chance to touch each other. Hughes's concern over the cut on your forehead." Stoney looked at each of them, shrugging his shoulders, an innocent gesture that seemed to apologize for what he had seen.

Hughes glanced at Barleigh, his eyebrows raised, then turned his attention back to Stoney. "I know what you *think* you saw," he began, "but—"

Stoney held up both hands, palms out. "Please." He continued. "I'm not here to pass judgment on your private business. But others will. They'll pass judgment, all right, then pass the shotguns while they're good and riled up. Seems here in this Great Salt Lake of a City, a man can have as many wives as he wants at one time. Seven even, if he sees fit. But they won't tolerate two men having tender feelings toward one another Hell, that would get them run out of town. Or killed. Even I know that, and I'm an . . . an uneducated grunt from Arkansas."

"Stoney, you don't know what—" Barleigh tried to reason.

"All I'm saying is," interrupted Stoney, "if I've picked up on it, it won't be long before others do, too. You best be more careful." He threw back another slug of the Valley Tan whiskey, making a wincing face and shuddering his shoulders as it went down.

Barleigh bit her cheek to keep from laughing and looked at Hughes, who was stifling a laugh as well. In a low voice, she said, "You're right, Stoney needs to be brought in on my secret. I'll tell him first thing in the morning after he sleeps this off and a pot of black coffee sobers him up."

"Splendid idea, Barle . . . Bar," said Hughes.

"You two can stand there whispering till morning if you want." Stoney's body swayed with the effort of his words. "I'm going to bed and dream up my own religion where I get as many wives as I can stand, all at the same goddamned time. G'night."

*****

The next morning, Barleigh left the hotel before Stoney awoke, wanting to take a long walk to clear her mind—something different, not on horseback for a change. The unseasonably warm weather invited the casting off of coats and gloves, but not the casting off of troubled thoughts. She headed out of town toward the foothills with a canteen full of black coffee and a mind jumbled and confused.

She thought telling Stoney would be easy—just come right out with it—but figuring out the best way to tell him, which exact words to use, proved tricky. As she walked, she tried out a few scenarios, practicing her speech out loud.

"Hi, Stoney, I have a secret to tell you. I'm really not a homosexual carrying on a flirtatious relationship with another man. I'm really a girl masquerading as a boy. So, I guess for all the world to see, it does appear that I am a homo . . ."

Discarding that one, she tried another.

"Hi, Stoney. I'm a girl. Pretending to be a boy. But you can't tell anyone, even though you've sworn on the Bible to be honest and trustworthy and I have too, but I have to ask you to lie for me and to not tell anyone . . ."

Shit.

Draining the last drop of coffee from the canteen, she looked around, surprised at how far she'd walked. As she turned back toward town, she saw a lone rider approaching at a steady canter, silhouetted against the rising sun. As he rode nearer, the shape of a sombrero glowed like a soft yellow halo in the morning light.

"Stoney, how'd you know I was here?" she said with a nervous smile. Despite her apprehension, she was ready to get this over with.

"Cookie said you filled a canteen and took off walking. This is the one place I knew to look, after I didn't find you at the barn."

"How's your headache?"

"Aww, takes more than a little whiskey to give me a pounder. I'm fine. But I need to haul your ass back to town—you have a run to get ready for. Mario said this one has some urgent letters of some sort. Hop on."

"Thanks." She grabbed hold of Stoney's arm and threw a leg over the back of the saddle, riding double behind him on the big chestnut gelding. The horse's easy stride was smooth and fast, the town growing larger on the horizon.

"Stoney, remember last night when—"

"I remember. I remember that's it's none of my business. I sure as hell don't understand it, but that don't change our friendship if that's what you're worried about."

"That's—I'm relieved to hear that—but what I have to tell you *might* change our friendship. The secret that we spoke of last night—"

"Should stay a secret. I don't want to hear. I don't want to know. I don't. I meant what I said, Bar. Whatever's going on between you and Hughes is—"

"Stoney, listen to me. What I'm trying to tell you is that. . . . Damn it to hell—I'm a girl."

"Girls say things like 'damn it to hell.' A Man would say 'fuck.' So you're the girl in the, uh, relationship. I was wondering how that all worked. I tried not thinking about it, but I confess, I wondered. I guessed you'd be the girl and Hughes the—"

"Stoney. Listen to me. I'm not a boy. At all. Period. I. Am. A girl." Barleigh wound her arms tightly around Stoney's waist and pulled herself close to him, hugging forcefully to his back and pressing her chest against him. "Do you feel these? These are breasts. *My* breasts."

"What the—" Stoney twisted himself in two as he spun around in the saddle to get a good look at Barleigh, his eyes as wide-open as his mouth. The quick movement caused him to jerk on the reins and pull too hard on the horse's mouth, which brought the gelding to a grinding stop. The combination of the horse's abrupt stop and Stoney's own centrifugal force spun him right out of the saddle, bringing Barleigh tumbling to the ground with him.

"Holy fuck," said Stoney, stumbling and dusting himself off as he grabbed for the reins. "But, I thought you—everyone thinks you—you're a boy. Are you going to tell me what the hell's going on?"

"Yes, yes I am. Everything I've told you about myself—"

"You ain't told me much except you're an orphan from Texas. Shit, I've learned more about you in the last twenty-four hours than I have since we joined up in Arkansas. About your grandpa teaching you cards. You wishing you wasn't his kin. And now this. It's no wonder you kept to yourself. I thought you was just the quiet type. But good God a 'mighty."

"Listen, Stoney, I need this job. I need the money. This is the only way, the only *decent* way, a single girl can earn a respectable wage." Barleigh's mind flashed over the remembrance of Mr. Goldthwaite and his indecent proposal, the memory giving her body a shudder.

"Holy fuck, and good God a 'mighty," Stoney said again, scratching his head.

"I'll tell you everything, but I'm begging you to keep my

secret. If you can't, I'll understand. I'll ride away and go back to Texas. I won't ask you to do anything against your conscience."

"Who said I had a conscience?" Stoney grinned and reached to shake Barleigh's hand. "I don't see any reason I should go blabbing your personal business around. Hell, I don't think anyone would believe me anyway. I want to know everything, but first, I want to know how you keep them . . ." He pointed at her chest. "I mean, what do you do with them when. . . . Well, ain't that something!"

"Normally, I keep them tightly bound. I wear baggy boy's clothes," she said, emotion overwhelming her. "Thank you, Stoney. You're a good friend." She shook his hand, one firm pump like a man. "Keep your horse at a slow walk back to town. There's a lot to tell you."

Stoney picked his sombrero up off the ground and knocked the dust off of it. He placed the big yellow hat onto his head, tightening the bolero under his chin. Grinning from ear to ear, he gathered the reins as he stepped into the stirrup, swinging over and down onto the saddle. He offered Barleigh a hand to assist her as she mounted behind him "Well," he laughed. "Well, ain't *them* something!"

CHAPTER FOURTEEN

NOVEMBER 26, 1860

Hughes awoke from a light, troubled sleep to the sound of footsteps in the hall. They were leaving from the room next door, the room that belonged to the Pony Express riders. He'd listened to those quick, sure footsteps before. He knew to whom they belonged.

Slipping out from under the warm covers, Hughes strode to the window and drew back the curtains, watching as Barleigh left on foot. She was carrying a canteen, but she didn't go to the stables as he anticipated she would. Instead, it appeared she was heading in the direction of the foothills. He wondered why she was walking. Then, his mind still in the half fog of sleep, he recalled the kisses they'd shared the previous night, of how good her body felt pressed against his, and he wondered why she wasn't here in his arms—or in his bed.

He shook his head and pounded his fists against his temples, then rubbed his eyes as he tried to get his mind straight. He was here to do a job for an old friend—to keep an eye on her daughter—and he'd strayed of course. How'd he let that happen? He'd better rein in that sense of protectiveness before it got him in trouble. But last night, it was a lot more than a sense of protectiveness he'd felt toward Barleigh.

When he'd returned to the hotel, a telegraph from Jameson had been waiting for him. It now lay open on his bedside table. Hughes reached for it, reading it again for the fourth time. It was brief, simply stating that Miss Leighselle Beauclaire was near death and that Doc Schmidt was keeping her sedated and peaceful. He offered little hope for an optimistic outcome.

Hughes threw the telegram in the trash. Sitting on the side of the bed, he leaned his head in his hands, raking his fingers through his hair. "Fuck." He pounded his fist on the table.

Restless, his mind unsettled, he paced the floor. On the mantel, the black marble and gold filigree clock ticked away at his thoughts as he walked back and forth between the walls of his room. He inspected his nails, picked at a grain of dirt, and looked again at the telegraph crumpled in the waste basket. Sending a reply to Jameson could wait—what he wanted to say couldn't be said. Yet.

Sooner or later, though, he'd have to tell Leighselle he couldn't continue keeping her secret—if Leighselle didn't die first.

He went to the window and threw it open, breathing in the cool, crisp air, clearing his mind. Feeling caged in, seeing the mountains, he had an urge to be outside. Moments later, Hughes was dressed and out the door.

After a brief stop in the kitchen, he hurried over to the stables. He ran a brush over his mare's glistening winter coat that had grown thick and dark. Picking up each hoof, he inspected the shoes, then saddled her while she finished her oats.

"All right, girl, let's go for a ride." He slipped the bridle in place and led her from the stall.

"Morning, Mr. Lévesque," said Mario as he forked hay into each stall. "Everyone's out and about early today. Bar took off afoot about an hour ago, then Stoney not too long after him. Now you. Seems everyone wants to leave town this morning. I might as well leave, too. Go someplace warm. Naples . . . or Venice."

"Good morning, Mario," said Hughes, swinging up into the saddle. "Did you wake up on the wrong side of the bed this morning? Feeling a little homesick, maybe?"

"Italy hasn't been 'home' in a long time. I'm just tired of my toes being cold. That's all. I hate cold toes. They put me in a sour mood." Mario leaned against a horse stall, frowning.

"I know what you mean, sir. I hate them, too." Hughes

made a mental note to buy Mario a warm pair of socks first chance he got. Reining his mare around and out the door, he almost collided head-first into Stoney's horse.

"Whoa," Hughes said, drawing back the reins.

Barleigh slid off the back side of Stoney's gelding, hopping to the ground. "Morning, Hughes. Mario." She ducked into the barn, grabbed a pitchfork, and busied herself with filling the remaining empty troughs with hay.

"Morning, Bar," Hughes said. "Stoney, how are you? All that pie and whiskey last night keep you awake with nightmares?"

"As a matter of fact, sir, I slept like a baby." Stoney dismounting and led his horse into the barn.

"Like a baby, eh," said Mario, standing in the doorway. "So what'd you do? Cry, then piss and shit the bed? Have fun cleaning that mess up."

"Ain't you ever the comedian?" Stoney slid the saddle off his horse, setting it on the stand in front of the stall, then looped the bridle over the horn.

"Bar, put down that pitchfork and go get some breakfast," said Mario. "Don't stray too far. Be ready to jump and ride. Supposed to be urgent mail coming out of California on this run."

"Can I take this run?" Stoney asked. "You don't have to pay me extra—I just need to get out of here for a while. Clear my head."

Mario looked at Stoney with a concerned expression. "You all right, son?"

"Fine, sir. I just miss my old eastbound route. I don't get to run it often enough. Not that it matters—the westbound run is fine, too. You know how it is. A man feels nostalgic every now and then —wants to revisit his beginnings. That all right with you, Bar?" he asked, a grin spreading across his face.

"If that's what you want to do, Stoney, it's all right by me," Barleigh answered.

"I'm glad we got that settled," said Mario, hurrying off with his pitchfork in hand. Then, shouting over his shoulder, "Like I told Bar, Stoney, don't stray too far. Be ready to jump and ride."

"I'm headed to the foothills, Bar. I wouldn't turn down

some company," said Hughes. "Weather this nice in November won't last long."

Their eyes met for a brief second before she turned away. "I don't know. I—"

"Go. It's a pretty day for a ride," said Stoney. "Here, I'll resaddle this gelding for you. He's probably wondering why such a short ride this morning, anyway."

"I can saddle my own horse, thanks." Bar led the gelding out of the stall and tied him to the grooming post. "What? You want to treat me like I'm your little sister?" She spat on the ground, then with her free hand readjusted her crotch. Looking at Hughes, she spat again for good measure.

Stoney gave a nervous laugh and looked from Barleigh to Hughes. "Hey, I didn't mean nothing. Just offering."

"What's got you so riled?" asked Mario, walking back in with a pitchfork full of fresh hay. "I saw you dance and get a kiss from Dorthea last night at the pie-eating contest. You should be in fine spirits this morning."

"Maybe Bar's in poor spirits because that's all he got, a dance and a kiss. That's still better than what some of us poor bastards went home with. Saddle up. Let's ride." Hughes spurred his horse away from the barn, anticipating Barleigh would follow. When he heard the sound of hoofbeats behind him, he eased his mare into a trot, pointing her toward the craggy, snow-capped mountains that flanked the sleeping city.

Silence lingered between them as they rode. The clear air, blue sky, and mild temperature induced a variety of birds into venturing out of their nests, the birds seeming happy to fill the quiet space with chattering and chirping.

As they neared the turn-off for the passage to the secret cave, Barleigh broke their silence. "A dance and a kiss is still better than what some of us poor bastards went home with? What were you expecting to go home with? A kiss you stole from me in a dark alley, which you led me down under unknown pretense—plus what else?"

Hughes threw back his head and laughed. "I was playing along, Miss 'I can saddle my own horse because I'm not your goddamned little sister' or whatever it was you said to Stoney. And for the record, I didn't steal that kiss in the alley. I took it. Taking and stealing are two different things."

"Oh really? Your semantics lesson impresses me." Barleigh leaned back in her saddle as the horses began their descent into the canyon, lessening the weight her horse was bearing forward of his withers.

The steep passage into the cave required their precise attention, and conversation was sparse. The snowmelt and refrozen ground created a treacherous pathway. Rocks and gravel slipped under foot, and both horses dropped their noses to the ground, careful to pick and choose their way to safe footing.

"We should picnic here in the glade instead of in the cave," said Barleigh, once they had reached the hidden clearing. She dismounted and looped the reins over a low-hanging branch.

"Out in the open where you feel safe that I won't take advantage of you?" Hughes stood next to his mare and studied Barleigh, his eyes clouded and dark.

Barleigh cocked her head and looked at him, a confused expression on her face.

"I didn't promise you last night that I wouldn't want to kiss you. I promised you last night that I wouldn't kiss you again. I keep my promises." He turned away, the memory of the telegraph concerning Leighselle flooding his mind, and he couldn't look at Barleigh. He kept his promises, all right, even those he hated keeping.

"I meant out in the open where the sky's so blue and the weather's fine for a picnic. What's wrong?" Barleigh stepped forward and put her hand on his arm. "Are you all right?"

He stared at her hand on his arm—wanted to pick it up, to kiss each finger, to not stop there but to kiss her palm, the length of her arm, to kiss his way to her mouth and more. "Yes, I'm all right."

He patted her hand like one would a child's, then moved it away. "A picnic here in the glade is what we'll do, then." Reaching for his saddlebag, he lifted it from behind the cantle and set it on the ground. He removed the contents and arranged the plates and food on the unrolled blanket.

"You sure pack a fancy picnic," said Barleigh, picking up the linen napkin and the cut crystal glass.

"Growing up in New Orleans, I was used to my mother serving a fancy brunch on Sundays, complete with French champagne. She'd splash a little orange juice in it sometimes, for color. Here." He handed Barleigh a glass, the brush of her finger against his setting his nerves on edge.

Barleigh sipped. "Mmm. Wonderful. New Orleans? Is that where you're from? If you recall me saying last night, my grandfather spent time there."

"I recall a lot about last night. *À votre santé.*" Hughes lifted his glass and sipped. "To your health."

"*À votre santé.* Are you sure it doesn't mean 'let's change the subject'?"

Hughes smiled at her. "I grew up in New Orleans. My father owns Lévesque Sugarcane and Shipping. He built Lévesque Plantation with the engineering plans from Thomas Jefferson's Monticello home. Besides sugarcane, he raises thoroughbreds."

"Tell me more, please." Barleigh sipped her champagne.

"Yes, ma'am," said Hughes, refilling their glasses. "Actually, the horses are my mother's doing. Father *allows* her to raise them. I have a twin brother, John-Pierre, who's taken over most duties with the businesses. I left New Orleans when I was eighteen or so—became a Texas Ranger. Now, I do certain jobs for the government that no one else will. That's my story in a nutshell. Now, may we call a truce for the day? You seem angry with me."

"I'm not angry. I'm nervous that if my secret gets found out and I lose this job—"

"Then what? What's the worst that could happen?" He handed her a plate. "Sorry, the food is a little sparse."

"Thank you." She nibbled on a small piece of smoked bacon. "The worst? I go back to Texas without enough money to pay the taxes on my ranch. Then the bank forecloses and I lose the deed. I told you. I'm not dressing up and pretending to be a boy for the thrill of the masquerade. This is not a game I'm playing."

"That poker stake you won last night isn't enough? How's

that cut on your head, by the way?" He reached out to inspect it but Barleigh drew back.

"It's fine, thanks," she said, pulling away from his touch. "The money helps a great deal, but no, not enough."

"How much are the taxes? I'll give you the rest of the money." Hughes shifted on the blanket and refilled the champagne glasses.

"Why? Because you're a wealthy plantation owner? How many slaves does it take to run a sugarcane and thoroughbred plantation? Do your slaves work at your shipping yards, too?" She swallowed the remainder of the champagne in one gulp, coughing at the stinging in her throat as it went down.

Hughes leaned back on his elbows, biting his tongue, trying to keep his anger in check. "My father is the owner of Lévesque Sugarcane and Shipping. Don't judge me based on what you think you know."

He settled a steady gaze on her, clenching and unclenching his jaw at the memory of his father shoving a pocketful of money at him—telling him not to come back. He'd learned more of how to be a man from Okwara, the plantation slave, than from his father.

"I was wrong to judge. The idea of you giving me money that was earned off the backs of slaves set me off. Please forgive me."

"Forgiven and forgotten. But boy, you sure can go from a friendship truce to firing with both barrels in the flash of an eye."

"My father said my fiery temper was a gift from my mother. I wouldn't know, firsthand. She died when I was born." Barleigh shrugged her shoulders.

"I'm sorry." Hughes drew in a deep breath, then let it out slowly.

"Besides the taxes, there's also the matter of rebuilding the house, the barn. Animals to replace. . . ." Barleigh shuddered, started to say something more, but looked away.

Laying on the picnic blanket watching her, Hughes tried to follow her gaze but it led to nowhere in particular that he could discern. Hearing her speak those words, saying that her mother died in childbirth, made him sick to his stomach. His jaw clinched, his eyes darkened, but he wouldn't allow her to see his reaction— he was well versed in the art of secrecy.

He waited in patient silence for her to gather her thoughts, hoping she would let down a little of the wall she'd built between them—the barrier she'd fashioned between her and the rest of the world.

She looked back at him, her brow furrowed, and said in such a soft voice that he had to sit up and lean forward to hear. "A midnight Indian raid. . . . The night of the Comanche moon. Birdie, Papa, and Uncle Jack, all were killed. Aunt Winnie and I hid in the goat shed down in the cellar with my new baby sister, Starling. That night, the moon was so big—so bright. Beautiful, yet terrifying. It spotlighted a swarm of Comanche up on the Brazos River ridge. I saw them as clearly as I knew they saw us."

Hughes put his hands on her arms, turning her more to face him. "That night, what else do you remember?"

"I remember Papa being worried about the worsening skirmishes between the Reservation Indians and the settlers in the area. But Papa said it wasn't the Reservation Indians doing the attacking." Barleigh's voice quivered.

"Who did he say it was?" asked Hughes.

"He said it was either white men doing it and blaming it on the Reservation Indians, or it was Quanah Parker's band of Comanche. There had been reports of Quanah raiding in the area, according to Papa's friend, Captain Goodnight. You might know Charlie Goodnight. He's a Texas Ranger, too."

"He's a friend." Cold sweat beaded on Hughes's forehead and his gut tightened. He sat his plate on the blanket and stood, removed his hat, and ran his hands through his hair.

But Quanah Parker was in San Antonio. Could he have traveled that far in a day or two? A Comanche on horseback riding hard can cover 250 miles or more in twenty-four hours, stealing fresh mounts along the way. It was possible. . . .

"What are you thinking? You look like you've seen a ghost," Barleigh said.

"I'm trying to figure out if Quanah Parker could have been

in—" Hughes stopped himself, trying to remember if Barleigh had shared with him where she was from, or if he was remembering it from his tracking her down.

"Been in what?"

"When, exactly, was the raid on your ranch? The date? And, did you tell me where in Texas you lived?"

"The raid happened Friday, September the twenty-seventh. Just after midnight. And, no, I haven't told you where I'm from. My land is in Palo Pinto, a half day's ride west of Fort Worth on the Brazos River."

"When you saw the mounted warriors on the ridge, could you make them out clearly? Could you see if there seemed to be a leader, or chief, and if so, what color was his horse?" Hughes drilled his questions, his words coming rapid-fire.

"There were so many, well over a hundred. I'm certain there was a leader who gave the signal to attack. I don't recall the color of his horse. White, maybe?"

Hughes paced back and forth, then walked to where the horses stood tied. He rested his forehead against his mare's neck, breathing in the woodsy, familiar smell of a sweaty horse. That smell always took him back to his first memory. It was the smell of his childhood and the hours he spent racing his pony through the mossy woods of his home.

"Damn it to hell." His booming voice and his fists pounding against the saddle caused his horse to nicker and shy away.

The words of Jerry Allsup, the obese blackjack dealer in San Antonio, rang in his head: "*Mark my words, but you'll regret not killing that son of a bitch while you had the chance.*" And he was right. Hughes now regretted not having killed Quanah Parker, even if his warriors would have filled him with their arrows.

"Hughes?"

He turned and saw her looking at him with fear and concern in her cat-like eyes that reminded him of Leighselle's, the only difference their color The tilt of her head, the slope of her nose, the point of her chin, her fine cheekbones, her gracefulness even while dressed like a boy, gripped his heart.

"You look so much like . . ." He ran a hand down his face, shutting off the thought.

"I look so much like what?" she asked, standing, moving cautiously closer.

"Nothing, Barleigh. You remind me of someone I know. End of story. We better go. I have a long ride tomorrow."

He rolled the plates and glasses together in the blanket, tossing the food aside, throwing out the rest of the champagne. One of the crystal glasses banged against a plate and splintered into a spider's web of cracks.

"Goddamnit." He hurled the broken glass against a rock. Picking up the other glass, he threw it, too, sending shards of fine, leaded crystal flying into the air.

Barleigh placed a gentling hand on his arm. "Hey. Hey. Easy. Let me help you with putting these things away. What's wrong?"

Hughes shrugged off her hand. "No. Don't. Just. . . . Please get on your horse. I'm in a hurry."

There was a letter to write. He would beg Leighselle to stop this damned lie—he couldn't do it anymore. If Barleigh knew she had a mother—that her mother had paid the taxes on her land— Barleigh would go home and would stop this dangerous masquerade she was playing.

"Hughes, what have I done? What's wrong?" Barleigh followed him as he slung his saddlebag over the cantle, tying it in place with the leather latigo. "Look at me. What have I done?" She stood close behind him, waiting for an answer.

Turning around, Hughes looked down and into her eyes, which were the color of the sky. He reached out his hand, stroked her cheek, rubbing his thumb across a smudge of dirt. Lifting her bangs and seeing her cut forehead, he traced around the bandage with his finger.

"I don't know how in the world you have everyone fooled into thinking you're a boy. You're so pretty. So very pretty." His voice sounded sad and weary.

"People believe what they want to believe, or what they're told to believe. What have I done to anger you? Something's changed."

"You've done nothing. I've just come to the conclusion that you've been right all along. I should've never kissed you. I don't have the time or the luxury to worry about you," he said, a firm set to his jaw.

"The luxury? I didn't ask you to worry about me. You appointed yourself to that role. And you don't have to speak to me in such a rude fashion. You don't have to speak to me at all, as far as I'm concerned. What I'm trying to accomplish would have far fewer risks if you and I never crossed paths again." She folded her arms against her chest.

"Have it your way. Barleigh." He turned and swung into the saddle, guiding his mare up the steep grade and away from the cave.

The ride back into town was even more silent than the ride out. Hughes rode ahead of Barleigh, keeping his mare at a fast trot. Each time she caught up with him, he would speed up just enough to make it obvious that he didn't want to ride side by side.

*****

Barleigh reined her gelding to a stop at the end of the road and watched as Hughes led his mare into the barn. He never once looked back to see if she was behind. She had wanted him to leave her alone. She had pushed him away—told him to never kiss her again, to never speak to her again. So why did she feel like her heart was shattering like the crystal glasses he'd smashed against the boulders?

Minutes later, she watched as he left carrying his saddlebags in one hand, something clutched in the other. He headed for the Salt Lake House across the street. Barleigh squeezed her heels and clucked, "Come on, boy, walk on." The gelding complied, responding to the gentle cue.

"Mr. Lévesque was sure in a foul mood," said Big Brody as he swept the center aisle of the barn. "Didn't say nothing to me. He scribbled a quick message for the Carson City mail, asked Mario to have Carson City telegraph it to San Antonio, and then he grabbed a bottle of whiskey and left."

So that's what he was carrying.

"I can't say. We rode together for a while before he took off on his own. Said something about a big job tomorrow." Barleigh finished currying the gelding and put him in his stall with a fresh pail of water and scoop of oats. "Stoney already gone?"

"He rode out a few seconds ago. That's his dust hanging on the wind." Big Brody nodded over his shoulder toward the wide, double doors that were slid open, allowing fresh air into the barn.

Barleigh peered down the road but Stoney was out of sight. "A bit late leaving, wasn't he?"

"Mail was late coming in. Some problem back down the line, don't know what for sure. Say, just so you know. . . ." Big Brody lowered his voice. "Mario ordered me to take that Mexican sombrero of his and burn it. Today. You might want to hide it someplace."

"Mario can go to hell," said Barleigh, giving Brody a thank you nod. A good spit on the ground was called for.

"I've been to hell," said Mario as he walked in the door, slapping Barleigh on the back. "Hell's living for eighty-seven days in the steerage of a cargo ship and fighting over who gets the fattest rat for your one meal of the day. It's seeing your mother and father's bodies tossed overboard along with the rest of the stinking trash. Hell's being ten years old and alone in New York City, someone stealing your shoes off your feet while you slept. Waking up hungry. Picking through horse shit with your bare hands, searching for the undigested oats. I've been to hell."

Big Brody rolled his eyes and shrugged his shoulders, and then went back to sweeping.

"I didn't mean that, Mario," said Barleigh. "Yes, sir, that sounds like hell to me, too."

"Don't mind me." Mario gave a dismissive wave of his hands. "My toes are cold. So, what'd you do, Bar? Lévesque came back sullen and looking for a good drunk."

"I didn't do anything," she said, a little too defensively she thought.

"Maybe he's lonely for his lady friend in San Antonio that he's writing to," said Mario with a mischievous grin. "Maybe his toes and other body parts need warmed."

"Maybe it's because I told him he couldn't have Dorthea, that I wanted her all for myself." Barleigh spat on the ground and left the barn, the sounds of laughter from Mario and Big Brody following her out the door.

Barleigh crossed the wide street as she made her way toward the hotel, wanting nothing more than to go back to bed, crawl under the covers, pull the sheet over her head, and hibernate for the rest of the day. She missed Aunt Winnie—missed Starling. She missed Texas. She wanted to go home, even if home was just a burned piece of land.

"Hey, watch where you're walking," said a gruff voice, reeling from the surprise impact of two people colliding. The speech was slurred, the clothes reeking with alcohol, dirt, sweat, and urine.

"Excuse me, I'm so sorry," said Barleigh. "I guess my feet didn't know where to be."

"In a holy place of worship is where you should be," said the old man, straightening his sour-smelling coat. "It's Sunday morning."

"And where should you be then?" asked Barleigh.

"That's none of your business. But if you could spare a few coins to cover my breakfast, I'll forget about your rude behavior." The stinking suit held out his hand.

Barleigh fished around in her pockets and came out with some coins, handing them over to the old man. "Enjoy your breakfast. I'll forget about your rude behavior, too."

"Thank you, miss. God bless you."

Barleigh stopped in her tracks and stared into the old man's watery, bloodshot eyes. "What did you say?"

"I said thank you, miss, and God bless you. That was all. You ain't going to make trouble for me, are you?"

"No. No trouble. Blessings, or whatever, to you too." Barleigh tossed him another coin and went into the hotel.

Thank you, Miss? Miss? What the hell am I doing here?

The room was dark, quiet, the four bunk beds that Big Brody and Yates shared along with the new stock handlers, Lars and Liam, were empty. The two single beds, hers and Stoney's, were empty as well. With everyone gone, she had the room to herself for a change. No having to lie here listening to farting and belching—no disgusting, raunchy humor about women's genitalia, and then pretending to laugh.

Barleigh lay across her bead, stretching out over the top of the covers, enjoying the quiet. Getting comfortable, she kicked off her boots, loosened the cord on her shirt, and untucked the ends.

She turned her head and looked at the wall between her and Hughes's room, trying to envision what he was doing. Would he be lying on his bed with his boots kicked off? With his shirt off? Would he be sitting by the window, sipping his whiskey? Why would he need whiskey this early in the day? Why was he kind one minute, then rude and sullen the next? Was he missing someone—his lady-love in San Antonio?

Why do I care about any of this?

Barleigh slid out of bed and tiptoed over to the wall, pressing her ear against it, trying to make out the muffled sounds next door. She heard voices and wondered who he was speaking to. Was he talking to himself? Did he talk in his sleep? She wondered what it would be like to sleep in his bed, to feel his naked body against hers if she woke up during the night. She pressed harder against the wall, imagining it was Hughes's body she was feeling pressing against hers in return, like their bodies did their last kiss.

The bedroom door swung open and Big Brody and Lars stood in the hallway, Lars's hand on the doorknob as they entered the room.

"What are you doing, Bar? Eavesdropping on Lévesque?" asked Big Brody.

Barleigh jumped away from the wall, kicking the bed frame in the process. "Ouch! Fuck that hurt." She bounced around on one foot, holding the big toe of the other. "You surprised me."

"We can see that. Why were you listening in on Mr. Lévesque's room?" Big Brody asked, looking suspicious.

"I, uh . . . I thought I might have heard a woman's voice in there with him. I just wanted to know what it sounded like when a man and a woman, you know, might be, uh . . ."

Big Brody belted out a laugh. "You mean you've never

been with a woman? You don't know what a woman sounds like when she's in the throes of passion?"

"I didn't mean any harm." Barleigh sat on the side of her bed massaging her sore toe. "Why are you looking at me like that? Just—just go fuck off, all right?"

Big Brody and Lars looked at each other, then at Barleigh. As if on cue, both had her by each arm, forcing her boots on her feet, grabbing her coat, and dragging her out the door.

"What are you doing? Put me down." Barleigh struggled, but it was no use. "I said let me go."

"Let's all go fuck off," laughed Lars. "Let's all go fuck off at the whorehouse."

"Exactly what I was thinking," said Big Brody, laughing even harder. "Bar, you won't have to wonder anymore what a woman sounds like. You'll experience it firsthand and then be thanking us from here to the other side of next Sunday."

Hughes's door opened a crack and he stuck his head out into the hallway. "What's all the commotion?"

"We've decided to take a little walk over to see some of Miss Maeve's girls. Bar seems to have a curious streak this morning that needs satisfying," said Lars. "If you're not already so engaged, please feel free to join us."

"That's an invitation I don't believe I should pass up. Give me a minute to pull on my boots." Hughes slammed the door.

"Those women don't work on Sunday mornings" Barleigh looked from one, to the other. "Do they?"

"In this town? That's when they're the busiest." Big Brody quickened his steps.

"Amen and Oh, God, Oh, God." Lars stepped up his pace to keep even with Big Brody.

*****

French perfume and sweet cigar smoke scented the air in the dimly lit rooms at Miss Maeve's Boarding House. Girls in scanty costumes and in various stages of undress lounged about on billowy pillows, some wearing gaudy amounts of rouge and lipstick, some wearing none at all. The ones wearing none at all saddened Barleigh the most—they looked so young, fresh, and unspoiled.

"Here's something for you, Miss Maeve," said Lars, handing her a silver dollar. "Pick someone nice for our friend, Bar. It's his first time going upstairs. Someone nice, like Berta." Lars and Big Brody winked at each other, then strolled over to the pillowed floor and selected rouged and lipsticked girls for their own pleasures.

Hughes motioned to Maeve, privately slipping her a five-dollar gold piece. "Buffalo Berta might be a little frightening for what we want to accomplish today. It's Bar's first time. He should have the most experienced woman here. Miss Maeve herself."

"Anything for you, Hughes," said Miss Maeve, batting her eyelashes like a shy schoolgirl. She held out a hand for Barleigh, the sound of her throaty voice filling the air. "Come with me, boy. But when we're done, no one can call you a boy any longer."

Barleigh laughed out loud.

Hughes took Miss Maeve by her elbow and pulled her aside. Whispering something to her, he handed her another five-dollar gold piece. Miss Maeve surreptitiously glanced at Barleigh for a mere second, nodding as Hughes spoke, smiling, and nodding again.

"My special service? I'd be delighted to give Bar my extra special service," Miss Maeve said loud enough for everyone to hear. She looked at Barleigh and winked.

An hour later, Barleigh and Maeve prepared to step out from the room. Miss Maeve pinched her cheeks to make them appear flush with color, mussed her hair and threw a lacy robe over her shoulders.

"What a pleasure it was meeting you, Barleigh. I must say, this was the most surprising morning I've had in a long time. And, the most pleasure I've had earning money, just by sharing a little 'girl talk.' Don't worry, honey, your secret's safe with me."

"Thank you, Miss Maeve. What an enlightening hour. I haven't had another woman to talk to in a while. I hope I didn't shock you with all my questions."

"Miss Maeve's not shocked by much." The woman gave a hearty laugh.

"Growing up without a mother, I've only had my imagination to guide me about the intimacies between a man and a woman." Barleigh blushed, recalling in vivid detail some of Miss Maeve's explicit descriptions. "I'll give some thought to what you said about Hughes—the way a man like him can go from kissing me one minute to almost killing two men the next."

"It wasn't just about Hughes, it was about most men. The good ones have a strong need to protect the weaker sex. You can't fight it or ask them to go against it. It's in their nature. Especially for a man like Hughes—it's *sacred* to his nature. You can use it to your advantage. Not manipulatively, but fairly, where each one gets what they need."

"But, I don't know what I need."

"Then you keep looking until you discover it. The trick is to never give up till you find it, honey. You'll do just fine. Now, speaking about all men, looks like your buddies are waiting for you. I'll put on a show of it. Watch this." She pinched her cheeks again, re-fluffed her hair, and proceeded to enthrall everyone with a breathless story of pure, sensual delight.

"Well, well, congratulations, Bar. Who would've thought a little guy like you had it in you to take care of a woman like Miss Maeve?" Big Brody slapped Barleigh on the back, a look of admiration on his face.

"And for a whole hour, too," added Lars. "My first time? I had my pants back up and cinched in less than five minutes. Or, did I even get them all the way down before I finished?" His thoughts and words trailed off.

"Lars and I want to stay here a while, see what other trouble we can scare up, then maybe go over to Whiskey Street. Want to stay with us? Romeo?" Big Brody laughed, slapping Barleigh on the back again. "Now that you've got your first one under your belt, you might as well give Buffalo Berta a ride."

"Thanks, but no. I'll wait for Hughes to, uh, finish, to come, to uh, come down the stairs. Then I'll head back to the house." Barleigh looked up the stairs, hoping to see Hughes.

"Oh, Mr. Lévesque didn't stay," said one of the young, fresh-faced girls wearing no makeup and lounging on the pile of pillows. "He said he had other important work to take care of." She pouted, trying to act affronted.

"You two have fun," Barleigh said, giving a knowing smile. "I think I'll go hibernate a while. A man needs his rest after all that excitement."

After thanking Miss Maeve again, Barleigh walked back to the Salt Lake House alone. With hands in pockets, she passed the large plate-glass window in front of the mercantile store. She stepped back and studied her reflection, wondering what Hughes saw when he looked at her.

She saw rowelled spurs strapped around tall-heeled, knee-high boots, the black leather polished but worn. Blue tweed dungarees tucked into her boot tops. Yellow buckskin shirt threaded up the front closure with a leather cord. Yellow bandana tied around her neck in place of a pearl necklace. Heavy, oil-skin slicker lined in thick sheep's wool that hung to the ground. Colt .45 strapped to her hip that she'd learned not to leave at home. Brown, short-brimmed, short-crowned western hat she tightened down with a sturdy latigo and a silver concho, the concho for show because she liked the way it looked. Boy-short hair in need of a cut and a comb. Fringed leather gloves to keep her calloused hands warm. An image of the weaker sex in need of a man's protection? Hardly.

Barleigh took a step closer to the window and contemplated her appearance a moment longer, taking in her expression, pondering the face staring back. Plain. No makeup. Like the young, fresh-faced girls at Miss Maeve's who looked like they didn't belong in their jobs, either. She turned and walked away toward the Salt Lake House, feeling tired and melancholy.

How fortunate, though, I only have to ride horses for a living.

*****

Someone banging on the door awoke Barleigh from her sleep, the insistent pounding growing louder. "Wake up. Are you in there?"

Where was everyone else? Barleigh felt disoriented. Normally, at least one other rider was sleeping in the bunk room at any given time. She shuffled to the door in her red long johns, the warm thermal underwear her basic uniform when not in riding attire.

"Coming. Hold on." Soft light filtering in the window around the curtains indicated it was not yet evening. A glance at the clock showed it to be half past four in the afternoon—she'd almost slept the day away.

"Yes, what is it?" She opened the door a crack and peeked outside.

Hughes was slumped against the wall in disheveled clothes, his hair a mess, a five o'clock shadow peppering his jaw. Too many whiskeys etched the lines on his face. She wanted to jump into his arms, or to pull him into the room, but she reminded herself that that's not what a Pony Express rider would do.

"Lévesque. You look like shit."

"Thank you. You look delicious," he whispered.

"You're drunk."

"You're astute." He held up a bottle of Baer Brothers' whiskey already three quarters empty and took another swig.

"Why are you here?"

"I went to the barn to check on my mare—"

"Even drunk, you remembered your priorities before passing out. Good for you." She stepped back, closing the door.

"Listen to me," Hughes said, brushing aside her remark, his boot forcing the door open. In a loud voice, speech slurred, he said, "Stoney . . . he's missing. His horse came back to the barn without him. The mochila's gone, too. There was blood—a bloody handprint—on the horse's neck." Hughes leaned against the door frame for balance.

"Oh, dear God. That can't be." Barleigh rushed back into the room, pulling on her clothes. Shouting over her shoulder, she asked, "Is there someone out looking for him?"

"Mario sent Big Brody and Brody's little brother—what's his name—Yates?" Hughes called from the hallway.

"Right, Yates." Barleigh ran out the door, pushing past Hughes, sending him spinning like a top. As she left, she grabbed Stoney's Mexican sombrero from the hat rack, putting it on for good luck.

Hughes steadied himself against the wall and stumbled toward his door. Nodding to the two men peering from out of their doorway that was across the hall from the Pony Express room, he raised his bottle in an invitation.

"Evening, gents. Share a toast?" He slung back another gulp and held out the bottle.

The door closed, the lock clicking in place.

Inside his room, Hughes emptied the tea from the whiskey bottle back into the silver tea server. Then, he refilled the whiskey bottle with its original contents of Baer Brothers' from his canteen, minus the two shots he'd allowed himself after the morning's ride with Barleigh. The third and fourth shots missing from the bottle had helped to steady him after he awoke from an unrestful nap and a fitful dream of Quanah Parker engaged in a bloody raid on a North Texas homestead.

After running a quick razor across his face and a comb through his hair, he pulled on his uniform of the night: black trousers, black shirt, vest, and topcoat. Black boots, black gloves, and black hat.

Looking at his image in the mirror, he told himself, "You don't have the luxury of worrying about her. You have a job to do."

He slipped out the window, closing it behind him.

CHAPTER FIFTEEN

NOVEMBER 26, 1860

A lone figure dashed from the Salt Lake House Hotel, almost running headlong into a scrawny lad standing out front on the sidewalk. Holding an extra edition for the *Deseret News – The Pony Dispatch*, the boy called out to passersby that the Southern secession movement was gaining momentum. He pointed to the headlines as proof. The bold type announced that South Carolina, Georgia, and Mississippi had called for a special session of the legislature for the election of delegates to a secession convention.

Barleigh apologized to the boy as she sped past, ignoring the headlines.

"Mario," she shouted as she ran into the barn, trying to push down the panic rising from her gut. "Mario, where are you?"

"Over here." He came out of a stall leading a small brown mare that was tacked up and ready. "I knew you'd be coming as soon as you got word. I can't tell you not to go, though I wish you wouldn't. Brody and Yates are already out looking."

"I have to." Barleigh took the reins from Mario.

"Don't forget, you're on duty tomorrow."

"I haven't forgotten," she said, double checking the cinch.

"Is Mr. Lévesque riding with you?" asked Mario, looking over Barleigh's shoulder toward the door. "I expected he would."

"Lévesque is drunk off his ass. He can barely walk, let alone ride." Barleigh stepped into the saddle, the reins heavy in her hands. The hard, oiled leather strips were beginning to stiffen as

251

the temperature started to slide.

Mario looked confused. "He was here earlier. Didn't seem drunk to me."

"He was beyond drunk," she said, annoyed again at the thought. "Anyway, what happens if I'm not back by morning?"

"What do you mean, if you're not back?"

"I'm not coming back until I find Stoney. What if it takes longer? What if I—" She dropped her gaze down to her gloved hands holding the stiffening reins. She slapped the leather hard against her palm.

A tangle of emotions caused Barleigh's breath to catch, and keeping her voice from shaking took considerable effort. The thought of heading back to Texas had been planted in her mind— the notion of quitting the Pony Express now a sprouting seed.

"After I find Stoney," she said, "it might be a good time for me to leave—to go home."

Mario patted the mare on the neck. "You'll like Little Brownie. She's surefooted and swift. Take an extra bedroll and an extra canteen of coffee. The nice warm day we enjoyed today was a teaser. There's a nor'easter blowing in. I can already feel the change."

He fixed the bugle and both canteens to the saddle horn and tied them with the latigo, then put an extra coat inside the bedroll, reattaching it to the cantle. "Lars or Liam can fill in if you're not back in the morning. We'll talk about you going home after you find Stoney."

"Yes, sir. Thanks, Mario."

"I'm glad to see you wearing that damned sombrero. The wide brim will help keep the snow off you," he said, a twinkle in his eye.

Barleigh gave Mario a salute, touching the edge of her hand to the sombrero, and nodded. "Yes, sir, it will."

"Be careful, son." As she rode out of the stables, Mario drew the barn doors closed against the chilling wind.

Reining the mare around, Barleigh rode east, following Stoney's mail route. A few stars poked holes into the darkening sky as a cold, gusty north wind spilled over the Wasatch Mountains.

The gale shook from the sky a few fat snowflakes, and they fell hard to the ground like round, white coins.

The way into Parley's Canyon felt familiar, and Little Brownie seemed to know the way. The route was clear and solid, the footing good, the pace even. She kept the mare at a fast, steady trot, listening, calling out Stoney's name, listening again. Barleigh kept her eyes peeled and ears open for anything out of the ordinary.

Through Emigration Canyon, up Mountain Dell and Big Mountain Pass, thoughts of the first time they rode into Salt Lake played across her mind. She recalled the excitement she and Stoney had felt at nearing the end of their first long ride. They had whooped and hollered, putting on quite the show of it for travelers on the Overland Stage

Like a wild banshee, Stoney's lusty whoops had filled the air. Waving his hat at the travelers, he'd dropped his horse right over the edge of the mountain, fearless, and rode it down like he was floating on a river current. The jubilant expression he'd had on his face was of pure joy. Recalling their shared experience on that ride, as she now covered the same ground on Little Brownie, hardened her resolve to find him.

At Webber Canyon Station, she caught up with Big Brody and Yates who had stopped to rest and change horses. She had changed once at Mountain Dell, but decided to change again, even though her pace had been slow and steady, the horse not yet played out.

"We're going to double back from here," said Brody. "They say Stoney never made it this far, that Big Mountain Pass was the last he checked in. I'm riding a bit off the trail to the north; Yates is riding a bit off the trail to the south. What's your plan, Bar?"

"I'll make a few circles around Webber Station, maybe go as far as Echo Canyon, and then come back here by morning," she said. Stoney could be anywhere in between if he were hurt.

It was near midnight when Barleigh left Webber Station. Snow fell nonstop and covered the ground several inches deep in places, deeper where the drifts blew against rocks and trees. The woolen poncho hung from her shoulders, draping over the saddle and covering her legs all the way down to her boots.

In the upper elevation, the snow was more powdery than what fell down in the valley, and the horse had to push through it instead of walking over a sold pack. The temperature dropped throughout the night until it settled near zero.

Riding northeast from Webber Station, Barleigh aimed for the foothills of the Red Bluffs that ran in an obtuse line against the level plane of the Webber River Valley. From there, she circled around to the northwest, then crossed Echo Creek to head south, making a sweeping circle of the icy valley as she curved northeast again to her starting point.

The moon cast a slight illumination across the snow, allowing some light to shine on an otherwise dark night. Barleigh decided to make her circle wider, going farther off the trail. Deeper into the trees and scrub brush, she crisscrossed the creek, fording the low-water crossing of the river.

On the bank of the Webber where the snow had yet to accumulate to more than a dusting, something caught her eye. Moonlight glinted against the shape of on object contrasting with its surroundings. Dismounting, she bent over what looked to be an arrow. She picked it up. The blue-gray flint tip was smeared with dried blood. After tying it into her bedroll, she remounted and spurred her horse toward Head of Canyon Station.

Colonel Hill, the station master, wasn't a colonel as far as anyone knew, but everyone called him Colonel because his fists were quick to remind folks that he preferred to be addressed as such. Colonel Hill said he had not seen or heard of Indians in the area, and was sorry to hear about Stoney.

"I like that boy. I sure hope you find him all right. But shouldn't you stay put till morning? At least till it stops snowing?"

"It could snow for days," Barleigh said, saddling a small but stout, coppery colored mare. "I'm riding to Cache Cave."

Because of where she had found the arrow on the Webber River as she rode out of Echo Canyon, she knew the logical place to look for Stoney pointed to Cache Cave. If she had Indians chasing her, that's where she'd try to get.

"You'll cross the watershed between the Bear River and the Webber River. The terrain should be frozen. Mostly. Where it's not, might be patchy quicksand. Be careful, son."

"Yes, sir. Thank you, Colonel."

Riding out in the open, she felt vulnerable, jumpy at sounds, suspicious of shadows. The snow had tapered off and the moon hung like a bright ball in the dark sky, with a scattering of clouds flitting by. The trees and scrub had become sparse, and the flat open ground between the two river valleys left little means of protection. She kept her eyes on the ground, looking for more arrows or other signs. She no longer called out Stoney's name for fear someone else might hear her, too.

Overhead, the full moon shadowed her, reminding her of the powers and perils of its beauty—to see and to be seen. She wondered what name was given to the moon by the people of the mountains.

Barleigh whispered a song under her breath, each word forming an icy cloud in front of her face. "I see the moon; the moon sees me. I ran away from the Co-man-che."

The ground surrounding the watershed was crunchy underfoot, but in several places her horse's balance faltered where the hard-pack wasn't frozen solid. The weight of the animal broke through the top layer and the mare lurched forward, seeking solid footing. Dismounting, Barleigh walked next to the horse to ease the animal's strain.

Wanting the warmth of the hot liquid in her belly, she reached for the canteen tied to the saddle. The two canteens were bound together along with the bugle, and the leather strap was dallied tight around the saddle's horn. Her numb fingers fumbled with the stubborn knot. Giving up, she took her knife and cut the leather, removing all three from the saddle.

"Whoa, whoa now. What's wrong with you?" She spoke softly, trying to reassure the frightened mare. Barleigh darted her eyes left and right, hoping to spy whatever had driven the horse into a sudden panic.

Sidestepping and rearing, head high, eyes wide, the mare whinnied in a horse's nervous way. Barleigh tightened her grip on the reins and followed the horse's movement, jogging forward toward the mare as the panicked horse shuffled backward.

"Easy, girl. Easy," Barleigh soothed.

The frightened horse whinnied again, shaking her head left and right. Rearing, pawing the air with slashing hooves, she jerked the reins free and bolted into the darkness.

Barleigh dropped to all fours, pressing low to the ground. She made a quick sweep with her eyes, looking in all directions, seeing nothing, but sensing—something. Huddled under the poncho, she crouched on her haunches, sipping from one of the canteens as the spotlight moon lent its soft, silvery light to the crunchy, frozen earth.

"Damn it to hell," she cursed. "And yes, Stoney, that's exactly what a girl would say."

Looking at the dark line of the rocky ridge and the formation called The Needles, she knew she must be close to Cache Cave. Hanging the two canteens and the bugle around her neck, she stood to leave when something in the low sagebrush—a flash of yellow—caught her attention. She settled back down under her poncho, waiting, watching. But, she was the one being watched.

A pair of eyes glinting in the glare of the moonlit snow peered out from the thicket of sagebrush about one hundred yards to the north near the base of the ridge.

What are you, wolf or coyote?

Barleigh waited several long minutes before the eyes disappeared, then reappeared moments later, closer, alongside another pair. And another. Then another. The hair on the back of her neck stood on end. Turning around, slow and deliberate, she saw two pairs of eyes, shiny and bright and reflecting the silvery moon. They watched her every move.

Left and right, more eyes appeared.

The Colt revolver she carried had only five bullets loaded. With the extra cartridge in her pocket, she had ten shots in all. Counting the pairs of eyes surrounding her, she realized that if every animal attacked at once, she'd be several bullets short of defending herself. That's if all shots hit their mark. She holstered the pistol, saving the bullets for a possible worse threat.

With Cache Cave to her right, she began easing backward

in its direction. Staying low, going slow, not making any threatening movements, she pivoted her head to the left, to the right, and to the rear, watching each side. Removing the sombrero, she gripped it in her left hand, the bugle in her right, and crept toward the cave.

One brave animal made an advance. She bugled her horn as loudly as she could blow and flapped the sombrero at the stalking creature. He shrank back into the darkness. Another approached. She bugled and waved. Again, it was frightened away. Another, then another tested, and each time, the noise from the horn and the flapping of the sombrero scared the hungry animals back into the shadows.

A male and female hunting pair advanced together, flanking left and right. Whirling around, Barleigh bugled and waved the sombrero, but only one shied away. The boldest of the pair moved in closer, lunging, baring its teeth. Barleigh slapped with the sombrero and bugled with all the breath she had left in her sore lungs. The wolf retreated, confused by the strange trumpeting noise.

Bumping up against a large boulder, Barleigh sat and huddled with her back against the stone. The advances and retreats continued throughout the night. Barleigh remained vigilant, bugling and swatting, which forced the hungry wolves to make their charges from the shadowy fringes of the brush.

At the moment when she felt she had nothing left, her energy drained, her body exhausted, her sore lips swollen and cracked, a pale pink glow washed the eastern horizon. It gave way to a hope that she'd outlasted the wolves.

The sun never rose in bold grandeur, the world simply became light. Soft gray clouds diffused the pink streaks and turned the sky into a mottled silver realm. With the morning's light, the wolves disappeared to their dens to await the next night of hunting some other prey.

Her cramped muscles ached. Barleigh stood, pressing a fist against her lower back, rubbing and massaging her stiff neck. The coffee in the canteen was bitter and cold but she drank it, holding the cold metal away from her sore, bruised lips. Picking up the sombrero, she turned it around in her hands, inspecting the bright yellow hat with the gold and black trim. Claw or tooth marks frayed a small area on the edge where the large gray wolf had lunged, getting far closer than Barleigh had realized.

Taking note of the topography, Barleigh saw that she was farther from the base of The Needles formation than what she'd anticipated. Feeling disoriented and confused—they were supposed to be on her left . . . no, on her right—she spun around, trying to get her bearings. The sun offered no directional help, with the sky a milky gray mess. Tracing the ridge with an imaginary line, she marked the spot where the last Needle pointed toward Echo Canyon. Breathing a sigh of relief, she turned around and began walking southeast, knowing Cache Cave was less than a mile away.

The crunchy, half-frozen terrain of the two rivers' watersheds gave way to slippery gravel. She picked her way with slow, cautious steps across the treacherous ground. The path skidded and slid, changing once again to deep sand, but she was almost there. Not too far away, maybe another twenty yards, she saw the gaping opening slashed into the side of the rock, the familiar tunnel that travelers knew as Cache Cave. Above the entrance, small dark clouds drifted in an easy circle, floating high above the opening.

A slow, cold dread settled over her. The clouds formed into shapes. Barleigh shouted, running toward the cave, realizing the circling figures were not dark clouds at all but buzzards, crows, birds of carrion. She trumpeted the bugle, waving her arms and the sombrero. As with the wolves, the commotion drove the scavenging birds away.

Approaching the entrance to the cave, Barleigh exchanged the bugle in her hand for her pistol. Five Indians lay dead in rusty, freeze-dried pools of blood. Off to the left were two more, then one other to the right. Upon entering the cave, she saw two more who lay sprawled together in an unsuccessful effort at fleeing. Barleigh stepped over the last two, unsure of what she'd find farther in the cave.

And then she saw him.

Stoney was slumped, half leaning, half lying, near the wall. His Colt revolver was gripped in one hand, the other hand holding fast to the mochila. He opened his eyes as Barleigh dropped to her knees next to him.

"My sombrero," he whispered in a weak voice. "You brought me my . . ." He pointed at the hat, his voice trailing off.

"I did, Stoney. I brought it to you. How bad are you hurt?" The blood that pooled on the ground under him frightened her.

"They thought I was dead when they shot me off my horse. They took the mochila. But I followed them . . . here. I got . . . got the mochila back," he said, his voice raspy.

"You did some fine shooting, Stoney. Looks like you got them all." Barleigh took him by the shoulders, easing him forward, peering over his shoulder at his back.

Three arrows were embedded down the middle next to his spine, above what appeared to be a bullet wound. The arrows bore the same feather fletching as the one Barleigh had found earlier on the banks of the Webber River.

"I didn't get all of them. The tall white man . . . got away." He struggled for breath.

"One got away? A white man? Not Indian? Stoney—talk to me. Stay awake, buddy." She gave him a sip of cold coffee from her canteen.

"A black ghost was here. He told me—I don't know—he talked to me. Ghosts are supposed to be white." His rattling breaths were shallow and labored.

"That's right, ghosts are supposed to be white. Keep talking to me, Stoney. I'm going to lay you down on your side, easy now, like this, and see about getting these arrows out."

Memories flashed: Uncle Jack's body, Aunt Winnie tugging at the arrows. The lance, leaning on it, breaking it off.

She shook her head to rid it of the remembrances from that dreadful event, the vision of their horrifying discovery the morning after the attack. Concentrating on the task at hand, she willed herself to stay calm, for Stoney's sake.

"I'll pull these out. Then I can wrap my poncho around you, keep you warm while I go for a horse. Mine ran away. Wolves spooked her. I'll need a horse to get you to a doctor. Talk to me, Stoney. Stoney?" Her voice broke, shattering her calm.

Barleigh moved around to kneel in front of him. She lay down on her side close to him and took his face in her hands. Kissing his forehead, she soothed him as best she knew how with her soft words.

"Everything will be all right, Stoney. I promise. I'll bring back the swiftest pony I can find, one for you to ride away to the stars." She blinked back tears. "Wouldn't that be something, Stoney?" Stroking his cheek, she felt on his face the soft peach-fuzz of a boy not quite a man, and her heart broke.

Blood trickled from the corner of his mouth. He gasped for breath. His eyes fought to stay focused on Barleigh's, but then his gaze drifted. He looked through her, beyond to someplace she wouldn't know. One final rattling breath moved him from this world to the next. Stoney was gone.

"Oh, Stoney." She wanted to cry, to scream, to pound her fists. Her body tightened and heated, the anger and emotion choking her breath. But, she couldn't seem to find the relief tears would offer. She felt a never-ending circle of sadness hardening her heart, adding yet another calcifying layer.

Her hands trembled as she reached out to close his eyes—those eyes that were as blue as the river. "I'm sorry, Stoney. I am so sorry. This was my mail run, not yours. It should have been me."

Covering him with her poncho, she sat with his body, her back against the cave wall. She kept her gun in hand, at the ready. Sipping cold coffee, she worked through a plan in her mind. Hiking back up to Head of Canyon Station to get horses from Colonel Hill was the obvious choice. Weariness and bone-deep fatigue washed over her. She tried to fight it off, her head snapping back and falling forward, but soon she could not resist the pull. She fell into a deep sleep, sitting upright, canteen in one hand, pistol in the other.

*****

A noise echoing, a hand on her shoulder, startled her awake. Jumping up, she tripped over her spurs and fell to her knees, pointing her pistol, realizing her hands were empty. A scream caught in her throat as hands reached for her, took her by the arms, and raised her to her feet. Held her. Enfolded her in strong arms.

It happened so fast, she didn't realize it was Hughes until she was pressed against his chest—the smell of his body, the scent she remembered from the first time she wrapped herself in his coat flooded her memory.

Hughes held her close, saying nothing, waiting for her panic to subside. "Shhh, shhh," he soothed as her breathing returned to normal.

"I'm lucky it's you," she said, her voice quavering. She felt foolish, falling asleep, leaving herself vulnerable.

"It's all right, I'm here." Hughes looked over at Stoney and shook his head. "I told him to hang on till I got back. Damn it—I thought he could hang on. I had to go after Archer."

"What do you mean, till you got back?" Barleigh pulled away, Hughes's hands slow to release her.

"I've had my eye on the Archers. They're part of a larger group who've been tampering with the mail. They hire renegade Utes and Shoshones to do their dirty work so it'll appear like a common Indian attack. Tonight came as a cold surprise. I was expecting it to happen next week, but with the westbound mail to California."

"But you were drunk—so drunk you could hardly stand," said Barleigh, confused.

"I was on my way to a good drunk. When I learned this was happening tonight, I switched the whiskey for tea to put on a show for those watching."

"So it was a ruse," said Barleigh, putting the details of the evening in order.

"A ruse—yes."

"Stoney said the black ghost visited him, talked to him. That was you." She stole a glance at Stoney lying quiet and still under her poncho.

Barleigh fisted a hand against her mouth, afraid that if she were to remove it, a flood of unbearable sadness would come rushing out. It was better to hold it inside where it belonged, buried alongside the other memories she tried to hush.

"I guess I'm the black ghost," acknowledged Hughes. "Stoney handled the Indians just fine, but Johnny Archer had Stoney pinned. I shot once—it grazed him. Archer fled, but his blood made the trail easy to follow in the moonlight. That Stoney was a brave son-of-a-gun."

"Brave—yes, he was brave," she said, clenching her hands into her hair. She kneeled next to Stoney's body. "It should be me lying here, not him. It was my mail run . . ." Barleigh's voice trailed off.

"It's not your fault, Barleigh. Don't go down that road." Hughes knelt beside her, turning her to face him.

"I'm very familiar with that road," she said. This wasn't the first death for which she felt responsible.

"What are you saying?"

"First, it was my mother when she gave birth to me. Then it was Papa and Birdie and Uncle Jack, when I ran like a frightened child and hid in the cellar instead of fighting alongside Papa . Now, Stoney." She looked down at her hands, as if she might see blood.

"Stop it." Hughes's hands gripped her shoulders. "Don't do this to yourself. All this false guilt will do nothing but keep you from ever finding happiness."

"I'm not looking for happiness. I don't expect it's looking for me, either." She shrugged away from his grip. "All I'm looking for is a way to get back to the city. I'm horseless. Wolves spooked mine away. And I'm taking Stoney with me. I'm not leaving him here."

"I've got Archer's body outside tied to his horse. We can leave it in the cave, tell the authorities where to find him, and use his horse to get Stoney home. You can ride behind me."

After removing the arrows from Stoney's back, they wrapped his body in Hughes's bedroll and draped him over the saddle of Archer's horse. Barleigh tied the sombrero to the pommel, letting Stoney take it home. If they rode nonstop at a steady pace, the trek back to Salt Lake City would take well into the night.

Barleigh rode behind Hughes, holding onto his coat, and

tried not to think of Stoney lying across the saddle of the horse that trailed behind—tried not to think at all. She pounded her forehead against Hughes's back, over and over.

Hughes never flinched but reached a hand around to squeeze her thigh. The tenderness and the intimacy was almost too much for Barleigh to bear. She stopped pounding her forehead, and instead, lay her cheek against his back and tightly closed her eyes, staunching the flow of tears.

As evening wore on, Hughes decided to make a small campfire to reheat the coffee in Barleigh's canteen. His saddlebags weren't packed with his usual fancy picnic, so dinner was beans and sourdough biscuits. For Barleigh's starving stomach, it was a feast.

Sitting on a log close to the crackling fire, she sipped steaming coffee from the tin cup Hughes handed her. "When I took off looking for Stoney, I told Mario that I might . . . that I was thinking about going back to Texas after I found him. I didn't think I'd be bringing him back like this."

Hughes stirred the embers, adding more kindling. The flames sparked and danced upward like lightening bugs do in a warm summer sky. He glanced back over his shoulder, the look of relief evident on his face.

"You're going back to Texas? I am so relieved to hear you say that."

"I thought I'd made up my mind. But I can't leave Mario like this. I have to stay now. For a while, at least."

Hughes came to kneel in front of the log she was sitting on, taking her hands in his. "Barleigh, look at me. Stoney's dead. There are many others like the men who killed him. They'll kill anyone who gets in their way. The Archer brothers were a small fraction of those involved who'd like to keep certain letters from going between Washington and California. These Southern sympathizers will stop at nothing to convince California to side with the Confederacy. You have no idea the danger you ride into every time you pick up that damn mochila."

"Are you saying this is just the beginning?" A chill shivered down her spine, despite the warmth from the fire and coffee

"That's right," he said, his eyes dark and serious. "An intricate conspiracy with a far-reaching association is at work. Tensions escalating between North and South spur these conspirators to more heinous acts in their efforts to pull California's gold into the Rebel war coffers. Lincoln *has* to keep California loyal to the Union, thereby keeping control of its gold. Whichever way California sides could sway the outcome."

"You talk as if war is certain."

"I believe it is."

"Then that's all the more reason for me to help get the mail through. Look at what's at stake."

"Look at what's over there and tied to that horse." His voice was a harsh growl. "Are you willing to take that risk?"

"Maybe I am. Maybe it doesn't matter." Barleigh's eyes filled with sadness at the thought jabbing at her heart. "Starling would be better off being raised by Aunt Winnie, anyway. I'm not fit—"

"Look at me, Barleigh. That's not true." His voice was sharp, emphatic. "Your sister needs you. Purposely risking your life—taking dangerous chances you don't have to—is not the answer." Hughes tossed the rest of his coffee aside.

Barleigh stood, kicking sand into the fire. "Why can't there be easy answers, where decisions don't seem impossible?"

"Not all decisions are impossible. Damn it—I can't let this go on. It has to stop." Hughes walked over to Barleigh, his hard eyes reflecting the fire's flickering light.

"What do you mean? What has to stop?"

"There are things . . ." He paused, sucking in a deep breath, letting it seep out slowly through gritted teeth. ". . . that you need to know." Hughes rubbed the back of his neck and looked to the sky, as if the moon would give him the right words.

"Hughes? What are you trying to say?" She grew alarmed by the look on his face and the grave tone of his voice.

"It's killing me, seeing you like this. So torn up, so sad and guilt-ridden over something that didn't happen." Hughes held her at arm's length, fixing his penetrating eyes on hers. "You can't go on thinking that you're responsible for your mother's death,

Barleigh. Your mother didn't die giving birth to you. Your mother is alive."

*****

She had done as he had requested—listened and let him speak uninterrupted. He'd talked until the fire went cold, giving Barleigh an abbreviated telling of her mother's life. He'd spared a few details, he had said, that Leighselle might wish to keep to herself.

He told of the anguish he'd felt that Barleigh's mother might die before he could persuade her to change her mind about keeping this a secret. He'd tried, he said, to convince her to let him tell Barleigh the truth. Now, he wasn't sure if there would be enough time.

Barleigh felt assaulted by his words. They covered her with shame and filled her with sorrow. The words numbed every fiber and nerve of her being. In a span of time lasting less than one hour, he had undone her past. His story revised her history. It stripped away what she'd known to be true of the life she'd worn so comfortably.

She sat, listening, unmoving, a statue without feelings. Birdie, whom she'd always thought was so beautiful, so exotic— it's no wonder her papa had fallen in love with her. Birdie reminded him of his first love.

Barleigh remained frozen in place, hearing, absorbing, processing. The dark, frosty woods swirled around her. Noises far away made hollow echoes. A ghost wind skimmed across her skin, not touching, just passing over. Nothing seemed real.

"Barleigh, are you all right? I know it's a lot to take in. You haven't said anything."

"You wanted me to listen to your story while you spoke uninterrupted. I've listened."

"Please," said Hughes, taking her hands. "Say something now. Ask me a question."

"How much farther to Salt Lake?" She pulled away and walked to where the horses stood tied. Shaking her head, both arms extended, she pressed her palms outward against this foreign world closing in on her.

Unable to speak, she waited in silence for Hughes to

265

follow. Words that formed in her head crumbled to dust before escaping her mouth. Hughes let her have her silence. When he was in the saddle, she mounted the horse behind him, with the lead rope that connected them to Stoney's horse dallied around their saddle horn.

Barleigh's mind was tangled with distressing thoughts and images. Her entire life had been a lie. Did Papa know that her mother didn't die in childbirth? Did it not matter because he had grown to love Birdie? And Grandfather—Grandfather lied and manipulated the totality of her existence. Was Birdie complicit in the charade, or did she, a slave, not have a choice? A mother, alive all that time—all that guilt—that every birthday Barleigh had enjoyed was an anniversary of her mother's death.

And Hughes—hired to track her down—and, on finding her, knowing who she was, yet pretending not to. The telegraphs to her mother in San Antonio, giving her updates. Letting Barleigh think that he was falling for her with his kisses and his false worry. And Barleigh, falling for him.

The silent words banged around in her head until she couldn't think or breathe. A roiling panic swelled from deep within. Cold, prickly sweat beaded on her skin as waves of nausea washed over her.

"Please, stop the horse," she said with urgency. But before she could finish the words, her stomach betrayed her, retching the sourdough biscuits and reheated coffee. Leaning away, she tried to throw up so that it didn't foul the horse or Hughes.

Hughes reined to a stop and lowered her to the ground, retrieving a canteen of water from his bag. "Are you all right?"

"Am I all right? Am *I*? How can *I* be all right when *I* don't know who *I am*?"

"You're still you, Barleigh. *You* have not changed. Only your story's changed. You look pale," he said, dismounting and taking her by the shoulders.

"I feel pale."

"Barleigh, please understand. I was doing what I thought was right. I couldn't betray the promise I'd sworn to your mother. Now I have, and I hope she'll forgive me. But damn it—it was the right thing to do."

"Honoring that promise to her, but then selectively choosing which secrets to keep, or which lies or half-truths to throw at me? I don't understand you or your code of ethics. I don't want to understand. When we get back to the city, I don't ever want to see you again."

She shrugged away from his grip on her shoulders, knelt down, and scooped snow into her hands, washing her face and her mouth. She pressed her icy fingers against her cheeks, wanting to feel the biting cold on her skin, and she breathed the frigid air deep into her lungs until they burned and she coughed. Still, everything felt unreal, as if she were disconnected from each of her senses. Even the beauty of the rugged landscape, the smell of the pine trees, and the crunching sound her boots made in the snow seemed like forgeries.

"Since I've known you," said Hughes, "you keep your emotions in check, buried deep inside. Your world's been ripped to pieces today. I wish you could let it out somehow. Scream. Cry. Throw a fit. Hell, throw a punch or two. Release a bit of emotional steam."

"I did release emotion. I spewed it all over the back of your coat."

Hughes forced a grin. "I'm serious."

"I am, too. Your coat's a mess."

He took it off and inspected the stain. "I've seen worse." Then, rubbing a handful of snow on it, washing away what he could, he put the coat back on. "There. That should do the trick."

He swung himself back in the saddle and held out his hand for Barleigh to remount behind him. "Ready to ride?"

"Yes," she replied flatly. "We've a long way to go."

She put her foot in the stirrup to climb up behind him, but a wave of dizziness caused her to totter backward. Regrouping, she tried again. Before she could manage a third attempt, Hughes leaned down from the saddle, lifted her, and sat her in front of him sidesaddle. He cradled her against him, his arms encircling her as he held the reins in each hand.

With no strength to protest, Barleigh lay her head against

his chest, but her eyes remained alert and watchful. The steep trail wound its way down into the valley. Overhead, the bright, full moon cast silvery shadows of their procession onto the snow-packed, frozen ground.

*****

It was midnight when they rode into the Pony Express stables. Barleigh had moved behind Hughes, not wanting to give cause for questions or raised eyebrows. The streets were quiet, a few lights burned in windows, cats prowled in corners, and snow crunched under the weight of the horses' hooves.

The tranquil scene made Barleigh want to scream.

They were met by Mario, who took the horse carrying Stoney's body. "My God, my God. He was a fine young man. My God—" Mario didn't try to hide his tears. "I'll make arrangements to send him back to Arkansas and to his family. A boy should be buried where his folks can tend the grave."

"He wouldn't want that," Barleigh said, giving Mario's arm a squeeze. "He never wanted to go home again. He'd want to be buried here along the Pony Express trail."

"That's what we'll do, then," said Mario. "I'll tend to his grave. Get some rest now. I'll take care of things here."

"Stoney saved the mochila. We left it with Colonel Hill at Head of Canyon Station so it could continue on to Saint Joe. Stoney died saving the mail. Someone ought to be told about that. It was heroic, what he did." She gave Mario a brief description of events, Hughes filling in the gaps of her information.

"Everyone will hear of Stoney's story. It don't take long for something like that to make the rounds. But I'll send word to Carson City and have them telegraph headquarters to make sure the right people know, too." Mario removed the sombrero from the saddle horn and handed it to Barleigh. And then turning, Mario led Stoney's horse away.

Hughes and Barleigh walked to the Salt Lake House, climbed the stairs to the second floor, and said goodnight, she turning to her room, he to his.

"Are you going to be all right?" Hughes asked, turning back around.

"I wish you'd quit asking that."

"Are all the riders away? Do you have anyone to bunk with tonight?" Hughes looked at her, concern wrinkling his brow.

"Are you worried about me?"

"Yes, damn it, I'm worried about you, all right?"

"I thought you didn't have time to worry about me." She didn't wait for him to answer, but turned and opened the door to the bunk room. "It appears I have the room to myself tonight. Brody must be on Stoney's . . . on the eastbound run. I guess the new guy, Lars, is on mine."

"Give me a minute, please. I'll be back."

"Why?"

"Because I don't want you to be alone tonight."

"It's not necessary, Hughes. Besides, what if I want to be alone."

"I'll be quiet. You can pretend to be alone. Why do you always argue?"

"Why do you always assume you know what's best?"

"It's not an assumption." He turned and walked away.

A quick sponge bath from the basin vessel, a brushing of her teeth, a comb through her hair, and a change into clean long johns made her feel almost human again. She was in bed by the time Hughes returned. Though half asleep, she noticed he'd put on clean clothes, too.

"I'll be quiet. You won't even know I'm here." Bending over the bed, he kissed her on the cheek. "I'll be on the bottom bunk, if you need anything. I hope you sleep well."

But she didn't. She tossed and turned, fits and starts of dreams tormenting her sleep. Disembodied faces floated in and out, chasing, yelling, hovering. Grandfather's face, laughing. Papa and Birdie clutched in a skeletal embrace. Barleigh falling. Stoney trying to catch her but his hands were bloody and slippery and they couldn't hold her. He let go. Then he was tumbling down, down, down a mountain that never ended, but it was her bloody, slippery hands that let him fall. A wolf howled. Her dream wolf. He was shaking her. Wake up. You're all right. It's all right.

"I'm right here, Barleigh. It's all right." Hughes sat on the side of the bed, holding her hand, stroking her face. "Shhh. Everything's all right. I'm right here."

Barleigh bolted upright in bed, jerking away from his touch and drawing her knees into a protective shield. "I don't want you here. Leave. Leave me alone."

"You were having a nightmare," Hughes said, offering her a glass of water.

She pushed the glass and his hand away. "I'm living a nightmare."

Feeling buried under all the lies she'd been told all her life, now Hughes's lies, how he'd traded the truth for her affection, she began to hyperventilate—a cold panic rising, swelling, suffocating her. Kicking the covers away, she lashed out at Hughes and tried to push him off the bed with both of her feet. She kicked and clawed at anything that was him.

"I said to leave!" she cried out, half whimpering, half shouting.

"I'm not going anywhere," he said, his voice calm and measured.

Still shoving and kicking, she knocked the water glass off the nightstand as she tried to push Hughes away. With her foot, she shoved the wooden bedside stand; the water basin tottered, fell, and shattered to pieces as it hit the floor.

Hughes pulled Barleigh against his chest, encircling her in his arms, holding her tighter as she continued to kick and lash out. "Get it all out, but I'm not letting go until you're done."

"Don't you understand? All the lies. Everything's been a lie or a secret—Grandfather, Papa, my mother. Your lies. Look at me —I'm living my own lie." She broke down, the sobs coming in waves. "I don't know what truth is. All I know is that I want you to leave." Her final words were spoken in a broken whisper, her breath feeling like needles in her lungs.

"Nope. I'm not. But I'll turn you loose if you're ready to quit clawing at me like a tiger," he said, sounding somewhat hopeful.

"Why did you tell me?" Barleigh put up a halfhearted attempt at a struggle to free herself from his clutch. "My life was fine, even if it was a farce—the memories I had of what my life was, without knowing about all this . . . this craziness."

"You were in a very dark place, Barleigh," he said, his words spoken softly against her ear. "A dark place, and you were spiraling into a dangerous void of unmerrited guilt."

"You've shown me that my life has been nothing but a damned lie. You've effectively erased my history, my memories. For that, I hate you."

"You can hate me all you want for telling you," said Hughes, cradling her against his chest. "But I told you to give you something to live for. You have a mother who loves you."

Moments passed. When Barleigh's breathing returned to a shaky version of normal, he relaxed his grip and she pulled away. Then, gathering the covers onto the bed that she'd kicked to the floor, she turned to face the wall, pulling them over her head and burying herself under the mound of blankets.

"Sleep, Barleigh," said Hughes, watching her cocoon herself in the downy duvet. "I'm not going anywhere. I'll be here when you wake up."

*****

Hughes pulled a chair next to Barleigh's bed, sleep a far thought from his mind. He watched the shape under the covers move with each breath, at first panting and seething, then more evenly, and finally, calm and measured. He moved the blanket away from her face, making sure not to waken her.

He wanted nothing more than to crawl into that bed and hold her. To take her in his arms and tell her that everything would be all right, to lie with her all night with her head on his chest.

He wanted to assure her that his affections for her were real —and he knew that hers were real, too. Or, that they once were.

He wished he knew that everything would be all right, but he didn't.

So, he'd just sit there. And he'd be there when she woke up in the morning, just like he said he would.

Then, he would leave.

Chapter Sixteen

November 29, 1860

Sunlight filtered through the dark velvet drapes, puddling on the floor in big, uneven spots. From the angle of the shadows, morning was melting into noon. Barleigh blinked hard, rubbed fists over her eyes, yawned, stretched, and bolted upright, pulling the blankets up to her chin.

"Uh . . . ," She drew in a sharp breath. "What are you doing here?"

Hughes sat in the chair, watching as Barleigh woke up. His bloodshot eyes gave evidence of his all-night vigil. "Don't you remember? When we got back last night, I tried to leave and go to my own room, but you begged me to stay—said you didn't want me to leave you alone."

"That's not how I remember it, now that it's coming back to me. Is that coffee?" she snapped. She reached for the cup. Her stomach pitched at the notion of their fingers touching. She now dreaded the physical contact that she once found pleasurable.

"Yes." He handed it over. "I promised you that I'd be here when you woke up and I didn't want to break that promise—have you wake up to see me gone. But you were snoring so loudly I figured you were in a deep enough sleep I could chance a run to the kitchen."

"I don't snore. Do I snore? Really?" She sipped the coffee and handed him back the cup.

"Yes. Really. But in a cute, girlish sort of way. Actually,

that's not quite precise. It's more like a grizzly bear defending her cubs."

"You could have left it at cute and girlish," she said, embarrassed.

"Probably, but I made a promise to myself last night that I'd never tell you another lie or be dishonest with you. Ever."

"I could look the other way when it comes to things like describing my snoring."

Thinking about honesty and deceit made her want to roll over and pull the covers over her head. The enormity of revealed secrets weighed on her shoulders like a thousand-pound cloak.

Hughes sipped the coffee and handed her the cup. "Being honest with you means being honest with myself, too."

He stood and walked to the other side of the room, drew back the curtain, and cracked open the window, allowing the fresh, cool air to seep in. He turned and looked at Barleigh with a puzzled expression. "How can you wake up looking so beautiful, and these yahoos not look at you and see that you're a woman? You've gotten away with being *Bar* Flanders longer than I would've bet."

She felt a blush rising and looked away. "I better get dressed so we can go to check on Stoney's arrangements."

"Before we do, there're two more things I need to tell you," he said, walking over to the chair.

"More?" What else could there be, after all he'd said last night? She stiffened, bracing for hurtful words sure to follow.

"First, if something happens, your mother's will leaves you a tidy sum of money along with some New Orleans real estate. When I wrote to Leighselle to let her know I'd found your trail, I filled her in on the details. I told her since I was heading to Saint Joseph anyway on business, I'd continue looking for you. A wire waiting for me there said she'd taken care of the taxes on your ranch, and put money in your account to more than cover next year's, too."

"I don't understand. Why is she unwilling to meet me—get to know me—to tell me these things in person—" Barleigh flung herself back against the pillows, pulling the duvet up over her head.

274

"It's not that she's unwilling. She didn't want to interrupt your life. She felt your knowing about her would disrupt what she'd hoped was a happy life. Leighselle carries an enormous sense of guilt that somehow she was responsible for Grandfather Flanders taking you away from her. A lifetime of guilt, even if it's unearned, can color the way a person sees reality, even a good person who means well, like your mother. Like you."

"That's a lot to think about," said Barleigh, her words muffled coming from under the covers.

"You said you grew to wish you weren't your grandfather's kin. You have more in common with your mother, a woman whom you've never known, than with your grandfather who raised you." Hughes smiled, his eyes lighting up.

"Really?" She peeped out from under the covers, then sat up, leaning forward. "Do I remind you of my mother?"

"Yes. Besides your beauty, you've got your mother's gumption—her fearless determination to set things right. Leighselle passed on to you her love of animals, her kindness, her ability to bluff at poker, and her fondness for the color yellow. I've noticed you always wear that yellow bandana around your neck."

"I've always been drawn to the color." The thought of common traits warmed her, like the yellow rays of the sun. "You said there were two things you had to tell me. What's the second?" She reached for the coffee, taking the last drop.

"This is the part where I'm being honest with myself." He leaned back in the chair, then sat forward. "The night before Leighselle came to San Antonio, I'd been on my way to Fort Worth to pick up a prisoner to escort him to Austin for trial. Partway there, the horse I was riding gave out and died, so I set off walking back to San Antonio."

"Go on." She noticed the anxiety grow more evident on Hughes's face. His eyes darkened, he clenched and unclenched his jaw, his brow furrowed into deep lines.

"I knew I was being followed, and before I could think, I had three lassoes on me. It was Quanah Parker and his warriors." Hughes swallowed, his mouth dry, and he reached for the coffee before remembering it was empty. He smiled at Barleigh as she shrugged and mouthed "sorry."

He told her the story of how he had to think fast and figure out a way to keep his scalp, how he'd talked Quanah into a fight for bragging rights, in order to save his life. Quanah had killed one of his own men—it would have been nothing for him to kill Hughes, too.

"Thankfully, they have a fearful respect for wolves, and the spirit of the wolf," he said.

"I don't understand."

"*Waya Agatoli* is the shortened version of the name the Comanche had given me. Man Who Sees With Wolf Eyes. I used their superstitions to my advantage."

"Ah—I see." She thought of her recurring dream of the wolf with the amber-colored eyes, the way he would watch over her while she slept, keeping the nightmares at bay. She wondered if the Comanche didn't have it right—that there was nothing superstitious about it.

"I should have killed him right there. But I knew if I did, his warriors would have filled me with arrows before Quanah's heart quit beating. Quanah honored our agreement. He let me go free, and made his warriors honor it, too."

"And this was during the time of the Comanche moon?" she asked.

"Yes. After that, it's possible Quanah headed north for the Llano Estacado, one of his band's hunting grounds. That would put him passing through Palo Pinto around the night of your family's tragedy." Hughes leaned the chair back onto two legs and sucked in a deep breath, easing the chair down as he exhaled.

"If you'd—" Barleigh started.

"If I'd killed Quanah when I'd had the chance, you'd still have your father and Birdie, Winnie would have Jack." He leaned forward, putting his head in his hands. "I could have prevented it." He pounded his fists onto his knees. "Goddammit."

Barleigh slid out of bed, walking around to his chair. She lay her hand on the back of his head for a moment, not knowing what to say or do, what to feel or to think. Footsteps in the hallway drew her attention to the door. When she saw the knob turning, she hurried away from Hughes. Moving to the armoire, she pulled out clean clothes to dress for the day.

Mario stuck his head in the door. "Bar, I was hoping you'd be awake. The undertaker has a place for Stoney up by the chapel close to the trail. He says he can bury him this afternoon at one o'clock if that's agreeable."

Barleigh looked up from pulling on her boots. "One o'clock. Thanks, Mario. You going back to the barn? I need to come talk to you about my job."

"I'll be there. Mr. Lévesque, see you at one?"

"Yes. Thank you," he said as Mario nodded and closed the door. Hughes stood and took the empty coffee cup. "I need some more—with a little fortification. You want some?" He pulled out his flask and splashed some amber liquid into the waiting cup.

"Sure. I'll come down with you."

"Bar," said Hughes, standing in the doorway. "I know less about the future than you do about the past, but I do know this. No more secrets, no more lies, not between us. You've made it clear you don't want anything to do with me. I understand. I'm leaving for California tomorrow. I don't know when I'm coming back. Can we at least part as friends?"

"That's the first time you've called me 'Bar' in a private conversation." She removed Stoney's sombrero off the rack and looped the bolo around her neck, letting the yellow Mexican hat hang loose across the back of her shoulders.

*****

The undertaker and his wife, a petite redhead who sang in the church for free but hired herself out for social gatherings and funerals, were waiting when they arrived at the small graveside chapel. Stoney's funeral had a few attendees: Barleigh, Hughes, Mario, the two new riders—Liam and his brother Lars—Big Brody and his brother Yates, the hotel cook, and a string of rangy Pony Express horses tied to the hitching posts. Off to one side, hiding in the shadows of a large pine tree, was a doe-eyed blonde-headed girl who made fine chocolate cream pies.

The undertaker chose to read a fiery passage from the Book of Revelation about pale horses and hell and death and destruction, after which his wife sang a popular love song, *When the Corn Is Waving, Annie Dear.* Barleigh didn't know which was more inappropriate, but both left her speechless and lightheaded. Or maybe the lightheadedness was due to the earlier consumption of fortified coffee on an empty stomach. Either way, all she wanted was to be alone, on a horse, and riding far away from there.

The others departed after the singing, with Mario leading the string of ponies, one of them riderless and draped in a black blanket. Hughes leaned against his horse, arms crossed, eyes dark and watchful as Barleigh placed a wreath of Christmas holly on Stoney's grave.

She sat down next to the fresh mound of dirt and thought of all the things she wished she'd said to Stoney, all the things she wished she'd asked him. Did his mama ever stick up for him when his daddy beat him with his fists, or did Stoney have to defend her, too? Did he have any happy Christmas memories from his childhood? Did he ever get what he wished for? Was there room in his small corner of the world for wishes?

The sky darkened with threatening clouds moving in from the west. The feel and smell of the air altered in the way it does before a storm settles over the valley, the kind of storm that declares it's here to stay a while.

"I know this has been hard for you," said Hughes, walking over to the grave. "Stoney was more than a friend. You haven't uttered a word to anyone since we got here. Are you speaking to me?"

She nodded her head, her best effort.

"Will you tell me that you're speaking to me? Please."

"I'm speaking to you. I just don't know what to say." Her voice was a whisper, barely audible even to herself.

"What did you tell Mario about your job? Did you decide to keep riding, or to go back to Texas?" Hughes knelt down by the grave, next to Barleigh, his shoulder against hers.

"I told him I hadn't made up my mind yet. I needed to sleep on it. Liam and Lars are riding with the regulars, Eagan and Haslan. They're learning the trail, so Mario said he's in good shape with riders for now."

"What's your plan between now and in the morning?"

She felt Hughes studying her face, trying to read her. She kept her profile to him, keeping her eyes to herself. He was always trying to read her—an impossible mission. With the walls she had built, she was finding it difficult even to read herself.

"Take a long ride. Think. Clear my head." She stood, looking over her shoulder at the line of the Wasatch Mountains against the charcoal sky.

"Don't ride far. The weather's turning. I worry about you." His eyes seemed to deepen in hue, with flecks of dark golden brown and russet, like the first sparks of a fire strengthening and catching hold.

"You're not very good at worrying. Anyway, I'm not yours to worry about." Barleigh turned and swung herself into the saddle. Never looking back, she cantered away.

*****

Hughes sat by Stoney's grave and watched her ride toward the foothills, watched for a long while until her form became a small speck on the horizon. An icy wind began to blow, snapping his attention back to the present. The clouds had thickened, the first flakes of snow dusting the ground.

His gut tightened like it did every time he watched her ride away by herself. She was right—he wasn't good at worrying. Swinging himself up into the saddle, he rode in the opposite direction into town. He had unfinished business before he left for California.

*****

George Archer had received word of his brother's death and the death of the ten Shoshone Indians they'd employed in their scheme to steal the Pony Express mail. That the mochila was rescued and sent through on its eastbound route infuriated him. Those letters from California's governor to the president of the United States should have been stopped. He was standing at the bar of the Salt Lake House speaking to two other men when Hughes returned to the hotel from Stoney's funeral.

Spying Archer along with the others in the bar, Hughes formulated a plan and put it to quick action. He pulled his flask

279

from his vest and stumbled up to the bartender, waving the flask in the air, speaking in a loud, slurred voice.

"Bartender, my whiskey's run dry. Gimme your best bottle." Turning to Archer, Hughes leaned close. "Don't you hate an empty flask? I do." He belched, for effect.

"What I hate is a rude, loud drunk. Back off and mind your own business," said Archer, his voice gruff and threatening.

Hughes nodded and stumbled backward a few steps. "Yes'sir, boss."

Turning to his two companions, Archer continued his conversation, lowering his voice. "Anyway, the one they say found the mochila, sent it on its way, then brought the dead boy's body back was the kid named Bar. I know which one he is—the little shit. I'll be watching their room again tonight. I guarantee he won't make it out alive. You two just do your part. Wait until dark, then go to the Pony Express stables, take out what's his name—Mario, the manager—then run off all them horses. Got it?"

The two men nodded, all three slung back one last shot of whiskey, and then all departed on their separate missions.

Hughes watched as Archer went upstairs and into his room. Then, hurrying outside, he looked to see which way the two conspirators went. Snow covered the sidewalk, their boot-prints easy evidence. Hughes bent into the wind, following the two as they made their way down Main, past Whiskey Street, and into the alley behind Marcum's Apothecary Shoppe.

Sprinting up the sidewalk, Hughes rounded the corner, coming out the backside of the row of buildings at the other end of the alley. He walked toward the two. They both looked up just in time to see fists being planted squarely on each of their noses, the punch knocking both men to their knees. Following up with kicks to the sides and fists to the backs of their heads, Hughes knocked both men out cold before they knew what had happened.

Hughes dragged the pair onto the back porch of the Apothecary Shoppe, then took the belts from their pants and cinched the men together. In what looked like a loving embrace, their arms were wrapped around each other, with the porch's cedar support post between them.

Walking back to the front of the store, Hughes spotted a young boy in the street playing fetch the stick with his dog. He took a paper and pencil from his coat and scratched a note.

"Son, I'll give you a dime to take this note to the sheriff."

"A whole dime? Really? Just to run a note up the street?"

"Hurry. It's important. Off you go."

Leaving the sons of bitches to freeze to death in the dirt was what he'd really wanted to do, he thought, as he hurried back to the Salt Lake House. But, the sheriff would have fun deciphering the note about mail thieves and murderers who use Indians for scapegoats. In the late afternoon glow of the gas lamps, a hard snow fell in a sharp slant against the hotel's window panes. The boot-prints he'd followed earlier were already obscured under the mounding drifts.

*****

Shaking the snow from his clothes and off his hat, Hughes took a long draw of whiskey from his flask, swishing it around, then swallowing, letting the warmth seep through his body as he made his way up the stairs. He banged on the door of the Pony Express riders' room, shouting out his slurred words, teetering back and forth. He kicked the door with his booted foot, hoping to draw the attention of the man in the room across the hall.

"Hey, anybody wanna join me for a drink?" He turned the knob, eased the door open, and peered inside the empty room. "I don't wanna drink alone. Anyone home?" He slammed the door and stood there a moment longer when he heard Archer's door behind him click closed.

Smiling to himself, he turned to Archer's door and banged with his fists. "Mister, wanna share a toast?"

No answer.

"Hey, mister?" He banged on the door again. "All right. I can take a hint. G'night." Hughes made foot-stomping sounds as if he were walking away. In a moment, he heard shuffling on the other side of the door, then the click of a lock, then saw the doorknob turning slowly.

The door inched its way open. Hughes shoved his shoulder against the door, pushing his way into the room. With a swift back-kick, he slammed the door shut with his foot. Propelling his weight forward, he knocked a surprised Archer backward into a table; the man and a ceramic lamp toppled to the floor.

Archer groped behind him and picked up the heavy lamp. He swung it as Hughes was bending over him, hitting Hughes in the forehead. Stunned, Hughes stumbled backward, tripping and falling to his knees.

Archer sprang to his feet and raced to the window, flinging it open. He threw himself out onto the snow-covered, sloping roof, sliding down, slipping over, and hanging onto the ledge by his fingers.

Climbing out of the window, Hughes eased himself down the sloping roof, balancing his weight against a gable. They were on the backside of the hotel, the alley below an enclosed pen for cattle in the summer, in the winter a depository for the ice and snow that shop owners shoveled off the walks in front of their stores.

Archer looked over his shoulder at the jagged ice below, then back at Hughes. "The drunk from the bar."

"Guess I handle my liquor better than you thought." Hughes reached out a hand to Archer, trying to grab his coat sleeve. "I've got your two pals all bundled up for the sheriff. I'm taking you in, too." He stretched out farther, then felt his boot slipping off the ice-covered wooden shingles on the gable. Sliding down, he braced both feet on the guttered ledge, stopping his fall.

"Pull me up," begged Archer. "I can't hold on."

Leaning his weight back against the roof for leverage, Hughes looked at Archer's fingers in a death grip on the roof's ledge, and then at the fear in the man's eyes. In one searing rush, Archer's words from earlier, bragging he would kill Barleigh before the night was over, rang loud in his ears. Hughes imagined Archer's fingers in a death grip on Barleigh's neck, or on a trigger, squeezing it, a bullet being released into Barleigh, that same look of fear in her eyes.

Hughes hesitated, his hesitation giving way to a simmering madness. He saw Archer's mouth moving, but the sound of his plea for help didn't register, the words falling silently like the snow. Hughes pulled his revolver from its holster, eased the hammer back, and took a steady look at the man on the other end of his gun. He felt—not hatred, not rage—but an unflinching assuredness that this person who wanted Barleigh dead didn't deserve to live. He aimed the barrel between Archer's frightened eyes.

The sound of his pulse beating loud in his ears and echoing in his head, the cold sweat trickling down his forehead, the shaking of his gun in his hand, the unsettled feel of shallow, fast breaths— clouded his thinking. A vision of Barleigh watching, waiting to see if he'd choose whether to cross that fine line that separates humanity from the dark side tugged at him, hovered over him.

He'd crossed that line before. He understood the cost it exacted.

For Hughes, not killing Quanah Parker when he'd had the chance had been an easy decision. That had been a matter of survival, of self-preservation. Not killing Archer went much deeper. This was a matter of preserving his own soul.

Hughes eased the hammer down and holstered his gun. He reached out his hand, grabbing for Archer's coat sleeve.

"Oh—oh, no—you ain't taking me in." George Archer yanked away, releasing his fingertip grip on the roof, kicking off the wall and flinging himself backward. He landed with a thud on the frozen ground below.

"You crazy son of a bitch." Hughes peered over the ledge at Archer lying on the rough ice, a bright red halo pooling around his head, and snow falling silently on his motionless body. He looked up at the open window and the steep slope of the icy roof, then across the roofline at the gutter running down the side of the building. He inched his way across the ledge, crawling down the gutter, then lowering himself to the ground.

Archer lay sprawled in the snow, his blood a contrasting stain against the icy whiteness beneath him. Hughes bent down and inspected the body. A sharp section of jagged ice was embedded at the base of his skull, the formation protruding from the snow like an iceberg peeking out of the sea.

Hughes wrote a note for the sheriff and left it with the body.

A whiteout obscured the sunset. Snow blew sideways. The deserted streets of Salt Lake City were choked with a foot of snow, more coming down nonstop since it began just after Stoney's funeral. Hughes stood at the window, watching for Barleigh. Pacing the room. Going back to the window again, and again.

Why aren't you back? I hope you've holed up somewhere safe.

Somewhere safe. Less unsafe.

He spun away from the window. Grabbing his coat, hat, and saddlebags, rolling up an extra blanket, he made a quick stop in the kitchen, stuffing the pouches full before heading for the barn. He was covered in snow when he walked into his mare's stall. "Sorry to do this to you, Rose, but someone needs our help."

Feeding the horse an extra helping of oats while he curried and saddled her, he put several extra portions into a bag and tied it inside his bedroll. He looked around to see what else he might need. An extra rope. Matches. Water canteens. Coffee.

Mario came in from his quarters off the west side of the barn, rubbing sleep from his eyes. "Mr. Lévesque, I thought I heard something. Sure was hoping I'd see Bar standing here. What'd you do to your forehead? You got a goose egg on it."

"I ran into a lamp. No, it's just me, but I'm certain I know where she is from the direction she rode after—" Hughes caught himself. He closed his eyes and dropped his chin to his chest. "Damn it. And I told her I was the best keeper of secrets she'd ever need."

Mario paused in the doorway, staring at Hughes for a long moment. "Bring her back safe and sound. Good riders are hard to come by." He gave a quick wink, and went back to bed.

Snow drifted hock deep in places, with most of the trail covered in a solid pack. The whiteout had diminished to a steady, heavy snowfall with the wind gusting in surprise attacks, laying low one moment, the next ripping through the valley with a baleful force.

The normal hour's ride to the secret cave took twice as long. By the time Hughes descended the steep slope into the level glade where he and Barleigh had last picnicked, his exhausted mare was blowing hard through her nostrils and her coat was clumped with ice and snow.

Hughes dismounted, trying to quell a rising panic. There were no footprints or hoof prints in the snow. No evidence or trace of human or equine activity. He turned around, listening, trying to get a feel for what he was hearing. There was something. There it was again. A sound. His mare whinnied, her alert ears pricked forward.

He kneeled on the ground, waiting, listening. Again. There. A strange echo. A clopping. Hooves striking on solid rock. Smiling, he led his mare down the narrow passage and into the cave.

"Hello, Hughes. I'm beyond the pool, up against the far wall."

"How did you know it was me?"

"Your mare nickered in the glade. I recognized Rose's nicker. She sounds more like a stallion. It reminds me of Deal, my horse back home."

"Maybe I'll get to meet him sometime. May we come in?"

"Please."

"I'm sliding you a box of matches. Keep one burning until I get this horse unsaddled and dried off, and we get our bearings."

"Of course."

Hughes fumbled around in the saddlebags, located the box of matches, and slid them toward Barleigh. "Coming to you."

"Got 'em." She struck a match and the smell of sulfur filled the air. And, for an instant, Barleigh saw the Man Who Sees With Wolf Eyes staring back at her.

The horses ate oats side by side off the damp floor while Hughes built a small fire, using as starter the extra cotton rope he'd brought along. He'd gathered an armload of branches from the pine tree in the glade, using some of the driest, setting some aside for later.

"I couldn't leave her out in the storm," said Barleigh, gesturing toward her horse. "She would have frozen to death."

"A blizzard's no place for a horse or a woman. I'd hoped

you'd be here."

The soft glow of the fire cast liquid shadows on the wall. Hughes sat next to Barleigh and reached for her hand, but she pulled back.

"Hughes, when I left Stoney's funeral, I wanted to clear my mind. I needed to rethink everything I thought I knew about my family history. The sudden, enormous detachment from my past—it's beyond confounding."

"I understand," he said. He knew what it was like to feel detached from one's family—at least from one's father.

"And poor Stoney—I just ache inside—the guilt is suffocating me. I'm drowning in sadness for him, for me, for my mother, but I'm afraid if I let go of it, if I give voice to it, it will live on forever in the air, somewhere out there, and will come circling back to haunt me, 'round and 'round the globe. Like a nasty wind."

Barleigh stood up and paced around the fire, walking over to the horses still munching their oats. "I want to scream till my throat's raw, to tear my hair out, my heart out, anything to feel a worse pain than I'm feeling inside."

"You can shout it all out and it'll go no farther than this cave. Get rid of it. Leave it in this cavern."

"How? How is that possible?" Barleigh began to shake, the emotions of the last two days and the lack of sleep overwhelming her.

Hughes stood, removed his boots and gun belt, slid out of his trousers, his vest and shirt, piling everything next to his saddlebags. In his long johns and bare feet, he walked to Barleigh, holding out his hand for her.

"What are you doing?"

"I'm going to show you how to get rid of your sadness, how to leave it here in the cave."

"Hughes, I'm not—" she stammered, shrinking away from him.

"Don't be silly. It's not what you're thinking. It's purely innocent. Take my hand. Trust me." He held out his hand, waiting.

She hesitated a moment, then took it. He helped her remove

her clothes down to her long johns, then led her to the pool, and together they slipped into the warm water of the hot springs.

The water came up to the level of his chest but was over Barleigh's head; she clung to the ledge. "Let go," he said. "Trust me."

She let go of the ledge.

With a hand on either side of her waist, holding her at arm's length, Hughes motioned for her to hold her breath and follow him. They ducked below the surface. The intensity of the heat on her face shocked her. She resurfaced, clinging to his neck, gasping for air.

"Next time, you'll be used to it. When you go under, scream. Let it all out. Scream. Shout. Curse. Release all the anguish you have inside. Get rid of all that's hurting you."

Barleigh nodded her understanding.

"Water will hold the sound—your words, your pain—and not let loose of it. Everything you give to the water, it'll hold forever." He held his breath, and she did, too.

He held onto her, and together they slipped below the surface. Barleigh screamed, cursed, yelled, tightfisted and kicking, Hughes's hands around her waist keeping her steady. When she could hold her breath no more, she pushed off of him, rising and gulping air into her lungs. Then, she dove below, and again he held her steady, letting her shout out her grief, releasing it into the water.

She dove below, again and again, until she was spent physically and emotionally, having nothing more to release, nothing more to give to the water. The last time, instead of pushing off of him for more air, she collapsed in his arms.

He swam to the side of the pool, placing Barleigh on the ledge. She lay still and quiet, steam rising off her body. Hughes eased next to her, rubbing her back, massaging her shoulders, waiting until she was ready to speak.

Long moments passed before Barleigh sat up, dangling her feet in the water. "I feel like I've purged something poisonous from my body. I feel better. Thank you."

"I'm glad," he said, relieved to see the relaxed expression

on her face.

"To dwell on the past can't help me now. It's done. But for the present, I'm starved. I hope you brought one of your fancy picnics with you."

They sat on the edge of the pool, sipping wine and eating dried fruit that Hughes had confiscated from the kitchen. His standard fine embroidered linens and engraved pewter plates with matching goblets made Barleigh smile.

"As for the future, I've decided to go back to Texas. I have a baby sister who needs me. Who knows better than I do what a child needs who doesn't have a mother to raise it?"

"What about us, Barleigh? Do I fit into your future?" he asked, feeling a mixture of relief and uncertainty.

"You said you were leaving for California. I thought you didn't want to worry about anyone but yourself. Especially not about me." Barleigh hesitated, then looked up into his eyes. "Do you want to fit into my future?"

"God. More than anything, if you'll let me."

Hughes lowered himself into the pool, taking Barleigh by the hand, easing her into the warm water. He sat her on the ledge that lay just below the surface. "I want the luxury of worrying about you. I'll hang up my badge forever. I'll walk away from everything to fit into your future."

"My future's not going to be very exciting, raising my baby sister and rebuilding the ranch. Your life is so thrilling, so—"

"All the thrill I need is seeing you wake up next to me every morning." He took her face in his hands and drew her to him, kissing her mouth, relieved to find it willing, seeking him, wanting him.

Her kisses were hungry, her arms and hands and fingers excited and eager to touch, to feel, to explore, to be explored. She wanted more. Standing on the ledge, she unfastened her long johns, peeled them down, and stepped out of them.

Hughes sucked in his breath, his eyes feasting on her wet, naked body. "My God, you're beautiful." He stepped out of his long johns, tossing them out of the pool. Reaching out for her, holding onto her, he lowered her into the water.

"Hughes—" Barleigh wrapped her legs around him, entwining her arms around his neck, letting him kiss her wherever he wanted, giving her body to him.

"Barleigh," he groaned, kissing and tasting every inch of her exposed body that was above the water's surface, his hands exploring the rest.

She whispered against his ear, kissing the words, caressing each one into place with her lips. "I want you to make love to me."

Hughes was sure of what he wanted—his body was sure. "Your strength," he said, kissing her, "and your beauty," he tasted her mouth again, "shatter me. Your eyes take me apart and put me back together, a better version than before." He brushed his lips across hers, then kissed her again, long and deep and slow, cupping her face in his hands. "From the first time I saw you, I knew you could turn my world upside down and I'd stand on my head gladly."

"You've set my world spinning back on its axis." She traced her lips down from his mouth, over his chin, kissing the small dip at the base of his neck.

"Have you ever—? Are you a—?"

"No, I've never—. Yes, I'm a—."

"Marry me. Tomorrow. I can't take something from you that you can never get back. If you won't marry me, then no, I won't make love to you." He kissed her again, his body hot and wanting hers.

"It's not just a 'want.' I've discovered what I need. I knew the first time I met you there was something different, something special about you, though many times I pushed you away. Not anymore. Make love to me."

She wrapped her arms around his neck, her legs tighter around his waist, pulling him to her, kissing him, tasting the wine on his mouth. The hot mineral water sloshed around them, over their heads, out of the pool and onto the granite floor as they twirled and splashed, their bodies entangling, clinging to one another.

Hughes held back, letting Barleigh move at her own pace. Steam rose off the surface of the water, off their bodies. Barleigh, clutching and gasping, screamed out Hughes's name while the winds howling through the canyons called out to spirits and ghosts.

The fire played out. Shadows faded. Snow drifted into the cave from the crevasse above and melted on the warm floor. Hughes lifted Barleigh from the edge of the steaming pool and lowered her onto the blanket. He covered her with his coat before checking on the horses and giving them another handful of oats and warmed water from the melted snow.

When he returned, she was sitting up. "How can I marry you? People think I'm a boy."

"Not everyone."

"What do you mean?"

"I spilled the beans. I'm sorry. It slipped out. If Mario had any suspicions, I erased all doubt." Hughes offered an apologetic smile.

"He can be the preacher. He used to be one, anyway, before hiring on with the Express, but not everyone knows. He felt private about that." Barleigh yawned and stretched, then sighed a deep sigh of relief.

"I guess that means you're going to marry me." Hughes looked down at her, waiting for an answer, but she was fast asleep.

*****

A jolt startled Barleigh from her dreams. She sat up straight. "Hughes?"

"I'm here. Nightmare?" He moved her off his arm, which had fallen asleep.

"Sorry, I made a drool puddle." She wiped away the shallow pool of drool on his chest. "Ouch—what happened here?" She touched his forehead with her fingertips, a fleeting panic seizing her, wondering if it was something she'd done in the heat of delirious passion.

"I ran into a lamp. Sort of. It knocked some sense into me, though. Made me realize how much I worry about you. That it's a luxury I look forward to, and . . . that I love you."

Barleigh shifted onto her elbow, propping her head in her hand. "I'm sorry—I just now noticed it. I woke up with this thought, and I had to share it."

"Are you ignoring that I said I love you?"

"Yes and no. I'll have to get used to that word. Is that all right?"

"Yes. And, if I wake up every morning with you drooling on my chest, everything'll be all right." Hughes yawned, then said, "So, what's the thought you have to share?"

"It couldn't have been Quanah that raided our ranch. Papa said he saw warriors watching from the ridge days before Birdie gave birth. Quanah was in San Antonio on those days, according to your encounter with him."

"That's right," Hughes said. "He was."

"On the night of our raid, he would've traveled hundreds of miles to have been there. Even if he were present the night of the actual raid, before that night, the wheels were already in motion. It would have happened anyway, with or without Quanah."

"You could be right," he said, considering the possibilities.

"Either way, you're not responsible. Please don't let that eat away at you. Leave those guilty feelings here in the cave, too."

Hughes took her in his arms, his tender kiss growing more passionate, urgent, and deep. "I love you, Barleigh Flanders. You'll have to get used to hearing that. What did you mean, earlier, that you've discovered what you need?"

"A conversation with Miss Maeve. She told me to keep looking until I found what I needed in life. I've found it." Barleigh felt a rush of happiness, of peace, lying in his arms.

"That makes me a happy man. What else did Maeve tell you?"

Barleigh blushed. The memory of that day's conversation brought a flush to her skin. She'd learned that there were many different ways a man and a woman can find intimate pleasure with each other's bodies.

"I had lots of questions for Miss Maeve, and she was generous with her answers," Barleigh said, a slow smile spreading across her face.

"Remind me to send her a generous tip and a thank you when we get back."

"One day soon, we can explore those ways, but right now I

want you to make love to me again." She pressed her body against his. Her urgent kisses, fingers caressing him, stroking him, teasing him, gave him all the encouragement needed.

He took her, took what she offered. This time, the urge to please her again, the hunger for her body, consumed him. What he'd denied himself the first time he'd made love to her in the pool, he would not, could not, deny himself now. Holding nothing back, when he felt the moment of Barleigh's pleasure, he let loose of his passion with a scorching wave, sending heat pulsing through both of them.

"My God, woman." He wrapped Barleigh in his arms as she lay on his chest. "That could send a weaker man to his death. And it wouldn't be a shameful way to die."

Wrapped in each other's arms, they lay in the darkness of the cave, breathing each other's breath, face to face, lips brushing, eyelashes tickling. Outside, the snow had stopped, clouds opened to the darkness behind them, and stars took their rightful place in the velvet sky.

*****

Barleigh awoke to the whispered words "I love you" spoken softly against her ear, Hughes's hand stroking her hair.

"I love you, too," she whispered.

"I've been watching you sleep, and I've been thinking."

"Uh-oh. Snoring again? Mama Grizzly in her cave?"

He laughed. "No—no snoring. I've heard it said that love grounds us. I disagree. I say love uproots us. Loving you has caused me to want to change things about myself, to be more like who I know my true self to be. What do you think?"

What did she think? Barleigh rolled over, resting her head against Hughes's chest, listening to the sound of his heart thumping, the sound of water dripping down the walls of the cave, to the horses moving about, to the sound of her own breath and pulse combined with his.

"I think with love, uncertainty is guaranteed. Love offers no guarantees. That's what makes it valuable, what makes it worth taking a risk at any cost. I'm just afraid."

"Love *is* worth the risk. But, what are you afraid of?" he

asked, kissing the tips of her fingers.

"That the people I give my heart to, the people I love, all die before I'm ready to let go," she said softly, not wanting to give power to the words or the thought.

"Cashing in your fear and letting go of your heart is the high cost of hope, my dear. Hope is what fuels the fire of love. Are you willing to cash in your fears, and let go of your heart?"

Barleigh glanced at the man she lay with, felt his arms holding her close, and she considered this question and all that it meant—the things that she feared, what she might lose if she let go of her heart—what she might gain if she did.

"I am. And I'm never looking back."

*****

A notice in the *Salt Lake City Deseret News*, the *San Antonio Sentinel*, and the *New Orleans Tribunal* read:

> ***Hughes Pierce Lévesque of New Orleans, Louisiana and San Antonio, Texas, and Miss Barleigh Alexandria Henrietta Flanders of Palo Pinto, Texas and Salt Lake City, Utah Territory, were married in holy matrimony on Thursday, November 28th, 1860. Officiating was Reverend Mario Russo of the Central Overland California and Pikes Peak Express Company. The bride wore a white lace gown with beaded pearl accents, and surprised her guests with a display of Western boots and spurs as her footwear of choice. In lieu of a bridal veil, she wore a bright yellow Mexican sombrero trimmed in gold and black accents. Official reception to follow at the Menger Hotel, San Antonio, Texas. Details to follow.***

"Get your riding gear ready—I've got to get you to Texas" were Hughes's first words for his bride, after the "I dos" had been said.

*****

December 31, 1860

When the stagecoach pulled into San Antonio, Texas, at noon on New Year's Eve, they found the town decorated in festive holiday colors. Barleigh pulled the telegram from her reticule, the small decorated bag a Christmas gift from Hughes when they'd stopped overnight in the township of Dallas. She held the fragile paper that was torn at the creases from the wear and tear of folding and unfolding it.

She looked up at Hughes, feeling the weight of his stare. "I just want to read it again," she said, casting her eyes down at the telegram.

Trying to keep the haunting anxiety from building, she concentrated on each word. Her mother's condition had worsened, Jameson's telegram had said, and time was of the essence if they wished to make a reunion possible. The telegram was almost fifteen days old.

Having said good-bye to Mario after he performed the quick nuptials in Salt Lake City, Hughes had sent three telegrams, one to Jameson, one to Winifred Justin, and one to Leighselle. He'd asked all three to respond as soon as possible, and to send their replies to the office in Saint Joseph, where he and Barleigh would be catching a stagecoach for San Antonio.

"If Leighselle still doesn't want to see you, and I can't imagine her *not* wanting to after I tell her our news, then, we'll have to accept her decision," he'd said. "But I'm going to do my damnedest to see you and your mother are reunited."

After one last night at the Salt Lake House Hotel, they made a final stop at the Mercantile. While Barleigh purchased supplies, Hughes arranged for a gift to be delivered to Mario. Hughes's signature card read, "I hope these woolies will keep your toes warm for many winters to come." Then, off they went, riding hard for Saint Joe. They changed ponies at the express stations, retracing backward Barleigh's and Stoney's first ride into Utah Territory.

*****

Winnie's telegram read:

Congratulations my darlings. I shall head to San Antonio with Starling and be prepared to stay several weeks. Will be leaving Hog Mountain Ranch in Esperanza and Julio's capable hands. Should be in San Antonio by Christmas. Will send telegram to Jameson at the Menger Hotel as you instructed. Love, Aunt Winnie.

Jameson's telegram read:

My best to the happy couple. Unfortunately, Miss Beauclaire's condition worsens each day. Time is of the essence if a reunion is possible. I've received Mrs. Justin's telegram and have secured a room for her and the baby adjacent to Miss Beauclaire's. Do Hurry.

Leighselle's telegram was the one Barleigh lingered over. Reread. Folded and unfolded, over again. She silently mouthed the words "I love you, Mother" to see how they felt in her mouth, in her mind. Each time she spoke the words, they became more a part of her, taking root in her heart, growing a fraction with each beat and pulse.

Hughes leaned forward, lifting her chin, seeking Barleigh's eye. "Darling, say it aloud. Practice how it feels to hear them spoken."

"Not yet. I don't want to jinx anything." Barleigh smoothed the paper on her lap and read it again.

Leighselle's message read:

I'm so happy for both of you. How very perfect. Hughes, I understand why you told Barleigh. Yes, you HAD to! I should never have asked you not to in the first place. I wish for nothing but to get to see her again, to get to hold her again before I leave this world behind. She sounds like a remarkable young woman. Tell her that I love her, have loved her always, until I can tell her myself, face-to-face. I'm doing my best to hang on. Please do your very best to hurry.

*****

The Menger Hotel was congested with hordes of people in town for the holiday season. Hughes took Barleigh's hand and led her through the crowded lobby full of festive folks in high spirits, past the shiny black grand piano, and toward the back stairwell. Taking them two at a time, he pulled her along with him. The burgundy and pink floral carpeting muffled the sound of their feet as they ran down the hall toward Hughes's old room, the room Leighselle now kept.

Standing before the door, Hughes looked at Barleigh and said, "Are you ready for this?"

She leaned past him and pounded on the door. "What does that tell you?" She smiled at him. "Yes. I'm ready."

After a long pause, Hughes knocked again. "Hello?"

They waited, their eyes meeting, holding, then separating.

Hughes knocked on the door, more insistent, speaking into the crack of the door frame. "Leighselle? Are you in there?"

Barleigh stood next to him, a gloved hand pressed to her mouth.

Hughes put a hand on the doorknob and turned. It opened. He pushed the door into the cold, dark room that smelled of lavender and lye. He stepped inside, looking around, taking note of what he was seeing, of what he was not seeing.

Easing out into the hallway, he turned to Barleigh, shaking his head. "The bed's been stripped to the mattress. No coals or ashes in the fireplace. It smells of rubbing alcohol and lye soap. This room's been vacant for a while."

"After all we did to get here, and we're too late." Tears rolled down her cheeks.

"Darling, I'm so sorry," he said, swallowing hard, holding back his own emotion.

"We didn't make it in time. I knew it. I knew as soon as I gave in to the notion of loving her that she'd, she'd . . . ."

Hughes took her in his arms and held her tight against his chest. "I'm so sorry, my love."

"I should have said it aloud. I should have set the words free, that I loved her. Then, they would be out there floating around somewhere and might find their way to her." Barleigh pulled her face into Hughes's lapels and sobbed.

"Let's go find Jameson and Winnie," he said, kissing the top of her head. "I'm sorry. I hate that I didn't get you here sooner." He closed the door behind them.

They looked into the room next door, after knocking and getting no answer. Barleigh recognized the coat and hat on one bed, and on the floor was a baby's doll.

"Well, at least we know Aunt Winnie and Starling have arrived. I wonder where they are." Barleigh picked up Starling's doll, placing it on the other bed.

"It's lunchtime. Let's head down to the Colonial Room, if we don't find Jameson in his room first."

Jameson didn't answer the knock at his door, so Barleigh and Hughes made their way to the crowded Colonial Room. Jovial hotel guests dined on a sumptuous feast and filled the room with boisterous conversations and bright laughter.

"I don't see Aunt Winnie," said Barleigh, glancing around the room.

Hughes turned around in a slow, complete sweep of the room, eyeing each table. "Jameson isn't here, either. Perhaps they've chosen the patio." He put his hand on Barleigh's back and steered her toward the side door.

Sunshine poked through thick palm fronds that hovered over the patio, creating a soft and inviting shade. The winter temperature in San Antonio was still pleasant for outdoor dining. At the farthest end and away from the door, Hughes spotted a table. White pressed linen cloths and silver butler service gleamed. Crystal glasses sparkled. A holiday floral arrangement was placed in the center, the candle awaiting the need for a fire.

Jameson, with his back to the wall for observing the comings and goings of others, stood and waved them over as soon as he saw Hughes.

To Jameson's left and right sat two well-dressed women, one holding an infant, the other sipping from a sugar-rimmed glass of lemonade with an infusion of dark amber liquid swirling throughout. Both women looked up and smiled.

Barleigh's breath caught in her throat. She reached for Hughes's hand, but her eyes were on the frail, thin woman sitting at the table across from Aunt Winnie who was sipping the lemonade. The delicate woman, whose smile, fine features, and cat-like eyes mirrored her own, held Starling against her shoulder, patting the baby's back, a half-empty bottle of milk on the table.

"That's her. That's my mother," said Barleigh, knowing, not asking.

"Indeed, she is. Leighselle Beauclaire has surprised me yet again," he said, his eyes crinkling at the corners as he smiled.

While the crowd of festive holiday travelers dined on their opulent feasts and the wait staff bore trays of food and drink to and from tables, a beaming Hughes Lévesque took his wife by the hand. Together, they made their way to the table at the far end of the sun-drenched patio.

Acknowledgments

While this book is a work of fiction and the characters are figments of my imagination, the swing stations and home stations mentioned are accurate according to the Pony Express route, and two actual riders are mentioned by name, Eagan and Haslan. The experiences my characters endure along the Pony Express trail are fabricated; however, some mirror purported factual events, such as the wolf scene where the rider was saved by bugling his horn to frighten away predators. Efforts to censor the mail, tamper with the mail, and steal the mail were abundant during the prewar years; however, the conspiracy specifically targeting President Lincoln's letters to California began as a seed of my imagination and grew into an actual plot.

Research for this book was made easy by having available two priceless and enjoyable resources: *The Pony Express Trail: Yesterday and Today*, by William E. Hill, and *Orphans Preferred*, by Christopher Corbett. I kept Mr. Hill's book open and on my desk for three years, referring to it many times for his invaluable knowledge regarding particular stations and trail conditions along the route. And, in an NPR interview about his book *Orphans Preferred*, Mr. Corbett's words fueled my imagination when he said: "The history of the Pony Express is rooted in fact, but layered in fiction." Hearing his interview spurred me to do two things: purchase his book, which was a fun and fascinating read, and then it motivated me to throw my own hat in the ring and add another layer to the fiction and the myth of the Pony Express.

While visiting San Antonio, I picked up a copy of *The History and Mystery of the Menger Hotel* by Docia Schultz Williams. Staying at the historic hotel was a treat, but alas, I never saw a ghost. However, I did have a fright when the bedside radio randomly turned itself on and off during the night. If you ever find yourself in the Alamo city, I highly recommend the Menger. You can learn more about the hotel at www.mengerhotel.com.

Along with the above mentioned books, I found other informative literature through the Saint Joseph (Missouri) Convention & Visitors Bureau, the Pony Express Museum, and www.ponyexpress.org and www.xphomestation.com.

While researching historical data on Quanah Parker and the Comanche raids in North Texas, I came across S. C. Gwynne's *Empire of the Summer Moon: Quanah Parker and the Rise and Fall of the Comanches, the Most Powerful Indian Tribe in American History*. I must have read it at least four times, and then kept it handy when I needed a reminder of the brutality of life on the western frontier.

Although I am part Native American Indian (maternal great-grandmother was full-blooded Cherokee and paternal great-grandmother was full-blooded Blackfoot), I don't pretend to speak any native tongue. The Lakota Siouan language I used for my book was taken from *The Full Text of the Lahcotah: Dictionary of the Sioux Language*, University of Pittsburgh Library System, authors J. K. Hyer, W. S. Starring, and Charles Guerreu (originally printed in 1866—not in copyright and no longer in print). I cross-checked this information with www.native-languages.org. Because of the many dialects of the Siouan language, I wanted to make sure the words I chose were correct. I apologize to any Native American if I've not done an accurate job—please email me—I'd value your coaching for future manuscripts.

I would like to thank graphic artist Carla Chadwick for designing the beautiful cover for *Orphan Moon*, as well as the cover for my contemporary suspense/thriller, *IF THE DEVIL HAD A DOG*. You can see examples of her lovely work at www.carlachadwick.com, and give her FB page some love at https://www.facebook.com/carla.chadwick2?pnref=story

Though the Pony Express operated for less than two years, it was during a critical time in America's history, and both the ponies and the riders captured our imaginations and our hearts. We're still writing (and reading) stories about them more than 150 years later.

A Note From the Author

This is the "*Thank You*" page—the most important page of the book. Then why is it at the back? I see it as being at the bottom of a pile of pages, holding everything up that's on top. Because, without all the people I have to thank who've helped me and who've encouraged me along the way, this book wouldn't have legs to stand on.

To my early readers, Renee Jordan, Megg Elliott, Beverly Helton, and Susan Bertram, I owe all of you much thanks, many sushi dinners, bottomless wine and endless chocolate, and more gratitude than I can describe.

To my adorable father-in-law Theodor Lukas, whose first language is German, thank you for being my first "official" reader and purchaser. Hearing your laughter and seeing your tears as you read showed me that a good story transcends language barriers.

To my dear friend Ines Eishen, whose words of encouragement when I was your student and you were my English Literature and Creative Writing professor gave me the courage to follow my dream, *grazie*. I'm grateful for our lasting friendship—it feeds my soul.

To Carol Dawson, author, editor, and courageous leader of the summer editing retreat in Alpine, Texas, sponsored by the Writers' League of Texas. Thank you for your kind honesty. It hurt cutting my first twenty-five beautifully written, eloquent, poetic pages, but you were *so* right. "Get to the nitty-gritty," you said. Yes ma'am.

To Sara Kocek and David Aretha at Yellow Bird Editors, thank you so much for your expertise in polishing my manuscript and in advising me with your straightforward answers to my many questions. I can't imagine having a more positive, professional experience during the editing, revising, and rewriting process. I'm looking forward to our next collaboration.

To Gary B. Haley, my old high school chum, thank you for

your eagle eyed proofing and critiquing. Gary is the accomplished author of the novel **The Attunement,** a fast-paced thriller reminiscent of the Jason Bourne stories.

To Baron, Ryan, Angie, Malachi, Erik, Marla, Miriam, and Krista, I love you all. Now, someone please pop the Almondage!

*****

And to you my dear readers, I offer my sincere gratitude for taking the time to read my book. I hope you enjoyed the story and characters, and perhaps learned something new about the American west and the Pony Express. If you feel so inclined, please leave a review on the **Orphan Moon** Amazon.com page and on Goodreads at www.goodreads.com. Search for the book by title or my name. Your review is invaluable and provides the feedback I need to become better at my craft. You can also leave feedback on my website at www.TKLukas.com and at the T.K. Lukas Facebook page. If you would like to receive periodic updates about my projects and excerpts of works in progress, including books two and three of **Orphan Moon,** please leave your name and email address at the following link: http://www.tklukas.com/contact-me-newsletter. You can look for books two and three of the **Orphan Moon** trilogy in 2016.

About the Author

T. K. Lukas, an accomplished equestrian and author of the award-winning contemporary short fiction *Of Murder, Mayhem, and Magnolias*, lives with her husband on a small ranch in rural Palo Pinto County in North Central Texas. Their three grown children are scattered across the globe. Along with international travel, she and her husband enjoy spending as much time as possible riding their horses through the woods, taking their dogs for walks, and watching their Belted Galloway cattle get fat. She is currently working on the second book in the *"Orphan Moon"* trilogy. Visit her at her website www.TKLukas.com and at the T.K. Lukas Facebook page.

The author with her appaloosa mare, Hollywood Jackie GN. "Holly" is the cover girl for the book. You can see how the cover art went from a photograph to the final masterpiece, an original oil on wood panel, by visiting www.TKLukas.com.

Original cover art by renowned Texas artist Sharon Markwardt. You can visit her website at www.sharonmarkwardt.com.